JILL
THE RIPPER

JILL
THE RIPPER

RICHARD GARNER

UMBRIA PRESS

Umbria Press
London SW15 5DP
www.umbriapress.co.uk

Printed in Poland by Totem
www.totem.com.pl

Paperback ISBN: 978 1 910074 19 0
E book ISBN: 978 1 910074 22 0

CHAPTER ONE

Toby Renton sighed as he listened to his father's voice on the other end of the telephone. It was the same call every Thursday and it always ended with the same question. "Shall we be seeing you on Sunday?" his father would ask. It was an innocent enough question but here he was: 34-years-old, single, just returned to London to live, with a flat of his own. He should be living it up and not feel a duty to go back and visit his parents every weekend.

He could see it from their point of view. Damn it! That was one of his weaknesses. He could always see things from other people's points of view. After all, his father had retired earlier that year without thinking of things to do in his retirement. He got under his mother's feet. He was always sitting there - forever watching the television. The two of them yearned for company to help them take them out of themselves for a little while. Hence the invitation to Sunday lunch. Hence, also, his agreeing to take it up - even though it made him feel as if he had never left home and was still tied to his mother's apron strings. Honestly, he felt that the famous sketch from Monty Python's Flying Circus where John Cleese replies to his mother's cooing of "who's a good little boy, then?" with the words: "Mother, I'm 43 and a cabinet minister" had been written with him in mind. Except, of course, that he wasn't 43 or a Cabinet minister. Perhaps there was time to change.

He replaced the receiver slowly and glanced at the surface below. There was a leaflet on it. It must have been left there by Gabi, the German assistant teacher to whom he had offered lodgings when she was kicked out of her own flat. That was another source of contention. Gabi. Of course, his parents did not think he should be living with her. There was nothing between them, no relationship, but the problem was the only telephone in the flat was in his bedroom and so when his parents called and she answered they knew she was in his bedroom and drew their own conclusions. They were surprisingly unenlightened for a couple who had been brought up in the sixties. Well, early sixties actually and that could explain it. Also, it rankled with them that she was German. No, not because of a throwback to the Second World War. They wanted their son to be spending his time looking for a nice English woman to settle down with. Someone like Rose who had been a previous tenant - and who had never answered the telephone in the bedroom.

His mind came back to the present and he looked at the leaflet again. It was headed: "North London Women's Revolutionary Action Group."Yes, he thought, obviously Gabi's. The lead item was headed "Jill the Ripper". It was calling for women to hit back indiscriminately against male sexual violence by taking out the men who exploited them. It argued that the police never took attacks against women, particularly prostitutes, seriously and so it was up to them to avenge the wrongs done to them themselves. It wasn't clear whether this action should be restricted to attacking men who had shown violence towards women or whether the attacks should be completely indiscriminate. He shuddered for a moment. Surely Gabi - a woman with whom he had shared several pleasant evenings drinking - could not agree with these sentiments?

He heard the flat door slam shut. It would be Gabi. He wondered for a moment whether he should raise the contents of the leaflet with her. He decided he would - although he left the actual leaflet by the side of the telephone. "Hi," he said on coming face to face with her in the living room. "I've just been on the phone to my parents."

"So, what's new?" she said. Her German accent masked

whether she was actually critical of him spending time talking to his parents or whether she was just making conversation.

She went into the kitchen and switched on the kettle. She did not offer to make him a cup. It was the way their relationship worked. They were both completely independent of each other and only socialised on those evenings when neither of them had anything better to do.

He hovered in the kitchen doorway - trying to think of how he could bring up the subject of the leaflet. He looked at her. She was significantly younger than him - 23 and as thin as a rake. She wore jeans, a sweater - even though it was the start of summer - and a scarf flung back across her shoulders. If he had been asked to sum up her appearance, he would have described her as striking rather than pretty or attractive. "So, what do you want?" she asked as she began to make her cup of tea. This time he felt he could denote a smidgeon of irritation despite the difficulty of interpreting the German accent. He was invading her space.

He cleared his throat. "I... erm ...," he began. He swallowed again. "While I was on the telephone, I noticed a leaflet," he said. "It was from the North London Women's Revolutionary Action Group."

"Oh, that," she said, the semblance of a giggle seeming to form on her lips.

"Yes, that," he said. "You surely don't believe...." His voice tailed off into the distance.

"That women should be indiscriminately and violently taking out men. Killing them. Why not? Men have been doing that to us for ages? As the leaflet says, look at Jack the Ripper. We never got back at him."

Words failed Toby for a moment. "But... ," he finally managed weakly.

"Relax, Toby," she said. "How long have we been living with each other?"

"About three months."

"And have you ever seen me fingering the bread knife with malicious intent?"

"No."

"Also, I have a boyfriend in Germany. I do not wish to kill him." She thought for a moment. "He is worried about me for a different reason," she added. "He does not like me living with another man."

"Oh."

"I have reassured him. I have told him he has not met you and - if he did - he would realise there was nothing between us."

"Oh," repeated Toby. She's toying with me. Teasing me. I don't know whether I should consider those last words as a comfort or an insult, he thought to himself. "Thing is," he added. "You've only just picked up that leaflet."

"So, it could have changed my mind as to how I view men?"

"Well, yes," he said. "That's what it aims to do."

"Toby," she said in a voice that seemed to want to be reassuring, "I went to this meeting of this group. We talked about a lot of things. We didn't even talk about that leaflet but - even if we had - I don't think the people I met would take it as an encouragement to go out and start killing men. It's meant to make you think. That maybe if somebody did go out and start killing men in the same way as Jack the Ripper killed women, it would be one way of drawing attention to the problem. Men would see how wrong they had been to tolerate violence and sweep it under the carpet. Maybe that would happen."

"Still looks like an incitement to murder to me," said Toby.

"Okay, but don't worry about it." She reached forward and touched his arm - a move that surprised him. She was one of the least tactile people he had known. Perhaps she really did like him and wanted to reassure him.

"Let's forget about it," said Toby. "Look, there's a film showing

4

on TV that I wouldn't mind watching - 'What's New Pussycat?' It's got Woody Allen in it."

She smiled."Okay, then," she said.

He went into the kitchen to make himself a cup of tea and sat down beside her to watch the movie - all thoughts of the leaflet gone at least for a moment. They resurfaced during one scene in the film when an angry girlfriend started banging the main character Peter O'Toole's head against a hard surface during a row they were having. Gabi laughed uncontrollably at the spectre. Toby just winced.

• • • • •

It was, Rivers reflected, simply one of the biggest mistakes of his life. He hadn't drunk that much. It was only a five-minute ride from the station to his home. What the heck? He would be all right. No problem.

All had been going well until he came to a sharp bend in the road near his home. He negotiated it all right but then a few yards later came to a shuddering halt as he crashed into the back of a parked car. Luckily, as a result of the bend, he had been going at no real speed at all but the airbag inside the car inflated and his horn started sounding.

He got out of the car, staggered for a moment and then pulled himself together. A woman came over from the other side of the road."Are you all right?" she asked."I could get you a glass of water."

"I think so,"he said thoughtfully. He looked at his hand. There was some bleeding as if he had cut it somewhere. His chest was also smarting from contact with the airbag. He reached inside his car and switched off the engine. The horn stopped blaring. He was aware of some people coming out of the house that the car he had rammed had been parked outside. He remembered it felt strange to him at the time that they made no move to come over to him. If someone had gone into my car outside my home, I would have gone out and started remonstrating with them, he thought.

"I've called the police," the woman who had rushed to help him. He nodded. It seemed a reasonable thing to have done. "I think you've been drinking," she added. "I can smell alcohol in your breath. And you staggered on getting out of the car."

He nodded. "I have been drinking," he confessed, "but I think the stagger was down to the shock not the drinking."

She went back into the house and came back with a glass of water. He took it from her with a "thank you" and walked across the road to sit on the low garden wall opposite. He looked towards where the three people had been standing. Now there were only two of them. One of them was an elderly man, quite portly. In his sixties, Rivers surmised. The other was a woman of about the same age. Well-dressed by the standard of people who, he thought, might just have been watching a spot of TV before the accident had occurred. They made no move to go towards the car he had hit. Perhaps it wasn't theirs. He looked at the car. He could see even in the dim lighting - the council had axed late night street lighting about a year ago, as a result of the austerity cuts - that it was a red car but he could not determine what make it was. He smiled for the first time since the crash. Even if it had been broad daylight he would probably not have been able to say what make it was. Cars weren't his thing. Just a means of getting from A to B.

Suddenly, he noticed someone emerge from the driveway of the house. Perhaps it was the third person who had been standing there a moment ago. Whoever it was got into the driver's seat of the car, started up the engine and drove off. Strange, he thought. You would have thought whoever it was would have waited to exchange names and insurance details. After all, what had happened was not his fault at all. From what little he could see of the figure, he could tell it was a man. The former policeman and private detective in him told him he should try and get the number plate. The trouble was, it was mangled from the impact of the crash and he could not read it. He wondered if he should go over to the couple standing opposite but what would he say. It was obviously not their car as it had been driven off by the third person. Anyway, it would be up to the police to sort things out.

He sighed and rested his head in his hands. What an arsehole, he thought to himself. As a former policeman, he had always been meticulous about not drinking and driving - even lectured friends and family on the subject. How are the mighty fallen, though, he said to himself. He had been drinking that night in London with his friend Mark Elliott who - ironically - lived in the same block of flats as he did. He had decided to leave early while Mark had met another friend. If only Mark had come home with him, this might never have happened. He had received bad news the previous day - that his brother had been diagnosed with bowel cancer, the disease a previous girlfriend of his had died from. It was no excuse for what he had done, he thought, but it was a reason.

Suddenly, he heard the sound of a siren and saw flashing lights. The police had arrived. Two officers got out of the car and made their way over to him. One took his notebook out. "How did this happen?" he asked.

"I don't know," confessed Rivers. "I'd just come round the bend and then suddenly crashed into this parked car."

"Which parked car?" asked the police constable.

"It's not here anymore," said Rivers. "Someone came out and drove it away."

The policeman looked at him oddly. "Who?" he said.

"I don't know," replied Rivers. He looked over towards the elderly couple who were still standing by the gate of the house where the accident had happened. "You could ask them," he said pointing towards the duo. "Whoever it was came out of that

7

house they're standing outside."

The policeman nodded. "Sir," he said, "I have reason to believe you have been drinking."

"Yes," said Rivers, "I'm sorry. It's out of character to drink and drive."

"You admit it?" said the PC surprised.

"There's no point in denying it," he said.

The PC smiled. "You'd be surprised how many people do. 'I've only just had the one' or 'that was hours ago'. Unfortunately, I cannot breathalyse you as I don't have the equipment - and it looks as though we should get the injury to your hand checked out. I'm going to have to take you to hospital for a blood test. You will have to remain in our custody until that procedure is finished."

Rivers nodded. "How long will that take?"

The PC shrugged his shoulders. "Depends on how busy the hospital is," he said.

Rivers nodded again. He was wondering whether he should ring his wife, Nikki, and tell her what had happened. He decided against it. She would only worry and get out of bed and try to come down and comfort him. He would see how long the procedure would take and - if it turned out to be that lengthy- ring her. He glanced at his watch. It was not closing time yet. She would not be expecting him home for at least an hour.

"Would you wait here a minute?" said the PC. "I just have to talk to the other party."

Other party? thought Rivers. How do we know they are the other party? After all, they didn't drive the car away.

The PC walked over to the couple while his companion busied himself by taking a statement from the woman who had brought some water out to Rivers. She had not seen the crash - only hearing a loud bang followed by the sound of a horn. When she had come outside, she had noted that the driver of the car that had gone into the rear of the one parked in the street was a little unsteady on his feet.

"Oh, Mr Morgan," said the PC on approaching the couple across the road. "I didn't recognise you. It's the street lighting."

"Yes. How can I help you?" His voice was curt as if he resented being bothered by the police.

"Was it your car that was involved in the accident?"

"The car outside my home was not 'involved in the accident' - as you put it. It was simply driven into by a driver who was obviously drunk."

The PC swallowed. Mr Morgan was a senior member of the ruling group on the local authority and a local councillor. He had met him before and decided to be as polite as possible. "We will, of course, be seeking to charge the driver with driving with excess alcohol," he said, "but, in the meantime, could you tell us who the owner of the other car was?"

"No," said Morgan. "I haven't a clue."

"That's funny," said the PC. "Mr Rivers - the driver of the other car - said he saw the owner coming out of your house and driving off."

"And you would believe the word of a drunk over an extremely sober member of the local council?"

"No, sir, I'm just putting to you what Mr Rivers said."

"And I have responded. Let that be an end to the matter."

At this juncture, their conversation was interrupted by the arrival of a breakdown van whose occupants made their way towards Rivers' car and towed it away. "I won't keep you a moment longer, Mr Morgan," said the PC. "Obviously, there's no point in an exchange of insurance details between you and Mr Rivers as the accident would appear to have nothing to do with you."

"I don't like your use of the word 'would appear'," said Morgan. With that, he turned on his heels and went back inside the house with the woman the PC assumed was his wife.

The PC watched him go. He shook his head. "Odd," he said.

He walked back to where Rivers was standing. The second PC gave Rivers a scrap of paper with the name and address of the breakdown company on it while his colleague still looked after the departing Morgans opposite. "Well," he said to Rivers, "he says he doesn't know who the driver of the car was - so at present I have no-one to give your insurance details to for a claim for damages."

Rivers gave a sheepish smile. "Well, I suppose that's the best bit of news I've had out of this evening," he said.

"Come on, let's get you to hospital," said the PC. He opened the rear door of the police car and Rivers got in. It took them half an hour to get to the hospital and another two hours to wait for the blood test. The police then drove him home - ready to face Nikki at two o'clock in the morning.

Meanwhile, back in the street where the crash had taken place, two cars left the home of the Morgans about half an hour after everyone else had dispersed. Morgan got into a small black Fiat while his wife revved up the engine of a four by four. An hour later, the four by four returned with Morgan in the driving seat and his wife as a passenger.

• • ● • •

Larry Green mopped his brow as he got out of the car. The detective chief inspector was prone to sweating at times of stress. He had been advised that the corpse would present quite a gruesome sight and was preparing himself for viewing it. He had arranged for his new deputy, Francesca Manners, to meet him at the scene of the murder but she had not arrived yet.

He had parked in the grounds of the disused warehouse next to where the body had been found.

Some PCs had already arrived as had the pathologist his station used. "What have we got here?" he asked Professor Saint as he approached him.

"Nasty one." He took Green over to where a body lay - under lighting hastily set up by the two PCs at the scene. A man lay on the ground. He was fully clothed from the waist upwards but his pants and trousers had been pulled down to reveal that someone had hacked his penis and testicles off. It was not precision surgery and there was a great deal of blood seeping on to his clothes and the ground.

"Oh, my God," said Green. He brought a handkerchief to his mouth as if to stifle any attempt to vomit. He was a seasoned police officer, though, and - despite being revolted by the scene before him - managed to retain his composure and put his handkerchief back in his pocket.

He shook his head. "I'll be retiring in two or three weeks' time," he said to the professor, "and I don't mind telling you I will be happy if I never see a sight like this again in my working life,"

Professor Saint nodded. "Male," he said. "Approximately 46 years of age."

"Approximately?"

"Well, actually," the professor confessed, "I looked at his driving licence. John Hedger. Signs of a blow to the back of the head. And strangulation." Saint pointed to ligature marks around the body's neck.

"What killed him?"

"The strangulation. The blow to the back of the head was severe but I think it would just have stunned him and knocked him unconscious."

Green took a look at the body again. "The severing of the penis?" he began.

"Did it happen before he died or after?" said Saint anticipating the question.

"Yes."

"I can't say. I'll know more when I get him back to the lab."

"And the time of death?"

"Ditto, but I would hazard a guess at between 10pm and midnight. The body's been lying here for a good few hours."

"Who found it?"

One of the PC's intervened. "A jogger on a morning run," he said. "He's over there." He pointed to a young lad who could only have been about 18 who appeared to be shivering as he sat in the back seat of a police car.

"I'd probably better have a word with him," said Green moving towards the police car.

"By the way, sir," said the PC.

Green stopped in his tracks. "Yes?"

"We found the penis. It's now in a plastic bag in the boot of the police car. It was about a stone's throw from the body."

"So someone just hacked it off and threw it away. What's that all about?" Green shook his head as if in disbelief. "God save us," he said.

It was at that moment he heard another car coming into the open ground at the disused warehouse. Out of it stepped Detective Sergeant Francesca Manners. There were no signs that she had been woken from her slumbers and told to report to a crime scene early in the morning. Her clothes had an immaculate look about them. Green felt he could have been forgiven for thinking she had just been invited out on a first date.

"Detective Sergeant Manners," he said. "Welcome to Hendon CID work. Your second day, I believe?"

"Yes, sir."

The two had met the previous day in the office but it had been a fairly routine occasion. No real crime to keep them busy. It had turned into a familiarisation session for Detective Sergeant Manners in her new job. In her late twenties or early thirties, Green surmised, she had transferred from Brighton CID where she had won plaudits for helping prevent an innocent man go to jail. The man had been fitted up by her senior officer but she had resisted all pressure to turn a blind eye to flaws in the investigation. That reputation did not endear her to Green who liked to feel free to cut corners if it would help him get a conviction. He decided not to judge her, though, and explained what had happened."Would you like to see the body?"he asked her.

"I can see it, sir. Not a pretty sight."

"And the penis? It's in the back of the police car."

"I think I know what a penis looks like, sir,"she said

"Yes, well,"he said slightly embarrassed."You're right. I don't think there's anything to be gained from viewing it. What do you make of all this?"

Francesca thought for a moment. "A crime with a sexual motive, obviously,"she said. She paused for a moment."It would suggest the deceased has been violent towards somebody. The severing of the penis would suggest that violence had taken place in some kind of sexual relationship. Is it a woman getting back at someone who has been violent towards her? Or is it a man gaining vengeance for violence the deceased has perpetrated on someone he knows?"

Green was impressed. "Very clear headed," he said to her. "Now, you go and interview the jogger who found her. Go easy on him. He's a bit shaken up by all this. I'll go and break the news of his death to his family. I'll have to get them to come and view the body."With that, he took the driving licence away from Professor Saint, noted that the address on it was only a couple of miles away and determined to go round to it immediately.

• • • • •

"How are you darling?" said Toby's mother as she proffered her cheek for a polite peck when Toby arrived for Sunday lunch. His father stood hovering in the background. The two had never quite worked out how to greet each other.

13

"Fine, mother," Toby replied. In actual fact, he wasn't. The previous night he had had a bust-up with his girlfriend who had all but told him he was too clingy, too needy.

"I'm sure your parents have made you that way," she had said, "but it's not what I want in a relationship. I want somebody who's a bit more confident in themselves. Someone who can plough their own furrow for most of the time."

Toby sighed. It was an all too familiar pattern. They had been going out together for about ten months - the same length of time that many of his relationships had survived. He had to face it. Women just seemed to get bored with him. Maybe the best idea was not to get involved with them in the first place. A song he had always fancied came into his mind. Ironically, he had found it amongst his father's collection of records several years ago-"I Am a Rock" by Simon and Garfunkel, a singing duo from the sixties and seventies - his father's time, with its lyric: "If I'd never loved, I never would have cried."

He was brought back to the present by his father. "You still with that girl?" he asked.

"Which girl?" He was aware he never really talked about his relationships to his parents - let alone introduced them to them.

"The German."

Toby smiled. "No, father, I was never with her."

"Oh, well, why are you living with her?"

"We're sharing a flat - just like Annette and Elsie. Nothing more to it than that." He smiled. Annette was his sister and she shared a flat in London with Elsie. They had never told his parents that they were a lesbian couple. That would have shocked them to the core. It was ironic, he thought, that their relationship had got the green light from his parents while he and Gabi, who had never slept together, were frowned upon.

"I could never work out why you gave up on that Rose girl."

"We were just sharing a flat, too, mother."

"She was good for you. Kept the place tidy." That was true,

Rose had been a friend of a friend who had lived on the south coast but been transferred to a London branch of her bank for a six-month stint. She had needed somewhere to stay and - as ever - Toby had obliged and offered her the spare room. She was grateful to him for helping her out and - as a result - was happy to cook his meals in the evening and do all the washing and cleaning. It wasn't a formal arrangement. She just took it upon herself to do it. Needless to say, his mother had been really impressed when she had popped round with his father to see how he was doing."I was very taken with her,"she emphasized.

"I tell you what,"said Toby."Just so as you don't think things have gone to pot since Rose left, why don't you come round to the flat and see for yourself?"He almost bit his tongue immediately on saying this. It would appeal to his mother's nosier instincts. She would be trying for all she was worth to detect signs that Gabi was sharing his bedroom. Let her, he thought. He almost had half a mind to steal a couple of Gabi's knickers and place them strategically in his bedroom to feed her suspicions.

"All right, dear, that would be nice,"said his mother.

Toby looked round to his father to see what his thoughts were."It'd get you out of the house, father,"he said."Bit of fresh air at least."

"Will the German girl be there?"he asked as if unconvinced by the merits of a trip to his son's flat.

"Not if I can arrange a day off during the week,"said Toby. "She'll be at school."

"At school? How old is she?"asked his father.

"She's the teacher, father,"said Toby irritated by his attitude.

A look of relief came over his father's face."Well,"he said,"I suppose a visit can't do that much harm."

Good, thought Toby. That at least will give them something else to talk about other than my love life.

His father glanced at his watch."Cricket's on the telly now," he said. They moved into the sitting room and turned it on.

At least it pre-empted the need for any further conversation between them for the rest of the afternoon.

• • ● • •

Gabi opened the door to the parish hall quietly and determined to slip into the back of the room without disturbing the meeting. It was impossible - there were only four people in the room and the slightest noise would have been noticed.

"Welcome." Hilary Sampson, a stern-looking woman with glasses and greying hair, dressed all in black, looked up from the notice she had been reading. "Good to see you again." Hilary was the chair of the North London Women's Revolutionary Action Group.

"We're just on feedback from the last meeting," she said. "I think you know everyone here - except for Jane Harris." She pointed at a stylishly dressed woman of about forty who turned around and gave Gabi an acknowledging smile. "Jane is a friend of Jenny's," said Hilary.

Ah, thought Gabi. The mad one. She remembered Jenny as being quite loud, always fidgeting, unable to sit still for any length of time. She had introduced herself as a freelance writer but Gabi had also learnt that she worked as a prostitute - which Gabi had felt was at odds with the aims and objectives of the women's group. No, Jenny had said firmly. If you had to engage with men, why not exploit them, i.e. charge them for the experience? Exploit them in the same way as they have always exploited women. It was an interesting argument, thought Gabi, but it was not one that she could empathise with. Jenny had then dismissed her as too traditional in her thinking. Gabi took a chair from where it had been stacked up at the side of the room and joined the other four. She looked round the room. Incongruously, there were notices advertising church services, Sunday schools and a range of other church activities.

A surprising meeting place for a women's revolutionary action group, she thought. As there were only five of them, why not meet in one of the women's front rooms, she had wondered aloud at the last meeting. It was Hilary who had answered her. They always leafleted the neighbourhood about their next meeting and Hilary was an eternal optimist and believed there was a distinct possibility that more people would turn out. She would have seen tonight's meeting as a success - the numbers had swelled by 20 per cent with the arrival of Jane.

"Do you have any feedback from the last meeting?" asked Hilary.

"Er... yes, I suppose I do." Gabi's English at that moment was halting - a word that could not normally have been used to describe her mastery of the language. It was as if she was reluctant to speak. "The leaflet I picked up from you. I left it by the side of the phone in my flat and my landlord picked it up," she said. Landlord, she thought, was not a term that really described Toby. He was not exploitative. He was doing her a good turn and had not made a single pass at her since she had moved in.

"What was his reaction?" said Hilary. "I assume it is a him?" She winced at hearing her own words. Not the sort of conclusion she would normally make, she thought.

"Was he frightened?" asked Jenny in a tone that demanded the answer: "Yes."

"I think, yes, he was. A little."

Jenny smiled. "And?"

"Well, we had a chat about it. I told him he had nothing to fear from me - that the article was just trying to make people look at relationships between men and women from another perspective and argue that, if a man went unpunished for violent attacks on women, why shouldn't the reverse be true."

Jenny sighed. "You should have made him sweat a little," she said.

"And if I had? He would probably have kicked me out, possibly gone to the police. I don't know."

"You probably did the right thing," said Hilary. Jenny shook her head vehemently. "I think we'd better move on to the next item on our agenda," said Hilary. It was a discussion of a dispute at a print works in Hendon. The all-female staff had gone on strike for more pay as it had been discovered the employer was paying them below the living wage. There was to be a march in the High Street on Saturday - an uncommon occurrence in that neck of the woods. It represented the best chance the group would have in a long time to encourage more women to join their group. Attendance on the march should be mandatory for the five at the meeting, said Hilary. They all nodded.

"If we don't get more women coming along soon, we're going to have to abandon the church hall," said Angela Curran - the other woman in the hall. She had the grandiose title of treasurer of the group. Grandiose because there was no money coming into it. Angela, Gabi remembered from the previous meeting, was the sensible one. To Jenny, she always seemed to be trying to limit the group's horizons. "If we believe in something, we should be prepared to pay for it," Jenny had said previously, Gabi remembered smirking. Had the battle for women's equality really come down to a row over whether they should pay for a church hall? she pondered.

Soon after the debate on the print works march, the meeting came to an end. There was an exhortation from Jenny to everyone to go for a drink at the local pub. Hilary and Angela declined but Gabi decided to join Jenny and Jane. As Jenny went to the bar to get the drinks - she was always the first to volunteer to buy a round - Gabi struck up a conversation with Jane. "I wouldn't have thought a meeting like that was your natural home," she said.

"You're right," said Jane smiling. "I've known Jenny for a long time, though. I thought I'd give it a try. I think the debate about the print workers' dispute was useful, though. We should be supporting people like that."

At that stage, Jenny came back with the drinks - which seemed to mirror the personalities of the people who had ordered them. Jenny was clutching a pint of Guinness while she handed a glass of white wine to Jane. She then went back to the bar to get Gabi her slimline tonic.

"How long have you two known each other?" asked Gabi.

"Oh, quite a few years," said Jane. "We're in the same line of business."

"Oh. Are you a writer, too?"

"No." Gabi let the answer sink in for a moment. If she was not a writer, then the answer must be she was into prostitution, too. That surprised Gabi, although surprise was not an emotion that often registered with her. To all intents and purposes, Jane was dressed as if she had been going on an outing to a West End show - her hair immaculately coiffured and an attractive two-piece suit with a knee-length dress. Before Gabi could speak, Jane started to expand upon her answer. "You think I don't look like a prostitute?" she said. "Well, if we had been writers, we could have been writing for very different markets - a downmarket raging tabloid or a more serious newspaper. Same with screwing. I work as an 'intimate therapist' - at least that's how the advert describes me - Jenny takes what she can get from the streets."

Gabi looked at Jenny. "That must be dangerous," she said.

"No more dangerous than my clients," said Jane - cutting in before Jenny could answer. "Just because people are better off it doesn't make them any less violent. In fact, Jenny has persuaded me to try my luck out with street adverts, too. Broaden my horizons."

• • • • •

John Hedger's home looked as if it had seen better days. It was in a prestigious cul-de-sac but it was obvious that the garden was not as well tended as those of his neighbours. The grass had grown and the hedgerow seemed to have expanded over the pavement.

Larry Green got out of his car and tucked his shirt in. He shook his head. No matter how firmly he tucked it in, it always seemed to come out again. He mopped his brow as he anticipated telling Mrs Hedger about the fate that had befallen her husband. He would keep the more gruesome bits out of it for the time being, he thought. At some stage, she would have to know, he thought, as it might become necessary to tell the press so as to give the public some idea of the kind of killer the police were looking for. Not today, though, he thought. Let her just come to terms with the fact of his death. He walked up the garden path and rang the doorbell. There was no response. Try the obvious first, he thought, and he attempted to open the door via the door handle. No joy. He walked round the side of the house and tried the back door. Again, no luck. He was just about to give up when a neighbour approached him as he walked back to his car.

"Can I help you?" the man asked.

Green fished his warrant card out of his pocket. "I was trying to contact Mrs Hedger," he said.

"You'll have a hard job," said the other man. "She hasn't been living here for the last six months."

"Lived here on his own, then, did he – Mr Hedger?"

The man from next door, who had obviously interrupted his gardening to confront the inspector – he was carrying a hoe in one hand. "You said 'lived'?'" he said latching on to the fact the inspector had used the past tense.

Green chided himself. It was not often that he let things slip by mistake. He thought for a moment. It was unlikely that the neighbour would prove to be an important player in investigating the murder of John Hedger although that hoe - it could have been a mighty effective weapon in the wrong person's hands. He stopped the thought there. Even he had been rendered a little squeamish by his find that morning. It would, he reasoned with himself, be quite safe to confide in the neighbour that John Hedger was dead.

"Did you know Mr Hedger well?" he asked.

"Not really," he said. "The wife and I were invited in for drinks a couple of times but since Mrs Hedger left, nothing."

"What happened?"

"We don't really know. The walls are thin. We heard shouting a couple of times, but I guess that's not out of the ordinary."

"No," said Green, stroking his chin.

"What brings you here?"

"Sad business," said Green. "Mr Hedger's dead. We found his body on waste ground a couple of miles away from here earlier this morning."

"Oh, my goodness. How did it happen?"

"That's what we're trying to find out but, first, we have to break the news to his wife and get somebody to identify the body? Did he have any other relatives? Children, for instance?"

"No."

"What did he do?"

"He was a salesman of some sort."

"Do you know where I can contact the wife?"

"Yes, she moved in with her sister. Lives in Cheshunt. I haven't seen her but I've no reason to think she's moved anywhere else. If you hang on a minute, I'll get the address. She didn't trust her husband to pass on the mail so she left me a key."

"That must have made it difficult between you and him."

"No. Not at all. I never had to use it. He always passed stuff on and he told me to keep the key - just in case anything happened while he was out at work." The man turned on his heels to walk back towards the house.

"Could you get the key?" asked Green. "I'd like to see inside the house."

The neighbour stopped in his tracks. "Don't you need a warrant for something like that?"

"Strictly speaking, yes," said Detective Chief Inspector Green. "But Mr Hedger's not going to object and his wife doesn't live there anymore. I am investigating a murder."

"A murder? I thought possibly he'd died of a heart attack or something?"

"No," said the inspector firmly. The neighbour needed no second bidding and returned from the house with a key and the address of Mr Hedger's wife's sister written down clearly on a piece of paper.

Once inside the house, Green began looking around. There was a file of newspapers on a bookshelf in the living room. They were all copies of the local paper. In a bowl on top of the bookshelf, Green found some business cards. "Not a salesman," he said showing one to him. "A marketing executive at the local paper." He grimaced. Executive was probably an overblown description of his work status. Many of these local papers were just three men and a dog outfits, he thought to himself. A brief reconnoitre of the place revealed an unmade bed, some dishes lying unwashed in the sink. Books, lots of books, stacked on shelves in the living room and in a room which doubled up as a second bedroom upstairs. "I'm going to get a team to come round here to look for potential evidence," said the inspector. "Do you mind if I keep the keys to pass on to them? I'll give them back to you." Meanwhile, he thought to himself, I'd best get off to Cheshunt.

The drive took him half an hour and, when he got to the address, it looked as if Hedger's sister-in-law was enjoying better times than he had. It was a semi-detached house set back from the road with a spacious driveway. A four-by-four was one of two cars parked in it. He rang the doorbell.

"Yes?" said a voice from inside. "Who is it?"

"Detective Chief Inspector Larry Green from Barnet police station. I'm looking for a Mrs Hedger."

"You've found her." The woman opened the door. She was wearing jeans and a T-shirt. Behind her was a woman dressed in horse riding gear. "This is my sister, Tanya," she said. "I'm Erica Hedger. How can I help you?"

"Do you think I could come inside?" he asked. "I'm afraid I have some upsetting news for you."

Erica Hedger nodded and ushered him into a living room which looked immaculate in comparison with the one that he had just left in Hendon. She motioned him to sit on a well upholstered sofa. "What could possibly be upsetting for me, Inspector?" she asked.

"I'm afraid I have to tell you your husband's dead. We found his body on waste ground in Hendon this morning."

The woman in riding gear moved towards her sister as if to offer a comforting shoulder to lean upon. Erica Hedger waved her away. She stood motionless in front of the sofa. "How did he die?" she asked in a matter-of-fact voice.

Green remembered his thoughts from earlier in the day that he should not tell her about the gruesome nature of her husband's demise. Her reaction, though, told him she might not be shocked if he did. He decided to hold back the information anyway. "That's what we're investigating," he said. "I understand from your erstwhile neighbour that the two of you split up several months ago."

"Yes, Inspector."

"In acrimonious circumstances?"

The other woman intervened. "Does anybody split up in happy circumstances, Inspector?" she said acerbically.

Yes, thought Green, if they have a better relationship to go on to. "There are all sorts of circumstances in which people split up," said Green diplomatically.

"Well, in my case, it was acrimonious," said Erica. "I haven't seen him for several months."

"Oh?"

"You see, Inspector, he was violent towards me. Hit me several times. I didn't feel I had to take it anymore. He had a temper."

"I see. Are you sure you haven't seen him recently?"

"What do you mean, Inspector?" asked Tanya.

"Like last night? He died a pretty violent death." Green decided he might as well go for broke now. "Where were you last night?"

"Erica was here with me, Inspector," said her sister. Yes, thought Green, and you'd say that wherever she had been.

"Can anyone else corroborate that?"

"My husband. Even my children if necessary."

The inspector nodded. If she was willing to offer the testimony of her children, she was probably speaking the truth, he reasoned. "Do you know if he had embarked on any other relationship since the break-up of your marriage?" he asked.

"I told you, I haven't seen him for months. I don't know."

"I see." He made as if to get up off the sofa. "Just one more thing," he said. "I wondered whether you would mind coming to view the body. We need someone to identify him."

Eric's sister stole a glance at her but she shook her head. "No, that would be fine, Inspector," she said.

"In which case I probably ought to warn you that it might be an upsetting sight," he said. He had previously been thinking of covering the body up with a rug and allowing her to identify him just by the face. That, he felt, would not now be necessary. "Would you like to come with us?" he asked. "We can arrange to have you brought back here." He turned to the sister. "And you madam, would you like to come with us? I think you should," he said.

The sister nodded and the three of them made their way outside to Detective Chief Inspector Green's car.

● ● ● ● ●

24

Toby had tried to prepare for his parents' arrival. He had advised Gabi to stay away. He just knew there would be no meeting of minds between Gabi and his mother. After all, she was German, left-wing, wore jeans most of the time. The only thing they had in common was that they were both quite cold in their dealings with other people but somehow Toby did not think that would be of any help. Of course, he knew his mother would nose around the place under the guise of "just tidying up, dear". Who knows what she would find? In actual fact, he did not care too much. It would be too much trouble to try and present a pleasant front to her in which everything would pass muster as she inspected the flat.

"I've made some lunch for us," he said as his parents arrived at the flat. "Would you like a beer, father?" He was already two brownie points down; men shouldn't cook in his mother's eyes and he should have realised his father couldn't drink as he was driving.

"No thanks, Toby," said his father. "Driving."

"Mother?"

"Ridiculous. You know I never touch the stuff."

"No, mother, I was just asking you what you wanted." In reality he had left it deliberately vague. It was his way of winding her up a bit. "I'll just have some water and dad will have some, too."

"Yes, mother." He busied himself with last minute preparations in the kitchen ready to serve them with a starter of tomatoes stuffed with prawns before producing a steak for the main course. It was his father's favourite - something his wife always reminded him about whenever they were in a restaurant. It was as if he could not remember by himself. Perhaps she was preparing for an imminent onset of dementia, thought Toby.

Toby had erected a table and chairs in the garden of the flats and brought out the starter. He could see his mother had already been rummaging about the house as she triumphantly produced a leaflet and put it on the table.

"What's this?" she demanded to know.

"It's a leaflet."

"And what's it doing in your bedroom?"

"Gabi must have left it there when she was answering the phone."

"What's it say?"

"Well, you can read it, mother. You know very well."

"It's talking about murdering men." His father began to take an interest in the conversation for the first time and reached over to pick the leaflet up from off the table. "It's dangerous."

"Gabi just happened to be at a meeting and picked up the leaflet. It's nothing to do with her."

"Then why did she leave it in your bedroom?" continued his mother. He almost replied by saying "because she leaves a lot of things in the bedroom" but stopped short just in time. His mother would misconstrue the answer. Knickers, bras, goodness knows what else, she would think. Toby thought for a moment. In actual fact, his mother probably would not think in so explicit terms but would conjure up her own version of what went on in the bedroom.

"Gabi just left it by the phone," he said. "She probably wasn't even thinking that she was in the bedroom at the time."

"Nevertheless, it is dangerous and constitutes a crime," said his father. "Incitement to murder at the very least. You should report it to the police."

Toby took the leaflet back from him. He made as if to rip it up but his father snatched it away from him. "I don't want to," said Toby. "It would be making a mountain out of a molehill."

"Well, if you won't, I will," said his father definitely. Toby looked at him for a moment. He had always had some respect for his father. Oh, he wished he would stand up to his mother a little bit more and not hide behind the thought of "anything for a quiet life" - but he never over-reacted to a situation. Toby could see he was very worried about the contents of the leaflet.

"Okay," said Toby. "Let's enjoy the rest of the meal, though."

His mother reached across the table and pocketed the leaflet. "We are taking it seriously," she said.

CHAPTER TWO

"Thank you agreeing to see us, Inspector," said Walter Renton. "We were quite worried about this." He produced the North London Women's Revolutionary Action Group leaflet from his pocket.

Green motioned Renton and his wife to sit down. "Where did you get it?"

"From my son's flat."

"Your son?" asked Green, surprised.

Renton smiled. "I apologise," he said. "He has a female lodger. A German girl." The accent was on the word "German" as if this was likely to shock Green and give him a steer as to whom he should blame for anything. Then he added after a pause: "Who we don't know very much about."

"That's putting it mildly," interjected his wife. "He always seems to hide her away when we go round. The only time we have anything to do with her is when we telephone him and she answers. The phone's in his bedroom."

"You're worried he may be at risk from her?"

"Yes, Inspector. Wouldn't you be if it was a child of yours who was involved?"

"Probably." It had never happened, thought Green. He was still single and likely to remain so for the rest of his life, he would tell people. He had never put sufficient effort into his private life. The job, he reflected, didn't allow him to. "Do you know anything about this group – the North London Women's Revolutionary Action Group?" he asked.

"Do we look as though we do, Inspector?" said Walter Renton.

"No," Green had to admit. "I had to ask, though."

"You ought to question this Gabi – this German girl," intervened Mrs Renton. "She's up to no good. I'm sure of it." She turned to her husband. "I wish he'd stayed with that Rose."

Green looked baffled.

Walter Renton smiled. "My son's previous lodger. My wife thought she was more suitable. She did the washing up."

Green smiled but he felt there was no need to pry any more into their son's private life. "Leave it with me, Mr Renton," he said. "I'll be in touch." He stood up and ushered them out of the room whereupon Green picked up the telephone. "Francesca," he said when a voice replied at the other end. "Can you come in and see me?"

Francesca passed the Rentons in the corridor as she made her way to her boss' office. She could hear them talking as they made their way down the stairs to the reception area.

"What did you think of him?" asked Walter.

"I don't think he's going to do anything. He didn't seem that interested."

"I suppose he's got to play his cards close to his chest."

"And in the meantime, someone acts on the leaflet and kills somebody?"

"There's not a lot more we can do, darling."

Francesca continued with her walk to Green's office. "Two dissatisfied customers out there," she said. "They don't think you're going to act on the information they supplied to you.".

Green shoved the leaflet across the table. "What do you think I should do about it?" he asked. "In the normal way, I'd completely ignore it. There must be hundreds of tiny revolutionary groups spewing out their poison in this area and it would take up all our resources to track them down and act on the kind of suggestions they were making."

"Yes," said Francesca tentatively, "but – on the other hand - we do have a murder on our hands which seems to copy the kind of suggestions they make in the leaflet."

"So, we should go and interview this German girl who had a copy of the leaflet?"

"Possibly but I think we should find out more about the people who produced the leaflet. The girl probably just picked it up. She's unlikely to have been the one who wrote it."

At that stage, Green's admin assistant came into the office with a couple of cups of tea. "I thought you might like these," she said putting them down on the table. She noticed the leaflet. "Oh, that lot," she said.

Francesca and Green pricked their ears up. "You know them?" asked Green incredulously.

"Yes," she said. She picked the leaflet up. "North London Women's Revolutionary Action Group. They were in the High Street at the weekend. Demonstrating with those women from the print works who are striking over their pay. I don't know. I mean we don't get that sort of thing in Hendon."

"No," said Green reassuringly - glad to have it confirmed that his admin assistant was not a member of a revolutionary band of women.

"They were putting out leaflets about their next meeting."

"Did you pick one up?" asked Green innocently.

"Good Lord, no. But there were a couple of lads from our station accompanying the march. They probably picked up copies. You should try them."

"Thank you," said Green. He turned to Francesca. "Well, let's be going," he said.

• • ● • •

Rivers threw his brief case across the room as he entered the small office space he had rented for Hoffmeyr and Rivers, his private detective business. "Fuck," he shouted.

"Good morning, Nikki, how are you?" said a voice from behind the other desk.

He looked up and saw his wife (he hesitated to call her that as it had taken thirty years of knowing each other before they had decided to get married) tapping away at a computer. "Sorry," he said. "Pig of a morning." He sat down at his desk. "You know, this is not going to work. Surveillance is impossible. All they have to do is get in a car and I'm lost."

It had been a few days since the accident and his arrest on suspicion of drunk driving. There was also the threat of driving without due care and attention or dangerous driving hanging over his head from the crash. His solicitor had warned him to expect a lengthy ban – there was the indication his breath test reading would have been higher if it had been taken at the time of the crash instead of three hours or so later at the hospital. All in all, it had made him feel there was no point in hanging on to the damaged car and he had come to a deal with the garage that had taken it in to repair it and sold it to them.

"There's no need to make the rest of us miserable in your company," said Nikki tartly. He looked at her. She was usually the epitome of sympathy – but she had had none for him since the crash. Maybe she was ashamed of him, he thought.

"Look, Nikki, I'm sorry."

"I've lost count of the number of times you've said that," she said, cutting in.

"Maybe that's because I really am." He got up and moved over to her desk and took her hands in his. "Look, I really am ashamed of what I did," he said. "Can you not acknowledge that and let us move on? Maybe we should reorganise things. Like you should do more surveillance work like the job I was doing this morning and I should handle more office-based jobs."

"You mean, I should go on jobs like the one you did this morning? It's not really the cutting edge of detective work." The company had been hired to tail the wife of a businessman whose husband suspected her of having an affair.

"It's the bread and butter of what we do," he said. Perhaps, he thought, Nikki was regretting given up her well-paid job in the fashion world to come and join him at the detective agency. She had done it in a moment of euphoria after a successful case – and just after he had proposed to her.

"The success of the case wasn't the only reason I proposed," he said as if he had got an inkling of what she was thinking. "You rescued me after Joanna died – and you had stuck by me for thirty years." Joanna had been a previous partner of Rivers' who had died from cancer. "We were really happy, then," he said.

Nikki relented. "Yes, we were, Philip," she said.

"And we can be. One of the rules I've always played by is don't dwell on disagreements. Sort them. Don't go to bed and let them fester. You'll feel much better when you wake up in the morning." He moved to kiss her on the lips. She allowed him to and then put her arms around him to kiss him passionately back.

It was at that stage that the doorbell rang. The two disengaged and Rivers went to open the door. Outside was the police constable who had arrested him on the night of the drunken driving charge. He noticed some lipstick on Rivers' cheek. "Sorry, have I called at an inconvenient time?" he asked.

"No," said Ripley managing as near a blush as he could muster. "This is Nikki, my wife and partner in the business sense, too," he said. For some unfathomable reason, he did not want the police constable going away with the impression that he had been snogging his secretary or made a habit of such louche behaviour in the office.

The constable smiled. "There are merits, then, in working with your wife," he said. "We wouldn't be allowed to do that in the police force. Kiss your wife on duty."

"I'm pleased to hear it," said Rivers. He had been in the police force himself. He could not have conceived that – in his day – police stations could be filled with the happy sight of police constables or detectives snogging each other.

"But I would suggest that wasn't why you came round to see me this morning," he said.

"No," he said. He took a notebook from his pocket and flicked through the pages. "We've revisited the scene of the crash - and we've also inspected your car again," he said, "with some rather disturbing consequences."

"Disturbing?"

"Yes," said the constable slowly. "On the road, just by where your car came crashing to a halt, we found blood. There was also a little smeared on to the mangled front bumper - passenger side - of your car. Did you see anything which could explain this?"

Ripley thought for a minute. He looked at Nikki who seemed to freeze in her chair and avoid his glance. "No," he said. "It could hardly have come from my car. I mean, that would have meant it came from the engine. It must have come from the car I bumped into."

"We don't know anything about that car," said the police constable. "Other than the fact that witnesses - yourself included - say it was red."

"And that I saw the driver come out of a nearby house and drive it away."

"That house belonged to the couple who were also standing by the roadside?"

"Yes, I'm pretty sure that was the case."

"Well," said the constable, "I've been to question them. John Morgan and his wife, Emily. Pillars of the community. He's a local councillor and chairman of the environmental services committee. She's big on the parish council. They say they have no knowledge of the red car and its owner."

"Well, whoever it was must have been visiting someone in that street. It's not the sort of place where you would park if you weren't. There are no shops, no pubs, anything nearby."

"I would agree."

"So, Mr Pillar of the Community and his wife are lying?"

"You might say that. I couldn't possibly comment," said the constable enigmatically. "We have to tread carefully before accusing someone as eminent as Councillor Morgan of lying to the police."

"Whereas I could be? But I can't see to what end? Just say I didn't really see a man coming out of what I now know to be Councillor Morgan's house, what do I gain from saying that I did?"

"I don't really think you've been lying, Mr Rivers," said the constable. "Think again. Could the man have come out of any other house?"

"No, I'm sure he came out of Councillor Morgan's house. I'm sorry, constable, but I don't think I can help you any further. This is all very curious, though. What do you make of it?"

"I'm not supposed to make anything of anything, sir," said the constable, "just try and find out what happened by painstaking enquiries."

"Let's go over what we've got," said Rivers to the constable. "Two cars involved in a crash. One driven by a drunken driver. The other stationary on the roadside. The police are called whereupon the driver of the stationary vehicle hotfoots out of the Morgan's house." He stopped. "Comes from nowhere and drives off. Conclusion?" His audience remained silent. "He has something to hide." He paused for a moment to let Nikki and the constable ruminate on what he had said. "Now," Rivers continued, "the red car disappears from the scene and the next morning in daylight it's found there's some blood on the ground near where the rear of that car had been- and on the bonnet of the car that caused the crash." He paused again for effect.

"Conclusion?" asked the police constable.

"That it must have come from the departing red car. I can swear that – even though I was drunk - I did not have a dead cat or a body concealed in the bonnet of my car. I don't remember the design of the red car that well but let's assume it was a four seater with a traditional car boot. To the best of my recollection, that's what it looked like. Well, the blood must have come from the boot of the car. The impact of the crash was not great enough to have penetrated through to the rear of the car."

"Conclusion?" asked Nikki, joining in.

"That the blood came from something or somebody that was in the boot of the car. Now, if you're driving someone home after a night out, you don't stick them in the boot of the car."

"And tests on the blood have shown it to be human blood," said the constable.

"So, someone had been dumped in the boot of the car who had either suffered some sort of accident or assault. It's quite possible they could have been dead. You have a job for CID on your hands, constable."

The police constable nodded. "You would make a good detective, sir," he said.

"I am a detective," Rivers stressed.

"Sorry, sir. I forgot." He proffered a hand to Rivers. "Well, it's been nice meeting you, sir," he said.

"So, what happens now?"

"I don't know. I'll report back on what you've said and someone will probably be in touch." With that, he departed.

"So," said Rivers when he had gone, "what do you make of that?"

"I don't know," said Nikki. "We're in a cleft stick until we find the owner of that red car."

"We?"

"You and me – or the police force."

"Call me cynical," said Rivers, "but I'm not sure that I'd put too much faith in the police force to investigate this one. You almost heard it from the police constable's lips – they are reluctant to do anything to ruffle Councillor Morgan's feathers. If I'm right about the man coming out of his house and Councillor Morgan denying it, that's exactly what any investigation would do."

"So?"

"If we want anything done, we shall have to investigate it ourselves."

"Isn't there a danger that if we ruffle feathers too much, it may come back to haunt us?" asked Nikki.

"That's never stopped me in the past." He thought for a moment. "I suppose the worst that could happen is that they could pin the blame for the blood on me but the only way I could be held responsible is if someone who had been dumped in the boot of the car was alive and the crash killed them. But surely the person who placed that someone in the boot in the first place is far more to blame for what happened than me? Besides, it looks as though Morgan doesn't want us to find out who was driving that car and if we - either us or the police - don't find the driver I can't see that there are any charges that could be brought over the blood."

• • • • •

"You know, I wondered if it wouldn't have been better if we had sent you in as some sort of undercover agent rather than go in guns a blazing," said Larry Green as he handed a coffee to Francesca Manners. They were sitting outside the church hall in Hackney where the North London Women's Revolutionary Action Group was holding their meeting that night. Luckily, the two police constables who had been policing the march the previous Saturday had kept a copy of the leaflet. At first glance, it did not look as though the exhortation to come to the meeting had had any effect. To date, Green and Francesca had counted only three women going into the church hall. Two more approached the door as they spoke.

"Do you think it's time we made an entrance?" asked Francesca. Green, who had been putting off the inevitable moment, nodded in the affirmative. Despite the fact that it was the cool of the evening, he began to sweat again. The two approached the door and entered the meeting – making the total attendance five.

"Excuse me," one of them, dressed in black and with greying hair, said on spotting Green. "This is a women's meeting."

"I know," said Green, now fervently wishing he had left this particular task in Francesca's hands. He pulled his warrant card out of his pocket. "Police," he said. "We need to have a word with you."

"Typical," said Jenny who had been doing some knitting while sitting on the chair next to Hilary – the woman in black. "It's a fascist state. We can't even hold a meeting."

"Nobody's stopping you from holding your meeting," said Green. "We just think you can help with an investigation we're carrying out."

Hilary, who had moved out of her chair to inspect Green's warrant card, then spoke. "Do you allow the woman to speak?" she asked.

"The woman is quite capable of speaking of her own accord," said Francesca. "She doesn't need permission to speak."

"Then perhaps she could ask us any questions that you have on your mind," Hilary continued. Francesca glanced at Larry Green who was perspiring profusely.

"There you are," cried Jenny who had noticed the glance. "She's seeking permission to speak. It's a masculine hierarchy."

Green was not sure how to react. He wanted to shout at them and ask them not to behave so childishly. On the other hand, if he and Francesca gained their co-operation, they might be helpful to his enquiries.

"Come on," said Angela Curran. "Let's get whatever they want over with and not be too grandstanding about it. Then we can get on with our meeting." Even Jenny did not come back on that.

Green withdrew to the rear of the room. "I'll leave it up to you, Francesca," he said. His detective sergeant nodded.

"Right," said Hilary, "you can address any questions you have through the chair - which is me."

"Thank you, chair," said Francesca. At the back of the room Green shook his head and sighed – not loudly enough for any of the participants in the meeting to hear, though.

"I don't know whether any of you have read the papers over the last few days?" said Francesca.

"We don't read the bourgeois press," said Jenny

Jane put her hand up. "Actually, I have," she said. "Is it about the murder in Hendon?"

"Yes," said Francesca. "A man was found strangled and beaten up on waste ground in Hendon. A gruesome murder and one of the most gruesome aspects of it is that his penis and testicles had been hacked off." At this point she was interrupted by Jenny starting to giggle. "In a manner that seemed to indicate that whoever killed him was trying to make a statement of some sort." She swallowed.

"And you think?" prompted Hilary.

"We linked it to a leaflet purportedly published by your group calling on women to fight back and take revenge for Jack the Ripper by launching indiscriminate attacks against men."

"So, you think we did it?" said Hilary.

"And that we're all homicidal maniacs waiting to pounce on men and kill them?" said Jenny.

I'm sure you are, thought Green. He decided against speaking out, though.

"Who wrote that article?" asked Francesca.

"It was anonymous," said Hilary.

"I know," said Francesca. "That's why I'm asking you."

"And we protect people's anonymity so people can feel freer to say what they really feel," said Hilary.

"At the moment, we're at an early stage in our enquiries," said Francesca, "but we would like to know if any of you know anything about the killing. Or if any of you know anything about the victim – John Hedger."

Green could have sworn he saw Jenny flinch at the mention of the name but stored her reaction up for future memory.

Francesca's question was greeted by silence from the group. "I shouldn't need to tell you how serious this is," she said. "I believe that piece is tantamount to an incitement to murder and as such..."

"Could you enlarge on the use of the word 'tantamount'?" asked Jane, butting in.

"Well, it is suggesting that women should rise up and attack men," said Francesca.

"Only I think you used the word 'tantamount' advisedly. In my book, it equates to 'nearly' and if it does mean nearly it means no crime has been committed and you're wasting our time here."

"There is another explanation," said Francesca, "and that is that the author of the piece is indeed the killer and – if that's the case – we're not."

"You have no proof of that," said Hilary,

"You're right," said Francesca, "but I have to tell you we are at the beginning of our enquiries not the end and – as we find more evidence – we may have to come and talk to you again."

"I can't wait," said Hilary

"Also, if the murder is connected with your piece, it is very likely that there will be others. After all, the piece is not calling for an indiscriminate assault on one man."

"So, are you putting us all under surveillance?" asked Jenny.

Francesca declined to answer this question and decided she had gone as far as she could in questioning the group. "Thank you for your time," she said. "That will be all – for now." She turned on her heels. Green followed her out of the door.

"Who told them we were meeting at this time here?" said Jenny. She turned to Gabi. "Was it you?"

Before Gabi could answer, Angela stepped in. "Don't be ridiculous, Jenny," she said. "We were distributing leaflets about this meeting in the High Street on Saturday. The police could easily have picked one up."

"What about the article, though?"

"I suppose it could have been Toby," volunteered Gabi, "but I don't think so. He seemed relatively calm about it."

"If I were the police and a man had had his balls hacked off and there was a leaflet from a woman's group urging people to do precisely that, I think I would have had to go and visit that group and find out precisely what's what," said Angela. "I don't think you should read that much into it."

"Whatever the truth of the situation, I don't think we should help them," said Hilary. "As editor of the newsletter, I should protect the anonymity of the person who wrote the article." They all nodded in agreement.

Once outside the church hall, Larry Green felt able to give vent to his frustrations. "Blimey," he said. "What a weird bunch."

Francesca smiled. "It was nothing more than I would have expected," she said. "Besides, they were not that weird. Of the five, one was a moderating force, one stayed silent throughout, a third was extremely intelligent – notice her querying of the word 'tantamount'. She was spot on. One was a fruit cake and the other was rather severe, stern. I think we could get somewhere with them if we talked to them individually."

"You reckon?"

"Well, it couldn't go any worse."

"Maybe," he reflected. "Maybe that's what we'll do next time. Get them all down to the police station. Shake a few oak trees. By the way, did you notice that when you mentioned the name John Hedger that noisy one, the fruit cake, seemed to flinch?"

"I didn't" confessed Francesca, "but then I was probably concentrating too much on what I wanted to say."

"We still have one or two avenues we need to pursue," Green continued. "For instance, talk to the publisher of the leaflet. And leave the word 'tantamount' out this time."

• • • • •

"Ring Toby, Walter," said Dorothy Renton. "Make sure he's all right." She was holding a copy of the local paper. Its lead story was about the murder of John Hedger and it lacked nothing in telling about the gruesome circumstances in which his body had been discovered.

Walter sighed. He was sure Toby would not appreciate the call. Still, it was Thursday and about time to make the weekly call to see if their son was coming round for lunch on Sunday. He rang Toby's number. "Toby?" he asked when the person on the other line read out the telephone number.

"Yes, father."

"I.,.. er .... I...."

"You wanted to know if I was coming round for lunch on Sunday." Toby prompted.

"Actually, your mother asked me to call." Why does that not surprise me, thought Toby. "She was worried about you."

More than usual he wondered, but neglected to put his thoughts into words. "Why?" he asked.

"Have you read the papers?"

"Oh, you mean this man?"

"Well, it does seem as if he died in the same way that that leaflet was suggesting men should be killed."

"I suppose so but I told you that it's nothing to do with Gabi. Father, I'm not in any danger from her. She's a normal human being who just happens – sadly from you and mother's point of view – to be German."

"I know, Toby, but do be careful. For your mother's sake."

As if I didn't want to be careful for my sake, he thought, and would be perfectly happy to be attacked and murdered if it wasn't for mother. "I will be careful, father, I always am," he said.

His father paused for a moment. "We went to the police," he said.

"About the leaflet?"

"Yes."

"I don't suppose they've come to see you."

"No."

"I thought not. They're not taking it seriously."

"You don't know that."

Walter Renton swallowed. "So, are you coming to lunch on Sunday?" he asked.

"I expect so, father," he said very much in the manner of someone who was indicating that he would if he had nothing better to do. Walter Renton could detect that in his voice but decided not to make an issue of it.

"He's all right," he said to his wife as he replaced the receiver, "and he's coming round to lunch on Sunday."

At that moment, the doorbell rang. Walter looked surprised but Dorothy seemed to know who it was. "That'll be Mark and Prunella," she said. "I invited them round for a drink. He's a journalist, you know. I thought he might know what to do about this awful business."

Walter opened the door and greeted them. Mark was a journalist for a tabloid newspaper and Prunella worked as a beautician. They had met at a social function about a year ago and got on well. Dorothy had insisted they keep in touch as part of her plan to get Walter involved in social events and out from under her feet.

"Hallo," she said greeted both of them with a kiss. She could turn on the charm as a hostess quite easily. Walter was more restrained in his greeting of them – although he did succeed in pouring them both a drink at Dorothy's bidding.

"So, how are you both?" said Mark rubbing his hands and then holding one out to receive the drink that Walter had poured.

"Oh, we're fine," said Dorothy, "but we wanted to pick your brains. Have you seen this story about the man who was murdered in Hendon?"

"Jill the Ripper?" said Mark. "At least that's the headline that our paper gave it."

41

"I don't think you were alone," said Walter. "The *Telegraph* had the same headline."

"Yes," said Mark, "bit worrying. Don't like to think there's a woman out there who wants to chop my ghoulies off." He shuddered at the thought.

"I have been tempted once or twice," said Prunella as she, too, relaxed with her drink.

"It's not really funny," said Dorothy.

"You see, Dorothy thinks it's someone who's sharing a flat with our son, Toby," ventured Walter.

"Good Lord," said Mark, shocked.

Walter explained about the leaflet they had found in Toby's flat and about Gabi, Toby's flatmate. "Toby seems convinced that she's got nothing to do with it but you can't help but get a bit worried," he added with a sidelong glance at Dorothy.

"I shouldn't worry too much," said Mark. "The leaflet must have been picked up by a number of people. Besides, if you are still worried, perhaps you should go to the police. After all, they are investigating this Hendon murder."

"We have been," said Walter.

"And?" asked Mark.

"We didn't think they took us too seriously."

"They've probably got a number of leads to follow up on," said Mark. "It's a high-profile case." He thought for a moment. "If you are really worried, though," he continued. Dorothy pricked her ears up. "There's a chap I know who lives in the same block of flats as me. He's a private detective. He's very good. Philip Rivers. I could arrange a meeting."

"Honestly, darling, you ought to ask Philip to pay you a retainer as his agent," said Prunella. "You're always putting work his way."

"Always is a bit of an exaggeration," said Mark. "There was this one case last year. He's very thorough."

"What could he do, though, that the police aren't doing?" asked Walter.

"Well, that's largely up to you," said Mark, "You'd be paying him. You could tell him what you wanted him to investigate. Get him to have a look at this girl. Check her background out."

Dorothy looked enthusiastic about the idea. "Shall we, Walter?" It was the sort of question to which he was not supposed to say no.

• • • • •

Rivers quickly worked out where the woman who had offered him sympathy on the night of his accident lived. The Glades was obviously a highly desirable residential area – and he reckoned the houses could have fetched at least £1 million on the open market. One of the priciest would have been the Morgan's house with quite a spacious driveway leading up to a building which resembled the manor houses of an earlier era. He decided against calling in on them yet. He wanted to gather some facts before he confronted them.

"Remember me?" he asked when the same woman who had comforted him opened the door.

She smiled. "Yes," she said.

"I'm just following up on the accident," he said, "especially the car I hit. The police weren't able to pass my insurance details on to the driver because he drove away and I was trying to find him."

"Oh, dear," said the woman. "I don't know if I can help you."

"Did you recognise the car? Had you see it before?"

The woman thought for a moment. She was a pleasant, bespectacled woman in her mid-fifties, probably. If Rivers had to guess what she did for a living, he would have opted for a librarian. That would mean her husband or whoever she lived with would have to be rich for them to be able to afford the house they were living in. "I think I have seen the car before," she said. "Only it's usually parked in the driveway."

43

"I wonder why it wasn't that night."

The woman screwed up her face as if thinking seriously. "I'm not sure," she said, "but I think there was another car there. A darker car. Black."

"Which didn't belong...."

"To the Morgans? No. At least I hadn't seen it before."

"I wonder if I could ask you to help me?" asked Rivers. "I wonder if you see the red car again, could you give me a ring – especially if you could pass on the registration number."

"It's very good of you to take so much trouble to try and pass on your insurance details," said the woman. "Most people would be glad to think they'd got away with it."

Rivers decided to be honest with the woman. "I do have an ulterior motive," he confessed. "When the police came back the following morning, they found blood by the roadside. There was also some on the bumper of my car. It must have come from the red car."

"Oh, my goodness," she said. She paused for a moment and then added: "Don't you think you ought to leave it to the police to investigate it?"

Rivers blushed. "Yes, I suppose so," he said, "but the trouble is I'm a private detective. It's just a natural instinct to try and find out what happened." He changed tack. "Do you know anything about the family over there?" he asked.

"I don't really know them that well. People in this road keep themselves to themselves a lot. I think they've lived here for quite some time. He's our local councillor. He comes round at election time to try and get our vote but – other than that." Her voice tailed off in a manner which suggested she was being critical of him.

"Maybe I should ask him if he knows the owner of the car," said Rivers.

"Maybe you should." She moved to close the door. He had detected that – following the mention of the blood – she had become a little more reluctant to get involved and he did not want to continue questioning her if she no longer felt like co-operating.

"Thanks for your help," he said as he moved off down the driveway. He decided to question a few more of the residents before turning his attention to the Morgans. The story that emerged was similar to the one given to him by the woman. Nobody else had seen the crash but a couple of neighbours – on having the red car described to them – did say they felt they had seen it before although they could not say whose it was. After about an hour, he decided to pluck up courage to knock on the Morgan's door. Emily Morgan answered. She eyed him suspiciously. She was dressed as if she was about to attend a formal function – two-piece grey suit with skirt, a white blouse with a large brooch pinned on to the top of it.

"We don't respond to any traders." she said.

"Quite wise, too," said Rivers. "I'm not a trader. I was the unfortunate who was driving the car that crashed outside your house a week ago. Philip Rivers." He proffered a hand to her which was not accepted.

"I don't know what you want," she said haughtily – much in the manner as if she had been dealing with a trader.

"Then let me explain," he said. "I was trying to find the driver of the car that I drove into."

"Surely the police would help you there."

He smiled. "You would have thought so. Unfortunately, whoever it was drove off and they haven't been able to trace him."

"What makes you think we know anything?"

"Well," he said, "it was parked outside your house. I thought whoever it was probably visiting you. You see, because the police have been unable to trace the driver, they haven't been able to pass my details on. I wanted to do that. I was, after all, responsible for the accident."

"And drunk, as I understand it."

"I had been drinking," Rivers agreed. "I am deeply ashamed about that."

"I respect your motives, Mr Rivers, but I still can't help you."

"Well," he said, "I could have sworn that I saw the driver coming out of your house before he drove off."

"You are mistaken, Mr Rivers, but then you were drunk. Now I have a parish council meeting to attend and I must get going."

"Do you think your husband might be able to help me?" asked Rivers.

"He's not here," she said, "but I don't think he knows any more than I do. Good day, Mr Rivers." With that, she shut the door - leaving Rivers hoping he had given her some food for thought as a result of his questioning.

• • ● • •

Larry Green groaned. He had had a couple of stiff whiskies the night before and the last thing he needed was another early morning call summoning him to duty. He picked up the receiver, though. "Yes?" he barked.

It was Francesca. "Sorry to trouble you, sir," she said, "but they've found another body. Same place."

"Same condition?"

"I haven't been down there yet," she said, "but I understand so."

"I'll see you there." He got out of bed and shuffled over to the bathroom - and splashed some cold water on to his face. He poured some into a cup and drank it quickly. Perhaps that would take some of the smell of whisky from his breath, he reasoned. He'd only had two glasses and it had been several hours ago, but he did wonder for a moment whether he should be driving to the scene of the murder. He shook his head. No, he would be all right. "Roll on retirement," he said as he tried to shave with an electric razor while making his way to the car. It took him about fifteen minutes to get to the waste ground where he was greeted by Francesca.

"Good morning, sir," she said. She was immaculately dressed - not a hair out of place. Green marvelled at how she did it. "Exactly the same as the last one," she continued. "Penis and testicles cut off."

"Have you found them?"

"One of the PC's did. Just thrown into the undergrowth again."

"Anything to identify him?"

"Wallet with driving licence in it. Again, he only lived a few minutes' drive away. Dan Peacock. Mid-forties. Don't know anything more than that."

"We'd better get round to his home," said Green. "There's not much more that we can learn from here."

Francesca thought for a while. "Did you notice something about the body?" she asked when she had collected her thoughts,

"I didn't take much of a look - to be honest," he said.

"His clothes," added Francesca. "Very 'lived in'. Not as smart as the other guy's. I would say he wasn't really that well off."

"And your conclusion?"

"Not really got one at this stage but it's worth bearing in mind."

Green nodded. "Why don't you leave you car here?" he said. "We can chat about the case as we drive to his home. I'll bring you back when we've finished."

Francesca got into the passenger seat of his car. Green started up the engine. "So, what are we looking at?" he asked. "Is it the indiscriminate attack on men that that leaflet was calling for?"

"Looks like it could be," said Francesca.

"Why have these guys been singled out?"

"Because they've been violent to women?" ventured Francesca.

"How does the killer know?"

47

"Because they've been with both men?" asked Francesca, "And that's where the clothing comes in."

"Eh?" Green obviously wasn't on her wavelength.

"Well, one was a reasonably well off guy - smart suit - good job. I ventured to think Peacock doesn't fit into that category so if we're right about both men having been with same woman it would have to be someone who moved in very different economic circles. Most women would strike up a relationship with people from a similar background to themselves. There's only one type of woman who definitely wouldn't."

"I think I can see where you're taking us," said Green slowly.

"A prostitute."

"Should we be warning men not to engage with prostitutes, then?"

"Bit early to come to that conclusion," ventured Francesca.

"Yes, but if you're right that it looks like somebody who's taken up the clarion call of the leaflet and someone who is engaging with a whole host of men as a result of her line of business, we'd probably better be bracing ourselves for a number of other bodies to be turning up in the weeks ahead." Green shuddered at the thought.

By this time, they had arrived at Peacock's home address. The information they had had led them to a council estate in East Barnet which looked as if it had seen better days. Peacock's house had obviously not seen a lick of paint for several years. There was rust around the perimeter of the windows, too. Green knocked on the door. There was no reply.

"I have a set of keys," said Francesca. "They were in his pocket." She put one in the lock and the door opened. They stood in the hallway. Green tried to switch the light on - although it was daylight it was quite dark in the corridor by the door. It didn't come on. He went down the hallway to the kitchen at the back of the house. Some plates and mugs from a recent meal had not been washed or cleared away.

"He's obviously not house-proud," said Green.

At that juncture, a small squat woman approached the doorway of the house. "What are you doing?" she asked. Green flashed his warrant card at her - as did Francesca. "Do you have a search warrant?" she asked.

"No," said Green, "but I don't think the owner would mind about that."

"What do you mean?"

"He's dead. We're trying to find some evidence of a next of kin - to inform them."

"Dead? But I only saw him last night."

"He died this morning."

"But he looked all right. He was in the pub."

"Quite probably he was all right," said Green. "He was murdered."

"Oh, my God." She shook her head. "I told him to be careful." Francesca pricked her ears up. "What do you mean?" The woman remained silent. "Come on," said Francesca. "If you know something you should tell us,"

"There'll be no next of kin. He was a loner. He mixed with prostitutes." Green gave Francesca a knowing glance.

"How do you know?"

"He told me. I went drinking with him occasionally. I'm on my own, too. He wanted to talk to somebody."

"Had he ever been married? Or had any partner?"

"No. I've known him for several years and there's never been any talk of anybody."

"Do you know any of the women he'd been with?"

"No," The woman looked indignant. "Do I look like the sort of person that would consort with prostitutes?"

Nothing surprises you when you've been a police officer as long as I have, thought Green. But no, he reasoned. She looked as if she had had quite a rough life but she must have been in her late fifties and - try as he might - Green could not envisage her working as a prostitute.

"No," he said, "but do you know where he picked up his prostitutes?"

"That wasn't the sort of thing that we would talk about," she said sniffily, "but I would imagine - just like any other bloke - he would look for adverts in telephone boxes, that kind of thing. I didn't ever see him using a computer so I doubt if he picked them up online."

"Did you ever see him with a woman? You know, in a normal relationship," asked Green.

"Not that I can recall."

"I was just wondering how he would have treated a woman," Green continued.

"I can't help you there," said the woman, "but he had a short fuse. He could be argumentative with both women and men. Not averse to using his fists."

Then why did you go out for drinks with him, thought Green. He didn't sound like such an appealing companion. He looked at her. She looked dowdy, certainly had no charisma about her and was probably lonely - just like the dead man had been. "Well, thank you for your help," he said. "We'll just finish up around here - see if there's anything that could help us find a next of kin." She took the hint and departed.

Green sighed. It was only ten o'clock in the morning but he was tired by now. Early morning calls didn't really resonate with him. "I think we'll get forensics to come round here - see if we can find any evidence of anyone else being on the premises," he said. "We'll come back mob-handed and go through the place with a fine toothcomb, see if there's anything to show which prostitutes he used."

With that, he turned on his heels and went back to his car. Francesca followed him. "So - two men brutally attacked," he said. "Both known to have had a history of violence. It probably is too soon to issue a general alert about associating with prostitutes. Maybe you're only in trouble if you're violent towards them."

• • ● • •

"I don't think we'll be troubled by the police anymore," John Morgan said to his wife as he put the telephone down. "That was a colleague of mine who is on the police committee. The police seem to accept that the car that drunkard drove into had nothing to do with me."

"Good, dear," said his wife Emily. There was a note of hesitation in her voice. It was as if she did not really believe the news that she was hearing was that good.

Morgan walked over to his drinks cabinet and poured himself a large scotch. "It seems they believe the word of a pinnacle of the community rather than a drunk," he said. He laughed. "And so they should," he added. "So they should. Would you like a drink, dear?"

"No, thank you, John," she replied. "I have a meeting later on tonight. It wouldn't be a good idea to turn up reeking of alcohol."

"No," he reflected. "That's not the image we're trying to cultivate." He finished his scotch and walked back to the drinks cabinet to pour himself another one. "On the other hand, I don't."

Emily looked a little apprehensive. "Do you really think we can cover up what happened last night?" she said. "Or that we should?"

"What's done is done," he replied. "There's no point in talking about it anymore," he added. "Now, go off to your meeting as if nothing has happened."

"Yes, dear," she said quietly – collecting her coat from the hallway before she departed.

CHAPTER THREE

"Morning, old boy," said Mark Elliott as Rivers answered his knock on the door.

"Let me introduce you to the couple I was talking about – Mr and Mrs Renton." He ushered Toby's parents into the living room. "I'll take my cut – 10 per cent or a snifter at the Greyhound."

Rivers smiled. "Payment will be made in the usual fashion," he said. "At the Greyhound."

Mark nodded. "No need for me to stay, old boy," he said. "All yours." With that, he was gone.

"Do sit down." said Rivers to the Rentons. He could tell they were a little nervous. "My name's Philip Rivers – private detective – I gather you're worried about your son."

"He's taken up with this woman – very unsuitable," said Dorothy Renton.

"Now, now, dear," said Walter patting her arm. "We don't know that." He turned to Rivers. "He, Toby, that is, has this lodger, Gabi, a German girl. She's an assistant teacher at a local school. We went round the other weekend and we couldn't help noticing this leaflet."

"It was in his bedroom," intervened Dorothy as if that fact spoke volumes. Rivers almost sighed audibly. What a mistake. Allowing your mother access to your bedroom, he thought.

"The only telephone in the flat is in the bedroom," said Walter

Rivers glanced from one to the other. "It really doesn't matter whether the two of them are having a relationship," he began.

"It matters to us," said Dorothy tartly.

"I'm sure it does," said Rivers a trifle icily. He was beginning to wonder about the wisdom of being commissioned by the two of them. After all, from the way Mark had described it, they wanted him to spy on their son. "It doesn't matter, though, for the purposes of my investigation," he added.

"No," said Walter trying to wrestle control of the situation. "There was this leaflet there," he added. "I'm afraid we haven't still got it. We gave it to the police."

"No matter," said Rivers. "I'm sure there are copies we can get hold of."

"It was from a group calling itself the North London Women's Revolutionary Action Group – I can remember the name only too well. It was calling on women to take the law into their own hands and start indiscriminate killings of men – a sort of revenge for the actions of Jack the Ripper."

"Yes, Jill the Ripper," said Rivers. "I saw the article in the local paper. It seems to have started, by all accounts."

"Mr Rivers," said Dorothy, anxiously touching the private detective's arm. "We want to know if our Toby is safe."

"You mean, you want to know if this lodger is a part of this revolutionary group – and if he's in any danger from her?"

"Yes, well, any danger from anyone, really."

Rivers thought for a moment. "So you mean find out about this group and whether this call is serious and what they intend doing about it?"

"Put like that, I suppose, it's a tall order," said Walter.

"No," said Rivers thinking. In actual fact, it made the scope of the enquiry more interesting. It was not just spying on poor Toby. "What about the police?" he added.

"We didn't think they were really taking our concerns seriously," said Walter. "They said they'd be back to us in due course."

"Was that before the murders?"

"Well, yes, I think so – or very soon after."

"I bet you'll find they're taking it a bit more seriously now."

"Maybe so," admitted Walter. "If you think it's not worth

taking the case on, we'd understand." Dorothy stood there glowering. Rivers realised she, for one, would not understand. Walter stood up as if about to leave.

"Just one more thing," said Rivers.

"Yes?"

"Does your son know you've come to see me?"

"No."

Rivers had thought as much. "I think it would be best if he did," he added. "Otherwise I'd have to snoop on him as well as on Gabi. If he realised I was following him for protection, it might put his mind at ease." Walter frowned. In truth, he did not relish telling Toby what he and his mother had done. "If you think it would sound better coming from me, I'd be quite happy to take on that responsibility," Rivers said. The tension in Walter's body eased. The whole essence of his relationship with his son had been based on non-communication. He was happy for Rivers to take the initiative. "On that basis, then, I'm prepared to take on the case," said the private detective.

• • ● • •

"Could I have a word with you before you go?" the matron at the retirement home said to Jane Harris as she spotted her sitting next to her father.

"Yes," said Jane as if glad to be distracted from her thoughts. She had arrived at the home early in the afternoon - as she did every Sunday. Her father had been awake at first and smiled upon her entry into the room. She managed to force a smile, too. The matron, Miss Durban, a portly woman who presented quite an austere front to the world, noticed that she did not kiss him. There seemed to be little warmth in their greeting. Week after week, it was the same, she reflected. Yet she still kept on coming. She would stay for about two hours and – indeed – seemed to be clock-watching from the time of her arrival. For most of the time, her father would be asleep, but she would touch his arm and smile as she was about to leave. As she did so that day, she made her way to the matron's office. "You wanted to see me, Miss Durban?" she asked.

"Yes," said the matron. "Please sit down." Jane looked surprised. It must be serious, she thought. "I was looking through your father's file and you are not named as his next of kin," she said.

"No," she replied. "I wouldn't be."

Miss Durban took a card out from a filing system she had already placed on her desk. "It's a Tom Harris," she said.

"Tom, yes. He's my brother."

"Elder brother?"

"No, younger, but father's a bit of a traditionalist. He doesn't think women can do things for themselves. He would never leave me with any responsibility."

Miss Durban nodded. "You're not close to your father, are you?" she said.

Jane reflected. Many people would have reacted by saying "what the hell's that got to do with you?" She did not, though. The question had not been posed aggressively. "No," she said without embellishing her answer.

"I don't know if you've noticed a deterioration in his condition of late," she asked.

"To be honest, no. As far as I can make out, he's spent most of his life asleep for these last few months."

"He's very weak. I don't think he's got long with us." Jane nodded. "This is difficult," began Miss Durban, "but I usually counsel families at this moment by saying if there's anything you need to get off your chest with father, now's the time to do it. Is there?"

"Is there what?"

"Anything you'd like to get off your chest."

Jane sighed out loud. "There isn't time for the amount of stuff

I'd like to get off my chest," she said. "And it would upset him too much. I wouldn't want him to spend his last few days reliving his quite shameful past."

I suspect, thought Miss Durban, it might upset you too much, too. "Quite shameful past?" she said picking up on Jane Harris' words. "Are there things that you think he needs to get off his chest?"

"Undoubtedly but you've seen him. He hasn't got the strength to do so. Besides, in his own version of history, he's done nothing wrong."

"I hope you don't mind me asking but why do you come every week?"

"I ask myself that sometimes," said Jane. "Duty. I can't imagine anything worse than spending your final days seeing no-one, talking to no-one, just waiting to die. I feel as if I have to – no matter what he's done – at least offer him some comfort." A tear welled in her eye as she spoke. The normally reserved Miss Durban put a hand on her arm.

"And your brother?"

"What about him?"

"He doesn't feel the same way?"

"No."

"You don't think he might regret it if he doesn't pay one last visit?"

"I'm sure of it. He lives with me. He can't understand why I come. I doubt if he'll even turn up to the funeral."

"Your father must have done something really bad?"

"That's a conversation I don't want to get into, Miss Durban," Jane said in a faltering voice. "Let me say this – I think Tom has taken the easier path. To his mind, he hasn't got a father. That poor pathetic creature over there," she gesticulated back to the living room, "who is in need of a little comfort and a helping hand doesn't exist. I have to provide what comfort he gets and –as you have observed – it's minimal. That's all I can bring myself to do."

Miss Durban nodded. "I think, though, you should tell Tom what the situation is," she said.

"I will," said Jane. She got up to go and was just making her way out of Miss Durban's office when she stopped and turned back to face the matron again. "Just to say- thank you," she said. "I realise your words were meant out of kindness – rather than prying."

Miss Durban smiled. On reflection, though, she admitted she would have liked to pry a little into the background of the Harris family.

Once outside, Jane made a beeline straight for the car. She had to fight back tears as she walked. At that moment, she almost envied families who could conjure up happy memories of loved ones when they were about to face death. She drove off, turning the volume up on her car radio as she listened to Classic FM. Tom was reading the Sunday newspaper when she got home. He did not ask her how she had got on. Their lodger, Beatrice, was also sitting in the living room playing around with her mobile phone.

"I'm sorry, Beatrice," said Jane. "Would you leave me and Tom alone for a few minutes?"

Beatrice gathered up some knitting and her mobile and made her way to her room. She had not often been faced with requests like this in the six months she had been renting a room in Jane and Tom's flat. Emotional heart to hearts was not their thing.

"He's in a bad way," said Jane once they were alone. There was no response from Tom. "He might die soon and matron thought you should be given the opportunity to visit him and make your peace with him before he goes," she said.

"And you thought?"

"I thought nothing, Tom, you know that. I'm not going to put any pressure on you to do one thing or the other. You should know that by now."

"Good."

"I take it therefore that you're not going to see him?"

"So, you are putting pressure on me?"

"If you think that's pressure, Tom, you need your head examined. I just want to know whether or not you'll go."

"No I won't."

Jane nodded. "Right," she said. "I think I could do with a lie down."

She moved towards her bedroom but Tom hailed her before she left the room. "Sis," he said. She stopped in her tracks. He moved towards her and placed an arm around her waist. "I know you've been having a tough time." He kissed her on the cheek. "You know, you don't have to keep on doing what you have been doing," he said.

She freed herself from his embrace. "I feel as though I do," she said. "Let me go, Tom. I do need a rest." He relinquished his grip and she disappeared into her bedroom.

A few moments later Beatrice reappeared from her room. "You all right?" she asked as she approached Tom. He nodded. She kissed him on the lips. "Remember, I'm always there down the corridor if you need me," she said.

"Thanks," he replied.

• • **•** • •

"I wish I wasn't a fucking psychology student," said Gary as he lay on the bed beside Jenny. "It makes me feel that I should understand you, but the truth is I haven't got a clue."

"That's literally what you are," said Jenny. "A psychology student who fucks. Not difficult to understand."

Gary turned to face Jenny and reached out to put an arm round her waist. She shook him off. He shook his head. "What do I get out of this relationship?" he asked.

"I've told you. No warmth. Men and women equals sex. I like sex."

"But you don't like men," said Gary.

"Not true. I can discriminate. There are some men I like. There are lots I don't like."

"As for me?"

"If you don't stop asking questions, I think you know on which side you'll end up," she said tartly. Then she relented a little. "Look, I like sex, I like stimulating conversation. You can provide both of those, but that's it."

Gary reached for the side of the bed and picked up one of Jenny's cards. "'Call Jenny'," he read from it. "'I'm naughty and need strict discipline'. Why, Jenny?"

"It's men exploiting women," said Jenny. "It's men hurting women. And they have to pay for it. That's women exploiting men. Just remember you're the only man who gets to fuck me for free and forget about the discipline."

"Happy to. I'm not really into discipline. I just wanted to explore your mind. It's what we psychologists do."

"Not a good idea."

"Why do you advertise yourself that way, though?" he persisted. "Others don't."

"Maybe it's my guilt complex," she said. "Look, if I followed in my parents' footsteps, I'd have ended up embracing the Catholic church and I'd probably become a member of Opus Dei. They believe in the pain theory of redemption. Instead, I became a prostitute and get to experience the pain theory of sex. Well, not theory – I get to enjoy a good spanking from time to time."

"Enjoy?" queried Gary as he hauled himself up from the bed. Jenny remained silent. In truth, she did not much relish talking about her work with clients with Gary. There were compartments to her life: one was the prostitution, one was Gary and the third was the women's movement. They were all separate as far as she was concerned and she did not want to mix them.

"I think I'd better go into uni," he said. "There's a lecture I have to attend and it'll probably be less taxing than spending a morning talking to you." He made his way into the kitchen to get himself a cup of tea. Jenny showed no signs of stirring from the bedroom. "Do you have any clients today?" he asked.

"Not for you to know," came a voice from the bedroom.

"I was just wondering whether I should make myself scarce," he said.

"Oh," she replied. Then after a moment's thought she replied: "I should stay away until tea time. Six o'clock."

He began drinking the tea. He had not made Jenny a cup. Whenever he suggested she make him a cup she would begin assaulting his eardrums with comments like: "It's not a woman's job to provide men with food and drink." Okay, he thought, then it's not a man's job either. He thought about her for a moment. He was still fascinated by Jenny. She would have provided an excellent case study for his psychology course. He had met her about six months ago at the students' union bar at his university. Her friend, Jane, had been studying on a part-time course there and invited Jenny along to a disco. It had not been either of their scenes so – when Jane decided to go home – they went out for a drink together. They had got on well together. Her father had been a vicar and she had gone to a convent school – after which she had gone to university where she had gradually been seduced by a radical feminist group. She had developed her theory about men there and had indulged in prostitution to help pay the fees. After leaving university, she had started a career in book publishing but her radical views did not sit easily with the need to make compromises with her employer so she gave the job up and concentrated on earning money through prostitution – interspersed with a little writing for radical magazines. The extras she offered helped to boost her income. On their first meeting, they had left the pub together and – empowered by drink – they embraced and Gary had lifted her skirt up when they were in a deserted alleyway and pulled her knickers down. He had then begun a little foreplay running his fingers across her vagina.

"That'll be £15," she said. He unbuttoned his trousers and began to penetrate her. "£25 now," she added, "but I'll let you off. You probably haven't got the money on you as you didn't make an appointment – and you are a student, part of the exploited masses as a result of tuition fees." He didn't say anything. He never did. After all, she had explained only too clearly that she didn't want any warmth in their relationship. There must have been something there, though, he thought. After all, as she said, he was the only one who got it for free.

As he left her flat on the council estate in Hackney where she lived, he noticed a smartly dressed man in a suit approaching the same door that he had just exited from. He could not help but wonder whether this was her first client arriving. After all, men in suits were a rare species on that estate. He decided against hanging around and trying to find out. Why would he need to know the identity of any of her clients?

Gary was younger than Jenny. Still in his early twenties and in the second year of his university degree. He had been bruised by an earlier relationship and was loathe to commit himself again. His politics were similar to Jenny's although if truth be known he was a little more mainstream in his thinking than her. In elections, he would vote for the most left-wing party that he thought had a hope of forming a government. Jenny would spoil her ballot paper by writing in: "None of the above." With a neatly trimmed beard and long curly black straggly hair, he had the look of a typical student which – he supposed – he was really. Jenny, he thought, as he walked to his lecture, I could do without her – but then again, I couldn't.

• • • • •

"My name's Rivers. Philip Rivers," said the private detective as he presented himself to Toby Renton on his doorstep.

"Yes?"

"I've been hired by your parents to find out whether there is any threat to you."

"From Gabi?"

"Yes, in the first instance."

"In the first instance?"

"Well, you may have read in the local papers that the type of action that the leaflet you spotted was calling for is already beginning to happen."

"What?" It was obvious that Toby had not caught up with this information. "Look, Mr Ri ...."

"Rivers," he said.

"Mr Rivers. I really don't think I need you to be spying on me. It's bad enough dealing with my parents on their own without some omni-present third force being at their beck and call."

"I don't intend to spy on you, Toby," said Rivers. "How can I? I've just introduced myself to you."

Toby eyed him for a moment. "Yes," he said, "that does seem a remarkably silly thing to have done."

"If my intention really was to spy on you," said Rivers. "But it's not. Look, would you mind if I came inside? I take it Gabi's not here?"

"She's not. She works as an assistant teacher at a local school. She's not here between eight and four thirty."

"I know. And your parents told me you often worked from home on Mondays."

"Oh?" said Toby surprised. "So, they do listen to some of the things I say." Rivers smiled. Toby opened the door a little bit wider and invited him in. Once inside, he made his guest a cup of tea.

"Can I ask you? You don't have a copy of this leaflet, do you?" asked Rivers.

"No, my parents took away my only copy – that is, unless Gabi has a spare one in her room."

"Would you mind if I took a look?"

Toby hesitated for a moment. "I suppose not," he said, "but I don't know what she'd say if she thought I'd been in her room."

"What kind of a relationship do you have with her?" asked Rivers.

"Oh, we're just good friends," replied Toby as he showed Rivers into his tenant's room.

"I didn't mean sexual." He was rummaging around in Gabi's drawers now – carefully putting back in place everything he had disturbed once he had had a look at it. "I mean, do you get on well together?"

"Well enough," said Toby. "We go for drinks together – although it's a little difficult to penetrate what I can only describe as a frosty exterior. She is an odd person in some ways." He described the incident that had happened while they were watching "What's New Pussycat?"

"So, she gets pleasure from seeing men in pain?" ventured Rivers

"I wouldn't have put it like that." Toby replied.

"How would you have put it?"

Toby thought for a moment. "I suppose like that," he finally conceded.

"Have you made a pass at her?"

"I was thinking of doing but then I thought, no. I didn't see any sign of any encouragement and I wasn't sure myself." He blushed. "I'm not very good at those sorts of things," he added, thinking he hoped the conversation would not turn to his lack of prowess in forming relationships. It didn't.

"Does she have a boyfriend?"

"Do you mean is she gay?"

"Or a-sexual?"

"She says she has a boyfriend in Germany."

"But you don't think so."

"Mr Rivers, it sounds terrible to say this – but I just can't imagine her fucking anyone."

"No," said Rivers. "That may be relevant information." He smiled. "There are lots of people we meet in life that we can't imagine fucking anyone. Where did you meet her?"

"In a pub."

"So, the two of you – you who have difficulty in making advances to women and she who gives out a strong aura of not having relationships with anybody – struck up an acquaintanceship?"

"Put like that, it does sound extraordinary, I warrant you," said Toy. "No, she was being chatted up by this rather leery overweight tabloid reporter. I could see she wasn't enjoying the experience so I just went over to her and said 'hi'."

So you do have the technique if you want to use it, thought Rivers. "Go on," he said.

"We started talking. I was with a friend who went to the bar with the tabloid reporter who apparently said to him: 'Your mate's trying to steal my bird' My friend said 'no, he's just trying to be friendly'. He managed to convince the guy he had had too much to drink and that he should give up on Gabi."

"So, what happened when you tried to start up a conversation with Gabi?"

"I apologised for butting in – but said I thought she looked as though she was not enjoying herself. I told her the guy was only after one thing."

"And that was?"

"That's precisely what she said to me. I said 'getting off with you'. She asked me: 'And you?' I said I have to get to know people a lot better before I reached a decision on something like that."

"Very diplomatically put. But she was in a pub on her own – happy to strike up a conversation with men she didn't know. And you still maintain she isn't interested in sex?"

"Put like that I can see why you might disagree with me."

"And, as a result of this chance one night conversation, you invited her to come and live with you?"

"You've got a way with words," said Toby. "It wasn't like that. I took her out for a drink a couple of times."

"And no thought of any romantic attachment?"

"At that stage, I'd come to the conclusion 'no'."

Rivers nodded. "And your overall assessment is that she poses no threat to you?"

"I'd hate to think that she does."

"And the women's group?"

"I don't really know much about that," he said, "but – if Gabi's not a threat to me – I don't see why I should be in any more danger than anybody else."

"No," said Rivers. "Logically that should be true." He thought for a moment. "Here's what I'll do," he said. "I'll shadow Gabi for a while and I'll find out what I can about the women's group. My first assessment is the same as yours. You're not under any more threat than anybody else. But your parents are paying me and – if I could find out anything that would help the police to solve these murders – so much the better. Are you happy with that?"

"I suppose so."

"Good," said Rivers finishing his search of Gabi's room. "There doesn't seem to be any leaflet here," he said. He made as if to leave but turned around at the door to give Toby a parting shot. "Oh, by the way, not a word to Gabi about what I'm doing."

"No, of course not," replied Toby.

• • • • •

Hilary returned to the bedroom with a couple of cups of coffee. Her partner, Buddy, had just woken up. "Thanks," she said, taking one of the mugs from her. "You look troubled," she added.

"Yes," she said. "I'm beginning to wonder whether I should have run that piece in the leaflet – you know, the one calling for indiscriminate attacks against men."

"Why? If you're a radical feminist group, you should be able to publish anything you want."

Hilary looked at Buddy. She was much younger than her. There was an honest indignation in her voice. It was what had attracted Hilary to her in the first place. She put her arm around her and stroked the back of her neck. She laughed for a moment. She would have liked to stroke her hair but Buddy sported a crew cut. There was no hair there.

"It's not a question of that," she said. "It's a question of whether it'll be more trouble than it's worth. There are so many things we should be concentrating on – the strike at the print works, for instance. Instead, we're just going to have the police buzzing around us like there was no tomorrow."

"Why?"

"Because someone appears to have taken the author of that pamphlet at their word. Two men have been killed locally in the past week with their balls cut off as if the killer is trying to make a statement."

"No," said Buddy as if shocked by what Hilary had just said. "And you think it's down to what you published?"

"It seems too much of a coincidence for it not to be," Hilary replied. "Anyhow," she added after thinking for a moment. "I suppose I ought to go to work." She ran a small printing shop which specialised in publishing left-wing leaflets and pamphlets – although she was known for taking on the odd wedding assignment to help the works make ends meet. Ironically, the print works was being flooded with clients at the moment as a result of the women's strike over pay. Hilary felt guilty that she was making money out of the dispute but consoled herself by reminding herself that it was to help the women's cause. If she felt that guilty, she reasoned, she could always give a donation to the print workers' cause. "It's a busy time for me at the moment," she said.

"And we all know why this is," said Buddy who got up from

the bed and made her way to the bathroom. "Who do you think is doing these murders?" she said as she passed her partner. "Is it one of the people from the women's group?"

"I hope not," said Hilary. "I really don't think murder is a way of promoting our cause."

"Surely murder is a legitimate tool in promoting some causes?" said Buddy switching the shower on as she spoke. "I mean the IRA, South African freedom fighters – would any of them got to where they are today if they had not been prepared to use violence?"

"You're not equating like with like. I mean, I haven't got much time for men but I don't think the women's movement has to resort to murdering men to get equality."

"So why did you print that piece?"

"Didn't someone once say 'I disagree with what you have said but I would fight to the death for your right to say it'?"

"Something like that," said Buddy. She emerged from the bathroom – naked now and carrying her night clothes with her. "You said the women's movement shouldn't have to resort to murdering men to get their way?"

"Yes." Hilary felt slightly ridiculous having this conversation with Buddy as she was washing and getting dressed.

"Well, why not? It is a legitimate ploy to get publicity for what you want and put pressure on the authorities to bow to your demands."

"Not if you can achieve them by other means."

"And the women's movement has achieved all it wants, has it?" said Buddy who was now fully dressed in jeans and what Hilary thought of initially as a cowboy shirt. She reproached herself mentally. It should probably have been described in less sexist terms. Buddy made her way into the kitchen as Hilary made her way to the door. She helped herself to some cereal. "Have a good day," she said to the departing Hilary.

Hilary turned and smiled but – as she reached the street

outside – she began thinking. Would Buddy really kill to get her own way – or had she just been making a point and speaking hypothetically? Come to think of it, what point had she – Hilary - been making by printing that leaflet? On both counts, at the moment, she could not provide an answer.

• • ● • •

James Curran knocked the top off his boiled egg and began to eat it. "Thanks, Angela," he said. The couple lived in a smart suburban home – two up, two down. They had no children but not for the want of trying. He worked as an accountant in the city and she as a supply teacher although there was no work for her that day. "What are you going to do today?" he asked.

"Oh, nothing in particular," she said. "I've got a bit of work to do with that women's group I belong to."

"You do seem to spend a lot of time on that," he said in a tone that was mildly critical. Angela just wondered how critical he would be if he discovered the kind of things the group were doing. She had managed to keep all the leaflets from him. He had no idea it was called the North London Women's Revolutionary Action Group. It was the kind of organisation that would not have been readily approved of in the cocktail circuit they moved in. He finished his egg. "I'd better go now," he said. She smiled and pecked him on the cheek before he made his way out of the door to his car.

Once he had gone, she fetched her briefcase from the living room and sat down in the room next to it that they had converted into a study. She brought some papers out of it relating to the hire of the church hall for their meetings and started totting up how much they owed the church. As she started working, she sat back for a moment and started thinking. To the women's group, she had always been considered the sane voice which brought them back to reality at times. James, though, would be shocked by the stance the group had taken on issues. She was beginning to wonder whether the duplicity – concealing her activities from James – was too much for her. Should she come clean about her political involvement despite the threat that it might jeopardise her marriage? Or should she cut her ties with the women's group and become a typical suburban housewife to fit in with James' image of her? As she had these thoughts, she began to weep quietly to herself. She felt unable for the time being to continue with getting the books straight for the women's group.

• • ● • •

"Let's review," said Green as Francesca entered his office that morning. "Where do we go from here?"

"The only real leads we've got are that leaflet about revenge attacks against men coming from the women's group," said Francesca. "Was it a serious incitement to murder? If so, did some serious plotting take place after the publication of the article?"

Green nodded. "Or were they just random hits?" he asked. "I think we can take it from the location of the bodies that the killer must have driven his victims to the disused wasteland. Is it, I wonder, a good idea to step up patrols around that area in case there's a third victim?"

"Probably," said Francesca. She looked at Green. She liked working with him. The two of them would discuss issues and it seemed he took account of what she had to say. It was a far cry from her memories at Brighton where her boss, Detective Chief Inspector Nick Barton, would just dictate the line they were to follow. She smiled and looked at Green. He may not have been charismatic. He may have been quite old school in his style of policing. But she was convinced he was straight as a dye.

"Right, let's do that," he said firmly.

"I doubt whether we'll get anything from it, though," Francesca added. "Whoever it is could have taken a risk there wouldn't be an extra patrol around there for their second hit. If they've got any sense. they'll realise they can't risk dumping a third body there."

Green nodded. What his detective sergeant was saying seemed to make sense. "Oh, I had a call from Professor Saint the pathologist this morning," he went on. "He seems to think the mutilation took place – in both cases – after the victim had been killed."

"So, it's a statement to us rather than an attempt to inflict more suffering on the victim?"

"Not much of a statement," said Green. "We don't know why these two men were singled out for killing – what it was about them that identified them as a target for killing."

"Maybe nothing," said Francesca Manners. "Maybe the killer just doesn't like men."

"In which case, none of us is safe." He pointed at himself here. "It's a chilling thought, sergeant." He paused for thought for a moment. "I think I'm about to make a sexist comment here," he said, "but surely the most likely place to find a woman who hates men that much is at that women's revolutionary group." Francesca did not seem offended by what he had to say. "So, we ought to start our investigation there," he added.

"Maybe."

"Correction," he said. "I think you ought to start your queries there. I'm not sure I'd even get to the point where they would allow me to ask a question. I'll have a word with the vicar – see if he knows anything about the group he hires his hall out to. I'll also drop in on the search of Peacock's home – see if they've found anything. Keep in touch if you find anything. Otherwise, we'll meet back here at six o'clock this evening."

"Mmmm, I think I'll start out by having a look at that German assistant Gabi. After all, she took the leaflet seriously enough to take it home with her and her landlord's family are convinced she poses a threat to their son."

"Good thinking."

• • ● • •

"I can't infiltrate a women's revolutionary group," said Rivers when he and Nikki finally got round to discussing the new case that had landed on his doorstep. "Besides, it's in Hackney and Hackney is notoriously difficult to access by public transport. The tube doesn't go there."

"So, the only reason you want me to take over that part of the enquiry is because of problems that you have rather than talents I have," said Nikki.

"I didn't say that," he protested.

"You didn't need to. It's all determined by your driving ban."

Rivers sighed. He wished he could turn the clock back. Last year when he decided to ask her to join the detective agency it was at a moment of euphoria. She had gradually nursed him out of his depression – the only person who had bothered to do that. She had stood by him when his former partner had died of cancer. They were getting on so well together than he had asked her to marry him on the last day of a successful case. They had known each other for thirty years, even lived together for a while at the beginning of their relationship. Surely when you had known a person for that long, there were no surprises in the relationship. You knew enough to know the relationship would work before you entered into a living together arrangement or marriage. Somehow, though, the euphoria of the previous year seemed to have slipped away. Maybe it was because they were both living and working together. No time for pursuing independent activities.

Nikki, for her part, was still dwelling on his drink-driving charge. How could he have been so silly? she thought. He had even crashed into another car. Could have injured someone or worse. That was not the Philip she knew and had loved. Had loved? It didn't bear thinking about. Surely, she could not have spent thirty years of her life always being there, being ready to pick up the pieces, for the relationship to fade so soon after they had taken the step of living together again and getting married.

"Look," said Rivers. It was almost as if he was reading her thoughts. After thirty years, though, he ought to have known her well, she thought. "I can't change the past," he said. "What's happened has happened. I feel as much remorse for what I've done as you clearly do. I trust you to take on the work that I can't do. Surely that's got to mean something?"

"Yes," she said. "I suppose it does." She at least realised something. In the past when Philip had come to a difficult stage in their relationship, he had walked away and moved on. He had done that with other women, too. Now he was trying to mend fences. Rivers realised that, too. You're growing up, he said to himself. Becoming a bit more mature. "So," she said, "I go round to the next women's meeting. What do you do?"

"There are two strands to this investigation," he said. "Does Gabi pose a threat to the son of my clients – Toby Renton – and who is behind these murders and therefore who is under threat now? You take the second strand. I take the first." He got up from his desk. "No time like the present," he said.

Larry Green parked the car at the end of the street. The address he had got for the vicar turned out to be a semi-detached cottage – traditional two up, two down. He sighed – remembering his early years in the job. Visiting a vicar or a priest wouldn't have been like this. There would probably have been a large rambling vicarage with someone on hand – usually the vicar's wife – to dispense tea to any visitors. He had got the address from the notice board outside the church. What had probably once been the vicarage lay behind the parish hall. It had been converted into flats long ago and was now probably a nice little earner for the church.

Green walked up to the door of the cottage and rang the doorbell.

"Coming," said a voice. The door was opened by a man who looked as near to retirement age as Green himself did. He was not so flabby, though. Indeed, he was quite thin. He was wearing a dog collar and a knitted jumper over a shirt. "Can I help you?"

"I hope so." Green took his warrant card out of his pocket and showed it to the man.

"Oh." He sounded surprised. "What have we done?"

"Probably nothing," said Green reassuringly. "I just wondered if you could help us with some enquiries we're making. Is it the Reverend Maurice Cruickshank?"

"The same," replied the vicar. "Come in." He ushered Green into what was obviously the living room to the left of the front door. A hallway led to a kitchen behind and there were stairs which must lead to the bathroom and bedrooms. "As you can see, modest living quarters," said the vicar. "Paid for by renting out what used to be the vicarage. I can offer you some tea. You can come into the kitchen and talk to me while I make it. No vicar's wife ready to dispense it. She's out at work – earning more money than I ever could. She works for a bank."

"Interesting," said Green hesitantly.

"Not what you were expecting, I suppose." He looked at Green closely as if scrutinising him for some clue as to why he was there. "You're old enough to remember the days of the rambling vicarage." he said. "They're long gone. But you didn't come here to reminisce, did you?"

"No," the detective replied accepting a cup of tea from the vicar. At least some things don't change, he thought. You still got served tea when you visited the vicar. "I want your help with a murder enquiry I'm pursuing."

"Murder?" echoed the Reverend Cruickshank. He sounded surprised.

"Yes, you may have read about it. Two men have been found

murdered and mutilated on waste ground not far from here. There appears to have been a sexual element in their killing." He was loathe to use explicit language in explaining what had happened to the man of God.

"Oh, yes," he said. "I read about it. They'd had their balls cut off."

Green spluttered over his tea-cup at this point. "Yes," he said, "as a matter of fact, they did." It was almost as if he was trying to dismiss the mutilation as insignificant.

"I don't see what I can do to help you," continued the vicar. "Neither of them were parishioners. I remember seeing their faces in the local newspaper."

"Then you'll have seen that the killings may have been linked to a revolutionary women's group which was calling for revenge attacks on men to get one back at Jack the Ripper. That women's group uses your parish hall for its meetings."

"Ah, Miss Sampson and her crew," said the vicar.

"Well, I wouldn't have described them quite like that," said Green. "I found them a bit more threatening. I visited one of their meetings."

"Well, you would have done. They don't want men at their meetings."

"I wondered how you found them?"

"Oh, always polite, but then they wanted something from me." He paused for a moment and saw a quizzical look forming on Green's brow. "I did invite them to attend one of my services but I got no response. Miss Sampson said that they wouldn't come to my services so long as I didn't come to their meetings. It was a bargain I was happy to strike."

"Do you have an address for her?"

"Yes, I always insist on taking an address for any group that hires the hall? Just in case. You know, they could leave something behind or something like that." He went to the end of the living-room where there was a filing cabinet with drawers. He opened one of them and produced a card with Hilary Sampson's name and address on it. "I'll write it down for you," he said, seating himself at a chair by the cabinet to do so.

Green took it from him. "Thank you," he said. "I don't think they'd have responded if I'd asked for it. Do you know the names of any other members of the group?"

"Let me see." He rummaged in the drawers of the cabinet. "There was another woman," he said. "She must have been the treasurer. I got regular cheques from her – mostly through the post. She put her address on the accompanying letter." He reached for another card. "I transferred it on to this – Mrs Angela Curran. Now she could have been a member of my flock. I remembered Miss Sampson was a bit austere but Mrs Curran looked like just the sort of woman you could find on the parish council."

"Thanks for that," said Green as the Reverend Cruickshank wrote this address down for him, too. "No others?"

"No," he said. "As I said, I never attended any of their meetings but I don't think they attracted many people."

"There were five there on the night I visited them," said Green.

The vicar looked a little worried as he waved Green to sit down again. "Are they dangerous?" he asked. "I don't really want the church to be associated with hiring a room to a group which is plotting murder on the streets of the parish."

"We've no evidence against them other than the words in that leaflet as yet," said Green.

"That's a pretty nasty thing to call for, though," said the vicar. "I've a good mind to suspend their bookings,"

"That's up to you," said Green, "but I would ask you not to take any action before we've had the chance to question them. It might alert them as to how seriously we're taking the threat in that leaflet. I would imagine it would only mean a couple of days delay."

"All right," said the vicar as he ushered Green out of the front door.

· · ● · ·

Francesca parked her car in the school car park and walked over to the main reception area.

Once inside, she produced her warrant card and asked if she could speak to the headteacher.

"Can I tell him what it's about?" asked the receptionist.

"I would prefer to do that myself," replied the detective. Within minutes, she was being ushered into Francis Durrant's office.

"What can I do for you, inspector?" the headteacher asked.

"It's sergeant, by the way," she said correcting him. "It concerns one of your employees – Gabi Dortman," she said. "I'm trying to build up a picture of her."

"Why?"

"I don't think it would be fair on her if I told you," said Francesca. "At this stage, she's not suspected of anything. She merely might have some knowledge of a crime that's been committed."

"Do you want to speak to her?"

"Not at this stage, no. Just find out a little about her background."

Francis Durrant nodded. "Fire away," he said, "but I think I have to warn you that I don't know that much about her."

"How long has she been working for you?"

"About eight or nine months. She started at the beginning of the school year."

"And how long does she plan on staying with you?"

"She has a contract until the end of this term. She had excellent references – from a teacher training centre in Bonn and the headteacher of a gymnasien in Germany."

"How does she strike you?"

"That's an odd question, sergeant. Subjective rather than objective."

76

Yet the answer may be more important to me than any platitudes written into her references, thought Francesca. "As I said I'm trying to build up a picture of her," she said.

"Well," the headteacher began. "As I said I don't know her very well but I have sat in on one or two of the lessons she's been helping out with. I'd say she was efficient. A German characteristic."

"Efficient?" queried Francesca.

"Yes, she's not warm," said the headteacher. "Her presence is invaluable for the children. They wouldn't actually get to speak the language they're learning so much without her being there. But I wouldn't say she shows any warmth towards the children. Just delivers what she has to deliver – efficiently."

"Does she socialise much with other members of staff?"

"I wouldn't know about that. You'd be better off asking our head of languages about that."

"Would it be possible to call him so I could have a word with him?"

"He's taking a lesson at the moment but if it's really important I could go down there and stand in for him and send him up here."

"If that wouldn't be too much trouble."

The headteacher nodded and made his way out of the door. A few minutes later, a younger man with longish curly black hair presented himself to the head's study. "Simon Fry, head of languages," he said. "I gather you wanted to speak to me."

"Yes," said Francesca. "Come in and sit down." The only seat that was free was the head's and the teacher seemed reluctant to sit on it. "It's all right," said Francesca. "He won't be coming back until we've finished talking." Simon overcame his reservations. "I want to talk to you about Gabi Dortman," Francesca continued.

"Yes," the teacher said. "The ice maiden."

Francesca picked up on his terminology. "The ice maiden? What do you mean by that?"

"She's very reserved. You don't learn much about her. When she first arrived, I took her out for drinks a couple of times but it was quite a boring experience. She didn't seem to want to say very much about herself."

"Could it have been a language barrier?"

"No, I don't think so. I speak German. I wouldn't have any problems on that score. No, I just think she didn't want me to get to know her."

"Does she have any particular friends? Boyfriends even?"

"She did once mention a boyfriend back in Germany but I don't think she's seen him since she's been over here. I think she gets on quite well with the bloke who's lent her a room in his flat. She's talked about him a couple of times – but I don't think she's made many other friends. She's good at her job, though. She speaks fluent German to the pupils – which is why we hired her."

"How close is she to this bloke – her landlord?"

"I don't know, really," said Simon. "I don't think there's any romantic liaison between them. I mean, she never talks of them doing things together."

"Thank you." At that juncture a bell rang outside and – within minutes – the headteacher was back amongst them. "I think I'm finished here now," she said. "I'll get back in touch with you if I need to."

By this time, Simon Fry had gone leaving Francesca with the headteacher. "Should I be worried about your enquiries?" he asked. "I mean is it safe for pupils to be left in her charge?"

"As I said, we have no evidence of her being involved in any criminal activity. If that changes and I think she could constitute a danger to your pupils, I would get back in touch but – at this stage – I think it's extremely unlikely."

"Thank you," said the headteacher. "I'll see you out."

Francesca was walking back to her car when she saw a familiar figure coming through the school gates. "Philip?" she said. "Philip Rivers?"

The private detective looked up at her. "Francesca?" he said. "Good God, what are you doing here?"

"Trying to conjure up a profile of someone who's involved in a murder investigation."

"Don't tell me – Gabi Dortman?"

"Yes. How did you know?"

"I'm following her because someone's parents believe she may pose a threat to their son."

Francesca pricked her ears up. "I think we should exchange information," she said. "Hop in – we'll try and find a café where we can have some tea."

Rivers got in her car. "What an extraordinary coincidence." he said. The two of them had worked closely with each other when Rivers had been trying to get his client off a charge of murder in Brighton. Francesca had helped him.

"I've got a new job in Barnet," she said. "Started just over a week ago."

"So, tell me about Gabi Dortman."

"I'm investigating the murder and mutilation of two men. She belongs to a women's group which had been calling for revenge on the male species for the killings of Jack the Ripper. We think the two things may be linked."

"And I've been hired by the parents of her landlord who think he may be in some danger from her."

"Is he?"

"He doesn't think so and I've no evidence so far to suggest he is. That's why I was coming to the school. What did you find out?"

"Nothing much," said Francesca, "Her colleagues call her the ice maiden – they say she gives nothing away about herself and is just efficient at her job."

"That shouldn't necessarily be a source of complaint," said Rivers.

"No, I agree. They said she was quite friendly with her landlord. Anything going on there?"

"No," said Rivers. "Toby admits that when he first met her he saw her as a possible girlfriend but now – well, they're just friends. Go out for drinks on odd occasions. He gave her the room because he felt sorry for her. She was being bullied by her landlord who had switched the heating in her flat off in the middle of winter."

"So, what do we do now?"

"Well, I think I ought to meet her, talk to her, perhaps try to chat her up. Find out a little bit more about what makes her tick."

"I think we ought to pool resources," said Francesca. "If you don't have any luck getting to know more about her, perhaps I should arrange a chance meeting, too."

"Good," said Rivers. He offered her a hand to shake.

"Can I offer you a lift anywhere?" she asked. He said where he lived and described where it was. "I think that's on the way back to the police station," she said.

He did not like to disillusion her. He took time to study her as they drove back to his flat. She was still as smartly dressed as he remembered her being during their days at Brighton. A handsome woman, he thought, as he disembarked from the car. He was pleased to see her again.

Nikki was aware of five penetrating pairs of eyes looking at her as she walked into the parish hall that evening. "Is this the women's revolutionary action group?" she asked – only too well aware that, try as she might, she could not mask her middle-class accent.

"Who wants to know?" asked Jenny sharply.

"My name's Nikki Hoffmeyr," she said. "I picked up one of your leaflets and thought I'd like to come along and see what you were doing."

Hilary intervened at this point. "Don't be put off by my colleague's rather gruff manner." she said. "It's just that we've been having a spot of bother recently from the police."

"Oh, well, I can assure you I have nothing to do with the police," said Nikki.

Hilary smiled. "We were just discussing what we could do to help the local women print workers with their dispute," she said. "They've got a public meeting on Friday night. We feel we should be there."

"Absolutely," said Nikki. Jenny screwed her eyes up at this juncture. To her, this potential new recruit sounded like an extra from the TV programme "Absolutely Fabulous".

Nikki hovered on the edge of the meeting. "Come and sit down." said Hilary friendlily. "You're aware of the dispute?"

"Oh, yes, they had a protest march in the High Street a couple of weekends ago," said Nikki, accepting Hilary's intervention. "I think it was then that I picked one of your leaflets up."

"Were you on the march?" asked Jenny, this time sounding more enthusiastic.

"No," Nikki replied. "Sorry to disappoint you. I was just out shopping."

"Do you have any questions for us?" asked Angela. She was smiling at Nikki. It was as if she recognised a kindred spirit. Someone with not quite so much revolutionary fervour as Jenny or Hilary – but someone who would sympathise about her predicament of melting into middle-class suburbia once the meeting was over.

"As a matter of fact, I do," said Nikki. She appeared nervous. "I saw another leaflet," she began.

"The one calling for indiscriminate attacks against men?"

"Yes. I wanted to know. I mean, is that your policy?"

"No," said Hilary, "and in fact that's what has got us to the attention of the police."

Nikki was hesitant but only for a moment. "I want to be frank with you," she said. "I don't really want to get involved with an organisation that sanctions violence."

"Oh, how prissy," sneered Jenny who appeared to have veered back to being sceptical about the new arrival.

"We don't as a group," said Hilary. "We open up our leaflets to people who want to express an opinion – anonymously or not. That was how that article came about. Well, I suppose it came through me as I publish the leaflets. I thought that was a legitimate expression of opinion."

"So you didn't write it yourselves?"

"Why do you want to know who wrote it?"

"I don't necessarily. I just wanted to find out whether it was the collective opinion of the group before I decided whether or not to join."

"I don't trust you," said Jenny sharply. With that, she reached over and snatched Nikki's handbag from her and began opening it.

"Excuse me," said Nikki in a futile attempt to get it back. She turned to Hilary. "Do you treat all newcomers like this?"

"We do if they're private detectives," said Jenny holding up a business card she had extracted from the handbag with a flourish. "Hoffmeyr and Rivers – private enquiry agents," she added. "What are you privately enquiring into? Us?"

Nikki reached out for her handbag. "I think I'd better go now," she said.

Jenny flung it on the floor. "I think you better had," she said. Nikki picked it up and made her way to the door – those five pairs of eyes staring at her in a penetrative way again. "I'm sorry to have interrupted your meeting," she said, "but I think I can tell my clients you're not as dangerous as they think you are."

"Come back and spy on us again and you might find out that we are," said Jenny. As Nikki left the hall, she turned to her fellow members. "You're all too nice for your own good," she said. "She could have been working for the press."

"No," said Jane firmly. "They'd have sent one of their own."

"I think we'd better be careful," said Hilary. "No more meetings here and no more new members until this has all blown over."

"Yes," said Jane. "We could find ourselves outnumbered by

disguised policewomen, private eyes and journalists if we're not careful."

Once she was away from the meeting Nikki rang Rivers on her mobile. "I'm afraid I was rumbled, Philip," she said. "Sorry. Next time we want an undercover job done I think you'd better do it yourself."

"I think I'd have stuck out more like a sore thumb than you in this instance," he said dryly.

"What I did find out, though, is that it isn't the group's policy to launch indiscriminate attacks on men. It was just a one-off article that was submitted to them. It needn't necessarily have been from one of the group, I suppose."

"They're not that well known." said Rivers, "so it probably was. We need to know who wrote it. Listen, coincidence this afternoon. I met up with Detective Sergeant Manners – you remember, from Brighton? Well. she's up here now and investigating this case. I reckon we should pool our information with her and see where it gets us."

· · ● · ·

"How's it going?" Green asked the detective constable as he arrived at Peacock's home that evening.

"Not much," came the reply. "A load of old takeaways stuffed in a bin. Clothes thrown on the bedroom floor and not hung up or put away. No photos of loved ones, nearest and dearest or anything like that. Looks like the home of a loner who didn't pay too much attention to himself or how he looked."

"Fairly routine, then?"

The detective constable nodded. "Oh, there was one thing," he added.

"Yes."

"Two or three cards – with telephone numbers on them. Prostitutes, I would think."

Green's eyes lit up. "Show me," he said. There were three of them. One urging people to call if they wanted an "intimate relationship", one inviting a caller to meet Jenny – a "naughty" girl who needed firm discipline and the third just a picture of a naked woman with a mobile number attached.

"Right, let's arrange appointments with all three for tomorrow morning," said Green. "We'll call round and bring them in for questioning. You take the naked woman, I'll take the naughty one and I'll fix up an appointment with the "intimate" one and Francesca can go round and collect her. He handed the naked woman's card to the constable and began dialling the number for the intimate relationship. A woman's voice answered. "Hullo?"

"I saw your card earlier today," said Green. "I think an intimate relationship is just what I could do with."

"Good," came the reply in a soothingly sexy voice. Well bred, thought Green. Why does she need to advertise on the street?

"Do you take appointments during the day time?" asked Green.

"Yes."

"How about eleven o'clock tomorrow morning?"

"Look forward to it. What's your name?"

Smith would be too obvious, thought Green. He also didn't think it would be right to use his real name. "Jones," he said. "Larry Jones."

"I look forward to seeing you tomorrow morning, Mr Jones."

"Larry, please."

"Larry." She gave him an address that he wrote down and then rang "naughty" Jenny and went through a similar rigmarole.

"Can I ask you one thing?" he said. His voice had changed from the husky tone he had adopted with Ms Intimate. Now he was more Essex man. He took a punt that this persona was more likely to appeal to Jenny.

"Yes," she said.

"How naughty are you?"

"We can negotiate that tomorrow morning."

Hmph, he thought. No Ms Intimate here. A hard-headed businesswoman, he thought to himself. "Does it involve spanking?" he asked as the detective constable arrived back in the room. He looked shocked.

"It could do."

"Right, I look forward to seeing you tomorrow." With that he turned his mobile off and put it back in his pocket. There was no reciprocal comment from Jenny.

"Don't you think you're getting into character a bit too much, sir?" asked the detective constable.

"I'll admit I was getting into the swing of things," he said. "But I thought it would make me seem like a legitimate punter. I'm just going to bring them in for questioning tomorrow morning. Nothing more." He scratched his head. "You know, I think I recognised the voice of the naughty one. I think she may be a member of the women's revolutionary action group – the group that was calling for indiscriminate attacks on men."

"Interesting, sir," said the detective constable.

CHAPTER FOUR

Green was aware of a young guy with long curly hair hanging around outside the entrance to Jenny's flat that morning. His eyes seemed fixed on her flat as if he wanted to vet anyone coming or going. Green approached the door, accompanied by a young policewoman.

"Who is it?" came a voice from inside.

"Jones. Larry Jones."

The door opened revealing Jenny wearing a short gymslip and white shirt with the first two buttons undone. "You're not Larry Jones," she said – instantly recognising the police officer from his visit to the women's group.

"No, and I'd hardly expect to have found you here operating as a prostitute with your views about men," he said.

"Many prostitutes don't like men." she replied. "What do you want? Why the need for subterfuge?"

"I think you'd have refused to an appointment if I'd told you who I really was," said Green. "I need you to come down to the station to answer a few questions for me."

"Am I under arrest?"

"No, you'd just be helping us with our enquiries."

"And if I refuse?" she said. "Helping the police has never been strong on my priority list."

"If you refuse, I may have to arrest you. It's up to you."

"So, it's heads you win and tails I lose? I shouldn't have expected any more from a fascist arm of the state."

Very naughty, thought Green. She deserved some firm discipline, he thought, and then banished the idea from his head. He had to admit to being a bit distracted by the garb that she was wearing but the presence of the young policewoman helped him to concentrate on the job in hand. He decided not to react to being called a fascist. "Then you'd better come with me," he said reaching out with his hand to guide her from the flat to the car.

"Don't you touch me," she said angrily – withdrawing from his grip. "I'd like to change into something more appropriate before I accompany you to the station."

Green nodded. "That's OK," he said. He motioned to the policewoman to accompany Jenny to her room. "Just in case you make a bid for freedom through the back window," he said.

"I know you're good at stitching people up," said Jenny, "but you haven't got a thing on me. I'll be back here sooner than you know it."

"I admire your confidence," said Green. "We'll see." He waited while she changed into a pair of jeans. She had also done the two buttons up when she returned from her bedroom. "Let's go," he said.

At the same time as her boss was knocking on Jenny's door, Francesca Manners had arrived at the home of the woman offering an "intimate relationship". She, too, was accompanied by a policewoman. She knocked on the door. "Mr Jones?" came a voice from inside. "Do come in." Francesca obviously did not reply because she would blow her cover away. A woman opened the door. She looked shocked by what she saw. "You're Detective Sergeant Manners." she said.

"Yes, and you're Jane Harris from the North London Women's Revolutionary Action Group." replied Francesca.

"I wouldn't quite define myself in that way," she said. "I suppose you'd better come in." Francesca could see there was a young woman hovering in the hallway. Jane turned to her. "Beatrice," she said, "it's all right. I don't think I run the risk of being beaten up by Detective Sergeant Manners – although you never know." She turned to Francesca. "Beatrice operates as my chaperone in case one of my clients gets violent. She stays in her bedroom – but can come in a minute if I call her."

"So, it's quite a professional set up you have here?"

"You didn't come to chat to me about that," said Jane.

"No, there are a few questions that we want you to answer. I'd like you to accompany me down to the station." Jane did not put up any resistance to this request.

● ● ● ● ●

"So, we have two prostitutes in for questioning – both of whom are members of the North London Women's Revolutionary Action Group. The naked woman was in a police cell at the time of one of the murders," said Green once they were back at the station. "It's all about this group, isn't it? Let's get them all in. We know where the woman who chairs the bloody thing lives and the treasurer. And you visited the school where that German assistant works. Pull them all in and make sure they all realise that every one of them is here before we start questioning them. I'll stay here while you organise it. Meanwhile, we'll put these two in the cells." Francesca nodded and departed. They walked past the cells where Jenny and Jane were being held. There was a banging on the grille from Jenny. Green opened the flap. "Yes?" he asked.

"How long are you going to keep us here?"

"We have to wait a while. We're arranging for more people to be brought in."

"More people?"

"Yes, I think you may recognise them. If you weren't here, you'd probably be holding a meeting."

"A meeting?" It dawned on Jenny that the rest of her group was being rounded up. "This is harassment," she said.

"No, it's good police work."

"You've got nothing on us. Nothing."

"We'll see when the others arrive. Now, if you wouldn't mind just waiting."

Five to go, Green thought. Within half an hour, Hilary, Angela and Gabi had arrived at the station accompanied by police officers. Gabi's "Ice Maiden" demeanour had vanished. She had been embarrassed at being hauled straight from her classroom down to the police station. It would be bound to reflect badly on her with the headteacher, she thought. Perhaps her job would be on the line.

Angela also looked worried. Her husband had been out at work when the police called but she could not help thinking that – were she to be detained for questioning after six o'clock in the evening – she would have an awful lot of explaining to do to him. She could not really ring him and tell him that supper would be a little late that day because she was being questioned about a murder.

Only Hilary appeared unruffled by what had happened. There would be no recriminations against her. Buddy would understand and accept her explanation that she had nothing to do with the murders. Her print business was her own and she could resume working at it immediately she was released from the police station.

"Well done," said Green to Francesca as she followed the three women into the reception area. "We'll question the prostitutes first," he said. "I'll take the mad one. You take Ms Initimate. We'll have to bring them out of the cells first and take them to interview rooms. We've only got four cells. Make sure they walk past their friends on their way to interview."

Francesca nodded as police constables released the two women from their cells and took them to separate interview rooms. A look of shock dawned on the faces of Hilary and Angela as their two colleagues were marched past them. Gabi, though, was beginning to regain her "Ice Maiden" composure.

"What's all this about?" Hilary asked Green as he followed Jenny into the second interview room.

"You'll find out soon enough. Can you organise the taking of these three women to the cells?" he asked the desk sergeant.

"Excuse me, inspector," said Angela.

"Yes."

"Are we here to help you with your enquiries or are we under arrest?"

"To help us with our enquiries."

"In other words, we're here voluntarily?"

"Yes."

"Then why do we have to be placed in a cell?"

Green thought for a moment. "It's easier to manage that way," he said. The woman had a point, he had to admit. There was nothing to stop them walking out and going home. "Okay," he relented. He opened the door to a waiting room. "You can stay in there," he said.

The trio trouped into the room. "Round one to us," said Hilary. "Well done, Angela." Gabi smiled at her, too.

"I do have legal training," said Angela.

By this time Francesca had already sat down opposite Jane in one of the interview rooms. She was accompanied by a detective constable. "You may know, Miss Harris," she began, "that there have been a couple of murders in this area recently. In the second case, a search of the victim's house revealed he had a card on him with your telephone number on it – offering him an intimate relationship if he'd like to give you a call." Jane made no verbal response – but a look of surprise came over her. Francesca took a photograph out of a folder and pushed it across the table. "Do you know this man?"

Jane took her spectacles out of a case to look at the photograph. What she saw horrified her. "Oh, my God," she exclaimed. It was the photograph of Danny Peacock's mutilated body. Jane turned away from the photograph.

"Do you know this man?" persisted Francesca.

"It's awful....what's happened to him," she stuttered.

"Do you know him?"

"I don't recognise him."

"He would appear to know you. He had your telephone number in his flat and he telephoned you the night before this happened."

Jane turned to look at the photograph. "Yes, yes, I do recognise him," she said. "I'm sorry but I couldn't concentrate on the face with....that." She turned away again and pointed to his mutilated body with her finger.

"When did you last see him?"

"I've only seen him once. It was three nights ago."

"The night that he was murdered?"

Jane paused for a moment. "If you say so," she said. "He was alive and well when he left my flat."

"You work as a prostitute?"

Full marks for deduction, thought Jane. "Yes," she confined herself to saying.

"Why?"

"Why?" repeated Jane. "What's that got to do with this case?"

"Just answer the question."

"Well," said Jane hesitantly. "I suppose it's because I enjoy sex."

Francesca thumbed her way through the folder again and picked out another picture of Peacock. This had been taken from his flat. It showed him fully clothed. "With this man?" she asked. "Crumbled suit, pot belly, dirty shoes, lived on a run-down council estate. You could have done so much better for yourself."

"I said I enjoy sex – not every sexual encounter that I have. This one," she said, pointing to Peacock. "No."

"How many times did you see him?"

"Just the once."

"And would you have seen him again?"

"No."

"Why not?"

"For the reasons you describe. Also, he was a bit rough."

"Rough?"

"Yes, he hit me. I nearly had to call my flatmate for help but – in the end – I persuaded him to go."

"So you discriminate over clients?"

"Yes." Jane paused for a moment. "Have you ever had a sexual encounter, Detective Sergeant?"

"That's not relevant," said Francesca, a trifle haughtily.

"It might help you to understand the situation. Have you never had sex with someone and thought,' oh, that was a mistake, I won't go there again'? It's the same with me. Just because you're a prostitute it doesn't mean you don't have feelings. Emotions."

Francesca thumbed through the file again. "What about this guy?" she pushed a photograph of John Hedger across the table. It was a holiday snap, not the mutilated picture that had been taken at the time of his death.

"Yes, a couple of times."

"When was the last time you saw him?"

"A week., ten days ago. I don't write down the names of clients in my appointments book. Sometimes I don't even know them myself."

"So, if I told you his body had been found on Tuesday morning a week ago – mutilated just like the last one?"

"It would have been round about that time that I saw him. I can't be more precise than that."

"And would you have seen him again?"

"No, I gave him the benefit of the doubt first time but he was rough, too."

"You don't seem to be having much luck with your clients, do you?" said Francesca.

"I have more than two a week," replied Jane coolly.

Francesca decided to change tack. "You're a member of this women's group, aren't you?"

"Who are all spending a day in police custody? Yes, I am."

"Do you believe in their philosophy of indiscriminate attacks against men in revenge for the hurt Jack the Ripper inflicted upon women?"

"It's not their philosophy. It's just something that somebody wrote."

"Did you write it?"

"I am not a violent person, Detective Sergeant. It's not a philosophy – if that's what you call it – that I would agree with."

"Did you write it?"

"I repeat – it's not a philosophy that I would agree him."

Francesca wondered whether she had chosen a clever form of words to avoid being caught out lying. "Yes or no?" she asked again.

"You've had your answer on that score."

Francesca closed the folder on the table. "That'll be all for the time being" she said. "If you wouldn't mind waiting in the waiting room, we may need to ask you further questions later."

The detective constable escorted Jane from the room and returned with Gabi in tow.

"Sit down, Miss Dortman," said Francesca. "Do you know why you're here?"

"You want to question me, I think, about a murder."

"Two murders, actually. You, actually, came to our attention before these murders were committed. The parents of your landlord were worried that you could pose a threat to their son."

"A threat? How?"

"You had a copy of a leaflet from a group you were a member of – calling for indiscriminate attacks against men."

"Oh, that."

"Oh, that?" mocked Francesca. "Yes, I suppose it was of no concern," she added sarcastically. "All it was asking people to do was murder men indiscriminately – which is, in fact, what happened."

"I did not write that leaflet," she said.

"No."

"I did not want to do what that leaflet was calling on people to do."

"Yet you have a violent past?" asked Francesca.

"What?"

"You pulled a knife on a fellow pupil at your school in Germany when you were ten years old, I believe."

"I was never charged with anything. The boy's parents decided they didn't want to bring charges."

"The boy, yes." She looked at the folder in front of her. "It was an indiscriminate attack on a boy, I understand?"

"It never came to court. No-one ever knew what the boy had done to me."

"Now's your chance to tell," said Francesca.

"It has nothing to do with this case."

"Whatever it was that this boy did to you – and the file doesn't help me there – did it scar your opinion of men?"

"No. I have a boyfriend in Germany."

"How convenient," said Francesca sharply. She pushed the two photographs of the mutilated men across the table. "Do you recognise these two?" she asked.

Gabi gave them a cursory glance. "No," she said pushing them back across the table. Francesca noted she did not seem at all distressed or disgusted by the photographs. A very much colder reaction to them than Jane had shown. "Have you ever worked as a prostitute?" she went on.

"No, I told you – I have a boyfriend in Germany. I can give you his address if you want me to. He will tell you I have quite normal sexual desires if that's what you're really interested in." The "Ice Maiden" seemed to be getting a little irritated at the way the interview was progressing.

"That won't be necessary," said Francesca. "Can you tell me, though, where you were a week ago last Monday evening and three nights ago?"

"I think I was in the pub both evenings. I go there quite a lot for peace and quiet. It's better than sitting in a living room watching television with somebody you don't know very well who is trying to make a forced attempt at conversation."

"Do you pick men up in these pubs?"

"No. How many times do I have to tell you – I have a boyfriend in Germany?"

"Thank you," said Francesca. "That will be all. Give us the name of the pub and we'll check out your alibi. If you wouldn't mind waiting, we may have some more questions for you later."

She motioned to the detective constable to escort Gabi back to the waiting room and asked him to see if there was anyone else waiting for interview. A few moments later he ushered Angela into the interview room.

"Angela Curran," said Francesca reading from her notes. "Housewife, married to an accountant, living in a smart suburban house. You're the oddball of this group."

"Me?" said Angela,

"Yes, you. There are five of you – two prostitutes, one lesbian, and a woman with a history of violence against males. You're a respectable suburban housewife. Very much the fish out of water. What are you doing with this lot?"

"I feel very strongly about women's issues."

"So strongly that you're prepared to kill men indiscriminately to obtain your rights?"

"Eh?"

"Well, that's what the leaflet your organisation has produced is suggesting."

"I don't agree with that."

"Did you write it?"

"Of course not," she said emphatically.

"Who did?"

"We have not been told."

"Where were you on the nights of a week ago last Monday and three days ago?" asked Francesca.

"With my husband at home," she said confidently.

"And he will verify that?"

"I'd rather you didn't ask him," she added quietly.

"Why not?"

"He doesn't know about the women's group. Well, he knows I'm involved with a women's group but he doesn't know how radical in nature it is."

"If we don't verify your alibi, you will remain a suspect," said Francesca. "I'm afraid we'll have to."

With that, Angela broke down and wept. "I've never killed anyone," she sobbed. "I've never been remotely violent towards anyone. You have nothing to suggest that I have been - yet you want to ruin my life."

"I don't want to ruin your life. It's your involvement with this women's group that has done that – if it happens." Angela was still wiping away a tear from her eye. "Look," said Francesca, "why don't you try telling your husband what's happened? If he's a reasonable man and you have nothing to do with these events, you might be surprised by him. He might be sympathetic to you." Angela remained silent. Somehow Francesca sensed she had not been reassured by what she had said.

• • ● • •

"Sit down," said Green to Jenny once they had arrived in the interview room. He picked a couple of photographs out of a folder and virtually flung them across the table at her. "Know either of these men?"

Jenny barely cast a glance at the photographs and then flung them just as decisively back across the table. "Fuck off," she retorted.

Green picked the photographs and walked around the table to the other side. He eyeballed her – so much so she could smell his breath. It was not a pleasant smell, she thought to herself. "Look at them," he said placing them on the table in front of her.

She sighed but did as she had been told. "They're men with

their willies off," she said.

"Not a trace of emotion," said Green. "I show you the mutilated corpses of two men whom we believe have been attacked by members of your group and you show not the slightest trace of emotion and try to make a joke of it."

"It is a joke. You've no reason to believe any of us had anything to do with either of these killings. It's the typical response of the fascist state. Pin the blame on the nearest left-wing group in town."

Green walked round to the other side of the table with the photographs. He put the one of John Hedger back in the folder but pushed the one of Peacock across the table again. "We know you knew him," he said. "Your telephone number was found in his flat. He telephoned you a couple of days before he died – probably to make an appointment. What was it, Miss Naughty? One of your spanking sessions going too far so you had to retaliate? How did you dispose of the body?"

"I thought I was coming voluntarily to help you with your enquiries," said Jenny, "which means I can walk out at any time. I don't have to listen to your insults."

"Do you like men, Miss Creighton?" Green decided to make formal use of her last name to try to bring the interview back to a less aggressive confrontation.

"Not particularly."

"So why do you fuck them?"

"Because I'm exploiting them. Charging them for something they could get for free if they had any wit about them."

"Bit of a gloomy existence. Fucking men just because you don't like them? Does it ever irritate you? Irritate you so much that you want to do away with them? Carry out indiscriminate acts of murder against them? Is that what happened with Mr Peacock?"

"Is that his name?" said Jenny. "Bit unfortunate. He seems to have lost the cock bit but then I guess he can't pee either."

"Your sense of humour is deeply disturbing," said Green. "You

97

haven't told me where you were three nights ago."

"Lying flat on my back in bed with some ape fucking me," said Jenny.

"Mr Peacock?"

"Not the unfortunately named Mr Peacock. No."

"Can anyone corroborate what you've said?"

"What do you think, inspector? They're probably married to a poor nervous woman whom they beat the shit out of every day – a punchbag that might finally pluck up the courage to leave them if they confessed to going with prostitutes."

"Do you get the shit beaten of you? Did Mr Peacock beat the shit out of you?"

"I control the aggression. I offer them favours for money."

"Like spanking?"

"You seem obsessed with spanking, inspector. I'm sure we could come to some kind of arrangement for a fee." The detective constable sitting next to Green blanched at these words.

"Did you offer Mr Peacock favours for money?"

"I'm not going to help you do your job any more. You'll have to find out for yourself."

"Did he go too far, Miss Creighton? Did you have to resort to violence to stop him?"

"No comment."

"I take that as a 'yes' then."

"You can take that however you like. I just don't feel like co-operating with a fascist bully from the state any more. I'm sure you're well capable enough of concocting some spurious evidence and trying to convict me and other members of the group if you want to."

"Why do you think the fascist state would want to waste time trying to falsely convict a little jerk like you?" said Green.

Jenny smiled. "I take it from what you've just said that I'm free to go," she said.

"For the moment," said Green. "Just for the moment, though,

I'd be grateful if you'd hang around until we have finished interviewing your colleagues."

"Out of a spirit of comradeship with them, I will do," she replied, "although I'd hate to do anything that would make you grateful."

Green nodded at his colleague and Jenny was escorted from the room. The detective chief inspector reflected for a moment. Maybe Jenny would have been less antagonistic if Francesca had carried out the interview. On the other hand, she was just as much a member of the fascist state's police force as he was. His concentration was broken as the detective constable returned with Hilary in tow.

"Sit down." said Green. He resolved to be less aggressive in his interview with her than he had been with Jenny. "You are the leader of this group?" he asked.

"The chair, yes."

"So, let's be clear. You're responsible for publishing and producing its leaflets."

"I publish them," she said.

"So, you would maintain you're not responsible for them?"

"I know where this is leading, inspector. Contributors are responsible for their own articles. They're not necessarily a reflection of my opinions."

"While that may be true, Miss Sampson, I think you'll find as publisher you have a legal responsibility for the articles."

"That's as maybe."

"Did you write the article advocating indiscriminate attacks against men?"

"No comment."

"Why not?"

"We preserve the anonymity of contributors. If those of us who didn't write it told you that was the case, you could arrive at the author's identity by a process of elimination."

"Do you like men, Miss Sampson?"

"That's a sweeping question, inspector. There are so many different types of men – as there are of women. I'm not interested in entering into a sexual relationship with a man. In the context of this case, I suppose I could put it that I have no interest in their willies – neither in touching them or cutting them off."

"Thank you, Miss Sampson," said Green. "That's very forthright of you. I'd just like you to tell me where you were three nights ago and – again – a week last Monday."

"A week last Monday I went to the cinema with a friend – I can give you her name. Three nights ago I was at home with my partner, Buddy."

"Thank you, Miss Sampson. We will check those details out." With that, he brought the interview to an end and followed the detective constable and Hilary out of the room. Within a few minutes, he had been joined in the reception area by Francesca. "Let's go over what we've learned," he said to her. "You first," he added when they were alone in his office together.

"Well," said Francesca. "Jane Harris. She admitted to having had sex with the two men - but seemed genuinely distressed when I showed her the pictures of their mutilated bodies. I don't think she wrote the article. She wouldn't give a categorical no, though."

"That, apparently, is group policy," intervened Green.

"Call it a gut feeling, I really don't see her as the violent type."

"Right."

"Gabi Dortman: she's a cold fish and she does have a history of violence in her past. On both the nights in question, she says she was on her own in a pub. She seems to spend a lot of her time on her own in pubs. What does she do there? Does she pick men up? I don't know."

"We need to find out more about her. We need someone to try and pick her up in a pub."

"I think I know just the man for that," said Francesca, smiling.

"Oh? Who?"

"Philip Rivers. He's a private detective I've worked with before. He's been hired by the Rentons to protect their son, Toby."

"OK," said Green.

"Angela," said Francesca. "She's the misfit in all this. Her alibi is her husband, but she's terrified of us contacting him."

"Keep a watching brief on her." Green thought for a moment. "Your private detective, could we use him to find out more about Jane and Angela, too?"

"I don't see why not," she said. Then she added: "What about your interviews?"

"Jenny Creighton. She has to be a suspect. She withdrew co-operation during the interview. Said she didn't want to be bullied any more by the fascist state. Refused to confirm whether she'd seen either Hedger or Peacock. I can imagine her hacking them to bits, though, and enjoying it. You know she made a joke out of Peacock's name – saying the cock bit didn't apply to him and she doubted whether he could pee any more, either."

Francesca smiled. "That is quite funny, sir," she said. She saw that Green was not amused. "In a black humour sort of way," she added.

"I think we should visit her home again," said Green. "Does she have a life outside prostitution? Then there's Hilary."

"Yes."

"She's responsible for the article appearing – although she wouldn't say if she'd written it or not. She seems unmoved by the male of the species – certainly not fired up like Jenny to want to do away with them. No need for further action yet but we ought to think about what we should do about the fact that she was responsible for the article being published."

• • • • •

"Jed? It's your dad here."

"Yes?"

"I think you should stay away from here for the time being," Councillor Morgan said to his son. "Or at the very least don't bring your car over here. We don't want to risk it being seen around here. In fact, you'd be better off selling it and getting a new one."

"Yes, Dad."

"I've managed to pull a few strings. The police accept that the red car that drove away from here on the night of the crash had nothing to do with me. They're not going to pursue the matter of the blood. They say they have no leads to follow up. The only thing is this chap Rivers has been asking a few questions. Says he wants to contact the driver of the car because he feels responsible for the accident. I'm not sure he's telling the whole truth about that. He may suspect something but he won't get anywhere if he doesn't find your car."

"What about Jones' car?"

"Nobody will find that. It's burnt beyond recognition."

"Okay, Dad. I'll keep my distance."

• • ● • •

Rivers opened the door to his office to find the PC who had attended on the night of the crash outside.

"I may be the bearer of good news," he said. "There's to be no prosecution for dangerous driving or anything like that. You were only just over the limit so you face the minimum sentence. We won't be arguing that – at the time of the crash – your count would have been higher because of the amount of time that had elapsed since the incident."

"And the blood in the road?" asked Rivers.

"No leads for us to follow up. Maybe it didn't get there as a result of the crash."

"You know that isn't true," said Rivers. "There was a spattering of blood in the engine of my car."

"As I said there are no leads to be followed up. You know, you ought to be happy at this outcome. It couldn't have worked out better for you."

"I know," said Rivers, "but my private detective's nose is out of joint. Something happened there that night involving someone at least being seriously injured in the boot of the red car. I can't help but think it's at least possible that I may have killed someone as a result of the collision."

"No," said the police constable. "If they had been stashed away in the boot of the car, they would have been dead already. You don't put passengers in the boot of your car."

"So, you are admitting that a serious crime is being covered up?"

The police constable sighed. "We've been told it's not worth the resources or time to follow it up as there are no leads," he added.

"I'm going to give it a go," said Rivers. "Try and find out what happened."

"Be careful," warned the constable.

"Why?"

"Well, whoever it is may have already killed. It shows they've got no scruples."

"Do you know much about this Councillor Morgan guy?" asked Rivers.

"No, not really. I've seen him at council events I've had to attend."

"So, you wouldn't form a view as to whether he was capable of killing someone?"

The police constable laughed. "I shouldn't have thought so," he said. "He's only a small-time politician on a two penny halfpenny council. What's there to kill for?"

"Precisely," said Rivers. "What?"

• • • • •

Angela paid the taxi driver and hurried up the driveway. She had refused Detective Chief Inspector Green's offer of a lift home in a police car following her interview. He had made the offer as a gesture because he felt that – of the five women the police had been questioning – she was the least likely to have had any involvement with the crimes. She had declined – largely because she had been worried about what James' reaction might have been – if he had seen her arriving home escorted by the police.

She was relieved to see there was no car in the driveway. It meant James was not home yet. Her relief was short-lived, though. No sooner had she turned the key in the lock than she heard a car behind her turn into the driveway. "James," she said breathlessly – showing a little surprise.

"I don't know why you're surprised," he said. "This is the time that I normally get home. What's for tea? I'm ravenous."

"Oh, I haven't put my mind to that yet. I thought we might go out for a meal tonight."

"Go out for a meal?" he said. It was almost as if she had suggested they should commit some crime together. "But we never do – not on weekday nights."

"Well, maybe we should break the habit of a lifetime. Live a little."

The idea obviously did not appeal to James. "You know I work hard and get tired during the week," he said, "and it's not as if you've got anything else to do."

"Actually, I've been quite busy," she said defensively – and then bit her lip. She would have to offer an explanation of why she had been busy.

"Why? What have you been doing?"

"Oh, this and that."

"This and that? What does that mean?"

"Well, if you must know I've been doing some things for our women's group," she said. It was not really a lie, she thought. She had been questioned by the police as a result of their suspicions about the group.

"I don't see why you have to belong to that organisation." he said.

Because of people like you, she thought to herself. Men who think the only thing women have to do in life is cater for them. "I enjoy it," she said. "Debating, discussing political issues, meeting like-minded friends during the day time." Like the two prostitutes, the lesbian and the ice-cool German assistant teacher, she thought.

James relented at this. "Yes, I suppose it can be boring left on your own all day with nothing to do," he said. Angela smiled. Boring would not have been the way she would have described her day – but she let it pass. "Let's compromise," he said. "Let's get a takeaway and then you can tell me all about this women's group." She went into the kitchen and poured him a drink. By the time she had done this he had taken his coat off, relaxed on the sofa and was listening to the local news on the TV. The lead item was about how five women from a local women's group had been helping police with their enquiries into a double murder. The five, it later added, had now been released by police. "Angela?" shouted James. "Is this your group?"

"I... er," she floundered.

"Do you know any of these five?"

Should she come clean or not? she pondered. Her silence spoke volumes to James.

"You do, don't you?" he said. "Christ, Angela, you're not one of them are you? This and that didn't mean a visit to the local police station, did it?"

"Yes," she finally admitted.

James grabbed her by the shoulders. "What have you been doing?" he said eyeballing her intensely.

"Nothing, James."

"But the police don't believe that."

"I've not been charged with anything."

"Oh, great. So the police don't think you're a murderer yet. What a relief. What if your names come out – in the local paper? What shall we tell the neighbours? My family? You idiot. What have you got yourself involved with?"

"Look at the end of the story. All five were released. In other words, they don't think any of us did it."

"Why did they think you had anything to do with these murders in the first place?"

"I don't know."

"Yes you do," he said, shaking her furiously. "The police must have told you why they were questioning you."

"Let me go, James. You're hurting me."

"I want to know the truth, Angela."

"The truth is these murders have got nothing to do with me – or with any other members of the group. It was just a line the police were pursuing and they were wrong." She wrenched herself free from his grasp and sat down on the sofa sobbing. "I've had a trying day, James," she said. "Called into the police station and questioned about something I had nothing to do with. Can't you understand that?"

James started pacing around the living room. "You'll have to resign from this group," he said. "I'm not having you have anything more to do with it. It's about these attacks on men. Goodness, they've been revolting."

"I couldn't agree with you more, James – and that's why you should respect the fact that I had nothing to do with them."

"Don't you see, Angela, if you resign it will show the police you're disassociating yourself from the group and that you had nothing to do with the murders?"

"Nor did they, James. Nor did they. And that's why I should stand by them."

"No," he shouted. "You resign. You resign immediately or – I don't know what I'll do."

A thought flickered through Angela's mind. We should fight back indiscriminately against the male bullies – it was the words from the leaflet. She said quite coldly and calmly to James: "If you don't know what you're going to do, then

I don't know what I'm going to do. All I do know is I have done nothing wrong therefore I don't have to resign."

He was out of earshot by that time. He took his coat off the stand in the hallway. "Suddenly," he said, "going out for a meal seems a good idea. On my own." The front door slammed shut.

Thanks, James, she thought, for standing by me.

• • • • •

Toby Renton staggered out of bed that morning and made his way to the front door. There were a couple of letters on the mat. One was a missive from a local estate agent's offering a free valuation of his flat. The second had the heading: "Private and Confidential." It was from his bank, warning him that someone at his address had defaulted on their payments and – as a result – their account had been closed. It must have been Gabi but he could not for the life of him think how she had managed to overspend. She was not an extravagant soul and she had a regular income coming in. He knocked on her bedroom door. There was no reply. He shrugged his shoulders. She probably would not have told him anything anyhow. He was just about to make his way back to the bedroom when there was a knock at the front door. It was Rivers.

"Hallo," he said. "This is early."

"Ten o'clock? Not for me."

"What do you want?" Toby sounded grumpy but did not mean to be. In truth, he had not really woken up yet.

"Have you seen Gabi over the last twenty-four hours?"

"Come to think of it, no," he said.

"Did you know she was hauled out of school yesterday morning by the police and questioned over these murders?"

"Good God, no. What happened?"

"Well," said Rivers. "She was released but, apparently, they still suspect her. Did you know she was on police files?"

Toby stared at him in amazement. "No," he said. "I had no idea."

"Some boy she hit at school in Germany. It was never proved. They think it shows that she has a temper."

"I've never noticed that," said Toby motioning Rivers to sit down and fetching him a cup of tea. "Except that thing about 'What's New Pussycat?' She seemed to find it funny that a woman was hurting a man." He thought for a moment before handing the letter from the bank to Rivers. "Then there's this," he said. "I wouldn't have thought that a bank should be doing that – sending a letter to someone else about a client defaulting on their money."

Rivers studied the letter. "It serves a twofold purpose," he said. "It's warning you that she's a bankrupt." Toby raised his eyebrow. "Well, nearly a bankrupt but it's also subtly warning you of the consequences if you default."

"Thanks a bunch."

"The police want me to find out what would happen if I chatted Gabi up in a pub," he said. "That's why I came round."

"I wouldn't fancy your chances, mate," said Toby. "For a start, you're more than twenty years older than she is. Secondly, I don't think she's the type that picks men up."

"Then why does she go to pubs on her own such a lot?"

Toby shrugged his shoulders. "To drink?" he suggested. "Also, all human life is there. She's a keen student of that."

"Where does she go?" asked Rivers.

"I don't know," he said. "Probably the Tavern just down the road."

Rivers nodded. "Thanks, I'll try that this evening," he said.

"Good luck," said Toby.

"I don't really want to succeed with her – otherwise I could end up here later on this evening." He thought for a moment. "Has she ever brought a man back here?"

"No," said Toby.

"And has she ever arrived back here late at night? I mean very late."

"I've been to bed before she gets back sometimes – and then I don't know what time she returns."

"Can you remember any dates when she was last back late?"

"Mmm. Tuesday this week?"

"The night Danny Peacock was killed. Your lodger deserves more scrutiny, I feel."

"Maybe," said Toby. He ushered Rivers out of the flat and poured himself a glass of white wine on returning to the kitchen to calm worries that he was beginning to feel. As he drank it, he began to ponder. Here he was – aged thirty-four, single and unable to form any attachment. He had lacked the courage, he thought to himself, to make an advance to Gabi. Just as well, maybe, if it turned out she was behind these attacks that were going on. He sipped his wine again. No, he couldn't believe it. Anyhow, it wasn't just Gabi he had been too shy to make a pass at. That had been the story of his life and – when he had plucked up courage – he never seemed to know when to advance into a relationship. Never knew when to get serious. To a certain extent, he blamed his parents and the way he had been brought up. There had been an absence of emotion in his upbringing at home. As if it was a weakness to show it. He idly flicked through the pages of the local paper as these thoughts started to dominate him. He spotted the lonely hearts column. Wow, he thought, some of these are quite explicit. He read one: "Wanted, man – age immaterial, preferably married – for discreet fun". Blimey, he thought, it might just as well have read. "Needed –someone to fuck me – anybody." Maybe what he needed was the certainty that the other person would consent to sex rather than that awful dilemma of whether to make an advance. One advert caught his eye. The caller was asked to telephone to arrange an "intimate relationship". He decided to give it a try and fixed an appointment for the following evening.

• • • • •

"She wants me to follow up on the prostitutes, too," said Rivers when he got home to Nikki that evening. "Apparently two of the women's group are working as prostitutes and that leaflet did make it sound a bit like it was the prostitutes' revenge. She's given me their addresses."

"So while you're hobnobbing with prostitutes and chatting up women in pubs, what should I do?" asked Nikki.

"There's not a lot else to do," he said. "Just stay in the office and see if any more calls come in."

"Who's paying you for all this surveillance work?" Nikki asked.

"The Rentons," he said. "They want to find out if their son is safe from murderous women on the rampage. All this will help me find out."

"Bit unfair on the Rentons," suggested Nikki. "You could tell them it's all in the capable hands of the police now - and there's nothing more for you to do."

"I could," he said, "but – when I start a case I always like to finish it – and if I did as you said I'd have no reason to see it through. Besides, the police aren't paying me for what they want me to do."

"Don't they pay informers?"

"Is that what you think I am?" he asked.

"In a way, yes."

"I beg to differ," he said. Then, he added, as if trying to broach a delicate subject: "Nikki?"

"Yes?"

"I wonder – are you still happy you gave up your job to join me in the agency?"

"It's not as glamorous as I thought it would be," she confessed. "This case is a bit seedy."

"So was the last one. A woman kidnapped and held as a sex slave. You also got shot if I remember rightly."

"We were doing something worthwhile," she said. "This case

is sleazy by comparison. Men being mutilated. Women calling for violence against men."

"But if we find the perpetrator we'll be saving some innocent people from getting killed. Look, Nikki, I wouldn't be upset if you decided you wanted to go back to your former career – although I must admit I like that Hoffmeyr and Rivers sign on the door. Think, though. You may just be unlucky with this case in that it involves work that a man can do better than a woman."

"You mean chatting up women?"

"Precisely."

"It's not, though, as if when I was given things to do that I did them well. The women's group soon sussed me out. I'm no good at undercover work."

"They would have been suspicious of any stranger at that stage. That's why Francesca Manners has asked me to check them out individually – rather than as a group. Don't act hastily, Nikki, but if working full-time here with me is beginning to grate on you. I would understand if you left."

"I think I've burnt my bridges with my former employer," she said. "I'll give it a go for now."

Rivers smiled. "So, what would your dream assignment be?" he asked.

"Being paid plus expenses to tail some rich aristocrat while he was on a holiday in the Caribbean," she said without hesitation.

Rivers grinned. "I'll bear that in mind," he said.

• • ● • •

Emily Morgan arrived on time for her parish council meeting that evening but – as she drove into the car park at the parish hall – she felt faint. She rested her head on the steering wheel for a moment. It'll pass, she told herself. She got out of the car and walked into the meeting and gave a wan smile to some of her fellow parish councillors.

As always, the Vicar opened the meeting. The first item on the agenda was whether to place speed bumps in the Glades where she lived. It had been something that was dear to her heart and she was the councillor who had insisted they should debate a motion calling on the local authority to install them. She seemed distracted, though.

"Emily, it's your motion," said a voice to the right of her. The woman who was speaking to her nudged her as she did so.

"Sorry," said Emily. She rummaged in her handbag for her glasses and stared at the agenda in front of her. "I'm sorry," she said. With that, she slumped forward. "I'm sorry, I'm feeling faint." At that the parish councillor to her right got up and poured a glass of water for her. The glasses had already been put on the table by the vicar.

"I don't think you're at all well," said the parish councillor. "Shall we ring for an ambulance?"

"No, I'm all right," she insisted – sitting up again. "Don't ring for an ambulance. It would annoy John."

"Annoy John?" the parish councillor replied. "Come on – you're our number one priority here. Don't worry about annoying John."

"I'll be all right," she said. "It's just been a stressful few days."

"With that drunk crashing outside your home? Yes, I can imagine. All the more reason to pass this motion." Emily nodded. "At least let us telephone John to come and get you," said the woman.

"You can leave your car in the car park until tomorrow morning," volunteered the vicar. "John can come and get it then."

Emily nodded. "All right, then," she said. "I think it would be better if I went home."

Her fellow parish councillor took a mobile phone out of her pocket and – with the help of Emily – dialled John's number. He answered quite quickly. "It's Rosemary Peebles from the parish council here," she said. "Your wife's not well. I wondered whether you could come and collect her from the parish hall."

"No," he said firmly – much to Mrs Peebles' surprise. "I've been drinking. I can't risk being caught out for drinking and driving."

"I wouldn't expect you to," said Mrs Peebles soothingly. "Maybe you could get in a cab and come and collect her yourself?"

"No," he said again. "Stick her in a cab and send her home."

"That's a bit unfeeling," said Mrs Peebles. "What about your son? Would he be able to drive over here and collect you and take you home?"

"No," said John firmly again. Goodness, he thought. We can't risk his red car being in the neighbourhood again.

"I just think it would be best if she was accompanied on the way home – in case she has a funny turn again."

"If you're so worried about her, why don't you accompany her?" asked John.

"There's no need to adopt that tone with me," said Mrs Peebles haughtily. "I will, though, seeing as you're unwilling to help." With that, she brought the conversation to an end.

Emily had detected that the conversation with her husband had been difficult. "What's wrong?" she asked.

"He's been drinking," she said in a tone that marked her disapproval. Without hesitation, she rang for a cab and insisted to Emily that she would accompany her home. As they got into the cab, she turned to Emily and asked: "Is everything all right at home?"

"Yes," said Emily faintly. Mrs Peebles was not convinced, though. She delivered Emily to her front door and then stayed with her until John answered her ring. "Look after her," she said a touch of irritation.

John was more emollient this time. "Thank you, Mrs Peebles," he said. "I will look after her now." He shut the front door firmly once Emily was inside. "You don't want to go drawing attention to us," he said equally firmly to her. "This will all blow away in a few days – but, in the meantime, it should be business as usual."

"Yes, dear," said Emily, "but I think I will feign illness until it does."

Her husband sighed

CHAPTER FIVE

Gary arrived back late that evening to find Jenny closeted in the bathroom. "What's wrong?" he asked.

"I've been attacked."

He opened the bathroom door to find Jenny administering iodine to a red mark on her backside. "My God," said Gary looking at the bruises and cuts which sat next to the red mark.

"He took the invitation to discipline me a little too seriously," she said. "There are bruises to my leg, too." Gary could not see these as she had just lowered her jeans far enough to deal with the red mark on her bottom. She had taken her provocative clothing off and changed back into her jeans. Perhaps, psychologically, she did not want to be reminded of what she had been through. As if she could forget with the red marks and cuts to her backside.

"You shouldn't have to put up with this," he said.

"No, right," said Jenny.

"So give it up. You're an intelligent woman. You could get another job."

"I know," she said, "but I'm not going to allow some violent man to dictate to me how I should live my life."

"Who was it?"

"He gave his name as Ted Brown. It's probably not his real name, though."

"How did you get rid of him?"

"With a saucepan," she said. "I told him I needed to go to the loo and he let me out of the bedroom. I went into the kitchen and picked up a saucepan and threatened to beat him over the head with it if he didn't leave. Luckily, he left."

"Had you had him before?"

"No ... and, before you ask, I won't be having him again."

"My God, if I ever catch up with him, I'll kill him."

"And you think that will be helpful in the current climate?" said Jenny.

· · ● · ·

Larry Green was surprised to find the pathologist, Professor Simon Saint, waiting for him in his office when he turned up for work the next morning.

"Bit late, aren't we, Larry?" he said looking at his watch and trying to sound reproachful.

"I'm approaching retirement," said Larry. "I should be granted the opportunity to ease myself out of my job."

"Unfortunately, there's a serial killer on your patch who doesn't see it that way."

"Tell me about it," said Larry. "Anyhow what do you want? You didn't come here to chide me on my lateness, I'll be bound."

"No, I wanted to bring you up to speed on my thoughts as well as developments."

"Go on."

"It's going to be terribly disappointing for the tabloid press – but I rather doubt that we've got a case of Jill the Ripper here."

As he spoke, Francesca walked into the office. "Good morning," she said to the two of them.

"Good morning," said Larry. "Professor Saint is just sharing a theory he has with me."

"Yes," said the professor. "As I said, your killings may not have been the work of a Jill the Ripper. They needed considerable force – especially John Hedger. He was quite a fit, lithe middle aged man. The killer had to be sure they would knock him out with an instant blow and then strangle him while he was still alive and able to struggle. Just a thought."

"Worth bearing in mind," said Green stroking his chin. "So what do you conclude?"

"Isn't it obvious?" replied the other man. "The killings needed so much force that it is likely they were committed by a man."

"So we're looking for a man who hacks penises off. What statement can he be trying to make?"

"Some men dislike violence to women, too," volunteered Francesca.

"So we're looking for a feminist sympathiser in the male community who hacks penises off. Does this mean we've been wasting our time interviewing the members of the revolutionary group?"

"Not necessarily," said Francesca. "It's not for the professor to say – but there could still be a link there."

Larry stroked his chin. "Too much information for so early on a Monday morning," he said.

"Yes, it is still early in the morning despite your snide remarks about being late for work," he added to the professor.

"Touchy," said Professor Saint. "Well, that's it. Must get off to the golf club now. I'm booked in to tee off at eleven o'clock. Down to serious work this afternoon."

• • • • •

Gary made his way straight to the kitchen to prepare a cup of tea as soon as he and Jenny woke up that morning. "What do we do now?" he said sounding impatient.

"What do you mean?"

"About that guy who abused you last night."

Jenny eased herself into a chair. "Forget him."

"We shouldn't have let him get away."

"Remember. I was on my own last night. You shouldn't use the royal 'we' to refer to me. I don't like royalty"

"This is no time for humour, Jenny," he said. "If you meant

what you said in that article, this guy is one man who shouldn't get off scot free."

"Who says I wrote that article?"

"Oh, come on Jenny, I saw it in your computer."

"What gave you the right to go into my computer?"

"It was on the screen one time when you just took a break to go and get yourself a cup of tea."

Jenny closed her eyes in frustration. "You mustn't tell anybody that," she said.

"Do you think I would?" He received no reply. "How did he inflict such pain?" he asked, changing the subject.

"He had a stick. I was smarting in pain on the floor. I could see he had a satisfied smile on his face. I knew I was in for more of the same. I shouted 'get out' but he raised his stick to beat me again. I grabbed it and – for just a moment – I caught him off balance. It gave me time to get into the kitchen and get the saucepan I told you about last night. I came back into the living room screaming 'get out' again and again hysterically and brandishing the saucepan. He took the hint and left."

"Describe him."

"What?"

"Describe him."

"No, Gary, no. I think it might be time to lie low for a while. Look, I've already been taken in for questioning by the police this last week. Now is not the time to start going out and taking revenge on people – especially bullying men who have just been violent towards a prostitute."

"Are you going soft?" asked Gary.

"No, just for the first time in my life, I'm being pragmatic. I know Detective Chief Inspector Green." – She spat on the floor at the mention of his name – "said the state wouldn't waste resources on trying to frame a twerp like me but I think the evidence of the last two days shows they would."

"You? Pragmatic?"

"Yes, I know it's a dirty word and – believe me – if I had got hold of him last night I might very well have killed him. But I'd have been the one languishing in jail – he would have been the so-called victim. Just leave it for the moment." She wanted to add "and look after me" but it would have sounded like a weakness. She was still in pain from last night's ordeal, though. She could not, however, bring herself to say the words. After all, what was her philosophy? No warmth in any relationships she had with men. "Look after me" would have made her sound pathetic.

Reluctantly, Gary acquiesced and went to make her another cup of tea.

• • ● • •

"Do I look all right?" Rivers asked nervously as he prepared to go out on his fishing expedition with Gabi that night.

"To pull a twenty-something blonde?" asked Nikki. "No, I think you'd have to go into Dr Who's time traveller machine before I could assure you of that. But if she's into picking up men for random sex and then killing them I think you'll do."

"Thanks a bunch," he said. "I can't help thinking I should have more protection with me in case."

"In case she's dangerous?" asked Nikki. "Well, you can't have me or your close friend Detective Sergeant Manners. Gabi has seen both of us."

Rivers picked up on Nikki's use of the word "close friend" to describe Francesca. Did she suspect something was going on? He wondered. Well, no matter. There wasn't anything between him and the detective. Time to get on with the job in hand, he thought. "Well, here goes," he said. He was dressed casually – cords, an open-necked light blue shirt and a blue blazer-style jacket. He looked as young as he possibly could by the time the taxi arrived and took him to the Tavern pub near Toby's home.

It was eight o'clock in the evening – time for Gabi to have got ensconced in the pub. As he walked in, he could see who he thought was her sitting in a corner reading a book. He decided he would not go straight over to her. That would be too obvious. Instead, he bought a pint and sat on the opposite side of the room. As he sat and sipped his beer, he saw another man go over to Gabi's table. They chatted pleasantly it seemed for about five minutes but then the man got up and moved away. Rivers was just finishing his drink by this stage and decided now was as good as any time to approach her. He had decided earlier he would adopt the persona of a previous client of his – a journalist who wrote about education. It would mean that he and Gabi had something in common. He had picked up some hints about his client's modus operandi during the time he had been working with him.

"Do you mind if I sit here?" he asked her as he approached her with his second pint.

"No," she said, gathering her books up. "It's a free country."

The gathering of the books was a good sign, thought Rivers. It meant she was prepared to engage in a conversation with him. "I've only just moved into the area," he said. "I thought I'd just try this pub out." Gabi nodded enthusiastically. "The name's Philip Rivers," he said. He held out his hand. He had decided that – while he would adopt a different C.V. – he would stick to his real name. Toby, he was sure, would not have talked about him.

Gabi took it for a handshake. "Gabi Dortman," she said.

"Not English?"

"No, German."

"Working over here?" he asked.

"Yes. I work in a school as an assistant teacher. Just down the road."

"Interesting," he said. "I write about education for a national newspaper." He gave the name of his client Roy Faulkner's newspaper in the hope that Gabi was not an avid reader and follower of its education coverage.

"I'm afraid I do not read it," she said.

"Never mind," he said with some relief. "You're missing out, though."

"I will get it tomorrow," she said.

That would be all right, thought Rivers. By then he would hopefully have made his mind up about her. "How long have you been here?" he asked.

"Since September," she said. "I have to go back soon. My contract expires at the end of this term."

"That's a shame," he said. He was not reading her replies well, he thought. They were all spoken with a slightly staccato voice which betrayed no sense of emotion. It could have been because she was speaking a foreign language, he mused. "Have you made many friends since you've been over here?" he asked.

"Not really. I have a room in the flat of somebody I met in a pub – like you," she said. For the first time a smile broke out on her face. "He helped when my landlord was putting pressure on me to go from the place I had been living in," she added.

"But he's not your boyfriend?" he asked.

"Why do you want to know?" she replied defensively.

"Oh, no reason, I suppose," he said. "Just interested."

Gabi nodded. "And you? Do you have a wife or lover or anything?"

"Anyone," he corrected. "No, not really," he said. "I had a partner but we split up a few months ago. That's why I moved over here. I had to find somewhere else to live."

"Oh."

"Tell me," he said. "What do you think of our education system?" On reflection, he thought it was not the best chat up line that he could have used but he reasoned it might get her talking a little bit more freely – despite the fact that he realised he might struggle to hold his end up if they got into a debate.

121

"The pupils," she said. "They do not have as much respect as we get in Germany." They were away. Both offered their thoughts on why this should be the case. He decided to be a bit provocative and suggest it was a legacy of the days of the Third Reich when Hitler had insisted on firm discipline in schools. "You are joking?" she said.

"Only half," he said. "So, which system would you prefer to teach in?"

"I think over here it is more challenging," she said.

"Very diplomatic," he said. He noticed she had finished her drink. "Can I get you another one?" he asked, pointing to her empty glass.

"That would be nice," she said. "I am drinking white wine."

He got up from the table and went to the bar, coming back with another pint of beer and a glass of white wine. "You know, I was wondering whether I should come into this pub on my own," he said. "Silly – but I don't often do that. I'm glad I did, though. It's been good meeting you."

She smiled. "I do it all the time," she said. "If I don't find someone to talk to, I think it is a good way of observing the British. I learn more about your country in pubs than I do in your schools."

"Do you often get chatted up by someone like me?" he asked.

"No," she said. "Normally, they're more upfront about what they want. They don't want to spend too much time chatting me up. It's a quick 'do you want to come round to my place?'"

"And what do you do?"

"That's when it's nice to have someone like Toby around," she said. "By the way are you chatting me up?" she asked.

He ignored her question. "Toby?" he asked.

"The guy I was telling you about. My landlord. He stepped in when a particular drunken right-wing slob was trying to chat me up. I was most grateful."

"So, if it wasn't for the Tobys of this world, what would you do?"

"Depends how I feel."

Their drinks were finished by now. It was still only half-past nine but he sensed it was time to find out what her reaction would be to developing their acquaintanceship. "Do you fancy moving on?"

"Moving on?"

"Going somewhere else? You could come back to my flat. I have some more wine. Or we could go for a meal. There's a good Greek restaurant that I've found nearby."

Gabi smiled. "I have to start school at eight o'clock in the morning," she said. "I think I should be getting home."

"Could I take your telephone number and get in touch with you sometime?"

"Yes," she said. "That would be nice." They exchanged numbers and he offered to walk her home. "It's not that far," she protested but eventually acquiesced. At the end of the short walk, she turned to him. "Well, this is where I live. Goodnight."

He moved as if to kiss her but she brushed him off. "Sorry," he mumbled. He turned on his heels and made his way to the nearest main road in the hope of picking up a cab. As he walked, he reflected on the evening. She had given no clue as to what she thought about him and had rebuffed any advances – but still held out the prospect of a date at a later time. It was a thoroughly normal evening, he concluded. One thing had emerged, though, she appeared grateful and to have a soft spot for Toby. Surely, he thought, she held out no threat to him – which was what his enquiry was supposed to have been all about.

• • • • •

"I've been thinking," said Larry Green. "Suppose we take Professor Saint's comments seriously. What if it is a man?"

"We shouldn't exclude that from our investigations," agreed Francesca.

"Who would that put in the frame? Jenny has a boyfriend. Jane has a brother. Angela Curran has a husband."

"You can't really suspect him, can you? They're a typical middle class family."

"Doing the best things so conservatively. Really, Francesca, I'm shocked at you. I never thought you would suggest to me that conservative minded people wouldn't commit murder."

"I didn't mean that," protested Francesca.

"I know you didn't." He reflected for a moment. "No, I wasn't thinking of them. I think we should see Erica Hedger again."

"Why?"

"Her husband was a violent man. Maybe there was another man in her life who disliked the way he treated her. It could be worth a try."

"But that wouldn't explain the murder of Danny Peacock," said Francesca. "He had no woman in his life as far as we know."

"I still think it's worth leaving no stone unturned."

The two of them decided to leave it until late afternoon to go round to Erica's sister's house, giving her time to get back from work. As luck would have it, both women were in when they called. Tanya answered the door.

"Good afternoon," said Larry Green. "We'd like to have another word with Erica if we may."

"Why?" asked Tanya.

"There have been new developments in the murder of her husband," he said. "I wanted to discuss them with her."

"Discuss?"

"Yes, no more than that."

"It's all right, Tanya," a voice piped up from the sitting room. "I don't mind talking to the detectives."

"Thank you," said Larry Green as he brushed past Tanya before he was formally invited into the house. She looked at him in an irritated fashion. Francesca motioned to her to go through to the living room in advance of her.

"Do you mind if I sit in on this?" said Tanya.

"I'd rather you didn't," said Larry Green – believing Erica might feel freer to talk about intimate relationships if her sister was not in the room.

"It's all right, Tanya, I'll be okay," said Erica.

"I'll be in the kitchen if you need me," her sister replied.

"Thank you, Mrs Hedger," said Green when they were sitting down in the living room. "It's just that we've had news from the pathologist who thinks that the force of the attack on your husband makes it likely that a man was responsible."

"Oh."

"I have to ask you whether you know of any man who might have a grudge against your husband."

She thought for a moment. "No," she said, "I would have thought that all those who had a grudge against my husband would have been women."

"I can see why you might come to that conclusion," said Green. "Can I ask a delicate question? Did you have – or have you had – any romantic attachments either at the time of separating from your husband or afterwards? Someone who might have resented the way he treated you and sought revenge as a result?"

"You mean am I dating a murderer?"

"I wouldn't have put it that bluntly," said Green.

"But it's the gist of what you meant. No, inspector, I have to disappoint you. I have had no other relationships either at the time of splitting up from my husband or afterwards."

"Well," said Green. "I think that's all." He got up as if to go as did Francesca. "If you do think of anything, please don't hesitate to call either me or Detective Sergeant Manners."

"Thank you, inspector." At this moment Tanya returned from the kitchen to show the two detectives to the door – making them think she had been listening in all the time.

"Does what they said surprise you?" said Tanya to her sister once they had gone.

"To be honest, it does nothing to me," said Erica. "I really couldn't care how John died."

· · ● · ·

Toby arrived home from work that evening at around seven o'clock. It was a warm, barmy June evening so he was not surprised to find the door to the flat open. He assumed Gabi was still there or was perhaps in the garden that backed on to the flat. "Gabi?" he said. There was no reply. He entered the living room and – to his surprise – found that the fire was full on. "Gabi," he called again. On receiving no reply, he entered her room. To his great surprise, he saw that all her belongings had gone. He scoured the house. There was no farewell note. He had known that day would be her last at school but – as she had said nothing – he had assumed she would come back and collect her things and possibly go the next morning. She had said that her boyfriend, Rudolph, was in London and he had made it clear to her that he was happy for him to stay overnight as they were planning to holiday together in England after she had finished at the school. He got his mobile out of his pocket and telephoned Rivers. "Something odd," he said when the detective answered. He explained what he had found.

"I'll come over," said the private detective.

Toby put the phone down and started clearing up to get the flat ready for Rivers' arrival. The first thing he did was to turn the fire off. He suddenly remembered he had left some papers in his car and walked up the alley between his flat and the next block. Just as he was about to open the gate leading to the road, he became aware of a noise behind him. He was just turning around when he felt a heavy object hit the back of his head. He fell to the floor, dimly aware of a voice talking to him. He could make out the words indistinctly. "That's to tell you not to mess with other people's women," it said. If it had not been for the seriousness of the situation, he would have replied; "Chance would be a fine thing." He thought the better of it and – in the blur that was before his eyes – he could see a man raising an object above his head, presumably to strike him again. He covered his head with his hands to protect himself from the blow which he managed to fend off. At that time, he heard the sound of a car coming to a halt on the road just outside the flats. Whoever was in it must have seen what was happening in the alley way. A voice he thought he recognised shouted: "Hey, you, put that thing down."

The blurred image who had been attacking him dropped the object he was holding, opened the gate and ran off. The man whose voice he now identified as Philip Rivers and who had arrived in a taxi started giving chase but it soon became obvious to the private detective that Toby's assailant was faster and fitter than him and he gave up, returning to see if Toby was all right. Once he had ascertained this, he turned back to the taxi driver and paid his fare.

"What the hell's happened here?" he asked when he was back by Toby's side.

"I don't know," said Toby. "Whoever it was told me to stop messing with other people's women." He felt the top of his head gingerly. "I wouldn't mind," said Toby, "but I'm not."

"Somebody obviously thinks you were. The only person who could have come to that conclusion would be somebody who had designs on Gabi. There are no other women in your life, are there?"

"No women, period," said Toby.

"Some people assume if you're living in the same house as a woman that you're having a relationship with them," said Rivers. "You know that. Didn't your mother and father come to that conclusion?"

Toby managed a smile. "Yes, but I don't think either of them beetled round here to give me a blow on the back of the head."

"Come on, let's get you inside," said the private detective.

"I want to have a look at that bump. We probably should go to the local hospital and get it seen to."

"I'll be all right," said Toby stoically.

"No, you're not," said Rivers. He sat his client down and brought him a glass of water. "Drink this," he added.

Toby gulped it down. "This is all a bit strange," he said. "I can't think what Gabi could be up to leaving the door open so burglars could get in and the fire on."

"She doesn't seem the type," agreed Rivers. "I was coming to tell you I didn't think you had anything to fear from her. I had a very pleasant evening in the pub with her last night but – when I attempted to make a move on her – she made it clear that was not what she wanted."

"And now you find this has happened."

"There is an explanation," began Rivers.

"Yes?"

"It's not her. Maybe it's her boyfriend. He could have leapt to the conclusion that there was something going on between you. He could have got hold of the key somehow – she would probably have left it in an obvious place for you to spot – come back, put the fire on, then heard you coming and made off, hanging around outside to see if an opportunity presented itself to attack you. He may not have been planning that in the first instance. Could have been worse. He could have been planning to set fire to the place before he was interrupted."

"In which case, she may be in danger. Maybe we ought to try and find her?" said Toby.

"He's most likely to have left her in the pub while he came back here," said Rivers. "Shall we go round there?"

Toby nodded but there was no Gabi when they arrived at the Tavern. An enquiry of one of the bar staff by Rivers elucidated the fact there had been a blonde girl there about fifteen minutes ago, but she had left with an intense looking dark haired man. "No point in looking for her," said Rivers. "It'd be like trying to find a needle in a haystack. I'll tell you what I will do – I'll stay overnight with you. Just in case he comes back again. Remember, he's probably got a key."

"Thanks," said Toby, "although they're probably long gone. Gabi was planning a holiday with him when she finished school."

"We'll try the school in the morning," said Rivers. Then he remembered he had a court appearance on his drink driving charge then. "It will have to be later," he said.

"There'll be no-one there. She finished today."

"It's still worth a try." The two of them had a quick drink at the Tavern and then made their way back to Toby's flat. As they sat there drinking some wine and eating a takeaway they had ordered, Rivers turned to Toby. "You know, there could be an explanation for Gabi's bankruptcy, too," he said. "Maybe she was giving him money."

"Doesn't sound like the sort of thing a member of the North London Women's Revolutionary Action Group would do," Toby pointed out.

"Maybe that's why she went to them," said Rivers. "She wanted some advice on what to do about him?"

"In which case, he may be in more trouble than I am," said Toby, a smirk suddenly emerging on his face. "Maybe she'll be putting the skills she learnt while watching 'What's New Pussycat?' into effect."

Rivers smiled. "I don't know," he said. "Your parents hire me to protect you from a revolutionary gang of women and you end up getting beaten up by your lodger's boyfriend. I'm not quite sure how I explain this to them."

• • ● • •

"I thought I might find you here," said Nikki as she walked into the magistrates' court and saw Rivers sitting with his legal advisers in the reception area. "Where the hell did you get to last night?"

"Toby Renton's. He was assaulted last night. I thought I ought to stay with him and offer him some protection seeing as I'd been hired to make sure he was safe."

"You should have rung."

"I should have rung," he repeated. "I meant to but we started drinking some wine and I fell asleep."

"Fine protection you would have been," said Nikki.

"Excuse me," Rivers' barrister butted in to the conservation. "Philip's case is coming up in about a quarter of an hour," he said. "I can think of better ways to prepare for it than having a marital tiff minutes beforehand."

Nikki glared at him for a moment and then softened.

The barrister then decided to brief Rivers on the proceedings. "We've had a word with the prosecution. There'll be no need for you to go into the witness box. I'm afraid it will be the mandatory one year ban – probably with a little extra added on because of the crash."

Rivers nodded but then asked: "Doesn't it strike you as odd that I crash into a car, blood spurts out on to the pavement and in to my engine and nothing is said about it?"

"I'd have used the word convenient rather than odd, Philip," said the barrister. "Certainly for one party,"

"My enquiring mind finds it difficult to let it go," said Rivers.

"Suspend you're enquiring mind for about half an hour – then you can think all the thoughts that you like."

They were interrupted by the clerk to the court calling out Rivers' name and they were ushered into the court room – Rivers to the dock with his legal team in the front row and Nikki to one of the public seats at the back of the court room. The prosecution team was already in place but there were no other members of the public around. Rivers sat through it while the prosecution outlined their case. He had been drinking with a friend in the centre of London and decided to drive home on returning to the station. He had then crashed into the back of a parked car and was found to be just over the limit. He had co-operated with the police at all stages, said how sorry he was for what he had done and acknowledged that he had been drinking. There was no mention of dangerous driving, driving without due care and attention or anything else. His barrister then got up to re-emphasize how sorry Rivers had been and that his actions were completely out of character. There was a character witness letter from Mark Elliott saying how ordinarily he would never have considered drinking and driving. Rivers could not help but smile. If only the magistrates had known what an inveterate drinker Mark Elliott was. The three magistrates then talked amongst themselves for about a minute before they announced a 14-month ban – precisely the sort of sentence that Rivers had been expecting. The magistrates signalled to him to go and he walked bemused from the courtroom.

"You were right," he said to his barrister as they assembled outside.

"You were lucky," said Nikki as she squeezed his arm.

"Thank you for representing me," he said. "I guess that's it?"

"Yes, it's one of those occasions where you say you hope you never have to see me again."

Rivers smiled. "Precisely my sentiments," he said. He then turned to Nikki. "I've got one or two things I've got to do now. Investigate what happened to Toby."

"I'll just go back and man the office phone then, shall I?" she said. He detected a note of irritation in her voice.

"Please," he said. With that, he disappeared from the court.

●　●　●　●　●

The Rentons were waiting outside the office when Nikki returned from the court house. "Apologies," she said as she unlocked the door. "Have you been here long?"

"About five minutes," said Walter Renton stiffly. "We wondered what you were playing at."

131

"What do you mean?"

"Toby was assaulted last night. You're supposed to be making sure he's OK."

"Things could have been a lot worse if Philip hadn't been around," said Nikki. She may have been critical of him when the two of them were together but she was fiercely defensive of him when he was under attack from others. "I gather he saw off Toby's attacker – and he stayed with your son for the night to make to make sure he came to no harm," she said.

"We told him he should come back and live with us."

I bet that went down like a lead balloon, thought Nikki. Instead she feigned innocence. "And what did he say?"

"He wouldn't," said Walter. "I don't know. He sometimes makes it difficult for us to protect him."

"Anyhow," said Nikki once she had got inside the office and ushered the Rentons to seats. "What can I do for you?"

"We came to end the contract we have with you to protect Toby," said Walter firmly.

"Because?"

"What do you mean?"

Nikki realised that would be the last thing Rivers wanted. He was enjoying being so close to such a major murder investigation. "Well, it seems to me there's more evidence of him being in danger now than there was when you first hired us," she said. "Also, your son seems to have developed a bit of a rapport with Philip." Certainly, if the wine consumption by the two of them the previous evening was to be believed, thought Nikki.

"You know, she might be right," said Dorothy tugging at her husband's arm.

"All right," said Walter, "but get Mr Rivers to stick a little closer to Toby in future. And we're going to inform the police about what happened."

"Will do," said Nikki. Phew, she said to herself after she had ushered them out of the door.

CHAPTER SIX

Rivers had to admit to surprise as he approached the school where Gabi taught. There were pupils playing in the playground, the car park seemed full to the brim and one or two teachers patrolled outside to keep a check on the pupils as they played. Definitely not holiday time, he thought to himself. He showed his card to the receptionist. "I wonder if I might be able to speak to the headteacher," he asked politely.

"Can you give me some indication as to what it's about?" she enquired.

"Gabi Dortman."

No sooner was the name uttered than a look of understanding that the matter was urgent came over the receptionist's face – a look that surprised Rivers. He felt there was some secret about Gabi to which he was not privy. The receptionist picked up the telephone and dialled the head's number. It only took a few seconds from him answering for Rivers to be informed that Francis Durrant would see him now.

"I gather you're a private detective," said Durrant after he had sat Rivers down in his office.

"Yes."

"Well, we've had the police here twice to enquire about Miss Dortman. What is it you want?"

"I'm trying to find her."

"Why?"

"I believe she may be able to help me over an assault of a client of mine." He looked around him. "Something tells me that term is not yet over at this school," he said.

"How perceptive of you," replied the headteacher with a

touch of sarcasm in his voice.

"Miss Dortman packed up her belongings from her flat yesterday morning saying she was leaving because her contract had come to an end."

"I wish that were true. She left hurriedly yesterday afternoon and should have been taking a class this morning."

"Left hurriedly?"

"Her colleagues had been planning a small party to say goodbye to her after school yesterday but she left before lessons were over. Someone came to collect her at the gates at around 3.30pm and she was gone. I don't think she was expecting him to come just then. They appeared to be having some sort of a row or discussion when he arrived at the school gates."

"What about?"

"It was in German. I wasn't close to them at the time but the people who were said they did not know what it was about. I think some of the staff who were closest to her were upset at her sudden departure but to be honest with you, Mr Rivers, I wasn't exactly forlorn at the fact that she had gone."

"Oh?"

"She had been in trouble during the past week. First, the police arrived trying to build up some kind of character portrait of her. Then they returned and took her away for questioning about these revenge attacks on men."

"But she hadn't in fact been found guilty of anything," interrupted Rivers.

"No, but you must understand – would you like parents to read that a teacher in charge of their children was being questioned by the police over a grisly murder? Now, if you don't mind, it's the last day of term and I have a lot to do. You're not going to be able to find her any more easily by any more questions here."

"No, probably not." He got up to go. In an ironic twist, he saw Francesca Manners striding through the gates as he was about to depart."I've beaten you to it this time," he said as their paths crossed.

"Yes," she said. "We were informed about the attack on Toby by his parents. I wanted to question Gabi."

"She's gone. She left a day early. She should have been teaching today. Come and have a cup of coffee and I'll fill you in. At least that way we can spare the headteacher the trauma of having to go through two interviews about Gabi Dortman."

"So, where is she?"

"She's gone off on holiday with her boyfriend," said Rivers. "They were planning to go on holiday after she finished her work but I think he arrived early and didn't like what he saw – Gabi living in the same flat as Toby Renton, demanded she leave and was very probably responsible for the attack on Toby last night. He got inside the flat and turned the heating on, was very possibly about to set fire to the place when Toby came back and I turned up at the flat."

"And that's an end of the matter as far as you are concerned?"

"I don't think Toby's in any real danger now. As to Gabi, well, she's not my problem. I was hired to make sure Toby was safe. I'm going to hang around for a bit just to make sure that I'm not wrong but I think she's just a quiet girl in a relationship with a guy who's a bit of a bully. She probably went to the North London Women's Revolutionary Action Group because she hoped an organisation like that would be able to give her confidence in how to deal with her situation. Unfortunately, she got involved with this revenge killing stuff instead."

"Well," reflected Francesca. "I suppose I should still pursue the case. After all, if you're right, she has gone off with a guy who might very well be guilty of assault."

Rivers nodded. "She's the one we should be worried about. Not Toby." he said.

• • • • •

The desk sergeant looked up from his book as the woman with mousy hair gingerly approached him. "I'm sorry to trouble you," she said.

"Yes?" he said making no attempt to put her at her ease.

"He's gone missing." The sergeant eyed her up and down. I'm not surprised, love, he thought to himself. She was quite plainly dressed and her clothes would not have looked out of place in the 1950's rather than the second decade of the 21st century. "I wouldn't have bothered you – only it's been weeks now. My friends told me I should wait." Tears welled in her eyes " They said he'd come back but there's no sign of that happening."

At that moment, Larry Green came out of his office. He was making his way to the door when he noticed the woman. "Everything under control, Sergeant?" he asked.

"Yes, sir," came the reply in a manner that was meant to convey that he should not want to be bothered with this case. Green looked at the woman. Something struck him about her. She seemed so utterly defeated that he imagined she must have plucked up enormous courage to come to the police station in the first place. "Tell me what's happened," he said sympathetically to her. He looked at the empty waiting room opposite. "Come on," he said, "we'll chat about it in there." The sergeant looked at him as if to register some kind of protest. "It's all right, sergeant," he said. "I can cope."

He looked at the woman again when they were sitting in the waiting room. He had had his fill of arrogant women during the past forty-eight hours with Jenny, the mouthy whore from Hackney and posh Tanya, Erica's sister. Here was somebody who appeared to be quite down-trodden by comparison. She would probably downplay everything and have been fobbed off quite easily if the sergeant had had his way. He felt she deserved a sympathetic ear.

"Thank you, sir," said the woman as she brought out a handkerchief to wipe her nose.

"Just tell me what happened in your own time," he said.

"Well, Brian – that's my husband – went missing just over a month ago. At first I thought, well, he sometimes did stay out all night but then, as time went on." She cleared her throat. "I didn't want to trouble you. Brian had had his troubles with you in the past."

"What sort of troubles?"

"Oh, he used to arrange loans for people in financial difficulties. It was sometimes hard to get them to repay the money they owed him." So, he used to crack their skulls, thought Green, just to encourage them to come up with the money. "One or two of his collectors got a little over-zealous in trying to get the money back," she said. "Brian himself lost control once – and he spent a few months inside. He wouldn't have wanted me to get the police meddling in his affairs. But it's been so long now I really worry that something's happened to him. He wouldn't just up and leave me. There's the kids. He doted on them."

The picture Green had built up of Brian didn't include him doting on anyone but he just nodded to allow the woman to continue. "Tell me what happened the night he left," he said. "Where was he going?"

"He was going to collect some debts," she said.

Perhaps, thought Green, the boot was on the other foot this time and he had found someone who was quite capable of resisting his threats and giving as good as they got. "When did he go missing?" he asked.

"It was the first Thursday in June."

"Was he with anybody?"

"Well, he's got two mates who help him out – Bruiser and Eel." The woman managed a little giggle. "He's called Eel because he's very slippery. I don't think he was with them on the night. He said this one guy had been bugging him because he couldn't pay. He didn't tell me his name, though."

"No," said Green. "It probably wouldn't have meant anything

to you, though, eh?"

"Probably not," she said snivelling again.

"Can I ask you, Mrs ....," he began.

"Oh, Nita. Just call me Nita. It's short for Anita." Not very, thought Green. "Nita Jones."

"Nita. Can I ask you about your relationship with your husband?"

"Oh, we were all right. I'd always try and make it that his dinner was ready on the table by the time he got home."

"And if it wasn't? Did he get annoyed? He was, after all, a violent man." Green was beginning to think there may be a link with the other murders he was investigating.

"Oh, I wouldn't say that, inspector."

"Well, he'd served a prison sentence for attacking one of his clients."

"But he had to. Attack the client, I mean. There was no other way he'd have got the money back."

"Did he ever have to attack you?"

"Eh. I'm not sure what you're getting at, Inspector. You don't think I ..." Her voice tailed off as she realised the implications of the inspector's question.

"I don't think anything, Mrs Jones – Nita. I just have to fill in a full picture of all the circumstances."

"Well, I mean I suppose it happens in any relationship. We'd had our ups and downs. He had hit me – but that was a long time ago."

Green sighed. He wondered what he was getting into here. Over the last week, it was almost as if every relationship he had come across had involved violence of some sort. He was becoming obsessed with finding the revenge killer and weaving it into every investigation. Probably best to treat this case as a missing person until it proved to be otherwise. "Does your husband have any records of the people who owe him money?" he asked. "Or a diary or anything?"

"I've never seen a diary," she said, "but he had got a little office at home. It might have details of his clients. I don't know. I've never been in there."

Green nodded. "I'll send someone round to have a look at it tomorrow morning," he said. "You'll be in?"

"Oh, yes. I don't work. It's the kids."

"I understand," said Green. He escorted the woman from the waiting room.

As they passed the reception area – where the sergeant still had his head buried in some paperwork, the woman turned to Green. "Thank you, sir," she said. "Thank you for listening."

• • • • •

"Have you made a booking?" came the woman's voice from inside the flat. The door remained firmly closed.

"No," said Rivers. Her tone made it sound as if he was going to the theatre or something like that. As he waited for a response, he surveyed the Hackney estate surrounding him. It had seen better days. There were youths gathering at a couple of the corners of the estate. Chilling out. Possibly selling drugs. It was an environment not designed to make him feel comfortable.

"Well, you've got half an hour and it'll be £30," said the voice. It was enough to confirm to Rivers he was at the right address. It had been given to him by Francesca so he had been pretty sure this was one of the prostitutes who belonged to the North London Women's Revolutionary Action Group.

"That's very kind of you," he said eventually, "but I'm not a client."

"What are you then?"

"I'm a private detective."

"What do you want with me?"

"Let me inside and I'll tell you."

"Think I'm falling for that one?"

"Please," said Rivers. "I'm representing the son of a couple who fear he may be at risk from this killer who's carrying out revenge attacks on men."

"And you think it may be me? Very brave of you to come in the circumstances. I'll just go and get the kitchen knife."

"Look, Jenny, I mean you no harm. I just want to know a bit about the circumstances under which that challenge to women was made – to carry out indiscriminate attacks against men."

"I've been questioned by the police over this," she said. "I really don't want to get involved any more. This is typical of the harassment that the Left faces."

"You're on the Left, then?"

"Obviously, if I'm a member of the North London Women's Revolutionary Action Group. We're not a bunch of fascists."

"I never suggested you were. Nor am I, by the way."

At long last Jenny opened the door. She was back to wearing a revealing gym slip and shirt unbuttoned to expose the top of her breasts. "You might as well come in," she said, "though how I can help you – or whether I should want to – I don't know."

"Thanks, Jenny," he said as he gained access to the room.

"You're being a bit over familiar, aren't you?"

"You advertise yourself on your card as Jenny. I don't know any other name to call you by."

Jenny ignored his reply. "What do you want to know?"

"The name of the person who wrote that article calling for revenge attacks."

"Why?"

"So, I can ask them what they hoped to achieve by it."

"You're asking the wrong person. Hilary Sampson is our chair – and she is the publisher of the leaflet. But I think I should warn you – she and we set great store by preserving the anonymity of people who write controversial articles for us."

"Do you sympathise with the strategy spelt out in that article?"

"And if I say I do the next question is whether I have carried out any random killings along the lines suggested by its writer."

"Thank you for asking it for me."

"Fuck off," she said. "There was no reason for me to help the police and I see no reason to help you either. Your time is up, Mr private dick." She seemed to revel in using the word "dick" to describe him and appeared to be looking for some sort of reaction. At that stage, though, they were interrupted by the opening of the door.

"Gary?" said Jenny surprised.

"Yes."

"I've told you to stay away during the day time when I'm entertaining clients."

"Is this a client?" he asked pointing at Rivers.

"This isn't a client," said Rivers. "Who are you?"

"A friend." He looked Rivers up and down. "This isn't the man who came round last Saturday night, is it?"

"No, of course not. Do you think I'd have let him in if he was?"

Gary moved nearer to Rivers until his face was within inches of the private detective's. "If he was, though, I couldn't think of a more fitting end to this encounter than that his body should be found on some waste ground – mutilated like the rest of his violent chums."

Rivers felt he had had enough of the present company. He had only called round to try and build a picture of Jenny Creighton. He felt he had done that adequately by now. "Look," he said, "you've both been charming company but I don't want to outstay my welcome. I think I'll be getting going."

As he left and shut the door behind him, he was aware of a row breaking out behind him. He thought he would loiter around and see what he could pick up.

"Look," shouted Jenny. "You don't come back during the day. This is out of bounds for you."

"I'm only trying to protect you, Jenny."

"I don't need protecting and I certainly didn't need protection from the likes of him."

"Only a couple of days ago you were terrified after your encounter with that guy on Saturday night. If I got my hands on him, I know what I'd like to do to him."

"We all know what you'd like to do with him."

"It's what all men who are violent towards women deserve."

"Well, that guy wasn't," said Jenny. "It's no use threatening everyone I meet. That guy was a private detective – not a client."

• • ● • •

"The crime rate seems to have gone up since you joined us from Brighton," noted Green as he greeted Francesca the next morning. "We've had two murders and a vicious loan shark has gone missing. Still, they all seem like unsavoury characters so perhaps it'll go down in the long run. We've still got to try and solve them all, though."

"Yes, sir."

"We're not making much progress in that regard."

"No sir."

"Time to rattle some cages again," said the inspector. "We can make one arrest." He paused for effect. "Hilary Sampson."

"How?"

"Incitement to murder for publishing that article in her leaflet."

"But where does that get us?"

"Well, as far as the boss classes are concerned, it'll look as if we're making progress if we've got someone behind bars. I'll warrant you Hilary deserves more respect than some of the members of that group – but it might smoke out the person who actually wrote that article. It might even show that she wrote the article herself. It'll at least get us some more publicity.

'Women's group leader accused of incitement to murder'. The tabloids will lap it up."

"Well, that's all right, then." Francesca had had her fill of working with people who wanted instant headline results rather than slowly piecing together who was responsible for the crime.

Green could see, for his part, that he had not convinced her of his strategy. "You know, this crime has got Thomas à Becket syndrome written all over it," he said. Francesca stared at him. It was certainly a more philosophical statement than she had come to expect from her superior. "It starts with 'will nobody rid me of these violent men?'. Then four women take her at her word. We may not be looking for the same killer – but the only thing the victims have in common is that they were violent towards women. There you are. We are getting there somehow." While he had been speaking, he had been making a paper dart out of some paper on his desk. He thrust it into the waste paper bin with a flourish.

"And the other case?" asked Francesca. Green looked puzzled. "You mentioned a vicious loan shark had gone missing."

"Oh, yes," he said. "Well, I'm pretty sure that's entirely separate but we mustn't forget it. I want you to get round to his wife sometime today and look up his list of clients. There's no absolute hurry for this one. He's been missing for weeks and he probably isn't coming back. Also, if he has been killed, it might be a case of good riddance to bad rubbish but that shouldn't detract us from going after the killer. I just hope it's not the wife. She's had enough to put up with in her life. I don't think it's her. Well, chop, chop. These things aren't going to solve themselves."

• • • • •

That morning Rivers decided to go and visit the second prostitute involved in the case. As with Jenny, he had obtained the address from Francesca Manners. He smiled inwardly as he made his way to the Hampstead flat where "intimate relationships" were on offer. He had never found a police officer who had been quite so willing to share information with a private detective. They had formed a close friendship during a previous case they had been working on. She was a very attractive woman, he thought, and maybe, just maybe, she thought he was an attractive man as well. Whatever, it was good to work with her.

He put these thoughts behind him as he approached the address he had been given and knocked on the door. "Philip Rivers, enquiry agent," he said identifying himself to the person on the other side.

"Come in," said a voice. It was a better reception than the one he had endured at Hackney. He looked around him as he was ushered into the living room by the elegantly dressed Jane Harris. Paintings adorned the wall and there was a well-stocked bookcase in the corner of the living room. "I don't suppose I need to guess what you've come here about," she said.

"The revenge murders."

"Yes, and you'll know that I had a sexual relationship with the two victims."

"In one case, at least, on the night he died."

"Yes. I can't call you inspector, can I? You're not one."

"No. You can call me Philip or Rivers. Most people call me Rivers."

"I can assure you, Philip, he was very much alive when he left here that night. As was the other guy on the last occasion that he visited me – although I can't remember the exact date on that one."

"Why do you do what you do?"

"I'm sorry?" The line of questioning did not seem fundamental to the case in Jane's eyes.

"Well, forgive me, but this flat doesn't look like a brothel."

"I wouldn't like you to think of it as one. I advertise intimate relationships with my clients. I like to get to know them. I like the relationship to be a little more than just 'wham, bam, thank you ma'am."

"But these two men?"

"Don't quite fit in with the stereotype I have just outlined. No, they were a mistake. I tried a little experiment. I had read that if you advertised on the street, surprisingly, you were no more likely – indeed it could be less likely – to meet a violent man. Violence is not what I offer."

"Unlike Jenny?"

Jane smiled. "You've met her?" she asked. Rivers nodded. "Our Jenny is a deeply troubled woman. She won't let anybody get close to her. I'm different."

"I can see you are," said Rivers. She was just a little younger than him, he surmised. Intelligent, elegant, deeply attractive, not scarred by the demands of her profession.

"The first victim," she said. "He came from my advert in the local newspaper offering an intimate relationship. He was violent, though; I had to get Beatrice – my flatmate – to get him off me. That was what prompted the experiment. It didn't work, though. One of the first people I attracted was this man Peacock. Same thing – although I didn't need Beatrice's help that time. I do kung fu – and he wasn't very fit. I still maintain that he was in rude health when he left, though."

"You still haven't answered my question. Why do you do it?"

"I enjoy sex, Philip." She moved a little closer to him on the sofa as she said this. "I like pleasing my clients." She remained silent for a moment. "I don't think that ever enters Jenny's head," she added.

"It's not only the clients she doesn't want to please," said Rivers before he could stop himself.

"You have met her, I can see," said Jane.

"But if you like sex why don't you get yourself a boyfriend? Somebody as attractive as you wouldn't have any difficulty."

"It's a complicated story, Philip. My parents – it was a bad marriage. My father was quite violent towards my mother. Something psychological snapped inside me as a result. I couldn't envisage a one-to-one relationship with a man. Better to keep them at arm's length."

"You know it's not inevitable that a one-to-one relationship will end up in violence."

"So people tell me, Philip. I have yet to find out and I don't want to take the risk."

"Do you do anything else?"

"Other than fuck, you mean?" It was the first time Jane had used a crude word and it seemed to disturb Rivers a little. "I write," she said. "I've had a couple of plays performed at fringe theatres."

"Can I ask you – what did you think of that article about revenge killings in the leaflet?"

"I could see what the author was getting at. There's a sort of ghoulish satisfaction with reading about Jack the Ripper. People tend to forget that there were prostitutes that were murdered at the end of the day. He seems instead to come across as a cult figure. I figure that the person who wrote it meant to point out it really was a case of violence against women but would the same conclusions be drawn if it was the other way round. Would a female Ripper be viewed as a cult figure or just someone who was inherently evil? It was badly expressed, though."

"Very," said Rivers. "Do you think it was responsible for these killings?"

"In a word, no. People have to take responsibility for their own actions."

"Well," said the private detective. "Thanks. I'd better get going. It's been very pleasant chatting to you."

"And in a normal situation in a man/woman relationship you'd be making a pass at me now?"

Rivers smiled. "Very possibly," he said, "but I am married."

"That's no barrier," said Jane. "So are most of the people I have intimate relationships with."

"And I don't really want to pay for sex."

"Do contact me if you change your mind." With that Rivers departed. He shook his head once he was outside. Two more different people than Jane and Jenny he could not imagine. He also found it hard to stomach that he had been so attracted by Jane. It was tempting to change his mind and contact her, he thought. Tempting but – no. He had been married for only a year.

He walked down the street in the direction of the tube station. For a moment after leaving the flat he got the feeling that somebody was following him. His instincts were normally good in such circumstances. Once when he turned around, he thought he could see a man on the street corner suddenly stopping to light up a cigarette – as if trying to disguise the fact he had been stalking him. He turned another corner and – just as quickly as he had noticed him – the man was gone. He shrugged his shoulders. Perhaps it was nothing after all.

Back in the flat, Beatrice had come out of her bedroom as Rivers was leaving. "Bit of a shame," Jane said to her. "He was nice but he didn't want sex. Or at least he didn't want to pay for it."

· · ● · ·

The telephone rang late that evening in Jane Harris' flat. It was the landline so she knew it wasn't a boozed-up punter trying to fix an appointment. They would only have had her mobile number. At any rate, if it had been, she would have refused to grant him an appointment. She didn't do drunks at closing time. She picked the receiver up. "Good evening, Miss Harris," said a woman's voice on the other end of the line. "It's Miss Durban from your father's retirement home here. I'm afraid it's your father. He's taken a turn for the worse. I've had to call the doctor out. He doesn't think he'll last the night."

"Oh."

"I thought I ought to call you so you could come in and see him if you wanted to."

"Yes, thank you, Miss Durban. I'll be over shortly." She replaced the receiver slowly as if lost in thought.

"Who was it?" asked her brother, Tom, who had been hovering in the background.

"Miss Durban – from the home."

"I thought so."

"Dad's dying." Tom remained silent. "I ought to go," she said. "He may not last the night."

Tom shrugged his shoulders. "Do what you have to," he said.

"Tom," she said. "I don't like him any more than you do but he is a human being."

"Barely."

Jane ignored the remark. "And he's our father and he's dying. At least we can give him some comfort by being there when he goes."

"Exactly," said Tom. "Give him some comfort. Why would I – we – want to do that? After what he did to mum."

"We'll have no-one left when he goes," said Jane. "You said I should do what I have to do. Well, I will and that involves going and sitting with him while he dies. It's the caring thing to do."

Tom fought back tears. "He's responsible for turning you into what you are," he said. "A prostitute."

Jane snapped at him. "How dare you?" she said.

"Don't pretend, Jane. You can't form any lasting relationships with men because you saw the way he treated our mum. That's true, isn't it?"

"Yes, but 'turning me in what I am'? Where's that come from?"

"I'm sorry, Jane. I shouldn't have said that but sometimes I can't help thinking my little sister….." He put his arms on her shoulders. "My little sister, I wish she had a family relationship just like any other woman and I could be invited round for weekends to play with my little nephews and nieces and have

148

a beer with my brother-in-law who, incidentally, would be a member of the caring professions, not a merchant banker."

"And my big brother?"

"Yes?"

"What about you? I can't remember you having a girlfriend. You can't make relationships, either."

"I have you, Jane. Maybe that's all I need."

"Or can cope with? Look, Tom, I've got to go. I think you should come to. I think you might regret it later if you turn down the opportunity to say goodbye to him. I can't tell you what to do but I am going."

"You go, Jane." He released his grip on her. As she left the flat, he sank back in the armchair in the living room with a sigh. Moments later, Beatrice appeared from her bedroom. She sat on the armchair next to him and took his hand in hers. He smiled at her and kissed her on the cheek.

"You know, your sister was wrong about one thing," she said. Tom eyed her suspiciously. "You can make relationships." He smiled and turned to her again, this time kissing her on the mouth with more passion. She led him to her bedroom.

Jane, meanwhile, got in the car and drove off towards the retirement home. As she drove, she reflected on her father's life. He had been violent. There was no doubt he would often hit their mother when he returned home from the pub of an evening. She knew little about his upbringing – if indeed there was anything in it that had caused him to act in the way that he did. All she did know was that it had become too much for her mother and she would never forget the day she returned from school to be greeted by Tom saying he had found their mother unconscious having taken an overdose of sleeping pills. The medics who arrived a few moments later had pronounced her dead in the family home. Their father could not be contacted and – when he did return later that night – he was drunk and fell over in the living room. Neither of them felt like going to his aid and helping him to come around. He did, though, and was gone by the time they woke up in the morning – in search of somewhere he could find a drink – and leaving them, or more particularly Tom, who was sixteen, to make the funeral arrangements with the help of their mother's sister. Their dad turned up for the funeral. He even shed a tear during the service but was gone again soon afterwards and out of their lives for a good ten years. It was only when he was admitted to the retirement home and they had asked him for an address for a next of kin that the home traced Tom and Jane and Jane was reunited with her father.

Jane arrived at the home and rang the doorbell. She was greeted by Miss Durban who had often in the past seemed quite officious as head of the retirement home. She could not have been warmer in her greeting of Jane, though. "Come in," she said. "He's still holding on. He's in pain and the doctor has prescribed some morphine." Jane entered her father's bedroom and sat down next to him. For once, she reached out and held his hand. She felt it relax in hers. He knew someone was comforting him. They sat in silence as they had done so many times during her visits recently. Miss Durban asked if she could get Jane anything. She shook her head but a cup of tea arrived five minutes later. "I expect you'll want to be alone with him," she said.

"I don't know," she said. Then she composed herself. "But you must have got other things you need to do," she said.

"At three o'clock in the morning?" said Miss Durban. She then turned on her heels. "I'll be in my office if you need me."

"Thank you," said Jane as she resumed her silent vigil. She started sipping from her cup of tea wishing it could have been something stronger – but then, at the end of it all, she would have to drive home. She must have been there for a couple of hours and was barely managing to keep herself awake when she became aware of a rustling noise behind her. She blinked to clear some of the sleep that had formed on her eyes and turned around. To her amazement, she saw a familiar figure standing in the doorway. "Tom," she said. She got up and flung her arms round her brother.

"I've come for you – not him," he said, kissing her on the cheek.

"Come and sit down," she said. As he did so, she noticed her father moving his arm slightly up in the air – as if he was aware that something had happened and there was someone he ought to greet. It was too much for him, though, and his arm slipped on to the bedding where it came to rest. A good ten minutes later, their father started coughing weakly. He opened his mouth and appeared to be mumbling something. Jane bent over him in an effort to hear. "I'm sorry," he said and then he appeared to slump into unconsciousness.

Jane looked at Tom. "I think he's gone," she said. "I think you'd better go and get Miss Durban." Tom nodded and left the room. It was as if he was consciously not looking at his father's dead body in the bed. Jane though, could see that a tear had formed even in his eye.

• • • • •

Larry Green was beginning to feel weary – almost as if he couldn't wait for his retirement in less than three weeks' time. Or more, he reflected soberly. He would stay on to see this case out. He eased himself out of his car and rubbed his brow to rid it of sweat. He realised that Hilary Sampson, the woman he was about to arrest, was intellectually superior to him and did not relish the exchange they were going to have. At the end of the day, though, he was going to arrest her – the first positive move he had made towards cracking this case.

He rang her doorbell. Buddy answered.

"Is Miss Sampson in?" asked the inspector.

"Yes. What do you want?" The question was delivered in a surly manner as if the questioner had had quite enough of the police.

"I want to talk to her - not you," said Green as he attempted to enter the flat.

"Hold on," said Buddy. "I haven't invited you in."

"Tough," said Green

"What is it?" Hilary emerged in the hallway.

"He was trying to barge his way in here," said Buddy.

"Detective Chief Inspector Green doesn't have to barge his way in here," said Hilary. "I'm quite happy for him to come in."

Green gave her a quizzical look. Normally she was sharp and on her guard but she seemed to be offering a friendly face this time. He accepted her invitation to come inside the flat. "Thank you, Miss Sampson," he said. "Hilary Sampson, I am arresting you on suspicion of incitement to murder. You do not have to say anything...."

The rest of his words were drowned out by an extreme reaction from Buddy who grabbed him by the lapels. "Hey, you," she said. "Are you off your rocker?"

"That won't help, madam," he said. "Take your hands off me or I'll have to arrest you, too."

"Do as he says, Buddy," said Hilary. "It'll only make matters worse." Green brought out a pair of handcuffs and was about to place them around Hilary's wrist. "Is that really necessary, inspector?" she asked.

"Procedure," he replied. By the time he had clasped them round Hilary's wrist two police constables had arrived at the open door. "Would you take Miss Sampson to the station?" Green asked them. One of them nodded and took Hilary by the arm. She tried to push him away to allow herself to walk independently out of her flat but to no avail.

"A question, inspector," she said. "Who is it that I have incited someone to murder? I notice there was no name attached to the charge."

"These questions are better left to the police station where you will face a formal interview."

Hilary stopped in the doorway as if she had something to say. The police constable started to pull her along but Green motioned him to let her be. He felt it would be best not to offer the public the sight of Hilary being dragged from her flat to a waiting police car.

"Buddy," she said. "Get hold of Angela. She's had some legal training. She'll know what to do."

Buddy nodded and – with that – Hilary allowed the police constable to take her from the flat. Buddy went inside and called Angela. "It's Hilary," she said. "She's been arrested. She asked me to call you."

"Oh, dear," said Angela looking at her husband, James, scoffing his tea. How could she explain to him that she was going down to the police station again?

"I think she wants you to go down and help her."

"I've had legal training but that was a long time ago." James' ears pricked up at the tone of the conversation.

"She's been arrested for incitement to murder," said Buddy. "It's really serious."

"Yes, I realise that." She looked at James again. Hilary's need was greater than his, she reasoned. And why had she been attending the women's group? Because she felt women should be more assertive in pursuing their own rights. She didn't have to tell him what she didn't want to tell him, she reasoned. "I'm off, darling," she said. "You can look after yourself, can't you?"

"Where are you going?"

Damn it, she thought. I am going to tell him. "It's Hilary," she said. "The police have arrested her. She's asked me for help and I'm going to see what I can do."

"What can you do, though?" he asked.

"A darned sight more than you would do in similar circumstances," she said. She was almost beginning to enjoy herself now. With that, she was off. James went back to his tea – shaking his head.

• • • • •

Rivers got back late from his afternoon visiting the two prostitutes. Nikki, who had been in the office all day, just gave him a cursory glance as he stepped into the living room. Things were going wrong in their relationship, thought Rivers. How could he have been so sure that it was going to succeed this time last year but now be faced with growing doubts? They had known each other on and off for more than thirty years. More off than on – admittedly because of his attitude, if truth be known. But surely if you started a relationship and got married to someone you had known for thirty years, you should know what you were doing? He reflected. He had felt warmer and more intimate during his questioning of the prostitute, Jane Harris, than he did with his own wife. Maybe things would get better when they got down to work the next morning.

· · ● · ·

"Yes?" The tone in John Morgan's voice could not have been less friendly as he answered the knock on the door that evening.

"Oh, Councillor Morgan, I don't know if you remember me – Rosemary Peebles –I helped your wife out when she was taken ill at the parish council meeting that evening."

"Yes?" The voice still sounded unaccommodating – as if he could not wait to get rid of his caller.

"Well, I just popped round to find out how she was," Mrs Peebles continued.

"Oh, she's still a little off colour." His tone seemed to relax. He knew he should put up more of a welcoming front as this busybody – as he saw her – might just get the feeling something was up.

"I wondered if I might see her."

John Morgan pondered the request for a moment. He did not want to be seen as turning it down out of hand. "No," he said finally. "I think it would be better if she rested. I'll tell her you called if you like."

"Thank you," said Mrs Peebles. She made no move to go, though.

"Will that be all?" Morgan asked – the note of irritation returning to his voice.

"Oh, yes," said Mrs Peebles. She turned on her heels and made her way back down the gravel path to her waiting car.

"Who was that?" called a voice from the living room after Morgan had shut the door.

"Oh, just someone from the parish council wanting to know how you were? I said you needed rest." He returned from the door and took her hand as he sat down beside her on the settee in the sitting room. "You know, you really ought to pull yourself together," he said. "People will start to suspect something if I continually have to turn them away."

"It was you who turned whoever it was away," said Emily. "I would have been quite happy to see them."

"I can't be sure of what you might say to them," he said. "You might land us in trouble."

"So might your attitude towards callers," she said reproachfully.

He ignored her. "I'm just going to fetch my book from the bedroom and then I'll make you a cup of coffee." Once upstairs, he noticed his wife's sleeping pills by the side of the bed. He picked them up and looked at them thoughtfully. He shook his head at the thoughts that were coming into his mind. No, he thought, better not risk another tragedy bringing attention to his household.

Meanwhile, Mrs Peebles had driven home from the Morgan household. Once inside, she made herself a cup of tea. She picked up the local paper which was lying on the table for a casual read. An advert caught her eye: Hoffmeyr and Rivers, private enquiry agents. She decided to give the number a ring and fixed an appointment for that afternoon.

CHAPTER SEVEN

Hilary Sampson was ushered into the interview room at the police station. Green had to hand it to her. She still looked composed. He waited for Francesca to join him before he started questioning her.

"Sampson Printworks Ltd," he said reading from the address at the bottom of the leaflet. "That's you?"

Hilary reasoned there was no point in denying her ownership of the print works. It would be easy for the police to check it out. "Yes," she said.

He thrust the leaflet across the table. "So, you are responsible for printing this leaflet?" he asked.

"I think I'd like to consult with my colleague before I answer that question," said Hilary. She had arranged for Angela Curran to come down to the station. She knew she had had legal training and thought she was the best person to help her.

"It's your print works that printed it. It says so at the bottom of the leaflet. You are responsible for the publication of this leaflet."

"As I said, I would prefer to consult with my colleague before answering that question," she repeated firmly.

They were at an impasse – which was only broken by a knock at the door. A police constable entered and whispered something into Green's ear. "It appears your friend is here," he said.

"Might I ask for some time to consult with her?" said Hilary. Green and Francesca withdrew from the room – to be replaced by Angela. "Thanks for coming," said Hilary, touching her arm to put her at her ease.

"What's happened?" said Angela taking a seat opposite her.

"I've been arrested on suspicion of incitement to murder."

"Not charged?"

"Not yet."

"That's something, I suppose," said Angela. She paused to take a breath. "Hilary," she said tentatively. "I'm not a practising lawyer – although I did qualify some years ago. Wouldn't you be better off hiring someone else?" She paused. "Not that I mean you're hiring me, of course, I'm just doing this for free as a friend."

Hilary smiled. "I never thought for a moment you wanted money. At the moment, I would just feel more comfortable with you in the room with me. We'll see what happens. I may need a practising lawyer later."

"I think you ought to be as honest as you can be. Be polite. Be as open as you can be."

"I'm not going to give up the identity of the person who wrote the article," said Hilary defiantly.

"I take it that it wasn't you?"

"If I tell them that, then I narrow the field of suspects from which the author can be drawn."

"Not by much," said Angela. "It could be me, it could be Jane, it could be Jenny, it could be Gabi. Or it could be from an unknown contributor from outside the group."

There was a knock at the door. "Are you ready?" asked Green from outside the room. Hilary nodded.

"We are," said Angela. She got up and moved to Hilary's side of the table. Green and Francesca re-entered the room.

"Are you representing Miss Sampson?" asked Green.

"I'm acting for her," said Angela. She produced a certificate confirming her legal qualification and passed it to Green. He nodded and showed it to Francesca. He then leant over to her and whispered. "I don't have any problems with that," he said. "She was a suspect but she's so far off the radar now." Francesca agreed. She switched on the tape recorder in the room – and all four gave their names. "You are Hilary Sampson and you are the proprietor of Sampson's print works?" said Francesca.

"I own it, yes," said Hilary.

"You are responsible for the publication of this leaflet," Green said, again thrusting it across the table."

"I published it," said Hilary. "I would question the word 'responsible'. The authors of each of the articles are responsible for what they have written." Goodness, thought Angela. Why did she need me to come and support her? She's more than capable of looking after herself.

"But you are the editor of what has appeared in this leaflet?"

"I published the leaflet."

"Why did you include this article?"

"That's easy," she said. "I found it interesting."

"It's calling for revenge indiscriminate attacks on men for the killings of Jack the Ripper. That's incitement to murder. Incitement to murder – interesting?"

"I think if you read it you'll find it is a little more thoughtful than that. It argues that – instead of being vilified – Jack the Ripper has received cult status in the eyes of many members of the public. Every night there are guided Ripper tours through the East End of London to show people where he murdered his victims. Glorifying him. It asks whether a female Jack the Ripper – a Jill the Ripper if you like – would be accorded such cult status and then suggests maybe we should test that theory out."

"By killing men," said Green. Hilary remained silent.

"What did you hope would happen as a result of publishing this article?"

"That people would read it."

"And act upon it? Surely it would have failed in its intention if they didn't act upon it?" Hilary remained silent again. "Did you write the article?"

Hilary glanced at Angela who nodded in her direction – indicating that she should answer the question. "No," she said.

"Who did?"

Hilary needed no confirmation from Angela this time as to her course of action. "The article, as you can see, is anonymous," she said. "We protect the anonymity of our contributors if they so wish."

"Even if they are killers?"

Angela intervened at this stage. "There is no suggestion that there is any intent on the part of the author to carry out the killings themselves," she said. She felt emboldened by Hilary's calmness under pressure.

"No, she's just calling on other people to carry out the killings."

"In which case, inspector, maybe you should be charging the author with conspiracy to murder."

"When I find out who it was, I will charge them."

"And my client will go free?"

"No, both the writer and the publisher will be charged," said Green. "Of course, were you to help us with enquiries and acknowledge how sorry you were to have published such an article, that could count in your favour."

His comments gave hope to Hilary. Perhaps he was just on a fishing expedition and did not intend to charge her at the end of the day. "I never intended anyone should get killed because of this article," said Hilary. "I never thought for a moment that would happen."

"But it did." Green looked at her. Her comments were not enough, he thought, to save her from ultimately being charged. "Do you know how this article first came to our notice?" he asked.

"I'm sure you're going to enlighten me," said Hilary.

"The parents of a young lad found it in his flat. He was sharing his flat with a member of your group. They were so worried by what they saw that they felt his life was at risk. Even now, they have hired a private detective to protect him. Is that the kind of reaction you wanted to create by publishing this article?"

"No,"

"You know what happened, of course, two weeks after its publication? A murder was committed. The mutilated body of a man was found on waste ground. Then a second body. You could argue that was a success story for the author of the article. And for you as editor of the publication."

"The article makes no mention of mutilating the body,"Hilary responded."Maybe the murders were not connected to it."

"A bit too much of a coincidence, do you not think?" Green continued."Where were you on the night of Monday, June 7?"

"At home with my partner, Buddy after going to the cinema with a friend?"

"And Wednesday the 9th?"

"Ah, we went out for an Italian meal. I think I still have the bill in my purse." She brought it out of her handbag and passed a scrap of paper over to Green, "There," she said. "Independently verified."

Green glanced at the receipt. "It says you paid at 9.45pm. The body was found much later – in an area near the restaurant," he said triumphantly."So what did you do afterwards?"

"We went home."

Green decided to change the direction of his questioning. "Tell me, Miss Sampson, what do you think of men?"

"I prefer not to categorise them,"said Hilary."Actually, I prefer not to think about them that much."

"It probably wouldn't cause you a moment's grief to think of a man's body being mutilated, his...." Green felt embarrassed to go further.

"Penis?"prompted Hilary.

"Penis being hacked off and cast away while he is murdered."

"I think I told you before that men's willies are of no interest to me,"she said icily.

Angela began to look alarmed. The comment was hardly likely to endear her to the detectives, she thought. She touched

Hilary on the arm. "What Hilary means is that she would have no motivation to carry out that sort of act," she said.

"And she didn't," said Hilary, referring to herself in the third person. "Nice try, inspector," she said. "Trying to present me as an enemy of all men simply because I am a lesbian. I think, though, you'll find life is a little more complicated than that."

"Miss Sampson, if you insist you are not responsible for these murders, you would so help your cause if you could find it within yourself to tell me the name of the author of this article," said Green. He gathered his papers up. "We are finished here tonight," he said. "We shall resume questioning in the morning. In the meantime, I shall have you escorted to a cell. You have already been arrested on suspicion of incitement to murder and cautioned."

He opened the door and called for a constable who then ushered Hilary away. She cast a glance at Angela before she left the room. The look on her face seemed to say: "I didn't expect this." "You will come back tomorrow, won't you Angela?" said Hilary. For the first time her friend could detect a look of anxiety on her face.

"They won't be able to start the interview without me," said Angela as she gathered herself together to leave the room.

Green turned to Francesca when they were alone in the room. "I'll be in touch with the Crown Prosecution Service tomorrow morning," he said, "but I think we have enough to charge her with incitement to commit murder."

"Come in," said Nikki as Rosemary Peebles arrived at her office that afternoon. "I'm Nikki Hoffmeyr and this is my partner, Philip Rivers." Rivers stood up and shook Mrs Peebles by the hand. Mrs Peebles felt reassured by the presence of Nikki. She did not look like a private detective, she thought. Her former career in the fashion industry led to her dressing a touch more elegantly than Mrs Peebles would have expected for someone in what she considered to be a slightly seedy profession. Nikki gave her husband a knowing glance which, roughly translated, meant: leave this to me. I think she feels reassured by being in the company of a woman.

"I just saw your advert in the paper," she began.

"Yes?" said Nikki as Rivers brought cups of tea for the three of them.

"I have a friend. I'm worried about her. She's worried about something. Something's troubling her."

"Can you be a bit more specific?" intervened Rivers. Nikki shot him a sidelong glance warning him not to press her too hard.

"She nearly fainted at the parish council meeting. Her mind wasn't on the matters in hand." Cynically Rivers felt he could sympathise with her on that. "It's just that the matter we were about to discuss was something she'd brought up and was rather keen. Putting speed bumps in the Glades."

Rivers' ears pricked up at the mention of the Glades. Hadn't the police constable investigating his drink driving charge also mentioned that the wife of John Morgan had been a parish councillor? "What's her name?" he asked.

"Emily Morgan," said Mrs Peebles.

Rivers glanced at Nikki and smiled. "What do you want us to do?" asked Nikki.

"Find out what's troubling her," Mrs Peebles said, "and put it right."

"You do realise that if you ask us to investigate you would have to pay us for our services?" said Rivers taking the lead in discussions. "I'm not really sure it comes under our remit as private detectives," he added. "We really only investigate when a crime's been committed."

"It might have been."

"In what sense?"

"Well, I get the feeling something happened at her house – something that her husband doesn't want her to talk about."

Rivers sighed. Much as he would have liked to taken her money for an investigation – it wasn't as if their coffers were exactly overflowing – he still felt it would be wrong.   She was a Good Samaritan who had brought something she was troubled about to light not someone at the centre of a criminal investigation. "I still think it's not quite our cup of tea," he said. "I think you should continue trying to visit your friend. If you find at the end of the day that there is something criminal for us to investigate, then by all means come back to us but I think it would be a question of robbery if we were to take a fee for what you have told us."

"Do you think I'm being silly?"

"No," said Rivers, "not for a moment but you might find – for instance – if it is a criminal matter at the end of the day, you should go straight to the police. It sounds to me that – if she's troubled by something – she might be better off talking about it to a doctor or a counsellor or somebody like that."

"Thank you," said Mrs Peebles as she got ready to leave. "It's nice to find somebody who doesn't just want to take your money at the end of the day."

Rivers smiled as Nikki escorted her from the premises. On returning, she turned to Rivers and asked forcefully: "What the hell did you do that for? I would have thought you would have loved to investigate that. It's where the Morgans live. It looks like he's trying to get her to cover up something that happened at the house. It's just what you said must have happened."

"Yes, I know and we will use it in our investigations – but I didn't feel comfortable taking money from her." He thought for a moment. "I do think you should take the lead in this. The Morgans don't know who you are. Call on them and see if you can get Emily Morgan on her own and find out what's worrying her."

"How do I get in to speak to her?"

"Pretend to him you're from the parish council."

"But she'll know I'm not."

"Tell her you're a friend of Rosemary Peebles and that she asked you to call round because she was worried."

• • ● • •

"It's an eyesore – a damned eyesore," said the rambler as he and his wife walked across the fields to get to their village pub. "Been there three or four weeks and no-one's come to take it away."

The burnt-out car had been left on the edge of the field. It must have been driven up the track from the nearby lane and just abandoned there. Somebody had obviously set fire to it after it had been dumped.

"I'm going to ring the police when we get to the pub," he said. "Joy riders, I'll be bound."

"Yes, sir, we have had one or two calls about it," said the police sergeant when the man got through to the police station. "I'll send somebody up to have a look at it this afternoon. I'm sorry for the inconvenience."

"It's just that it's a beautiful bit of countryside. Joy riders, I expect. They want flogging."

"Well, we won't be able to do that, sir," said the police sergeant, "but we'll be up there as soon as we can."

More's the pity, thought the couple. By the time they had finished their lunch and his pint, and they had started off on their walk back across the fields, the police sergeant had been as good as his word. There were two police constables pouring over the wreckage. "They haven't made as good a job as they thought of destroying the car," observed one. "There's what looks like the remains of a number plate under the back wheel."

"They probably didn't stay around to observe their handiwork," said the other.

The first police constable went back to his car and radioed in – asking headquarters to track the name of the owner of the car through the number plate. Within minutes, the reply came back to him. "Belongs to a Brian Jones," the constable told his colleague. "Been reported missing a few days ago. Seems as though we should be looking for a body."

"Well, there's not one here," replied the other man.

"We're to wait until detectives come along to take a look at the wreckage – although what they'll see that we can't I've no idea."

Within half an hour, Green and Francesca were on the scene. "Did you go round to Mrs Jones and have a look at his list of clients?" Green asked his subordinate.

"No, sir, I meant to – but I haven't had time."

Green nodded. He appeared to understand the time pressures on his colleague. "Well, perhaps we should go round there now and kill two birds with one stone."

The couple were still hanging around so Green went over to them.

"Are you going to take it away?" the man asked.

"Yes, sir, but it seems you might have stumbled on a crime," said Green. "I want to thank you for reporting it."

"Well, of course it's a crime. Joy riders."

"It may be more serious than that, sir." He received a withering look as if to suggest what could possibly be more serious than joy riders. "The owner of this vehicle is listed as a missing person. You may well have stumbled on the aftermath of a murder that went wrong." The couple went on their way at this while Green and Francesca resolved to make their way to Anita Jones' house.

It did not surprise Green that she was in – she looked shattered when she answered his knock. He reasoned that she did not have much in her life to take her mind off her disappearing husband.

"I'm sorry not to have been back to you before," said Green, "but we had little to report until now. We've found your husband's car. It's been abandoned in a field in Hertfordshire.

Somebody had set fire to it."

"Oh," she said.

"I'm afraid there was no sign of your husband," he went on. "He still remains missing but we are concerned about what might have happened to him."

Green's manner tended to suggest to Mrs Jones that they had not been concerned before they had found the car. "You think he may...." Her voice tailed off. "May have been killed," she finally said.

"We can't be sure either way," said Green, "somebody has tried to destroy all evidence identifying his car and that means they didn't want anybody to find it." He paused. "I seem to remember when you came into the station, you said you could lay your hand on a list of his clients?"

"Yes, I think so," she said. "He kept his records in the study." The study turned out to be too grand a name for a room which was strewn with paper and had a computer in it. It didn't take Green and Francesca long to find a little red book with names and addresses and figures in it.

"It shows how much each of his clients owed him," observed Francesca.

Green read through it. "There must be a hundred names on it," he said. "How on earth are we going to get through all these while still searching for our Ripper revenge killer?" He glanced at the list of names. None of them stood out or meant anything to him.

"Delegate this case to someone else?" suggested Francesca,

"No," said Green. "I've got a feeling in my bones this could be interesting. We'll hold on to it for the time being."

"We could start off by looking at those who owed him the most," suggested Francesca.

"We could ask his two partners if they knew anything about them," added Green. "What were their names – Bruiser and Eel?" He turned to Mrs Jones. "Maybe you know how to find them?"

"They run a scrap metal place in Hornsey," she said. "I can give you the address." Green thanked her for her information and the two detectives left – promising to keep in touch if there were any further developments. As he was approaching the car, Green's mobile went off. He answered it and then turned to Francesca. "That was the Crown Prosecution Service," he said. "They say we've got enough to charge Hilary Sampson. We'd best get back then."

· · ● · ·

"She's in real trouble, James. I have to go and help her," said Angela as she tried to tell her husband she was going back to the police station that day.

"You should cut yourself adrift," he said. "You don't want to get caught up in all this mess. I know you, Angela. All this politics – it's not your kind of thing."

You don't know me, James, she thought. "Politics?" said Angela. "It's not politics. It's a murder investigation."

"You know what I mean."

"Get off to work, James. I'm just trying to warn you I might not be back in time to get your tea." What a ridiculous situation, thought Angela. Here am I – a supposedly liberated woman in the eyes of my friends in the women's movement having to get permission (or so it seems) to get out of making my husband's tea when a close friend is being held on a murder charge.

"Anyhow, if she is in real trouble, she needs a properly trained solicitor. Not you," said James firmly.

"I am properly trained. Just not practising."

Precisely, thought James. "I'll not argue with you anymore," he said. He walked out into the hallway and took his hat from the hat stand. "You know my feelings. I'll see you this evening."

When he had shut the door, she flicked a V-sign in his direction. "Men," she said out loud in a desperate voice. He thinks his tea is more important that Hilary being on a murder charge, she thought. Of course, it wasn't that simple. He liked to think of her being at home and being at his beck and call. Well, she would see about that. When the business with Hilary was over, she would see about getting her own job. A first step might be to go back to that legal work she had embarked upon several years ago.

She rang the police station and asked to be put through to Detective Sergeant Manners. "We're waiting for an official response from the Crown Prosecution Service," the detective had said. "Then we will be able to proceed. We've been told we will get it in writing by four o'clock this afternoon, we've been promised that. I'm sure your friend will contact you if she wants you to represent her."

Angela put the receiver down. She busied herself with some household chores while she awaited a telephone call. By three o'clock it had still not come so she resolved to go down to the police station and wait there. At least she would be on hand when the deadline approached.

"I'd like to see my client, Hilary Sampson," she said to the desk sergeant on arrival at the police station.

"I'm sorry, madam, but you'll have to wait," he replied. "We're too busy."

At that juncture both Detective Chief Inspector Green and Detective Sergeant Manners swept through the reception area. Francesca stopped on seeing Angela. "We'll be with you in a minute," she said. "We've just got to fetch Miss Sampson from the cells. You can wait in the interview room if you like."

Angela did as had been suggested. Within minutes she had been joined by Hilary and the two detectives. Hilary had also been accompanied by a police constable. The meeting was formal, curt and to the point. Hilary was charged with conspiracy to commit murder and had her rights read to her. "You will be held in custody," said Green, "and be brought before the courts tomorrow morning."

The police constable took Hilary by the arm and began leading her from the interview room.

"Wait a minute," said Angela. "Could I have a moment with my client?"

"I can't see what harm it would do," said Green grudgingly. He turned to the police constable. "Leave them for a moment," he said, "and escort Miss Sampson back to the cells when they've finished."

Hilary had her head in her hands. She looked up when they were alone together. "So?" she said. "What happens now?"

"You heard what he said," Angela replied. "You're to be kept in custody until tomorrow morning when you'll be brought before the courts."

"Do you think I'll get bail then?"

Angela sighed. "I haven't a clue," she said. "This is getting beyond my pay grade. I think you'll have to go and get yourself a solicitor."

"From in here?" She sighed. "You've done well so far. Couldn't you carry on?"

"I seem to remember there's an all women firm of solicitors in Hampstead. Maybe I could get someone from there to take the case on." She glanced at her watch. "If I hurry, I might be able to get to them before they shut for the evening."

Hilary reached forward and touched her on the arm. "You do that," she said. "And thanks for everything."

With that Angela bustled out of the room. When she had gone, Hilary buried her head in her hands again and tears began to well in her eyes. She pulled herself together as the police constable came back into the room to escort her back to her cell.

• • ● • •

Nikki marched up to the Morgans' door later that afternoon. Once Rivers had decided she should carry out the investigation, she saw no reason why she should delay. She knocked at the door. As luck would have it, John Morgan was out at a council meeting and Emily answered her knock. She looked tired, thought Nikki, but no worse than that. "Yes, can I help you?" she asked.

"I'm a friend of Rosemary Peebles," said Nikki. "She asked me to call round to find out how you were."

"But," Emily stammered, "she only called round this morning and I was too weak to receive visitors."

"Are you?"

"No, I feel a bit better now – but I don't know who you are."

"As I said, I'm a friend of Rosemary's. She thought you were worried about something. May I come in?"

Emily looked flustered. "I'm not sure I should allow you in," she said.

"Why ever not?" said Nikki. "If you have got something on your mind, it might be best to talk about it with someone. Sometimes you can feel freer talking to a complete stranger than a friend."

"I suppose so." She invited Nikki into the sitting room and then offered to make her a tea or coffee. However, while she was still making it, the sound of a car turning into the driveway could be heard and a few moments later John Morgan entered the house.

Nikki stood up. "Hallo," she said offering him a hand to shake. "I'm Nikki Hoffmeyr – a friend of Rosemary Peebles from the parish council. She asked me to call round and find out how your wife was."

Morgan rejected the handshake. "She'd feel a darn sight better if she wasn't being pestered all the time by the likes of you," he said. "I told Rosemary Peebles this morning that my wife was too tired to have visitors and she still is. Now, if you wouldn't mind leaving." He pointed the way to the door as he spoke.

His wife returned with the drinks before Nikki could go,

though. "That's a bit inhospitable, John, isn't it," she said. "I've just made her a drink."

"I'm only thinking of you, darling," he said, "but maybe you should have your drink and then go." Nikki smiled and sat down with the tea Emily had prepared. Morgan sat down opposite her. It was obvious that he was not going to give them the opportunity to be alone together. Nikki tried to make polite conversation as she sipped her tea. She noticed a photograph on the mantelpiece above the fireplace. "Is that your family?" she asked. It was a picture of a man, a woman and a younger man standing outside a pub. "Is that your son?" asked Nikki. Emily nodded. "Handsome young man," said Nikki. But what had caught her eye more was the red car the three of them were standing next to. "Nice car," said Nikki. "Your son's?"

"Yes," said Emily.

"He must be doing well for himself," Nikki said. She could see as she turned back to sip her tea and face the Morgans again that a worried frown had formed on John Morgan's brow. She felt she should make her excuses and leave as soon as possible now. Once outside, she contacted Rivers on his mobile. "I got in," she said.

"Good. Did you learn anything?"

"Not really, John Morgan came back within minutes of my arrival. I thought I'd struck lucky because Emily Morgan was on her own when I arrived."

"Never mind," said Rivers. "It was worth trying."

"I did learn one thing, though," she said. "The Morgans' son has a red car. There was a photograph of them standing by it on the mantelpiece. John Morgan looked distinctly uncomfortable when I drew attention to it."

"Good," said Rivers. "That must have been the car I drove into."

• • • • •

"No rest for the wicked," said Green as he got into his car and bade goodnight to Francesca. "I'm going to see the eloquently named Bruiser and Eel to see if they can shed any light on which clients Brian Jones might have been visiting on the night he disappeared."

"Good luck," said Francesca. "I can't imagine they'll be of much help to you."

"Oh, I don't know," mused Green. The scrapyard Bruiser and Eel ran was about a quarter of an hour's drive from the police station – near the waste ground where the two victims of the revenge killer had been found, Green recalled. That was mere coincidence, though, he thought. The scrapyard wasn't known as Bruiser and Eel's but McCarthy and Higgs. Far more respectable, thought Green. He stepped out of his car and walked over to a ramshackle office where a gaunt, thin man sporting an ancient trilby which looked as if it had seen better days was sitting at a desk amidst a sea of paperwork. At least they had some paper work, thought Green. "Good afternoon," he said. "I'm looking for two gents called Bruiser and Eel."

"Who wants to know?" said the man gruffly without looking up from his desk.

"Detective Chief Inspector Green," he said producing his warrant card from his pocket. "I'm investigating a potential homicide,"

The man looked up at him. "Then you must have come to the wrong place," he said.

"Don't get me wrong," said the inspector. "These two gents – Bruiser and Eel – are not suspects. It's just that they may be able to help me track down what happened to a friend of theirs."

"A friend?" It was said in a way which seemed to suggest the man didn't understand the concept of friendship.

"Yes, or work colleague. Brian Jones."

The man suddenly looked shocked. "Brian Jones has been murdered?" he asked as if thrown by the idea.

"I don't know but it looks like it," said Green.

The other man lowered his guard. "I'm known by some of my friends as Eel," he said extending a hand of friendship to Green. Green accepted the offer.

"And I'm Bruiser," said a voice behind him. Green looked around to see a squat man riven with tattoos and sporting a jemmy in his hand. Green did not know whether he had originally picked it up because he was contemplating hitting him over the head with it. In the new spirit of friendship he had found with Eel, Green extended his hand to Bruiser, too. He was rebuffed. "State your case and say what you want," said Bruiser.

"You do business with Brian Jones, I believe? You help him out with the collection of debts."

"It is a service we provide – debt collection," said Eel.

"Then you may be able to help me. We found Brian Jones' burnt-out car in a field near Hertford," said Green. "His wife had reported him missing several days ago. He hasn't been seen for over a month."

"That would explain things," said Eel.

"Like what?"

"Well, he'd asked us to collect from three of his clients. We'd normally hand the money over at the Three Fellows pub in Ware on a Sunday evening but he hasn't been there to collect."

"Weren't you a little concerned about that?"

"Why? It meant we could hold on to the money for a little bit longer. It was his to collect."

"Besides," said Bruiser entering the conversation for the first time. "It pays not to be too inquisitive in these circumstances, don't you agree, inspector? You never know what you might turn up." He kept tapping his hand with the jemmy as he spoke.

"I have here a list of his clients." Green brought a sheet of paper from his pocket. "Could you tell me which were the three clients he asked you to visit?"

Eel held out a hand to look at the piece of paper but Bruiser snatched it from him. "No," he said. "I don't remember – and nor does my colleague."

"You're worried that I might go round and talk to them – and I'll find out you didn't strictly play by the Queensberry rules when you went to collect the debt?" Bruiser remained silent and it seemed as if his silence was having an effect on Eel's earlier decision to co-operate. "I can understand that you are loathe to believe me," Green continued, "but that was not the purpose of my question. I think if he handed their names on to you it means he was not intending to visit them again and so that probably rules them out as suspects in his disappearance."

It was like drawing blood from a stone. Neither of the men spoke. Eel broke the impasse, though. "Would you give us a couple of minutes on our own, inspector?" he said.

"Okay," said Green and he walked back to his car, opened the door and sat in it. He wanted Bruiser and Eel to realise that he did not intend to eavesdrop on what they were saying to each other.

"Why don't we co-operate with him?" said Eel. "Taking him at face value, it could help him find out what happened to Jonesy – and we'd like to know that. It would be in our interests. If he's found dead, we could keep the money." Bruiser failed to respond. "Also," continued Eel, "if he is bluffing and trying to catch us out, surely those three wouldn't squeal on us? They'd be worried about the consequences after what happened last time."

"All right," said Bruiser sullenly. He jerked open the door. "You can come in, Inspector," he said. He picked up the piece of paper. "These are the three that we visited," he said, making a pencil mark next to their names. The scrap of paper indicated the three names on the list that owed Brian Jones the most.

"So, can you tell from this list who Brian Jones might have been likely to visit?"

"He had a system," said Eel. "He'd make a visit to those who'd fallen behind with their payments. He'd tell them that – if they didn't come up with the money in a week – we'd be sent round to collect."

"Did he threaten them?" asked Green.

"Depends on whether you think a visit from us would be threatening," said Bruiser. He still had the jemmy in his hand.

"I take your point," said Green. "So, logically, it would be the ones with the next highest debts that he would be visiting." Neither Bruiser nor Eel said anything. "Your silence speaks volumes," the inspector added. He scrutinised the scrap of paper again. "That narrows it down to about half a dozen," he said. "Thanks, Gents, you've been most co-operative."

Eel smiled. "No police officer has ever said that about Bruiser before," he said. His colleague did not appear to appreciate the humour of the situation.

"One thing, inspector," said Bruiser. "Don't come back and tell us you've found whoever was responsible for Brian Jones' disappearance. If he has been murdered I expect we'll read about it in the papers. No need for you to visit us again. It would be bad for business."

"I'll be off then," said Green. He walked back to his car and turned on reaching the door. "Oh, by the way," he said. "I forgot to ask you. Which one is Mr McCarthy and which one is Mr Higgs?"

"You don't need to know," said Bruiser.

No, thought Green, I don't. Memo to self, he thought, if you ever have to arrest either of these two gentlemen, make sure you arrive with reinforcements.

• • • • •

"Francesca," said Rivers as he opened the door to his office. "What a nice surprise. What brings you here?"

"The urgent need to down a couple of drinks with somebody who does not work for the police service," she said. "Are you game?"

"Yes," he said. He started packing up the papers on his desk. "You're lucky to find me in," he added. "Nikki decided she wanted some outdoor work so she's doing a visit for me. I've volunteered to do the books for a few hours. Any distraction is welcome."

They walked down the High Street to the nearest pub, the Bull, and ordered a couple of drinks. "I've left my car at the police station in anticipation of drinking," said Francesca.

"This is not like you," said Rivers. "You're usually so cool and in command."

"I can do cool and in command with a couple of drinks inside me," Francesca responded. "Anyhow, I wanted a little help with something. It's nothing to do with the Jill the Ripper case – as the tabloids are calling it. It's a crime that's taking up some of the time that we should be devoting to going after the Ripper."

"Go on."

"About a week ago, the wife of a loan shark comes into our office and declares her husband missing. Turns out she hasn't seen him for a month or so."

"Right."

"Then yesterday his car turns up burnt out in a field and abandoned."

"No sign of him?"

"No, so the conclusion that we – that is Detective Chief Inspector Green and I – draw is that maybe he isn't just a missing person. Maybe he's been murdered."

"Quite natural."

"Anyway, we go and visit his wife and she gives us a list of his clients. There's a hundred of them. We haven't got the time – or inclination – to visit all of them. The DCI beetles off to a couple of debt collectors – the ominously named Bruiser and Eel – to see if they can help him narrow the list down. I haven't heard how he got on – but I wondered if you could have a look at the list and see if any thoughts come to light."

"I'll have a go," he said, "but there's no reason why it should."
He took the photocopied list from her and began to read it.

"You've been around the area a long time," she said. "It's just
that you may have come up against one or two of these people
in the past."

"Bernie Thompson," he said jabbing his finger down on the
piece of paper. "Small time villain. Bit like a weasel. Always in
trouble – but I wouldn't have thought murder was his style."
He read on. "No," he said, "there's one or two names I recognise
from court reports in the local papers but – again – murder
would seem to be a little bit out of their league." He suddenly
came to a halt in his reading. "What colour was the car?"

"Is that relevant?" asked Francesca.

"It may be very relevant. Was it red?"

Francesca shook her head. "It was badly burned but there
were bits that were not destroyed by the fire," she said. "It would
have been black, though, I would have thought."

"Hmm," said Rivers, still ruminating about whatever he had
seen on the scrap of paper. "Jed Morgan," he said, pointing to a
name in front of him. "Worth checking if that's Councillor John
Morgan's son."

"Why?"

"The reason I'm able to drink freely with you tonight – having
lost my licence on a drink driving charge. I drove into the back
of a car outside Councillor Morgan's home."

"Which was a red one, presumably, from what you've just said."

"Yes – and likely to have been owned by Morgan's son,
according to something Nikki has come up with this afternoon."

"Oh?"

"She was visiting the Morgans." He paused for a moment. "I
think I can tell you why you didn't find a body with the burnt-
out car. I went into the back of the red car and the following
morning the police found blood stains on the road and in my
engine which could only have come from the back or the boot

177

of the car I drove into. Whoever owned it drove off before the police arrived. Very suspicious. Jed Morgan's got a red car. Maybe he and the loan shark were both at Councillor Morgan's house in separate cars that night. He drove away with the loan shark in the boot of his car and they then got rid of the loan shark's car."

Francesca smiled at him. "I'm glad I asked you to look at the list," she said. "Makes my life so much easier."

"Would you like another drink?" asked Rivers.

"Yes – and while we're having it perhaps you could solve the Ripper murders, too," she said.

He went up to the bar and came back with another pint and glass of white wine. "I think I should pay Councillor Morgan another visit tomorrow morning," he said.

"That might not be wise," said Francesca.

"Why not?"

"He may tip his son off if you tell him what we suspect."

"I'd like to see the fat bastard squirm," said Rivers. Francesca was surprised at his tone of voice. "He's a prominent local councillor and I think that may have played its part in squashing any investigation of this."

"Be careful," said Francesca.

"I'm not going to be in any danger," protested Rivers. "He's got his position to think about."

"Maybe I should pay Jed Morgan a visit at about the same time tomorrow morning," said Francesca.

Rivers looked at her. She still did look cool and in command even if she thought she had had a rotten day. Stylish was a word that Rivers felt would be an apt way of describing her – even now. "We should do this again," he said finishing off his pint.

She leant forward and put a hand on his knee – much to his surprise. "I'd like that," she said. Stylish, cool and in command, thought Rivers. I'm not, he conceded to himself. He didn't know whether Francesca was signalling making an advance to him but – if she had been – there was Nikki to consider. Surely he didn't want to risk his marriage after only one year. Maybe Francesca didn't want him in that way, though. There was only one way to find out, he thought. He was interrupted by Francesca, though. "I'd better be off now," she said. "Maybe we should reconvene tomorrow evening after we've tackled the Morgans?"

"I'd like that," he said repeating her earlier words.

"Well, goodnight then," she said leaning forward to give him a peck on the cheek before she left. "That's for solving the mystery for me," she said.

"Let's review whether I have tomorrow night," he said. He watched as she walked out of the pub. Twenty-four hours to sort out his emotions, he thought.

• • • • •

Robyn Peters had a steely glint in her eye as she shook Hilary Sampson by the hand. "We're going to do our damnedest to get you out of here," she said. "Angela's been filling me in with all the details of the case. She's done a good job."

"She has," acknowledged Hilary as she reached out to touch her friend's hand across the table in the interview room at the magistrate's court. A policewoman stood outside the door – presumably to head off any attempt at escaping by Hilary.

"Now," said Robyn, "as they say – I'll see you in court. The policewoman (she gestured to the woman outside) will escort you into the court room and into the dock. We'll try for bail. I gather they're ready to start."

Angela and Robyn Peters left the room first. "Thank you for coming at such short notice," Angela said as they made their way into the court room.

"No – my pleasure," said Robyn.

"I didn't think I could do any more on my own. I represented her. I do have legal training but haven't worked for a while."

"Oh. Why?"

"I'm almost too ashamed to admit it," said Angela. "I got married and my husband's very traditional. He wanted me to be at home to look after the house."

"I'm not going to bite your head off for that," said Robyn. Her long black hair came to rest just below her shoulder line. She was elegantly dressed in a three piece grey trouser suit. "I'm glad you found us," she added. "We are the only women-only law firm operating in the area. Maybe you should consider resuming your work with us."

"With you?"

"I've been impressed with how calm Hilary is about these proceedings. A lot of that must be due to you."

"Oh, I don't know," said Angela blushing. "Hilary's a pretty calm person. She can give as good as she gets – even from the police."

As they took up their seats on the front bench of the courtroom a young woman – also dressed in a grey suit approached them. Angela did not recognise her at first. It was Buddy. "How's Hilary?" she asked. "I thought I ought to come along and support her."

Angela introduced Buddy to Robyn. "Hilary's partner," she added by way of explanation. Robyn smiled. She liked to put people at their ease in a courtroom situation.

"What will happen now?" asked Buddy. Before Robyn could answer, Hilary was brought into the courtroom. She smiled as she saw Buddy. Her partner blew her a kiss.

"Court rise," said the usher. At that the three magistrates entered the room. By now, the prosecution's solicitor had also come into the courtroom and set out his papers at the other end of the front bench. The charge was read out to Hilary. The prosecutor said he was opposing bail because of the seriousness of the charge.

"Madam Chair," said Robyn rising.

At that stage the lead magistrate intervened. "I am not a chair," she said icily.

"We haven't won that battle in Barnet yet,"whispered Angela to Robyn. The woman who was not a chair frowned at her for speaking – although she had not heard what she had said.

"My apologies, Madam,"said Robyn gracefully. She probably isn't a madam either, she thought to herself. "Madam, I am Robyn Peters from Buckland and Peters. I appear for the accused. I should like to make an application for bail on the grounds of my client's previous good character."

"Go on,"said the chief magistrate.

"My client is charged with incitement to commit murder – yet it is agreed that she did not intend to kill anyone. It is also agreed that she did not conspire with anyone in the sense that no conversation took place about killing anyone. She is not what you would call a flight risk. She lives in the neighbourhood near here, runs a print works and edits a bulletin produced by a local woman's group." It sounded so respectable, thought Angela, as Robyn spoke. How could James possibly have any disagreement with it?

"I've read the bulletin," said the chief magistrate gruffly. "I think women's group is a most inadequate way of describing it. These people are revolutionaries."

Robyn ploughed on as if unaffected by the intervention. "Nevertheless, the fact remains she has no history of violence and has never advocated it herself. On the surface, this purports to be a charge about murder – but in essence it is really about the defendant's freedom to publish what she wants."

The prosecutor got to his feet."My Lady, since the publication of an article by the defendant urging women to take part in revenge killings against men to avenge Jack the Ripper two men have been murdered."

"And there's been a terrorist attack in London," said Robyn, "but there is no connection to the article."

The senior magistrate intervened."I think we are in danger of trying the case," she said. "I think we are in possession of enough evidence to make a decision." She turned to her two fellow magistrates. One of them, a man, seemed to be arguing something vociferously. There were a lot of hand signals, anyway. "We shall retire to consider our decision," she said.

"Court rise," said an usher and the three of them trouped out,

"Well," said Robyn, "I think at least we've secured a division of opinion among them. The guy on the right is a local trade union official. I think he disagrees with her."

"And the other woman?" asked Angela.

"Never seen her before. We shall have to wait and see." They did not have to wait long. It took the three magistrates about ten minutes to reach a decision which their leader conveyed to the courtroom. "We have agreed to grant bail on condition the defendant surrenders her passport and does not attend any more meetings of the North London Women's Revolutionary Action Group," she said. It seemed to Angela as if the words had had to be dragged out of her – but nevertheless they had been.

With that, the magistrates retired. The policewoman standing next to the dock indicated to Hilary that she was free to join her supporters and the prosecutor left court without a word to anyone.

"Thank you so much," said Hilary to Robyn as she entered the body of the courtroom. Buddy, who had been jumping about as if she could not control a sudden release of energy, kissed Hilary passionately on the cheek.

"It's only the beginning," said Robyn, "but at least it will make things easier for you. You will, of course, still have to stand trial."

"Maybe before then we should try and find out what really happened to these men," said Hilary. "Angela, could you invite the others in the group round to my flat tonight so we can talk about it?"

"A meeting?" queried Robyn. "That would breach your bail conditions."

"No, a social," said Hilary firmly. "To celebrate my release on bail."

Robyn shrugged her shoulders. "Be careful," she said to Hilary.

CHAPTER EIGHT

Rivers knocked firmly on the door. A look of exasperation came over John Morgan's face as he opened it to see who his visitor was. "You again?" he said.

"Yes, me again," replied the private detective. "I think you have some explaining to do."

"Not to you I don't." He attempted to shut the door but found Rivers' foot in the way. "Do you mind?" said Morgan.

"I do and I'm wondering if I have to shout what I know from the doorstep, Councillor, so the good citizens you represent can hear us – or if we can discuss this in a more civilised manner inside."

Morgan relented. "All right," he said. "Come in. For five minutes."

Rivers was ushered into the living room. "The red car," he began. "You do know who owns it," he added firmly.

"Do I?" said Morgan, trying to feign disinterest.

"Yes," said the private detective. "Shall we start with a Brian Jones? A loan shark? You know him." Morgan failed to reply. "Well, he visited this house on the night of the crash. His wasn't the red car in the road, mind you. No, his car was parked in the driveway because he had come to see you to try and put pressure on you to pay off the debt your son owed him. He knew you were affluent. You had to be – owning a house in an area like this. He knew, too, that you were a pillar of the community."

"Thank you," said Morgan sarcastically.

"Oh, I don't doubt you've done good works for the community in the past," said Rivers, "but you're certainly not above using your influence to get things done or get people to back off. Jones threatened to expose your son's debts – and make the link between you and him. He thought you'd think 'anything for a quiet life'. But things started to go wrong from then on. Your son turned up – in his red car – the one shown in this photograph." Rivers pointed to the family photograph on the mantelpiece. Morgan looked puzzled. He couldn't work out how his visitor had known it would be there. Gradually, it dawned on him – the woman who had called round the previous afternoon must have something to do with his current visitor. "I don't know whether it was coincidence that your son was here," Rivers added, "or perhaps Jones had made it clear to him earlier in the evening that he was going to visit you to try and get the money from you and your son felt he had to warn you so he drove over here that evening."

"A fascinating story so far, Mr Rivers," said Morgan.

"Oh, I know it's true," retorted Rivers. "Let's move on. Jones' car turns up in a field. It has been set fire to but one of the number plates has not been destroyed so it is easy to find out who it belongs to. Jones' wife has reported him missing so it's a reasonable assumption to make that – as Jones had no reason to disappear off the face of the earth – someone else drove his car to that field to try and destroy it. That someone must have known what had happened to Jones – that he had been killed. Fast forward to the police going round to Jones' home and his widow gives them the names of a hundred debtors who are on Jones' files - one of them, your son, Jed Morgan. Go back to the night of the crash. An argument breaks out here – in your home - probably between your son and Jones. A scuffle ensues. Jones gets hit. Bangs his head on something. Perhaps the coffee table." He pointed to it. "Or something else in this room." He looked around him "The mantelpiece?" he added. "Anyway, Jones gets killed. You – collectively – now have to decide what to do. No point in going to the police. The pillar of the community will crumble in front of his public's eyes if he's connected with a killing like this. So you, your son and your wife decide you have to get rid of Jones' body and his car. You smuggle Jones' body in the back of the red car and Jed is just about to drive off with it when you hear the sound of the crash. That's me ramming the back of the car. Some blood seeps out from the boot but nobody notices it in the immediate aftermath of the crash. You know the police will be arriving in minutes. They've already been alerted by the woman across the road. You see her on her mobile. Your son drives off to get rid of the body and never returns. You want to pretend that red car has nothing to do with you. He gets rid of the body. Meanwhile, you have to get rid of Jones' car. You wait until the hubbub dies down. No-one has noticed it in the melee. Either you or your wife drives to waste ground where you attempt to burn it beyond recognition. The other half of the Morgan family follows the car to the waste ground and you both drive home in it."

At this juncture Morgan began to clap slowly, rhythmically. "Well done, Mr Rivers," he said. "Now gaze in your crystal ball again. What do I do now I'm in receipt of this information from you?"

"I presume you're thinking of getting rid of me," said Rivers. "After all, I'm not a police officer. I don't have back -up outside. You're wondering if I've even told anybody that I was coming to see you this morning. You might take a risk and think I haven't – but you'd be wrong. The police know about this, too. Right now Detective Sergeant Manners is arresting your son at his home on suspicion of murder. Harm me and you'll be implicating yourself in the cover-up of this crime,"

At that point the door opened. A young man with a key came in. "You're wrong, Mr Rivers," said Morgan. "Nobody's arrested my son. Can I introduce you to Jed?"

• • • • •

Francesca got out of bed early that morning and arranged for a cab to take her to the police station where she had left her car the night before. Once there, she drove off to the rather nondescript cul-de-sac that was given as Jed Morgan's address. As she approached the house, she saw a man getting into a red car in the drive-way and driving off up the road. Her instincts told her to follow him. It was not long before she was in an altogether more salubrious part of town. The man she believed to be Jed Morgan drove into a residential street and parked in the driveway of a house. She pulled up opposite and pondered what she should do. There was a chance, she thought, that Rivers would already be there after what he had said last night. If that was the case, he could be in danger on his own with Jed Morgan – a suspected killer – and John Morgan, a corrupt local politician. She radioed back to the police station for back-up but decided she would have to try and gain access to the house herself. She crossed the road. Nothing like the direct approach, she thought to herself, and rang the doorbell. She heard a voice from inside which she assumed to be Morgan's say: "Who can that be?" Nobody inside answered the call but she took it upon herself to make her identity known.

"It's the police," she shouted and pulled her warrant card out of her purse. A few moments elapsed before a slightly worried looking Morgan answered her knock. "What do you want?" he asked. "May I come in?" she replied. Once admitted to the hallway, she saw Rivers and nodded to him.

"I'm so glad you've come, inspector." Morgan was frantically trying to regain control of the situation.

"Detective Sergeant Manners, Sir." She showed him her warrant card.

"Detective Sergeant Manners," he repeated. He turned to Rivers. "This man is harassing me," he said.

"Oh, really?" said Manners in a tone which noted disbelief.

"Yes, he's been round here two or three times demanding to know the identity of the driver he crashed into outside my home a few weeks ago. I keep telling him I don't know but he won't take no for an answer."

Rivers walked to the door and looked out on the driveway. He turned to Jed Morgan. "Red car?" he said. "No wonder the neighbours said they thought they had seen it around beforehand. It's yours." He looked out at the driveway again. "They seem to have done a good job of patching it up," he said steeling Jed Morgan with his glare.

"I don't know what you're talking about."

"I think you do. Tell me, was it you or your dad that killed Brian Jones that night?"

"I had nothing to do with it," protested John Morgan, his cheeks turning red as if he was experiencing genuine rage.

"But your son did?" intervened Francesca,

"Dad," said Jed Morgan. He sounded almost pathetic as if pleading with his father to use his influence to fix things for him.

"I think your father is signalling that the game's up," said Francesca.

Jed Morgan, who still had his car keys in his hand, made for the door and ran out into the driveway, shutting the door behind him. Rivers made to follow him and found that he had got into the car when he emerged on the driveway. He was just switching the ignition on but Rivers managed to open the drivers' door and yanked him out of the car on to the driveway. Jed Morgan made as if to throw a punch at the private detective but found Francesca's hand gripping hold of his arm. "You're just making things worse for yourself, sir," she said.

At this juncture a police car arrived in the driveway and two constables got out and took care of handcuffing him. Francesca read him his rights and told the constables to take him to the police station.

"You came in the nick of time," said Rivers to Francesca. "I'd noticed there was a poker in the fireplace. I think Jed Morgan was going to use it on me."

Morgan now emerged from the house. "Are you both all

right?" he asked trying to sound as if he was concerned. "I am so sorry," he said. "My son – I can't believe what he's done."

"I can understand that, sir," said Francesca, "but – for a responsible elected official – I can't believe what you've done."

"What do you mean?"

"Attempting to pervert the course of justice, aiding and abetting a murderer." she said. "How about that for starters?"

"It wasn't really a murder," began Morgan. "They just had a fight – and Jones died. It was an accident."

"Then you should have contacted the police and reported it as such rather than try to get rid of the body. By the way, where is it, sir?"

Morgan hesitated for a moment. "I think I should consult my solicitor."

"Why?" interjected Rivers. "Does he know where it is?"

"No, of course not," he said.

"Mr Morgan, both you and your wife are likely to be facing serious criminal charges as a result of this," said Francesca.

"My wife? Leave her out of this."

"It needed three people to stage-manage the disappearance of the body and the cars on the night of the crash. She was the third."

Morgan buried his head in his hands. "I'll be ruined," he said.

"Very likely, sir," said Francesca. I don't think the council can come to your aid now, she thought to herself. "We shall be off to the police station to question your son and doubtless be back this evening to question you and your wife."

With that, Francesca and Rivers were off - Francesca giving Rivers a lift back to his office.

"Double celebration tonight?" he said.

"Maybe – if I don't have to go back to question the Morgans." Rivers nodded. "Give me a ring," he added.

• • • • •

"Thanks for coming," said Hilary as she kissed Jane on the lips. "I've been told I can't attend any meetings of the group but I don't think they've ruled out a social evening."

There were five of them in Hilary's flat that night. Buddy had stayed to support her partner. Jenny and Angela were already there by the time Jane arrived. "How are you?" Jane asked Hilary.

"Oh, bearing up," she replied. It was a question Jenny hadn't thought to ask, she reflected. Angela, of course, had spent most of the last few days with her and knew as much about her dilemma as anyone. "As you probably know, I have been charged with incitement to murder because of the article that was printed in the leaflet."

"Ridiculous. It's a witch-hunt. We should arrange a protest," said Jenny. The words somehow seemed to come out of her mouth without her putting a great deal of thought into what she was saying.

"I'm not sure it's as simple as that," said Angela.

"Simple?" shrieked Jenny. "Organising a protest is never simple. It takes time and energy to get people out."

"Which I won't be able to do," said Hilary. "Bail conditions," she added by way of explanation.

"Fuck that," said Jenny. "You have to stand up for your beliefs."

"Remind me, Jenny, which one of us is going to prison if I break my bail conditions?" said Hilary sharply. It silenced the other woman for the first time in a long time, others in the room reflected.

"What the police are desperate to find out is who wrote the article," said Angela. "I think the granting of bail to Hilary showed what a flimsy case the prosecution has against her. She hasn't colluded with anyone in inciting them to murder someone. No person was identified as the victim of this murder plot. They're on a fishing expedition. They want to find out who wrote the article. Then they can deduce what their motive was."

"They'd be better off trying to find the actual killer," intervened Jane.

"They just want to put the troublesome Left away," said Jenny.

"Jenny, your interventions aren't helping," protested Angela.

"It's true, though, isn't it?" continued Jenny. "We shouldn't be giving them any help at all. Just stay schtumm."

"And let Hilary take the rap?" said Angela.

"We didn't arrest her. We didn't charge her with incitement to murder. It's not our fault," said Jenny. "I don't know why you called this meeting."

"Because I like to think that some of you might want to help me," said Hilary.

"Have you told the police who wrote the article?" asked Jenny.

"No," replied Hilary.

"Good."

Buddy brought some sandwiches out on a tray at this juncture. "I thought as this was a social you might want to eat something," she said. She put them down on the table.

Jenny was the first to grab one. "Our best bet is to steer well away from this one," she said with a mouthful of sandwich.

"Then you'd better go," said Buddy taking the sandwich tray away from her.

Jenny frowned and reached across the table to grab another sandwich. "I don't see what we're worried about," she said. "The case against Hilary is flimsy. You said so yourself, Angela. We just wait for it to collapse."

"You've forgotten one thing," said Angela.

"What's that?"

"There have been two murders since that article appeared. Maybe the person who wrote it is responsible for them. Maybe there is no conspiracy. Maybe the person who wrote that article is doing what she suggested people should do – making random attacks on men."

"She?" queried Jenny.

"What do you mean?" asked Angela.

"You're assuming the person behind it is a woman. Sexist assumption."

"Jenny," said Hilary. "Why would men want to hack off each other's penises?"

Jane allowed a little levity to enter the situation. "Answers on two sides of foolscap," she said. The room dissolved into laughter.

"Look," said Angela. "The writer of the article must have been a woman and therefore it follows that if our thesis is correct and they started the revenge killings themselves the murderer is also a woman."

"What we should be trying to prove is that the killer had no connections with the articles at all," said Jane, "because – if that was so – there would have been no incitement to kill and we had nothing to do with what happened."

"Can you still be had up for incitement to murder if no murder took place as a result of your incitement?" asked Buddy.

"Good point," said Jane.

"I think you can," said Angela, her legal training coming back to her at this point, "but it's a moot point. I don't think the police would be over keen to prosecute if it was not connected to a murder."

Hilary suddenly began to feel very tired. "Thanks for coming," she said. "We're going round in circles. Maybe there isn't a role for us in the investigation of these murders. I just thought you should be brought up to date with what had happened."

Jane got up to go. "I hope it all goes okay," she said touching Hilary's arm as she made her way to the door.

"I'll come with you," said Jenny.

"I'd rather you didn't." said Jane. She made her exit before Jenny could get to her feet.

"What was all that about?" asked Jenny.

"I think she thinks you've been less than supportive this evening." said Angela.

"And guess what? She's not the only one," said Buddy.

Jenny scowled and made her own exit from the room.

"Just us again," said Hilary as she, Buddy and Angela were left alone in the room. "I don't know what I expected to get out of this meeting."

"A sandwich?" suggested Buddy as she proffered the tray to Hilary

Hilary took a couple. "Well, I've got a good legal team," she said. "Hopefully they'll be more energised with trying to help me than Jenny. You know, that one is skating on thin ice."

Angela stared at Hilary intently – as if trying to determine what she meant by that comment.

• • ● • •

"Let them stew for a while," said Larry Green as Francesca outlined the events of that morning at the Morgan household. "We have the son's confession that he killed Brian Jones – albeit he says it was an accident. We know therefore that Councillor and Mrs Morgan covered up a murder. We don't as yet have proof that they disposed of Jones' car. It's only a best guess. Maybe if we work on the son we can build on that. It's probably enough for the moment that we've ruined Councillor Morgan's career. Let's see where we can take it from there."

"That's fine by me, sir," said Francesca.

"So that gives us a night off. Let's use it wisely. Drink?"

Francesca thought about his offer for a moment. "No, sir," she said. "Thanks for the offer but I think using it wisely might mean getting away from police chit chat."

"I didn't mean when I said 'use it wisely' that you should use it sensibly," protested Green, "but I understand where you're coming from. I think I might go down to the pub. There are bound to be some people from the station in there."

"Yes, sir," said Francesca. With that, he walked out of her office. She waited for a moment then reached for the telephone. "Philip," she said when the person she had dialled answered her call. "I suddenly find myself with a free evening. There's an Italian restaurant just down the road from your office"

"I know the one," he interjected.

"Do you fancy meeting there for a bite to eat?"

"Yes, that would be great," he said. "Nikki has decided to have an early night after I sent her on surveillance duty in Colchester over a divorce today.""

"Right. I'll just go home and freshen up. Meet you there in about an hour?"

An hour later they were sitting at a table for two in the corner of the restaurant. Francesca was wearing a dark satin blouse and white trousers. Even Rivers had made an effort with white summer trousers and a black striped shirt. It was a warm summer's evening. They needed no jackets or coats. They ordered some wine. "Thanks for coming to my rescue this morning," said Rivers. "I think Jed Morgan was planning to become responsible for another accident when you arrived on the scene."

Francesca nodded. "It probably worked better that we caught them at Councillor Morgan's house. If I'd just arrested Jed Morgan at his home, I don't know that I'd have had the proof of his involvement in Brian Jones' killing. I think all I'd have been able to do would have been to make him squirm." She took a sip from her glass of wine. "Mind you," she said. "I think it was a bit foolhardy of you to set out for Councillor Morgan's place on your own. I don't know what you thought you might be able to achieve."

"Armed with the evidence of Brian Jones' debtors and his burnt out car, I thought I could shame him into admitting what had gone on or at least corner him. It helped, though, knowing about the red car and having it arrive when it did. That was the icing on the cake." He reached across the table and squeezed Francesca's hand. "We make a good team," he said.

"We do," she replied not resisting his touch. Well, Francesca, she thought to herself, you've always prided yourself on being a forthright person who knows what she wants and goes out to get it. Here goes. "Philip," she said gazing into his eyes. "Let's not play around. Do you want a relationship with me?"

He was slightly taken aback by the directness of her approach. No talk of "would you like to come back for a coffee?" or "I have a nice unopened bottle of Chardonnay back at my place, shall we do it some damage?" Do you want a relationship with me? He mulled the words over in his head. "That," he said, "would be nice."

It was not a definite yes, Francesca thought to herself. "What about Nikki?"

"We're having problems," began Rivers slowly.

Francesca sighed. "I don't want to come between you if you're still making a go of things," she said. "It's one of my rules. Don't play around with somebody who's in a relationship. But if you were free, I am too and I would love to." She held his hand. "Start up a relationship, I mean."

Wow, thought Rivers.

"I'll get the bill," said Francesca briefly withdrawing from contact from him. She signalled to the waiter and they were soon ready to depart. She ordered a taxi through the waiter and – when it arrived – slipped her hand in his as they left the restaurant. Rivers thought to himself. He had not rehearsed what would happen in these circumstances. He had assumed that it would be left up to him to make the first move. (He would have had to suggest going to the office as there was a chance Nikki might return to his home.) In one sense, it was the invitation that he wanted. He did have a feel for working with Francesca and there was no doubt that she was extremely attractive. He could not think why she did not already have a partner. On the other hand, he was slightly dreading what had happened. It was make your mind up time. Did he want an affair, a relationship, whatever, with Francesca? How did he feel about cheating on

Nikki? All that history and they had only been married a year. He began to realise the enormity of the step he might be about to make. He sighed. "I'm sorry," he said. "I can't do it. Nikki."

Francesca smiled. "Best that you're honest," she said.

They arrived at Francesca's and he let her leave the cab. "Goodnight," he said staring wistfully after her.

With that, the cab left the scene and Rivers felt sad.

● ● ● ● ●

Jane was wearing the most sombre dress and jacket that she could find for her father's funeral. Tom had agreed to accompany her for moral support. Beatrice was there, too.

"You know," said Tom to Jane as they approached the crematorium. "I can do this. It's much easier than I thought. I'm finally rid of him. More to the point, the world is finally rid of him. He can't harm anyone anymore."

"He hasn't been able to harm anyone for a while," said Jane.

"I know but just seeing him – it brought back those memories of what he used to do." Beatrice squeezed his arm at this point.

"I feel a sense of relief, too," said Jane. "I can't quite put my finger on it but it's as if something's all over now."

"Something?"

"A part of my life. You know I promise people an intimate relationship but what's intimate about demanding money at the end of every encounter?"

"You're not thinking of giving it all up, are you? The prostitution, I mean?"

"I don't know, Tom. I don't know. I don't need to rush into anything but I was thinking when that private detective came round that he was nice – and why did I have to demand money before anything happened? I don't know. I enjoy the sex. Mostly."

"There are one or two creeps you've had," said Tom. "You've talked about them. Violent like my dad."

"Your dad? He's mine, too. You don't have to shoulder the burden of his guilt all on your own."

Tom smiled. "No, I know." He fell silent as they approached the crematorium. There was a curate there to greet them but no-one else in the chapel. Their father had no family himself and their mother's family had never wanted anything to do with him because of his violence towards her.

"Two of the creeps died," said Jane reflecting on her life as a prostitute. "Murdered."

"It's probably not surprising, you know, with the lifestyle that they led," said Tom.

"You know, I think they went with Jenny as well," continued Jane.

"I've never met her."

"I should keep it that way," said Jane. "You know, she never had a word of sympathy for Hilary – who's been arrested on this charge of incitement to murder. It was all about her wanting to stage a protest. You know – she actually incites violence against herself. Describes herself as a naughty girl who needs firm discipline. And she gets it, too."

"There are women like that," said Tom, "but not our mother. She never deserved what he dished out."

He stopped speaking as the curate came over to speak to them. "I'm sorry there's not much of a turnout," he said.

"It's not as if it's a pop concert," said Tom awkwardly. "You can't advertise to get people to come in off the streets."

The curate smiled. "No," he said. "I'll just say a few words about your father – and then hand it over to you. Do either of you want to say anything?"

Good riddance, thought Tom, but he declined to speak out.

"No, I don't think we do," said Jane. "We weren't very close. We just felt we had to pay our respects."

The curate nodded. The service only took about fifteen minutes and then the trio were on their way again. "I could do with a drink," said Tom as he spied a pub across the road. Jane, who was driving, pulled into its car-park. "I'll have a pint," he said. "Jane?"

"Just a sparkling water."

"Beatrice?"

"A glass of white wine."

Tom went to the bar to get the drinks. Jane thought she would take the opportunity to talk to Beatrice. "You and Tom?" she asked. "Is it going anywhere?"

"I'd like to think so," said Beatrice.

"Good," said Jane. "He deserves something nice to happen in his life."

"As do you, Jane. Were you being serious when you were talking about giving up the prostitution?"

"I was talking out loud," said Jane, "but I'm beginning to feel that I'm having intimate relationships with the wrong people. I'm beginning to think I could form intimate relationships of my own – not just see sex as part of a business enterprise. After all, you and Tom have managed it."

"Yes."

"We could forget the past."

At that moment Tom returned with the drinks. He had overheard them. "I propose a toast," he said. "To the past being the past."

"The past being the past," Beatrice and Jane chorused as they raised their glasses.

• • • • •

Toby Renton had researched his field and looked at a number of the cards advertising the services of prostitutes. He was determined to give it a try. After all, his relationships had failed so spectacularly. One had caught his eye when he was visiting a friend in Hackney – a woman by the name of Jenny who described herself as a naughty girl who needed some strong discipline. That was why he set out that evening to the run-down estate where Jenny lived and found himself nervously knocking on the door.

"I booked an appointment with you," he said when Jenny answered his knock.

"Come in," she said aggressively. He stood awkwardly in the hallway. "We're not going to do it in here," said Jenny. "Come into the bedroom."

"I'm sorry," said Toby apologetically. "I've never done this before."

"I can see that," said Jenny abruptly. Don't expect me to feel sorry for you, she thought to herself. Or help you overcome your shyness. She was not the kind of person to sugar coat the pill to put him at ease, though. Jenny started undressing in the bedroom. "As I mentioned on the phone, it's £50 for straight sex and then there are extras."

"Extras?" said Toby, his mouth opened wide. Extras were something he normally associated with a cricket match.

"Yes. Discipline. Spanking with the bare hand knickers on – £15, knickers off £20, spanking paddle with knickers on £25, off £30. I have a paddle in here." She pointed to a cupboard opposite the bed.

"And you're happy for me to do that?" said Toby incredulously.

"Yes," said Jenny. "Just six times. I need to negotiate before we start because it's a bugger totting it all up as you're doing it if you haven't agreed in advance."

"Why?" said Toby.

"Look, you haven't been given an appointment so we can have a philosophical discussion. I suggest we make a start because you've only got half an hour." She moved over towards him and started unbuttoning his shirt and then removing his trousers.

"Wait," said Toby as she moved her hand towards his pants. "I think I've made a dreadful mistake. I don't want this."

"Why? What did you think was going to happen?"

"I thought we'd be a bit more friendly towards each other," he said.

"But we're not friends," said Jenny. "You might as well go if you feel like that. Stop wasting my time."

Toby pulled his trousers back on. He reached into his inside pocket and withdrew his wallet. "Look," he said. "Here's £50. No hard feelings."

"No feelings whatsoever," said Jenny sharply, She got dressed herself as Toby left the flat. She smiled at herself. She had wanted to put him off. Prostitution was no answer for a young lad like that. Then she chided herself for having feelings about him.

A few minutes later Gary emerged in the doorway. "What was he like?" he asked Jenny jerking his finger in the direction of the departing Toby.

"A total waste of space. He'd never done it before."

"Do you want me to go after him and get you some money?"

"No," said Jenny. "He paid for it. He just didn't have the sex. And I'll thank you for not loitering around outside when I have a client."

"It's since that violent bastard last weekend. I feel I should protect you."

Meanwhile, Toby was making as fast an exit as he could from the estate but – as he passed the telephone box where he had first spotted Jenny's number – he took her card out and tore it up. While he was doing that, another card caught his eye. It offered an "intimate relationship" with the client. That's got to be better than what I just went through, he thought to himself. I'll give this one more try, he concluded.

• • ● • •

"So, it's just you who's going to support me," said Hilary after she and Angela were left alone in her flat. Buddy had gone to visit a friend – a long-standing engagement. Angela had promised her she would stay with Hilary while they talked things through.

"And Buddy."

"I meant from the group."

"Well," said Angela. "Jane's got a lot on her plate at the moment with the death of her father. It's really Jenny who's no use."

"Interesting that," said Hilary, "when I could be the cause of so much trouble for her."

"What do you mean?" asked Angela.

Hilary remained silent for a moment. "I think I've said too much already," she finally said.

"I think I know what you mean," said Angela. "Jenny is the author of that article, isn't she?" There was no response from Hilary. "Your silence speaks volumes," Angela continued, "and – if what I'm thinking is correct – I could make life very difficult for young Ms Creighton, too. I'm going to confront her about it."

"Is that wise?"

"I'll make it clear I haven't got the information from you, don't worry."

"I mean, she's quite volatile. You've always claimed that the writer of that article was arguing a hypothetical case – that Jack the Ripper was awarded cult status as a result of what he did and that the same wouldn't be true if a woman were to take indiscriminate action against men. The article was just floating what might happen if a woman did – and hoped that it might have shown the dual standards over violence towards women and men. There was no real incitement for women to take the law into their own hands. I'm not so sure that Jenny thinks the same way as you. She may very well believe there is justification for a woman to go on a revenge killing spree to avenge what Jack the Ripper did. In that case, you should be very wary of tackling Jenny about it."

"Maybe we should tell the police," suggested Angela.

"No," said Hilary, "It won't come from me. I do believe very sincerely that the author of a controversial article has the right to remain anonymous and I won't breach that – even if it would be the best way of deflecting some of the heat over what happened from me."

"It's just so wrong that you should be facing charges," said Angela.

"I think we won round one of the defence against the charges when I was granted bail," said Hilary. "Hold in your mind what Robyn Peters said. There's no evidence of me inciting any individual to commit murder, there's no evidence of me wanting any individual dead."

"So do nothing?"

"Maybe that's the way forward."

Angela shook her head firmly. "No," she said. "The person who wrote the article is much closer to inciting people to commit murder than you are – much closer to the murders than you are. I'm going to have it out with Jenny."

• • • • •

Nikki was sitting curled up reading a book in front of the TV when Rivers returned that evening. "Oh, hi," he said as he opened the front door as if he was surprised to see her.

"How did the surveillance go?"

"We got final proof that the guy's having an affair. I've got pictures of him and another woman going into the bedroom of the hotel he was staying in."

"Good, well done."

"What about you?"

"Me?" he asked as if surprised by the question.

"Yes, you," she said. "Good day? Bad day?"

"Oh, good day," he said. "That's why I was late. I went out for a drink to celebrate. We've finally solved the riddle of the blood spattered red car. It belonged to Councillor Morgan's son and the blood came from the loan shark I was telling you about. The son's confessed to killing him – although he says it was an accident."

"Who did you go out for a drink with?" asked Nikki.

"Oh, Francesca Manners," he said. "You know, Francesca saved my life this morning," he added. "I think I was about to become another victim of an accident with a poker when she arrived at Morgan's house to arrest his son."

"Good for her. I hope you were suitably grateful." Not as grateful as I could have been, thought Rivers ruefully. "What are you going to do tomorrow?" Nikki asked him.

"I don't know," he said. "I suppose we should return to the original murders and I'd better check that Toby Renton is okay. I've kind of forgotten about him in the last couple of days."

"I'm sure he's all right," said Nikki. "We'd have had his mother and father on the phone if he wasn't. You know, it's good that Francesca Manners transferred over here. It makes it easier for police relations – although I think I have to be a bit wary about you and her."

"Er, yes," said Rivers. He changed the subject. "I think I'm going to turn in," he added. "It's been quite a day."

"Why don't we invite her round for a meal?" suggested Nikki.

"Well, I don't see why not," he said.

"Do you know if she's got a bloke?" asked Nikki.

"I don't know." Rivers replied. "She's never talked about one so I suppose she hasn't."

"She's a very attractive woman," Nikki went on. "I would have thought she'd have one." She paused for a moment. "Leave it to me," she said. "I'll set something up and I'll make it clear she's welcome to bring somebody along if she wants to. We could invite Mark and Prunella, too."

"Steady on," said Rivers. "Just suppose she is single. Won't she be a bit fazed by being in the presence of so many couples?"

"I hadn't thought of that."

"And what's brought all of this on?" he ventured to ask.

"Us," she said. "We hardly socialise at all and we've been getting on each other's nerves a bit recently. I'm determined to do something about that and clear the air."

"It's been my fault," he said, "but I really am tired. Can we make all these social arrangements some other time? I just want to go to bed." With Francesca, he thought for a moment but then he banished the idea from his mind. He looked at Nikki. They had known each other for more than thirty years. Most of that time their relationship had been in abeyance. To put not too fine a point on it, he had dumped her when they were in their late twenties because he had been feeling too trapped and tied down. The relationship had only resurrected itself when she selflessly turned up to comfort him when his previous partner died of cancer. He had needed her then. Maybe he had kidded himself he felt more for her than he did – and that was why they got married. One thing was sure, she had never doubted that she wanted a relationship with him.

"You're staring at me," said Nikki.

"I'm trying to summon up enough energy to put one foot in front of the other and go to bed," he said. With that, he did but he found it difficult to get to sleep that night.

Nikki detected his restlessness. "Are you all right, Philip?" she asked.

"Yes," he said. "I'm sorry. I keep on thinking of how close to death I came when I went round to the Morgans." It was a lie, of course. He was thinking of Francesca and what he had missed out on.

CHAPTER NINE

Francesca left for work early that morning. She reflected on the previous evening as she did so. Yes, she would have loved to have started a relationship with Philip Rivers but she was glad she hadn't. He was an attractive man. Straightforward. Easy to talk to and work with.

But it would have been messy. One of her cardinal rules was not to step in and play with somebody else's relationship. She would have been doing that if she had started an affair with Philip, she reasoned. She had adopted that moral stance after finding out a man she had thought of as her partner had been cheating on her. She could remember how much that hurt. She didn't want to be putting anybody else through those kinds of feelings.

She walked slowly and thoughtfully towards the police station. As she approached it, her mobile phone rang. She put it to her ear.

"Hallo, is that Francesca?" said a woman's voice.

"Yes."

"It's Nikki Hofmeyr – Philip Rivers' wife," the woman said.

"Yes, I know who you are."

"Philip and I were thinking last night it was about time we invited you round for a meal," she said. "Philip always seems to get so wrapped up in his cases he doesn't leave much time for socialising. I think it would do us some good."

Francesca froze for a moment. "Er....yes," she said tentatively. She felt it was a strange coincidence to be hearing from Nikki.

"Of course, you can bring round a partner if you have one."

"No, I haven't," she said.

"How about one night next week?" said Nikki. "Thursday?"

"Yes," said Francesca tentatively. "Of course, always with the proviso that something might crop up at the last minute."

"Great," said Nikki who then gave Francesca her home address. "Well, I won't keep you anymore," she said.

Francesca thought for a moment as she put her mobile back into her pocket. She would like to keep the appointment. She would like to be friends with both Philip and Nikki now the prospect of a relationship with him had been ruled out.

• • • • •

Thus far it had been an entirely different experience to meeting with Jenny, thought Toby as he sat on Jane's bed at her Hampstead flat.

"So Toby," said Jane. "Why did you decide to come and see me?"

"I should have thought that was obvious," said Toby who then reproached himself for sounding unfeeling. "Well, it was the way you advertised yourself as offering an intimate relationship. The whole idea was very different to the experience I'd had beforehand with a.... (he almost hesitated to say the word) prostitute."

"Don't think of me as a prostitute," said Jane. "Think of me as a sort of counsellor."

"Sex therapist," said Toby as he fumbled with her blouse,

"Don't worry, Toby, I'll take charge," she said. She could sense he was not that experienced.

What happened next, to Toby, seemed bliss. Far more loving, he thought, than most of the encounters he had had with women of his own age and warm enough to make his encounter with Jenny a distant memory. There seemed to be no time limit on how long they made love. At least Jane didn't mention one if there was one. He surprised himself as to how much stamina he had. They must have made love (it seemed more like making love than a casual fling with a prostitute, he thought) at least three times. After the third time, he lay back on the bed panting.

"Was that intimate enough for you?" she asked.

"You bet," he said. He looked at her. "You know, I can't think of you as a prostitute," he said.

"That's the general idea," she said.

"What made you go in for this game?" he asked.

"I liked sex," she said, "and – because of a whole host of things in my personal life – I couldn't make normal intimate relations with anyone. I panicked when I got too close."

"That's a bit like me," said Toby, "although with me it's that I don't know what to do. You know – should I ring them later – or fix up another date before I leave? I always seemed to get it wrong."

"Hopefully I can help and try and build your confidence up," said Jane.

"You mean, you'd like to see me again?"

"Yes," said Jane, "although in future I won't be charging. I'm beginning to get the confidence to start my own relationships without advertising for them." Jane reflected for a moment. It may have had something to do with the death of her father. The bad memories of his relationship with her mother were being exorcised by his death. "I've got a few clients to see until the end of the week – but after that I won't be taking on any more. Maybe see you next week some time. Maybe we could go out for a meal or do something. Talk."

"Yes," said Toby, "I'd love to."

"You see," said Jane, "that's where you should learn something from me. I felt confident you wanted to see me again and so I suggested a tentative date. You need to work out in your own mind whether things are going well enough to make another date – and then do it in a decisive manner. Don't dither."

"I see," said Toby.

He reached down by the side of the bed for his clothing but she put a restraining hand on his arm. "Not yet," she said, "I want to give you something to remember me by. Lie still."

"Will do," said Toby – a smile on his face now as he began making love to her again." When they had finished, he rolled over on the bed. "Thank you," he said.

"Now," said Jane, "I am going to charge you £50 for that experience but I don't want you to remember the money – I want you to remember the moments of intimacy instead."

"No difficulty with that," said Toby as he took his wallet out of his jacket pocket and parted with the money. He began dressing himself.

"Is there anyone in your life, Toby?" Jane asked.

"No, not really," he said.

"Do you think you may be able to find someone with a bit more confidence now?"

Toby thought for a moment. "I think I probably need one or two more lessons still," he said – a smile forming on his face. Or three or four or even five or six, he thought to himself.

She got dressed and escorted him from the flat. "Take care," she said warmly to him, kissing him on the mouth as he departed. It was something that prostitutes very rarely did, she reflected. As she returned to the living room, Beatrice was just coming out of her bedroom. Jane had almost forgotten she was in the flat.

"Well?" Beatrice asked.

"A lovely boy."

"Hardly a boy," said Beatrice. "He must have been in his thirties."

"But still quite inexperienced. Hopefully he won't be in future. I'm thinking of taking him on as a project after I finish with the prostitution."

"You are finishing with it?" asked Beatrice.

"I think so, Come and sit down and let's talk about it."

Beatrice looked anxious. "No," she said, "I've got one or two things I must do urgently. I can be with you in five or ten minutes. If you'll excuse me."

"Of course." She watched Beatrice as she made off towards her bedroom and disappeared. Maybe Beatrice needed help as well. She did not seem at ease with herself. Within moments, though, Jane had forgotten about Beatrice and began focussing on Toby again – and how she could help him develop into a more confident person.

• • ● • •

Angela knocked on Jenny's door - having summoned up courage to confront her about the leaflet.

"I know it was you who wrote it," she said when she had been invited in and was sat down on a rather ramshackle settee.

"Did Hilary tell you?"

"No, of course not," said Angela. "She prides herself on maintaining the anonymity of her writers. It's not difficult to work out, though. Gabi's English is not good enough to write it, Hilary said she didn't and I'm pretty sure Jane wouldn't harbour those sentiments. Oh, and I know I didn't write it."

"So – as a sister – what are you going to do with that knowledge?" said Jenny.

"So you admit it was you?" said Angela quickly.

"I asked you a question," said Jenny icily.

"I should go to the police," said Angela, "but if I do they'll jump to all sorts of conclusions and may try and pin the murders on you, too. If you go to them and admit it, you'll be in a much better position to deny that you had anything to do with the murders."

"And if I don't go?"

"You owe it to Hilary. They're only really charging her because they haven't got anyone else. The detectives are trying to give a message to their superiors that they're getting somewhere with their enquiries. If you admitted to writing it, they may drop the charges against her."

"And levy them against me instead?"

"It would be the sisterly thing to do to tell the truth."

Angela's response stopped Jenny in her tracks for a moment. "You're close friends with Hilary,"Jenny said to her."You'd prefer me to be charged rather than her. Well, let me tell you – I don't think we should give any information to help the establishment. They're only too willing to try and pin the blame on people like us when things happen. We shouldn't be helping them to do their job and hassle us."

"Change the record, Jenny,"said Angela with irritation."This is real life now. Two people have been murdered as a result of that article. Is that what you wanted?"

"You can't say that," said Jenny. "The murders may have nothing to do with what I wrote."

"Highly unlikely," said Angela."So you didn't have anything to do with them?"

"I'm not going to dignify that remark with a comment,"said Jenny frostily.

So not a denial, thought Angela. "What did you hope to achieve through your article?"she asked.

"I wanted to point out how the media glorify violence against women – and wanted to see what the reaction would be if women got as violent as men."

"Tell that to the police and they'll probably charge you with the actual murders and not just incitement. Jenny,"said Angela her tone becoming more urgent," you're in a whole heap of trouble over this. You'd better start thinking what you're going to do about this."

"What happened to the mousy Angela who's been coming to our meetings for months and wouldn't say boo to a goose?" asked Jenny.

"The mousy Angela realised she was being hen pecked and put upon by her husband at home – and decided to make a stand. The mousy Angela gained confidence to stand up to others, too. The mousy Angela is a close friend of Hilary's and doesn't like to see her being charged with incitement to murder when – as far as the mousy Angela is concerned – she hasn't put a foot wrong."

"Well, you're not going to guilt trip me into going to the police so you'd better be on your way."

Angela wanted to say "beware, the mouse has turned" but bit her lip. She didn't want to rile Jenny any further. After all, she could be talking to someone who had already killed twice. She had failed in her mission to get Jenny to act responsibly and own up to the authorship of the article. Now was the time to leave without dragging out proceedings any further.

"I'm sorry you won't see reason, Jenny," she said. "I'll be on my way." With that, she moved towards the door. Jenny made no attempt to show her out. Before she could get to the door, though, it opened and Jenny's boyfriend, Gary, walked in. He sensed there was an atmosphere in the room. "Excuse me, I was just leaving," Angela said as she made her way past Gary.

"What's been happening?" he asked.

"Angela's only been threatening to go to the police and tell them that I wrote that article in the leaflet," said Jenny.

"What?" asked Gary. "Is this true?" he said turning to Angela.

"I was hoping to persuade her to make the admission herself now that Hilary's been charged with incitement to murder. It seemed to me if there was any incitement going on it was being done by Jenny. I failed." With that, she left the room and hurried along the corridor and down the staircase before either of them could stop her.

Gary looked at Jenny once she had gone. "You're in deep shit, then," he said to her.

Jenny shrugged her shoulders. "If she goes to the police." she said. "They're hardly likely to act in a friendly way towards me."

"We've got to stop her," said Gary. "I'll go after her." He ran out of the flat and down the staircase. By the time he got to the bottom, though, Angela was nowhere to be seen. He sighed and returned to Jenny's flat. "Where does she live?" he said. "I'll go round and talk her out of it tonight."

"Don't do anything rash." said Jenny, her tone denoting a moderating influence for the first time that Gary could remember.

"Tell me where she lives," said Gary. Jenny remained silent. "Tell me where she lives," he repeated. "You must know. You've got all the group's names and addresses." Jenny nodded. She went to get her address book which was in a bag on the coffee table by the settee and handed it to him. "I'll get after her then," he said. With that, he was gone.

• • • • •

Larry Green bustled along the corridor that morning. The call from the chief superintendent's office summonsing him denoted a touch of urgency in the situation. As he left his office, he could feel a bead of sweat breaking out on his forehead. Summonses from Chief Superintendent Pratt (why did they promote people with such obviously inappropriate names, he thought to himself, and why did the superintendent always identify himself to his troops by saying "Pratt here" – it was almost as if he was defying his officers not to laugh) had that effect on him. They were hardly ever joyous occasions. The chief superintendent only tended to see his troops when there was something troubling him.

"Come in Green," the chief superintendent barked as his detective chief inspector hovered around the door.

"Yes, sir."

"Sit.," he commanded. It was almost as if he was talking to a dog. Green perched nervously on the edge of his chair. "This Jill the Ripper thing," he said. "How's it going?"

"Well, sir, we have one woman charged with incitement to

murder. As yet, though, we haven't got anyone in the frame for the actual killings – although we have a number of suspects."

"And if you'd come into my office yesterday what would have been your answer to my question." Pratt was a thickset man with horn-rimmed spectacles. His voice tended to boom so that you imagined anyone hanging around in the corridors outside his office would be able to hear what he had to say. He played with his spectacles as he spoke – taking them off from time to time and polishing them before putting them back on his nose.

"I'm sorry, sir, I don't quite follow," said Green.

"No, you wouldn't. My point is you would have said exactly the same thing. In other words, you've made no progress at all. What do you plan on doing to change that situation?"

"I plan to offer Hilary Sampson a deal through her lawyer. We'll consider dropping the charges against her if she names the author. All she did was publish the article. I don't believe she sympathised with its contents and I don't believe she actually conspired with anyone to carry out the killings. The same, though, couldn't be said for the person who actually wrote it." He then added as an afterthought. "I'll run all this by the Crown Prosecution Service, of course."

"Do you have any opinion as to who actually wrote it?"

"I've a pretty good idea, sir."

"Not good enough." The chief superintendent looked him squarely in the eye. "I want progress on this within twenty-four hours. You will come and see me at 10 o'clock tomorrow morning and if you don't have a different answer to that question I shall have to think seriously about whether you need to be replaced as head of this murder inquiry. Do you understand me?"

"There's nothing not to understand in what you've just said," said Green firmly. Roll on retirement, he thought to himself. Then I won't have Pratts like this threatening me at the beginning of the day.

"No," said Pratt who appeared slightly ill at ease at Green's response. A straightforward "yes" to his question would have sufficed.

Green, though, didn't feel threatened by what Pratt had said. He was too close to retirement to worry about the consequences. "Is that all, sir?" he asked.

Pratt waved him away but – just as he approached the door – he called him back. "There was just one more thing," he said. "I believe you have the son of a councillor locked up in our cells," he said.

"Yes, sir."

"I want that case to be watertight. It's a shame. His father's a really good councillor. My local councillor."

A personal friend of yours, Green thought to himself. I wouldn't be admitting that if I were you. "We've sent a forensic team round to Councillor Morgan's house today," he said. "We should know – as a result of their investigations – how deeply the councillor is implicated in the death of the loan shark by this afternoon. At the moment, it looks like he'll be charged with attempting to pervert the course of justice by getting rid of the body. His wife will face a similar charge."

"It's all deeply unsatisfactory," said Pratt, dropping his spectacles this time as he attempted to clean them with his handkerchief. "His reputation is in tatters, you know."

So it should be, thought Green but declined to say it. Instead, this time, he confined himself to: "Yes, sir."

· · **·** · ·

Rivers announced himself rather tentatively to the reception desk at the police station. "I'd like to see Detective Sergeant Manners," he said.

Within minutes he was escorted to Francesca's office. She bade him sit down. "Philip," she said. "I wasn't expecting you."

"No," he said. "I was trying to tie up some loose ends. Councillor Morgan?"

"I've just got the results of a forensic examination of his home," she said. "It's interesting." She shovelled a piece of paper across the table towards him. "As you can see, an examination of the poker by the fireplace reveals his fingerprints on it. Someone tried to clean it but those are definitely his fingerprints – and not those of his son. Also, there's still a bit of dried blood on the handle."

"You'd have thought he would have got rid of it," said Rivers.

"He wasn't expecting to be subjected to a forensic examination," she said. "As far as he was concerned he'd got away with it. He'd got rid of Brian Jones' car, he'd got rid of Brian Jones body. He'd persuaded the powers that be that there was nothing to investigate. Only you with your determination to find out what had caused the blood spatters in your engine and on the pavement seemed to pose a threat to him."

"Have you confronted him with the evidence?" Rivers asked.

"Not yet," she said. "It's a big deal so it may be Detective Chief Inspector Green that gets the job of doing this – rather than me."

"What about the son?"

"He's not been saying anything. Seems like he's happy to take the rap for his old man. I reckon he thinks he's caused what happened by falling into debt with the loan shark. His dad's quite a dominating figure. I think he's frightened of him."

"At any rate he was running to him to ask him to sort out his problems."

"And it appears he did – but in a more final way than we had previously thought. Was that all?"

Rivers shuffled uncomfortably in his chair. "Er, not quite," he said. "The other night." His voice trailed off as he uttered those words.

"Was nice," said Francesca. "As I said it should go no further as you're still with Nikki."

"No," said Rivers. "Possibly not." He had to confess he had not quite decided how he should handle this inevitable discussion.

"There are things about me that you don't know," said Francesca. "I was let down by a partner who cheated on me. I would never get involved in that kind of situation and nor – or so it would seem – would you."

"No, of course not," said Rivers soothingly.

"You've only been married for just over a year. Don't get me wrong. I think we could have had a relationship had things been different and it could have been rewarding – but it would have involved deception and that's not my scene. We work well together, Philip. Let's keep it at that."

In his heart, Rivers knew she was right. "Right," he said. "Perhaps I'd better go."

"One thing before you go." she said. "Nikki rang me today."

"Oh, yes, she had this idea of inviting you round to dinner. I'll understand if you don't want to come."

"No," said Francesca, "I'd like to. I think my life for the foreseeable future will not include a regular partner but that doesn't pre-empt me from having friends. I get on well with both you and Nikki."

"Sure," he said. "Let's give it a try."

"One thing," she added. "Don't tell Nikki what happened."

Francesca was right. He thought. After all, nothing really had happened. He was still thinking of Francesca when the door opened and Detective Chief Inspector Green entered. He stopped in his tracks on seeing the private detective. "Sorry," said Rivers. "I was trying to find out what had happened to Councillor Morgan."

Francesca rescued the file from her table. "You probably haven't had a chance to read it yet," she said, "but it appears to show that he was the person who killed Brian Jones."

"I'm not sure we should be sharing that information with a private detective at this stage," said Green. He turned to Rivers. "If you wouldn't mind," he said showing him the door.

When the two detectives were alone in the room together, he added: "I shall take great delight in arresting Councillor Morgan personally, Apparently, he's a friend of the chief super. I've never liked that man or rated his ability to suss people. Pratt by name, Pratt by nature. All I've got to do is remember there are less than two weeks left until I depart from here."

"Thank you, sir, for taking that off me," said Francesca,

Green shrugged his shoulders. "You've got to continue working with the Pratt," he said. "There is one other thing, though. We're in trouble over the 'Jill the Ripper' murders." He used the same shorthand as both the chief superintendent and the media had used for the case. It left Francesca feeling a trifle uncomfortable. After all, they had not proved the deaths were random attacks by women yet. "We've got to come up with a development in the case by 10 o'clock tomorrow morning," he said. "The trouble is I don't have a clue as to what that could be."

• • ● • •

"I thought I'd just check on how my charge is doing," said Rivers when Toby finally answered his knock on the door.

"Oh, fine," Toby replied vaguely.

"Not in any danger then?"

"I never thought I was," said Toby. "It was only my parents who were worried," He invited Rivers to sit down. "Oh, then there was that spat with Gabi's boyfriend but it had nothing to do with the revenge killings."

"Have you had any dealings with the women's revolutionary group since we last spoke?"

Toby smiled. "I think I have," he said.

"What do you mean you think you have?"

Toby sat forward in his chair as if to emphasize he was speaking in deadly earnest. "Nothing of what I am about to say must get back to my parents," he said.

"They are my clients," protested Rivers. "I feel duty bound to tell them things."

"Not this." Toby thought for a moment. "All you have to do is tell them things which are relevant to my safety. I don't think this is."

"Okay," said Rivers tentatively.

"I've been with a couple of call girls recently. I think they were members of the group. At any rate, they were hanging around in Hackney when the group was having its meetings."

"You? Call girls? Why?" said Rivers. He thought for a moment. "You do seem to be living dangerously." He was thinking it would be the type of information that would cause Toby's mother to have a blue fit. He also thought it was the type of information he would find it difficult to tell her about. Best just listen to Toby for the moment.

"Jenny and Jane their names were," said Toby. Rivers nodded. "That Jenny, she nearly freaked me out," Toby added. "Jane was nice, though."

"That would be the general consensus of people who had met the two of them," said Rivers diplomatically.

"I couldn't go through with it with Jenny," he confessed, "but Jane, she's invited me back."

Lucky bastard, thought Rivers. Then he chided himself. It was bad enough he had just contemplated a relationship with Francesca – he should put Jane out of his mind. "You didn't think that by going with prostitutes you were putting yourself precisely into the category of men that that article in the women's group newspaper was suggesting should be killed?" asked Rivers.

"It never occurred to me," admitted Toby. "I was never under threat from either of them for a moment. With Jenny, it didn't go that far. With Jane, the atmosphere was so good I can't imagine anyone being threatened."

"Intimate relationships," said Rivers nodding in agreement.

"There was one thing, though," said Toby as if he had suddenly remembered something. "When I left Jane's flat, I had the oddest feeling I was being followed," he said. "I saw a man

217

on the other side of the street. He got into a car as I got into mine. He took the same route out of Jane's block as me. I was kind of watching out for him in my wing mirror but then he suddenly disappeared. He can't have learnt anything about me - where I lived or anything like that. I was only a few hundred yards from Jane's flat when he was gone."

"Definitely a he?"

"I would have said so. He had a light Mackintosh on," he said as if women never wore that kind of garb.

"Had you ever seen him before?"

"I didn't get close enough to him to find out." Toby was obviously remembering things as he went along. "There was a guy loitering outside Jenny's flat, too," he said. "Could have been the same person."

"Did he follow you?"

"No, I didn't give him a chance. I scarpered from that estate as soon as I could. It didn't look like the kind of place one loitered around after dark."

"Did he have any connection with Jenny, do you know?"

"I think he went into her flat just after I left but I'm not sure. As I said I didn't hang around to find out. Bit farfetched to think he was hanging around outside both women's flats, isn't it?"

"Except the two of them were connected – by the North London Revolutionary Women's Group – the two of them were both prostitutes and the group had run an article suggesting revenge attacks for the Jack the Ripper killings. It's not a leap of faith to suggest that means the killing of men who have been with prostitutes. Oh, Toby, I think my work with you is far from up."

"What are you going to do then?"

"I don't know."

"Do you want me to do anything?"

"I think you've done enough already." Rivers then went silent for a moment. He was thinking that perhaps he should loiter outside

Jane and Jenny's flats to see if he could shed any more light on the man or men who seemed to be trying to stalk their clients.

● ● ● ● ●

Larry Green was accompanied by two police constables as he went to interview Councillor Morgan that evening. He knocked authoritatively on the councillor's door.

"Detective Chief Inspector Green," he said, "and PCs Conway and Fuller. Do you mind if we come in?"

"I don't suppose I have any say in the matter," said Councillor Morgan. He sounded wearisome. The fight and the arrogance seemed to have been taken out of him by what he had gone through. Morgan ushered them into the living room and invited them to sit down. They declined the offer.

"Is you wife in?" asked Green.

"She's upstairs. Why?"

"I'd like her to be in here to listen to what I've got to say."

"Emily," Councillor Morgan called. "The police would like a word with you."

"Thank you, sir." He waited until Morgan's wife was sitting on the settee beside her husband. He noted she looked a little dishevelled with rings under her eyes – not the sort of look that the wife of a man of influence would have if she was accompanying him on a night out.

"I believe you have met my colleague Detective Sergeant Manners," Green said. "She attended here on the day your son was arrested. He is being detained in police custody and has been charged with the murder of Brian Jones."

"That's right, Inspector." Morgan was holding his wife's hand by now – not to reassure her but to bolster his own confidence, Green surmised.

"Very dutiful, your son," said Green.

"Pardon?" queried the councillor.

"Very loyal and obedient," Green continued, "considering he didn't do it." He watched the two of them for their reaction. He thought he saw a flicker of relief in Emily Morgan's eyes. Her councillor husband showed no emotion at all. "Yes, he didn't do it," repeated Green.

"So, will you be releasing him?" asked Mrs Morgan.

"Oh, no," said Green. "The three of you are still facing serious charges. It's just that – with the help of your son – we may have brought the wrong charges against the wrong person."

It was quite likely that Councillor Morgan had never before sat as quietly during a conversation as he was doing that evening. The little colour he had left in his face seemed to be draining away. "So, tell me, Inspector, what are you going to do?" he finally summoned up the courage to say.

"You know we had a sweep of your house for forensic evidence?"

"Only a blind and deaf man could have failed to notice that, inspector, and then he would have had some difficulty in doing so," replied Morgan.

"Quite so," said Green. "Well, the results were interesting. We took away a poker which we believe to have been the murder weapon. An attempt had been made to clean it." Green paused again. He was hoping that Morgan would crack and admit that he had been responsible for killing Brian Jones. Even if he failed in that endeavour, he hoped the way he was delivering his evidence would make Councillor Morgan squirm a bit more. "Not a very good attempt," said Green. "You'd have done better to throw it away but then – I would guess you're not very experienced in covering up crime?"

"Get to the point, Inspector."

"The poker still had some dried blood and some fingerprints on it. Brian Jones' blood and your fingerprints. Not Jed's."

Councillor Morgan swallowed hard. "That doesn't prove a thing," he said.

"In my eyes, it makes it more likely that you are the murderer, sir."

"Why? As far as I recall I merely picked up the poker after Mr Jones had been killed to, as you say, wipe it down and destroy the evidence. I'll admit to that but nothing else."

"You were here on the night Brian Jones died, weren't you, Mrs Morgan," Green said turning to Morgan's wife. "Is your son a murderer?"

It was a few seconds before she replied. "No," she said quite firmly.

"Is your husband a murderer?"

"Hold on," said Councillor Morgan. "She can't testify against me – she's my wife."

"I think her silence speaks volumes," said Green.

Emily Morgan turned to face her husband. "John, it's time to stop all this," she said. "You've been bullying this family for far too long. It's not right that Jed should go through a murder trial because of what you've done. Be a man, John. Do the decent thing. Keep a shred of the decency that people who tugged their forelocks to you when you were a respected councillor thought you had. Please, John, stop Jed's nightmare." She sighed as she finished speaking. It was as if she had just released some pent-up stress.

Morgan closed his eyes and drew a deep breath. "All right," he said, "it was me but not before Jones had threatened to bring in a couple of heavies to rough up Jed if he didn't pay off his debts. I didn't think that little creep deserved any money from us. I'm afraid, Inspector, I lost it."

"I think it might have been a bit more calculated than that, sir. I think you had worked out in your own mind how you could get away with it. It was just unfortunate that a drunk private detective crashed into your son's car with the result that blood from Mr Jones spilled out on to the pavement and into the engine of the drunk driver's car. Not often we're beholden to a drunk driver, sir." He paused before reading Councillor Morgan his rights and arresting him on suspicion of murder. One of the PC's moved forward to handcuff Morgan and Green made no move to stop him – despite a beseeching look from the councillor who seemed to indicate that he was asking whether the handcuffs were really necessary. It would be a final ignominy for the once proud local councillor to be seen by his neighbours to be exiting his house in handcuffs. He was already relishing telling the Pratt the following morning all about this episode. As yet, though, he still did not have a clue what he was going to say about the other murders.

● ● ● ● ● ●

"You can admit it now," said Nikki after Francesca had departed for the evening.

"Sorry?" said Rivers abstractly.

"You seemed on tenterhooks all evening."

"I thought it went very well," said Rivers. "She's nice. Good company."

"I have a feeling you knew that before tonight."

"All right," he said. "I was tempted to have a fling with Francesca – but didn't. We're sorted on that. She doesn't want a relationship."

"And you?"

"Me? No, I want to get back on good terms with you," he said. "I don't want to see thirty years of my life wasted just like that."

"For most of them we were apart," said Nikki dryly. "You've had many other women in your life, Philip. Is it something you can't stop?"

"I really thought it was going to be different this time," he began.

"But it isn't?"

"I'm determined it's going to be," he said. He approached

her and put both his hands in hers. To his surprise, she did not withdraw from him.

"I hope you are," she said looking intently into his eyes.

"I think we have a problem working together and living together," he said. "I'm not sure you're all that happy with the work situation."

"I had a good career which worked out for me beforehand. I could go back to it. Stop us living in each other's pockets so much. There are plenty of openings in fashion events management. I still have some contacts from those days".

"Yes," he said. "It's not as if we have that much work that we need two of us at the agency – although I think it's good to have someone to bounce ideas off."

"One thing, then." said Nikki, cosying up to him and putting her arms round his waist. "I want the power of veto over anyone you hire to work with you."

"You mean I can hire an old battle-axe if it's a woman – or a man," he said.

"I think you'd be safe with a man," she joked.

"There'd be precious little chance of me going off the rails," he said.

"Do you want to?" she asked earnestly.

"I'll be honest with you," he said. "I get tempted. But, in the cold light of day if you ask me if I really want to go with somebody else, the answer would be 'no'."

"And Francesca?"

"Just good friends. I'd like to continue working alongside her but I think I can tell she doesn't want a complicated involvement – and I'm relieved that she doesn't. It'll make it easier working alongside her." He felt bold enough to kiss Nikki on the cheek by now. "I'm sorry I've been distracted," he said.

Nikki smiled. The doorbell rang at that stage. "Who can that be?" said Rivers annoyed. He opened the door. It was Francesca.

"I'm sorry," she said, "but I think I left my mobile behind."

"Oh," said Rivers, "come in and look for it." As she went over to the chair by the settee where she had been sitting before her meal, he made a point of going and sitting by Nikki on the settee and holding her hand.

Francesca picked up her mobile phone and looked over at the pair of them as they sat on the settee. "Good to see you two are OK," she said as she pocketed the phone and headed towards the door. "I'll see myself out," she said.

By the time she had reached her car, Rivers and Nikki had made it to the bedroom.

• • ● • •

The knock on the door sounded urgent. Angela finished putting the baking tray in the oven before she went to answer it. "Yes?" she said as she opened the door, Gary burst past her and into the living room. "Do come in," she said sarcastically. She followed him into the room and noticed he had a baseball bat in his hand. He seemed agitated, hitting his other hand with the bat.

"You can't say anything," he said. It seemed as if he was deliberately not looking at her as he spoke.

"What do you mean?" she asked. She was wearing an apron from her food preparation in the kitchen and to say his arrival had taken her by surprise would have been an understatement.

"You can't say anything," he repeated.

"About what?"

"About Jenny writing that article. She'll be in a lot of trouble." He walked menacingly towards her with the bat. "You'll be in a lot of trouble."

"Why don't you sit down and we can discuss this?" she said calmly.

"There's nothing to discuss."

"It's not fair that Hilary is shouldering all the blame for what happened," Angela persisted. "Jenny could help get her off the hook."

"Yes, and get herself on the hook instead."

"Well, maybe that's where she deserves to be," said Angela.

"What?" he said looking up from his baseball bat. "Look, it'll be the worse for you if you tell the police what you know."

"Are you threatening me?"

"No, I'm doing more than that, I'm going to show you what'll happen to you if you tell the police about Jenny," he said. With that he whacked her on the side of the head with the baseball bat. She lost her balance and fell to the floor. She scrabbled around on the floor trying to grab hold of a chair to steady herself as she tried to get to her feet. "Don't tell the police," he said. He lifted the baseball bat as if to hit her again. She put her hands up to protect herself and they took the force of the second blow so it failed to render her unconscious.

"Stop," she cried. "For heaven's sake, stop."

He looked at her as she tried to hold up her hands to protect herself again. "In fact, I might as well finish you off myself now," he said. "No messing. That would make sure you wouldn't tell the police."

"They'll know it was you," she pleaded. "The police will put two and two together."

"Why?" said Gary. "Nobody knows I came here this afternoon. Nobody will know. I haven't touched anything in here. There'll be no fingerprints. I can throw the bat away."

"Do you want to become a murderer? Can you live with that?"

Gary brought the baseball bat down on her again. It hit her hands forcing her to withdraw them because of the pain. He quickly brought it down again – this time hitting her hard again on the head. She collapsed to the floor.

At that juncture, the front door opened and her husband James walked in. "Hi, Angie, is tea ready?" came an enquiring voice from the hallway. She managed a scream. James pushed the door to the living room open and saw Gary standing there –

the bloodied baseball bat in his hand. "Who are you?" he shouted. "Get out." He reached for the umbrella stand in the hallway and grabbed hold of an umbrella. He swung it in Gary's direction, momentarily knocking the baseball bat out of his hand. He realised that the umbrella by itself wasn't enough to throw Gary off balance so he made a dive for the baseball bat before Gary could reach it. As he tried to gather it up from the floor, Gary jumped on top on him. They wrestled. There was no way James was going to win, an unfit man in his mid-forties in a sedentary occupation against a lithe student in his twenties. Gary grabbed the baseball bat again and as James was struggling to get up hit him hard on the back. He sagged to the floor again and Gary whirled the baseball bat above his head again ready to deliver the next blow to James. Angela saw her husband grab an ornament from the coffee table and fling it for all he was worth against Gary's head. It knocked the student sideways. When he steadied himself again, he saw James approaching him with a fruit bowl he had taken off the sideboard. Suddenly he panicked. He thought James was getting the better of him so he dashed out into the hallway, opened the door and was gone. James, puffing and panting, the fruit bowl still in his hand, stumbled to the door in time to see Gary rushing down the street and away. He sighed, held on to the door to steady himself and then – groggily – felt his way back to the living room where Angela lay unconscious on the floor. "Angie, Angie," he cried shaking her to see if he could find signs of life. To his great relief, he heard sounds of murmuring coming from her lips. He reached over her for the telephone and dialled for the emergency services. "Police and ambulance quickly," he said. "My wife's been attacked by an intruder." With that he gave the operator his name and address. As he put the receiver down and gasped again for breath, he felt a slight tugging at his sleeve. It was Angela. She was coming round. "Thank you," she managed to say before she lapsed into unconsciousness.

CHAPTER TEN

James Curran cradled Angela in his arms while he waited for the police and an ambulance to turn up. She appeared to drift in and out of consciousness – smiling at the moments when she was awake and looking up at him. "Thanks," she managed to get the strength together to whisper.

"Darling," he said. He stroked her shoulders, fearing that touching her badly bruised head might be too painful. "Darling, who was that?" he asked.

"Later," she said.

The police arrived first in the shape of two police constables accompanied by Detective Sergeant Manners. Francesca had been told of the 999 call from Angela's house by Larry Green. They both agreed that – as it was a member of the feminist community who had been attacked that it would be sensible for Francesca to go and investigate what had happened. Francesca took one look at Angela and realised she was not conscious enough to give any detailed account of what had happened. She turned to James. "What happened?" she asked simply.

"I don't know," he stammered. "I was just coming home from work when I heard these screams coming from inside the house. I opened the door and saw this guy attempting to batter Angela around the head with a baseball bat. It was awful. I manage to hit him and he ran off."

"Well done," said Francesca, sympathetically touching James' arm. "Did you see who it was?"

"I didn't recognise him," he said. "He was a young lad, though. I would recognise him again."

"Good," said Francesca. "Do you know what it was all about?"

"No," he said, "but my wife has been involved with this women's group. You know – the one that's been all over the newspapers with these killings. It must have something to do with that. We don't have any other enemies, I think." In truth, James was still a little bit bewildered about just what his wife had got herself into. He had barely thought about her women's group, considering it an irritation which got in the way of her looking after him. When he had thought about it, he considered it to be little more than a talking shop.

The two were interrupted by the arrival of an ambulance. Two paramedics got out and made their way over to Angela. "She's breathing, but she's badly hurt," said one turning to Francesca.

Francesca nodded. "How soon will she be able to talk to me?" she asked.

"Can't say," said one of the paramedics. "We'll have to get her to hospital and assessed by the medical staff before we can answer questions like that."

Francesca nodded. "Silly question," she mumbled. She turned to James again. "You'll want to go with your wife to the hospital?" she asked him.

"Yes, please," said James. "I want to travel with her in the ambulance."

The two paramedics had by then got Angela on to a stretcher and were ferrying her into the back of the ambulance. "Hop in," said one of them to James, "and then we'll be off."

"Great," said Francesca. "I'll join you at the hospital and then we'll get an identikit picture of her attacker drawn up with your help. The sooner we get after him the better. He's obviously a very dangerous man."

Francesca followed the ambulance to the hospital. As she entered the accident and emergency department, she spotted Larry Green hovering by the reception desk. "I thought I'd come and see what had happened for myself," he said. "It's your shout, though – especially when talking to Angela Curran.

I've arranged for an artist to attend - to draw up an identikit. He should be here in a few minutes."

"Good," said Francesca. "I've already primed Mr Curran about that. He's happy to co-operate." The two of them got directions to the operating theatre – where they found James Curran standing in the corridor.

"I should have been more supportive of her," he said. "I kept on demanding 'where's my tea?' – that sort of thing. I drove her into this women's group,"

"There's no point in thinking like that now," said Francesca soothingly. "Anyway, it wasn't the group that was the bad apple. It was individuals in it. It could just as easily have happened in any other organisation."

James did not seem convinced by this but he kept his counsel until the police artist arrived. Green found a room where the two of them could work together in private. James managed to give the artist quite a detailed description of the attacker – long curly hair, student type, jeans a T-shirt and a leather jacket – so that it did not take him long to draw a likeness which gained approval from James. They took the identikit to Green and Francesca. "I recognise that man," said Green. "It's the boyfriend of that prostitute – Jenny."

"Interesting," said Francesca.

"Why would he want to murder Angela Curran?" he said thinking out loud. "It must be connected to the murders." He turned to Francesca. "Look," he said, "you stay here. Get what you can from Angela when she comes round. I'll go round to Jenny Creighton's flat and see what I can pick up from there. If you get anything from Angela, let me know immediately but I think we ought to have Ms Creighton's man in custody as soon as possible."

James, who had been hovering in the corridor and listening to their conversation, approached Green as he was about to leave. "You know who it is?" he said.

"I have a good idea."

"Who?"

"I can't tell you that, sir. I may be wrong but rest assured we will be doing whatever we can to bring this guy to justice."With that, the detective chief inspector left the hospital. He motioned to the two police constables who had been with Francesca to join him."Get someone else to come and cover here,"he said to one of them."We have a suspect to arrest."The PC nodded and did as he had been bidden.

James watched them go but his thoughts were soon interrupted by a nurse. "I think your wife is coming to," she said. James went to be by Angela's bedside. The doctor who had examined her was still standing by.

"How is she?"asked James.

"She can talk,"said Angela butting in. James smiled.

"It's not as bad as it seems,"said the doctor."It's severe bruising to the head. We'll have to keep her in for twenty-four hours in case of concussion. She's cracked her elbow fending off a blow from her attacker but otherwise she seems unscathed. There's a swelling on her forehead that we'll have to monitor but the fact she has come round from the blows relatively quickly augurs well."He could see Francesca hovering around in the doorway. "I would just say one thing,"said the doctor touching Angela's arm."Don't over tax yourself."

Francesca came forward. "Is it all right if I ask her a few questions?"she asked.

"A few,"the doctor stressed. James held his wife's hand while Francesca got out her notebook.

"Do you know who did this to you?"she asked.

"Yes."

"Who?"

"Gary, Jenny Creighton's boyfriend."

Francesca noted the name down."Why?"she asked.

"I'd found out that Jenny was the author of the women's group leaflet calling for indiscriminate attacks against men in revenge for the Jack the Ripper killings. I wanted to go to the police with the information – but I thought I'd give Jenny the chance of owning up to it first."

"Right."

"Gary came in while I was at Jenny's. I said that – if she wouldn't go to the police (she was refusing to do so) that I would. I realised he didn't like what I was saying so I got out as quickly as I could. He obviously followed me home. He said he was going to kill me and would have done if James hadn't have come home when he did."

Angela was beginning to shake as she remembered the severity of the assault upon her. The doctor moved forward. "I think she's had enough," he said.

Francesca nodded. "Thank you, Angela," she said. "That'll be enough for now."

"Just one question," said Angela. "Will this be enough to get Hilary released from her charge?"

"Too early to say," said Francesca, "but we've always thought the author of the article was far more likely to have been involved in a conspiracy to murder than the publisher of it. For one thing, she believed what she was saying." Francesca paused for a moment. "You'll have to excuse me," she said. "I have to get in touch with Detective Chief Inspector Green with this information as soon as possible. He's gone round to Ms Creighton's flat to make an arrest."

"Make sure he gets that young man off the streets," said James. "I'm worried that he might come back and try to finish what he's started."

Francesca nodded and departed.

• • ● • •

Gary looked flustered as he let himself in to Jenny's flat. "Come on," he said. "We've got to go."

"Go? Go where?"

"Anywhere," he said making a wild gesture with his hands. "The police will probably be here in a minute."

"Why? What have you done?"

"It's what we've done."

"I haven't done anything," said Jenny firmly.

"I was only trying to protect you," he said as he went into his bedroom to pack a few things in an overnight bag.

"It sounds as if you haven't succeeded," said Jenny dryly.

"That bitch, Angela," he said. "I was trying to stop her from going to the police."

Jenny looked at him squarely in the eyes. "Oh, my God," she said. "You haven't killed her?"

"No," he said. "Worse than that. I could have got away with that. I tried to kill her but her husband came home."

"And you've killed him, too?"

"No. We started fighting and I had to run away."

"So, he can identify you?"

Gary nodded. "Come on, Jenny," he added. "We've got to go."

"No," said Jenny. "You've got to go. I can see that but I'm staying here, thank you."

"They'll come for you."

"No, they'll come for you."

"They'll know by now that you wrote the article. I didn't manage to kill Angela."

"Good," said Jenny.

"But don't you see? She'll have told the police about that."

"Writing an article is not the same as killing someone," said Jenny forcefully. "It's not the same as attacking anyone either. What state was she in when you left her?"

"She was unconscious, I think."

"Oh, no," replied Jenny. "Gary," she said slowly. "There's just one thing I don't get. Why did you think battering her to death and committing murder would be a help to me?"

"Because no-one would then know that you'd written the article. You wouldn't be charged with incitement to murder."

"My dear fellow." Jenny's voice reverted to the accent she would have had in her teenage years when she was being educated at a girls' grammar school in Sittingbourne. It was patronising, thought Gary. He screwed his eyes up in disgust. "My dear fellow," Jenny repeated. "What do you think would have happened if you'd been successful and had killed her?"

Gary shrugged his shoulders. "Nothing," he said.

"No," said Jenny her voice becoming louder. "Hilary would realise the murder had been committed either by you or me in an attempt to throw the police off our scent. So, then you would have had the dilemma of whether you would have to silence her – she would definitely go to the police if she thought we had killed Angela. She doesn't share my philosophy that you should never help the enemy. Then, as you bumped off the revolutionary left one by one, it would have been obvious even to the simplest of plods that I was the only one left that could have written that article."

"I'm sorry," mumbled Gary, "but are you coming with me, Jenny?"

"You're on your own," she said. "Your murderous exploits are nothing to do with me. Oh, and don't think you can silence me by getting rid of me."

"I never would, Jenny. I love you."

Jenny broke away as he attempted to grasp her hand. "I told you – we should never talk about feelings in this relationship," she said.

"Doesn't it mean anything to you that I would be prepared to kill for you to prevent you from going to prison?" he asked.

"In a word, no," said Jenny. "Now, if you're going, please get out of here." Her voice became louder as she completed the sentence.

"You won't tell them?" he said, dithering.

"I won't even tell them the time of day," said Jenny. "You know my views. They are the enemy and they will seek to pin anything on us. Sadly, you have just given them the justification to do that. Now please go." Gary sighed, picked up his overnight bag and made his way out of the flat. Jenny went to the door and shouted after him: "And don't come back." She watched him go, running down the stairs to the concrete below. She went back inside and began to pour herself a large glass of wine before sitting down on the settee and sipping it thoughtfully. What a prat, she thought as she recalled what Gary had done. He was right, she thought. They would be coming round. That Detective Chief Inspector Green had been longing to get his metaphorical claws into her. In fact, she had hardly had time to finish her glass of wine before there was a knock on the door. She answered it to find Green and two police constables outside.

"Come in," she said reluctantly.

"Is your boyfriend here?" asked Green.

"If you mean Gary, no," replied Jenny.

Green took one of the most cursory glances around the room and decided she was speaking the truth. "There are one or two questions I would like you to answer," he said.

"Go on," she said pouring herself a second glass of wine but declining to offer Green and his entourage anything to drink. They wouldn't have accepted the offer anyhow, she reasoned. Green, for his part, decided not to try and stop her drinking.

"Information has come to light that you were the author of that article in the women's revolutionary group leaflet," he said.

"That doesn't sound like a question," Jenny pointed out.

"Can you confirm that?"

"I will neither confirm nor deny that, inspector," she said. "You may have forgotten the stand I take against you. I will not help you in your attempt to persecute those whose politics you disagree with."

"This has got nothing to do with politics, Ms Creighton," said Green. "This is a murder investigation."

"The answer's still the same."

"It was your colleague Angela Curran who gave us that information - just after she had suffered a brutal beating at the hands of your boyfriend."

"I wish you'd stop calling him my boyfriend. It's so bourgeois a term."

Green coughed. He really did not want to waste his time discussing ideology with this wretched woman – as he saw her. "All right – at the hands of the man you live with," he said.

"Closer. Share a flat with would be preferable."

"You're testing my patience, Ms Creighton," said Green.

Am I? thought Jenny. Good. She finished her second glass of wine and decided not to pour herself another. She reckoned that she needed to keep her wits about her as the inspector was questioning her. "I'm sorry to hear that, Inspector," she said.

"Both Angela Curran and her husband have identified Gary Cole as her attacker. Mrs Curran is in hospital with serious injuries. She says the attack took place to try and prevent her from giving us the information that you had written the article. She was in no doubt Mr Cole would have killed her if he had not been disturbed by her husband."

"Then you should be out looking for him, Inspector. He sounds like a dangerous man."

"Have you seen him?"

"Yes."

"When?"

Jenny thought for a moment. She did not think that telling the police he had been in the flat a few minutes ago, but had now gone for good would compromise her principles. At least it would sever a connection between him and her. "I think that description of him as the man who shares my flat is – on second thoughts – a trifle out of date," she said. "He's packed his bags and gone."

"Did you know he intended to kill Angela Curran?"

"That's irrelevant, Inspector," said Jenny. "The point is I have not left this flat this evening and I have no knowledge of the events you are describing."

"Because if you did you could have stopped it."

"How?"

"By ringing us. In extreme circumstances, even someone of your obvious political persuasion would have done that in order to save a life."

"Maybe the fact that I didn't ring you tells you something?" said Jenny.

"Like what?"

"That I didn't know or have any part in what went on."

"Maybe," said Green, "but what you did do was to write an article which called for the indiscriminate murder of men. Jenny Creighton, I am arresting you on suspicion of incitement to murder." He then read her rights and then charged the two police constables with the task of taking her to the police station.

• • ● • •

"So you've charged John Morgan with murder?" said Chief Superintendent Pratt as Larry Green arrived for his 10 am appointment.

"He killed someone," Green replied.

Pratt shook his head as if in sadness. "Shame," he said.

"Yes, it was for the person concerned," said Green. "New evidence came to light showing him to be the murderer of the loan shark Brian Jones. I'm sorry sir, but I can't ignore the evidence. His wife has also given a statement to the effect that he killed Mr Jones. She's been charged with attempting to pervert the course of justice, too, on account of her actions in helping dispose of the body."

"You have been busy, Green."

236

"Thank you, sir."

"It's a shame," repeated the chief superintendent.

"I know," said Green – this time adopting a more sympathetic tone. "I believe he was a friend of yours?" he asked.

"We were members of the same golf club. He was also my local councillor."

Oh, thought Green, so he could not possibly have been a murderer then. Instead he was diplomatic in his response. "I know, sir," he said, "but if he will go round murdering people."

"This is not a matter for humour," said Pratt.

"No, sir," replied Green. Perhaps we should all adopt mourning clothes, black ties etcetera, he thought to himself. Best not to suggest it to the Pratt, he reasoned. You never knew how he might take it.

"Now can we get on to the other matter?" said Pratt. "The revenge killings."

"Yes, sir, well, we've made some progress in that direction, too. We have a woman in custody under arrest for incitement to murder."

"You had a woman charged with that yesterday," said Pratt.

"It's a different woman."

"And I'm supposed to take comfort from that?"

"No, sir, but we believe this charge will take us to the heart of the conspiracy. In fact, we will be questioning her today about the two murders – to see if she was directly involved in them."

"What leads you to believe this?"

"She wrote the article calling for the revenge attacks. When one of her colleagues worked out that she was the author, her boyfriend went round to her home – last night – and tried to kill her. He wouldn't have done that if she – or he – hadn't got something to hide, possibly about the murders, too, as well as the article."

"So when will you be talking to her again?"

"As soon as we're finished, sir."

"Don't let me hold you up, Inspector. I want a progress report again tomorrow morning."

"Very good sir." With that, he got up to leave the office. He headed straight downstairs to Francesca's office. "Well," he said. "We'd better get cracking on interviewing Jenny Creighton. We'll do it together."

Jenny was brought into the interview room looking a little bit frail. She had bags under her eyes as if she had not slept well. She didn't say anything as they set up the tape recording equipment for the interview. Green reminded her she was under caution and that it was her right to have a solicitor present.

"No," she said. "Not yet."

"Why did you write that article, Jenny?" Green began.

"It's none of your business. It wasn't aimed at people like you."

"Or me?" Francesca intervened. "Surely you wanted someone to take you seriously and start indiscriminate revenge attacks against men."

"All right," said Jenny, "I just wanted to see what the reaction would be if a woman behaved like Jack the Ripper. There'd be no adulation. She'd be reviled."

"There was no adulation for Jack the Ripper," said Green.

"That's your opinion." She realised that she was now cooperating with them – engaging in conversation with them – but she was beginning to think it would be in her own interests if she didn't act quite so provocatively towards them.

"Did you know John Hedger or Daniel Peacock?" Green asked.

"I sometimes don't know the names of my clients," she said, "so I wouldn't know if I knew them or not."

Green pushed two photographs across the table. "These are of them," he said.

Jenny gave them a cursory glance. "No," she said.

"They're both users of prostitutes. We found your number in Peacock's home."

Jenny took a second glance. "Maybe," she said shrugging her shoulders.

"They have both been known to act violently towards women," he went on. "Is that something your boyfriend – sorry, the man who used to share your flat - would have reacted to."

"I wouldn't have told him," she said.

"He could have seen for himself," insisted Green.

"You'd better ask him what he would or wouldn't have done. I can't speak for him."

"We will when we can find him. Do you have any idea as to where he might have gone?"

"No."

"Did he have any friends locally who might have been prepared to harbour him?"

"I don't know." She paused for a moment. "Inspector, from the line of your questioning, I understand you have nothing to implicate me in the murders of these two men. You're wasting your time asking me questions – questions that Gary (she emphasized his name as if it was something that they could agree on calling him) would be in a far better position than me to answer."

Green had to agree. He glanced at Francesca, raising her eyebrows. She nodded. "We shall terminate the interview at... (he glanced at his watch) ... 10.45 am," he said. "You will be charged and remain in custody until we can bring you before the magistrates' court this afternoon." A police constable was summoned to take Jenny back to her cell. "Well," said Green, "where do we start looking for Gary?"

"We could try the university to see if he had any friends but I wouldn't put any money on him turning up there. He's more likely to be sleeping rough."

"We should get night patrols out looking for him – armed with the identikit drawn up by our artist," said Green.

• • • • •

Toby could see through the glass door to his flat that the person who had rung the bell was tall and slim. On opening it, he was surprised to find it was Gabi.

"I thought you were long gone," he said. He stood in the doorway – initially not inviting her into his flat.

"I left something behind," she said.

"Well, maybe that could be considered as collateral for your attempt to burn down my flat – or get your boyfriend to beat me up," he said – still not flinching from his position.

"I am sorry for that," she said. "I didn't have anything to do with it."

"Believe me, so am I."

"If you will let me in to get my brooch, I will go – forever," she said.

Toby stood back from the door and let Gabi pass by him. She went straight to the bedroom that had been hers, rummaged around for a few minutes and returned triumphant with a brooch. "You have not invited anyone else to stay with you," she observed.

"No, I had rather a bad experience with a tenant last time," he said icily.

"I am sorry for that," she said again. Her voice still betrayed no emotion but Toby believed she was sincere.

"It wasn't your fault," he ventured.

"It was Rudolph. My boyfriend was jealous of you," she said. "He was convinced we were having a relationship."

"So, if he tried to burn my flat down, what did he do to you?"

"He is no more – but before that happened I convinced him I had resisted your advances."

Toby pondered the phrase "he is no more" but reckoned that – rather than being sinister – it came out worse than it was in translation. He then added: "But I didn't make any advances. And don't say 'I'm sorry' again." He let her pass him and exit through the main door to the flat. "I don't suppose we shall meet again," said Gabi offering a hand for him to shake. "I am going back to Germany tomorrow. I will not be seeing Rudolph again either."

Toby's hands remained steadfastly by his side and he watched as Gabi walked up the alleyway between two blocks of flats and disappeared from view. He could not help but feel sorry for her. Her "ice maiden" approach – he had learnt of her nickname at the school from Rivers – seemed to pre-empt any attempt to get closer to her. He wondered whether she was telling him the truth about Rudolph. It was only at that point that he decided to follow her – just in case Rudolph was still around. Gabi cut down a couple of side streets to the local pub where Toby had often taken her for a drink when she had been living with him in the flat. He observed her going over to a table. She took out a book and began to read after ordering a drink.

"Is he coming to meet you here?" asked Toby. "Is that it?"

"No," she said. "He has gone. He is no more. I just wanted to say goodbye to this place."

Toby went to get himself a drink. "I guess we shouldn't part on bad terms," he said. This time he offered his hand to her which she accepted. He then drank his drink quickly and departed from the pub.

As he left, he bumped into Rivers in the doorway.

"Mr Rivers?" said Toby surprised.

"I came to tell you about some developments in the murders," said the private detective, "I thought I might find you here." He looked over to the table where Gabi was sitting. "You're not sitting with her?"

"She's going back to Germany. This is probably the last I'll ever see of her."

"I shouldn't be too upset about that," said Rivers.

"Why?"

"Honestly, Toby, you do have a talent for putting yourself in tricky situations with members of the women's revolutionary action group. Your antics are increasing your parents' bill by the minute."

"You don't think I was in any danger from Gabi, do you?"

"Remember, she was turning a blind eye to burning your flat down. She didn't care that her boyfriend assaulted you. She was quite prepared for him to do that." Toby began to mutter a protest but Rivers waved to him to be silent. "She did all that without you laying a finger on her," he said. "What would she have done if you had made an unwanted advance towards her?"

"Surely, Gabi's not dangerous?"

"That's what I thought," said Rivers, "but just think about this for moment – the murders stopped when Gabi left London to go on holiday. Is that a coincidence?"

"But there's nothing to connect Gabi with either of the men who were murdered."

"And what did the article in the leaflet say? Carry out indiscriminate attacks against men in revenge for the Jack the Ripper killings. Indiscriminate. I'm not saying that Gabi was the murderer or that she conspired with someone – say Rudolph – to carry them out. All I'm saying is until we know who the killer is and they've been caught it's wise to be careful. Now. come on, let's get a drink," he said. "This is a pub, I believe."

"Okay. But she's left Rudolph and she's leaving the UK. She's no threat to me. Never was."

"You can be quite gullible, Toby," said Rivers

• • ● • •

Gary had slept rough that first night after leaving Jenny's flat. He had gone to the soup kitchen at Lincoln's Inn Fields and managed to get something hot from it. The truth was, though, that he had little money and little prospect of getting any. He knew the police would be after him now and any attempt to get credit from his bank would immediately have them rushing round to the cash point he was using and searching the surrounding neighbourhood. It was not a prospect that filled him with confidence.

Secondly, he was on his own now. He knew his relationship with Jenny was over as a result of his assault on Angela. Of course, Jenny had always insisted they had never had a real relationship. There were no feelings in it, she would always stress. He went along with her. She was too strong-minded a person to disagree with on something as fundamental as that. She was wrong, though. He knew that. How could the two of them have stayed together for so long without there having been some kind of feeling between them.

He reflected. All that did not help him now. He was almost destitute. He had nowhere to live. The only belongings he had were the clothes on his back and the baseball bat he had attacked Angela with. He sighed. That had to be his method of getting the money he needed to live on now. The baseball bat. He would have to pick his prey carefully. In some secluded street in the back streets of London. He had nothing to lose, the way he figured it. He was already facing an attempted murder charge for his attack on Angela – or a murder charge. He did not know how forcefully he had hit her and how much damage he had caused.

On leaving Lincoln's Inn Fields, he walked over to Covent Garden. There were always tourists there at whatever time of night. He walked down a side street just off from the main square and spotted a man standing outside a restaurant lighting a cigarette. Jo Allen's. That was the name of the restaurant. You had to have a bit of money to dine there, he reasoned. He waited for a moment while a couple of passers-by left the street. The man was still inhaling his cigarette. He slowly crept up behind him and then brought the baseball bat down on his head with as much force as he could muster. The man fell to the ground whereupon Gary reached for his inside pocket and withdrew

243

a wallet from it. He could see two people entering the street a couple of hundred yards away and resolved to make off as quickly as he could. He would rummage through the wallet for its contents when he had made good his escape.

He hurried off round the corner and soon found himself in the Strand with scores of other people enjoying a night out in the centre of London. He tucked the baseball bat under his arm in an attempt to make it look inconspicuous and made his way to Embankment where he veered off down an alleyway and sat on the wall to what looked like a small park to see what he had got in the wallet. He was in luck. He had chosen his prey well. The man had at least £70 in notes in his wallet. There were credit cards but Gary decided not to bother with them and threw the wallet away. He decided to go to a burger stand nearby and treat himself to a hot dog. He felt he had deserved it. Munching on the hot dog as he sat on a wall near Embankment station, he tried to concentrate and think about what he should do now. His university course was no longer an option. He would have to give that up. The police would definitely be keeping their eyes on the university in case he turned up there. He could not stop thoughts of Jenny coming back into his mind. He knew it was pointless but he admired her strength and the forthright way in which she dealt with people. He had attempted to kill one of her friends, though, even if it had been – in his eyes – from the best of motives. He had just wanted to protect her. As he thought about Jenny, a tear welled in his eye.

"Fuck it," he said angrily aloud. "I'm a hard man – I shouldn't be doing this." It didn't help. The tear soon become a flood and he was weeping uncontrollably – so much so that a passer-by put a hand on his shoulder.

"What's the matter son?" he asked.

"Leave me," said Gary tersely. "You don't want to know."

The man instantly drew back for a moment but – on seeing that Gary was still crying – made another attempt to console him. At this stage, Gary melted. His body relaxed and he dropped the baseball bat. As it fell to the ground, the man consoling him noticed it was blood spattered. He withdrew his hand from trying to console Gary and moved away to take his mobile out of his pocket. He's going to call the police, Gary thought. He immediately drew himself up to his full height and barged the man over before escaping down the alleyway to the small park again. When he felt he had put sufficient distance between himself and the encounter with the man, he stopped to consider his thoughts again. Get out of London, he thought to himself. The search won't be as intense if I can do that.

He toyed with the idea of going down to the West Country. He had spent some happy days there in his childhood. The search wouldn't have widened to that area. Get to Paddington, he thought. Buy a one-way ticket for a train journey. He had just over £60 in his pocket. One more mugging and he reckoned he would have enough money for the fare. Again, he ruled out buying a ticket with his credit card. The police would be alerted to where he was and – whilst they might not have arrived swiftly enough to stop him from boarding a train – they could well find out his destination. Where to find the next mugging victim, though. That was the question. He already felt he could not go to the Embankment or the Covent Garden area. There was a chance the police might have been alerted to both of those.

He walked on to Temple station and boarded a Circle line train, deciding to get out at Sloane Square. Not that he knew the area. The word "Sloane", though, conjured up images of affluence. He had heard of the Sloane Rangers. He felt if he walked around that area for long enough he would be able to find another secluded spot to single out another victim. On arrival at the station, he set off in search of a side street and within several minutes found himself in a residential cul-de-sac which did not seem to be attracting passers-by. As he entered the cul-de-sac, a man came out of one of the houses with a dog.

No, he thought, don't take on more than you might be able to handle. He did not have to wait long until another opportunity arose. A young man, quite thickset, entered the cul-de-sac. He did the same preparation as he had used in Covent Garden, mustering as much strength as he could to bring the baseball bat down on the side of the man's head. This time it did not go according to plan, though. Maybe the man caught sight of him wielding the baseball bat as a result of a street light focusing on it. At any rate, he avoided the blow and then threw himself at Gary. It was an unequal contest. The man was thickset, powerful. Gary could see now that he was built like a rugby player. By comparison, Gary was quite scrawny. As the man pinioned Gary to the pavement, he shouted out for help. "Dad, Mum, it's Chris, help," he said.

An older man emerged from one of the houses and together they held Gary prisoner. "Your mother's calling the police," said the older man. He smiled. "Lucky you built up your strength with your rugby training," he said. The pair of them held Gary until the police arrived.

• • ● • •

"Right," said Larry Green. "First things first. Hilary Sampson is downstairs reporting in to the station. Let's get her up here and tell her the good news."

Francesca smiled and left the room to escort Hilary to Detective Chief Inspector Green's office. Perhaps unsurprisingly, Hilary did not seem overly delighted at the request to accompany Francesca to Green's office. However, Francesca did her best to reassure her.

"There have been some developments which could be beneficial from your point of view," she said.

Green stood courteously when Hilary entered his office. Hilary noted she had not received any formal act of politeness from the police in the investigation so far. "Sit down," he said. He waited until she seemed comfortable in her chair. "We have decided not to pursue the charges against you," he said. "We will be formally dropping them when you appear at the magistrates' court again tomorrow morning."

"Thank you," said Hilary – a note of relief in her voice. "May I ask why?"

Green had thought she would be relieved, turn on her heels and just go. He wondered how much he could tell her without jeopardising his case. "We are satisfied you did not incite anyone to commit murder," he said. "We still believe it was an error of judgement to publish that article but we believe that any incitement was more closely linked to the person who wrote that article than to you. We now know who wrote that article."

"Oh."

"That person has now been charged with incitement to murder – and an accomplice with intended murder."

"An accomplice?" Hilary was trying to rack her brains to work out what had happened. "May I ask who you have charged?"

Green thought for a moment. "I don't suppose it would matter that you know," he said. "The person concerned will be appearing at the magistrates' court this afternoon. It's Jenny Creighton."

"Oh." Hilary stopped from making any comment. She still believed that any help given to the police in pursuing prosecutions stemming from that article would be a breach of the guarantee of anonymity that she had given the author. "And the accomplice?"

"Has been apprehended and is being brought to this police station this afternoon. The man she lived with."

"Gary?"

"Yes."

"So who did he try to kill? As far as I knew there had been no attempted murders – only successful ones."

"It won't have hit the papers yet. He won't be formally charged until this afternoon."

It was at this stage that Francesca intervened. She realised that Hilary knew nothing about what happened. "I think you ought to brace yourself for a shock," she said. "It's Angela Curran."

"Angela? Oh my God. How badly hurt was she?"

"She's still in hospital – but it only happened a couple of days ago," said Green. "The doctors are keeping her in in case of concussion but she could be free to leave fairly soon."

"I suppose it was Angela who told you about the authorship of the article," said Hilary. She felt that the silence of the two detectives on this point confirmed her thoughts. "And Gary tried to kill her to stop her telling the police?" Again, her deduction was greeted by silence. "That means, Angela must have confronted Jenny – given her a chance to tell you first." For the third time in succession the two detectives remained quiet.

"Ms Sampson," said Green. "We cannot really go into information which at some time in the future will be the property of the courts. I think we've reached the limit of what we can tell you. Detective Sergeant Manners will see you out."

Hilary nodded. "Thank you," she said. "And thank you for dropping the charges."

"I saw no reason for making an example of you." She had been a formidable adversary when he had interrupted one of the women's meetings, thought Green, but he had never detected any personal animosity towards him. Unlike some he could mention

"But you do of somebody else?" asked Hilary. Green smiled. Spot on, he thought.

Francesca escorted Hilary from the room. She was in two minds as she prepared to leave the police station. Should she go to the magistrates' court to hear what happened when Jenny appeared before them that afternoon – or should she go the hospital to offer some comfort to her friend Angela. She was still ruminating on this as she signed on at the custody desk – at the same time as two police constables were escorting Jenny to the court. Anger got the better of her. She approached Jenny. "You bastard," she shouted. "How could you let that happen to Angela?"

"I didn't do anything," protested Jenny. The two police constables tried to form a human shield between the two women. Francesca laid a restraining arm on Hilary's shoulder.

"No, you didn't, did you?" said Hilary controlling her emotions more firmly this time. "You didn't go the police station and confess yourself when you knew the game was up."

"Oh, Christ," said Jenny. "Listen to yourself, woman. When did the Left ever get anywhere by confessing what they had done to the police? Honestly."

"And you didn't stop your partner from trying to kill Angela after she had had the decency to offer you the chance to make your own confession."

"That was nothing to do with me either. Individuals are responsible for their own actions."

"Leave her in a room alone with me and I might disprove that theory." The words seemed to be directed at Francesca but – after they had left her mouth, Hilary began to regret being so aggressive. She really did not want a slanging match with her former comrade in the reception area of the police station, she reasoned. Francesca also seemed slightly shocked by the ferocity of her words.

One of the police constables took charge of the situation. She laid a restraining arm upon Hilary. "Clear a way so we can take the accused to the magistrates' court," she said.

"Of course," muttered Hilary as she stood back to watch Jenny being escorted from the station. "I'm sorry," she said to Francesca when they had gone, "but Angela's such a fragile creature. I can't bear thinking about what they've done to her."

Francesca nodded. "I understand," she said, "but – if I were you - I would revise my opinion of Angela as a fragile person.

She had great courage to go and confront Jenny about what she had found out. It was only a pity that Gary heard what had happened and decided to take matters into his own hands."

"Yes," said Hilary dignity now restored to her tone of voice. "I think I should now go and pay Angela a visit."

$$\bullet \quad \bullet \quad \bullet \quad \bullet \quad \bullet$$

Gary looked a bit feral when he was brought into the police station, Green noted. "Take him straight to the interview room," he said. "I'll be along in a minute." He then went up to Francesca's office. "Let's see if we can get anything by talking to him," he said. Francesca nodded and followed her boss to the interview room.

"Gary Cole," began Green. "I want to start off by questioning you about an incident last night."

"I want a solicitor," said Gary.

"All in good time," said Green. He began by cautioning him – and reminding him he had been arrested earlier that evening. "What do you know about Angela Curran?"

"I'm not saying anything."

"She was a friend of your girlfriend's, I believe. Jenny Creighton?"

This obviously struck a raw nerve with Gary. He wiped some snot from his nose. "She's not my girlfriend anymore," he said. He sounded like a truculent teenager in a school playground.

"But she was yesterday afternoon?" There was no response from Gary. "What happened?" Again, Gary remained quiet. "You must have done something to upset her? Gary, yesterday Angela Curran - your girlfriend's friend – was battered to within an inch of her life."

"So she's still alive then?" intervened Gary. He sounded relieved. There was some human emotion left in him, thought Green.

"Battered to within an inch of her life. You obviously did something of which Jenny Creighton would have disapproved. Can you see where this is leading – especially when we have two witnesses saying that you were the person who delivered the battering?"

"Two witnesses?" asked Gary.

"Yes. Why do you ask? Were you expecting there to be only one? It would still be a serious crime even with only one witness."

"But she was well enough to talk to you?"

"You seem to be taking great comfort from the fact that she is still alive?"

"Well, yes."

"You think that means you won't be charged with murder? Let me come on to that." Green fished the photographs of John Hedger and Danny Peacock out of a file on the table in front of him. "Do you know either of these two men?"

Gary did not look at the photographs of the two men very closely. "No," he said.

"Take a closer look," said Green, pushing them further towards him. "John Hedger was killed on the 11th of June and Danny Peacock a week after. Can you tell me where you were on the 11th and 18th June this year – in the evenings?"

"No."

"You mean you won't tell me or you don't know?"

"I can't remember."

"I suggest you try," said Green. "We believe both of these men were clients of your girlfriend's. Both of them acted violently towards her."

"No comment," said Gary. He had seen people saying this in TV police dramas and thought it safer to use that formula than say anything else.

"Presumably you wouldn't like anybody acting violently towards your girlfriend. If you're prepared to kill someone who suggests she goes to the police and confess her role in writing an article calling for revenge attacks against men, what would you do to someone who actually physically harmed her?"

"No comment."

"You could have found out where they lived by following them from your girlfriend's flat. You're in the frame for this, sonny, and it's a double murder charge."

"No comment."

"I think we'll let you get some sleep and think about this overnight. You've already been arrested for robbery and attempted robbery."

"That's not fair," Gary intervened. "In the second case, I came off worse."

"That can happen when you assault someone and that's why one of the charges is attempted robbery, sonny," said Green. "We will resume questioning you about the murders of John Hedger and Danny Peacock tomorrow morning." With that Green called for a police constable to escort him from the door. As Gary was about to leave, Green interrupted his progress. "Just a thought for you to mull over, Gary," he said. "Your girlfriend wrote this article calling for indiscriminate attacks against men. Two men who have shown violence towards women – including your girlfriend – have been murdered; possibly by her. How do you think she would react to a man who had beaten her friend half to death? Worth thinking about."

"So you haven't caught her?"

Green remained silent. "Just mull those thoughts over until tomorrow morning," he said.

CHAPTER ELEVEN

Jenny Creighton looked in awe of her surroundings as she entered the magistrates' court and sat down in the dock. Her eyes feverishly moved from side to side as she tried to take it all in. She felt like the type of shy little rich girl brought up in the leafy suburbs that she had once been – not the confident brash outspoken feminist who was a member of a women's revolutionary action group. She confirmed her name in a hoarse whisper to the magistrates and gave a nervous laugh after she had done,

"This is no occasion for levity," said one of the magistrates – a ruddy faced man who looked bored with the proceedings.

"No, I realise that," she said. She felt an urge to tell the bourgeois court – as she saw it – that she did not recognise their competence to try her. She wasn't going to be tried today, though. It was only a remand hearing.

The prosecutor got to his feet. "If I might address the court?" he said. The ruddy faced man now beamed with pleasure and granted him his wish. "There are enquiries going on which could lead to more serious charges than the one the defendant now faces," he said. "In view of that, we would urge a remand in custody."

"More serious than incitement to murder?" mused the ruddy faced man.

The solicitor appointed to Jenny got to his feet to make a plea for bail on the grounds she was of previous good character and lived in her own flat. None of this seemed to impress the ruddy faced man. He and the other two magistrates conferred. Fifteen seconds later – Jenny timed it – he spoke to her again. "Stand up," he said severely.

"I am standing," protested Jenny.

He ignored her comment. "Jenny Creighton, you will be remanded in custody for seven days," he said. He then looked at the warder closest to the dock. "Take her away," he said. With that, Jenny was escorted from the dock and back to the cells at the court. The warder opened the door for her and was just about to shut it when Jenny spoke. "What's happening?" she asked. "Do I stay here?"

"You'll have to wait. There are another couple of prisoners being taken to the same prison as you but they're not ready to go just yet."

"Prison?" Jenny asked. For some unknown reason, she had thought she would be transferred back to the police station she had just come from. It had not occurred to her she would be spending the next week in prison. "Hilary wasn't remanded in custody," she said. "Yet she faced the same charge as me."

The warder ignored her and just slammed the door shut turning the key in the lock. Jenny began to shudder uncontrollably.

• • ● • •

"My goodness, you do look a sight for sore eyes," said Hilary as she approached Angela's hospital bed.

In truth, she did. There was a swelling on the left-hand side of her head which was as big as a golf ball. Both her arms were in plaster and, for good measure, she was sporting a black eye,

"It's not too bad," said Angela. "The pain has been dulled."

"I want to thank you," said Hilary as she kissed Angela on her right cheek – thus avoiding all the bruising. "As a result of what you did, the charges against me have been dropped."

"Good," said Angela, "although I hesitate to say it was worth it. I think if I had to do this again – it would be 'sod it, I'm going straight to the police station with what I know'."

"You may have a point there," said Hilary.

At this stage, Angela's husband, James, emerged carrying a bunch of flowers. "I took a half day off work," he explained as he approached her bedside. He was not as adept as Hilary had been in picking out a part of her face to kiss to avoid the bruising and Angela winced a little bit with pain as he came into contact with her left cheek. She smiled. "Men." she said to Hilary.

"I wouldn't know," came the reply.

"James," said Angela. "This is my friend Hilary. She's a member of the women's group that I go to." Angela could see that James was a little bit nervous as to how to react. "It's all right," said Angela. "She's not going to bite."

James proffered his hand to Hilary. "Pleased to meet you," he said. By now he was also holding Angela's hand – a little gingerly. He was worried that any attempt to tweak it might cause her more pain.

"If it wasn't for James, I wouldn't be here," said Angela. "He came in the nick of time when Gary was beating me. By the way, have they found him?"

"Yes, I gather so," said Hilary. "He's still being questioned at the police station. Jenny has appeared at the magistrates' court today charged with incitement to murder – the same charge that I was on. I think they believe, though, that the two of them could have been involved in the murders."

"I'm not surprised," said Angela. "That Gary – her boyfriend – he was out of control." She reached out for James' hand again as she recalled the attack on her.

"How long are you going to be in here?" asked Hilary.

"Not for much longer," said Angela. "They're only worried about delayed concussion. What are we going to do about the group?" She could feel James tensing up as she spoke.

"A rather depleted group," said Hilary. "Jenny obviously won't be joining us. I don't know where Gabi is any more. As far as I know she might have gone back to Germany."

"And Jane?"

"No, I haven't heard from her. I never thought she was quite as committed to revolutionary politics as the rest of us."

James' brow became more furrowed at this point. Angela felt she had to intervene. "Excuse me," she said. "What about me?"

Hilary smiled. "You're right," she said, "Maybe nobody was as committed to revolutionary politics as Jenny and me." James seemed to be reassured at Hilary's acceptance that his wife had not been committed to revolutionary politics. "I suppose we ought to reconvene when this is all over," Hilary added.

"Maybe."

"Well," said Hilary. "I ought to leave you two to it." With that, she gathered up her handbag and left them on their own.

"I'm not going to interfere in anything," said James when Hilary had gone, "but be careful if you go back to the group again." He smiled as he took Angela's hand again. "It's not because I want my tea on the table when I return from work – but it has been quite a dangerous environment."

"I think your tea might not be on the table for another reason," said Angela. "I'm thinking of going back to practising law - taking a job for myself when this is all over."

James smiled. "The law should be a safer environment for you," he said. Angela smiled, too. If she had mentioned it a couple of months ago, he would have been dead set against it. At least the tribulations of the last few days seemed to have brought them closer together and to a closer understanding of each other.

• • • • •

"We're making good progress," Francesca told Rivers when she telephoned him that morning. "Both Jenny Creighton and her boyfriend have been remanded in custody – Jenny's on an incitement to murder charge and Gary Cole is charged with attempted murder."

"Attempted murder?"

"He tried to kill Angela Curran when he realised she had found out that Jenny was the author of the article and that she was going to the police."

"Right."

"We're now going to question them this morning about the two murders – John Hedger and Danny Peacock. We know they were both clients of Jenny's and that they have a history of violence. So, it appears, does Gary."

"You're sounding as if you think the investigation is nearing its end," said Rivers.

"Well, depending on what we get out of them this morning," she said. "I think this means your part in the investigation is over. It's over to us now."

"You've got no evidence putting them at the scene of the crime," Rivers pointed out. At that stage, Nikki entered their office. He waved at her indicating that he would be with her in a moment.

"Larry is under great pressure to come up with something from the chief superintendent," said Francesca. "This is the best we've got."

"Just one thought," said Rivers.

"Yes?"

"Do either Jenny Creighton or Gary Cole own a car?"

"What?"

"You heard and you know why I'm asking."

Francesca racked her brains. "I've never seen either of them with a car," she said. "It would be a simple matter for us to check."

"I'm surprised you hadn't thought of it beforehand," said Rivers. "After all, it would be very difficult for them to lug the bodies to that derelict wasteland without one. They could hardly go by public transport."

"They could have taken them prisoner and got them to drive them there," suggested Francesca.

"You're clutching at straws," said Rivers.

"Maybe," admitted Francesca. "I've got to go now. Larry wants a word with me before his meeting with the Pratt." With that, she hung up.

"Was that your favourite detective?" asked Nikki.

"No, it was Francesca," said Rivers dryly.

Nikki smiled. "Touché," she said. "It sounds as if you were putting a spanner in her works."

"It just came to me as we were talking. I just couldn't see how anyone could manage the murders without a car. The bodies wouldn't have been taken to such a remote spot if the murderer or murderers didn't have a car."

"So they're barking up the wrong tree?"

"Possibly. I think they're being carried away by their dislike of Jenny and her boyfriend – neither of whom have done anything to help themselves. They could have kidnapped Hedger and Peacock and forced them to drive to the wasteland where their bodies were found but I somehow doubt it. They'd have been better able to do that if they'd had a gun but there's no evidence that the killer had one."

"So where does that leave things?"

"At stalemate. They're under pressure to get a result and Jenny and Gary are the only meat they can toss to their chief super at the moment so they'll pitch that to him. I think I'm just going to carry on with what I was going to do."

"What's that?"

"Check out whether somebody is following clients of Jane Harris' when they leave her flat. I was going to run a similar check on Jenny Creighton but events seem to have overtaken that. I had a feeling someone was following me, though, when I went to Jane's flat and Toby had the same impression when he went to see her."

"Nothing came of it, though," Nikki pointed out.

"It's still worth checking out. I'll go over to her place this afternoon and just see what happens."

"Do you want me to be your driver?" asked Nikki.

Rivers grinned. "I'm stupid," he said. "For a moment, I'd forgotten I can't drive. And the client is hardly likely to be leaving on foot."

"I was wondering why you hadn't asked me," said Nikki. "I'll make us some sandwiches, too. We could be in for a long evening."

"Thanks," he said. "Why not make a picnic out of it? It's only a grisly murder investigation, after all."

$$\bullet \quad \bullet \quad \bullet \quad \bullet \quad \bullet$$

Francesca sighed as she put down the telephone to Rivers. She had to admit he had a point. Green detected a forlorn look on her face as she entered his office. "What's up?" he asked.

"A flaw in our case," she said.

"What?"

"How did they dispose of the bodies?"

"I'm not with you," said Green.

"They'd have had to have a car."

"Yes?"

"I've just checked. They don't."

"Bloody hell," said Green. "Why didn't I think of that? I must be going senile – only one week to go until retirement." He fidgeted with some papers on his desk. "Of course," he said, "they could have kidnapped Hedger and Peacock and forced them to drive them to the wasteland."

"But you don't believe that to be the case." said Francesca, "and nor do I."

"Look," said Green his hands sweating now as the implication of what his junior officer had said sunk in. "We're – or rather I – am just two minutes away from making my daily presentation to the Pratt. I can't go in and say my case has gone down the plughole. We'll have to stick with what we've got for the moment. Tell the Pratt we think it's Jenny and Gary and then go and question them for all we're worth. We can always tell him tomorrow that we couldn't find the evidence."

"He'll take it better tomorrow, will he?" said Francesca.

"No, but I'll be nearer retirement."

● ● ● ● ● ●

"Park over there," said Rivers indicating a parking bay for a block of flats just across the way from where Jane Harris lived. Nikki obliged. "It's a long time since I've done an observation operation," he said. "They can be quite boring."

Nikki nodded. She reached over into the back of the car and brought forward a thermos flask. "Cup of tea?" she asked.

"Thanks," he replied. "Of course, we don't know if Jane Harris has a client – or, if she does, what he looks like."

"Do you think we could tell whether somebody leaving the flats has been a client of hers or not?" asked Nikki.

"You mean will he be zipping his trousers up as he leaves? Somehow, I think he'll have done that before he gets outside. He won't want to draw attention to himself."

"Hopefully there won't be many men leaving flats in the middle of the afternoon," said Nikki. "It doesn't look like the kind of place where people are suffering from unemployment. Most people – men and women – will be out at work."

Rivers nodded. He looked around. "Doesn't look as if there's anybody waiting around to stalk anyone who leaves Jane Harris' flat," he said. "There are some garages below." He gestured to the right with his hand. "There may be somebody parked down there. I'll go and have a look."

"Don't make yourself too obvious," cautioned Nikki.

"No," he said. He pointed to a grass verge on an incline just opposite where they had parked. "If I go to the top of that mound of grass, I can look down on them but I don't think they'll be able to see me." He got out of the car and walked over to the top of the grass verge. On looking down, he could not see any cars. Mind you, he thought, they'd have been in the way of people wanting to leave their garages if they parked down there. He went back to Nikki. "Nothing untoward," he said.

"Cup of tea?" she replied.

"I should take you on jobs like this more often."

"I thought we were breaking up the partnership."

Rivers nodded. He drank his tea and put the car radio on. "Classic FM?" he said to Nikki. "That's a bit upmarket for me. I always had it tuned to Capitol Gold." They listened together for a while – occasionally swopping snippets of conversation. After about an hour, another car swung into the parking bay. Rivers was not good at recognising makes of car but he could tell it was an expensive make – probably owned by someone with money.

A man got out. He was in his mid-forties or early fifties and was wearing a suit. He was sporting a paunch and his trousers seemed to be a bit tight on him. "Going to seed?" suggested Rivers. "Do you think this could be our man?"

"Possibly," said Nikki.

"Can you tell when a man has sex on his mind?" said Rivers giving the driver of the car, which had parked opposite to them, a close look.

"No," said Nikki.

Rivers changed the subject. "The first floor flat on the left," he said. "That's where Jane lives." He looked up at it. He could not see far enough into it to tell whether Jane was there. The man walked across the road to the block in which Jane lived, pressed the buzzer on the intercom and soon disappeared inside. "How long does it take for him to do the business, I wonder?" mused Rivers. "He'll probably have booked in for half an hour or an hour."

"Know about these things, do you?" said Nikki dryly. Rivers was just beginning to think it might have been preferable to be doing the observation by himself when Nikki put a hand on his arm. "Only kidding," she said.

During the next quarter of an hour a couple of cars drove into the estate. One went down the hill to the garages, the other parked next to Rivers and Nikki. Both were being driven by women – presumably mothers – who appeared to be bringing their offspring home from primary school. They disappeared – one family into each of the block of flats. Another car soon followed them into the estate and also drove down the hill to where the garages were. It went too quickly for Rivers to get much of an idea about the driver but he was pretty sure it was a male. He repeated his trick of going to the top of the grass verge and looking below. To his surprise, the car was still there and had not disappeared into the garages. It was parked on the other side of the private road leading down to the garages – only it had turned around so it was facing the exit from the estate. He could see the driver was still sat in the car but even now he was unable to get a clear picture of him. He made his way back to Nikki. "I think we're on," he said. "That car is parked ready for a quick getaway – ready to follow our guy (he pointed at the posh car) when his hour is up." He looked up at Jane's flat. "You see the second window on the left," he said pointing. "Curtains drawn. That's her bedroom."

"You'd know, would you?" said Nikki sarcastically.

Rivers ignored her remark. "I know we're on," he said emphatically.

• • ● • •

"Laurie Fishlock. I have an appointment with you." the fat man said as Jane Harris opened the door of her flat to him.

"Do come in." She looked at her client as he made his way into the flat. He had a paunch which, she surmised, probably told of too many business lunches or too much alcohol.

He had a pleasant speaking voice – no accent, middle of the road south-eastern England she would have guessed. In terms of attractiveness, he was not a patch on young Toby who had visited her the previous week, she reflected, or that private detective who had not wanted sex.

Nevertheless, he was a client and she would do her best for him. After today, she was giving it all up so he was her last. "Would you like to come through to the bedroom?"

"Thank you," he said. He did not seem the conversational type. It worried her. It was not the kind of liaison she liked. She liked to talk to her clients and find out as much as they were willing to give about themselves. "This is your first time with me?" she said framing her words in the shape of a question.

"You know that," he said a trifle aggressively.

"Sit down," she said patting the bed. "Can I get you anything?"

"No thanks."

"I want you to have a good experience with me," said Jane, moving to undo the buttons on his shirt. He seemed to freeze while she did it. "Relax, Laurie," she said, "I'm going to give you a good time. How did you find out about me?"

"I saw your advert in a phone box."

Ah, thought Jane, one of them. They tended to be rougher around the edges than those who replied to her ad in newspapers. "What do you do for a living?" she asked in an attempt to make conversation.

"You don't need to know that."

"No, you're right, I don't," she said. "I just thought it might help relax you if we had some conversation and found out a little bit about each other."

"I know all I need to know about you. You're a prostitute and I've hired you for sex. Period."

"Ok, Laurie, then let's have some sex." His shirt was unbuttoned by now and she helped him take it off. She kissed his neck as she did so.

"I didn't think prostitutes liked kissing their clients," said the man. He could have been Laurie Fishlock or not, Jane thought. A number of her clients used false names. She knew that.

"That's true for many of them," said Jane, "but not for me." She moved to face him full on and started undoing his trouser buttons, kissing him fully on the lips as she did so. "I try to create an aura of intimacy in my relationships. We can both benefit from that."

He pushed her away from him and grabbed at the shirt she was wearing with both hands and ripped it off. He then pulled at her bra and started fondling her breasts and kissing them.

"Clothes are expensive," she said. "I'd prefer it if you didn't rip them off me."

"You prefer nothing," he said. "I'm paying for you. I'll give you extra to buy a new shirt."

She was beginning to get a little bit scared by this stage. "What do you want, Laurie?"

"I want to fuck you," he said. "That's all." By now he was naked, having taken his trousers and pants off himself. He undid her jeans and pulled them roughly off her and then did the same with her knickers. He then started to get on top of her.

"Whoa, cowboy," she said. "Slow down. I can make this much more pleasurable."

At that he slapped her hard across her left cheek and then hit her with his backhand across her right cheek. "Let's get on with it," he said.

"Wait," said Jane. "Paying for sex doesn't give you the right to hit me." She pushed him away from her. "I want you to go," she said. "You can have your money back. You've come to the wrong person."

"Let me be the judge of that," he said, raising his hand as if to hit her across the face again.

She brought her hands up to defend herself. "Beatrice," she yelled with all her might. Within seconds her lodger had arrived.

Beatrice seemed to have pre-empted what was happening in Jane's bedroom. She entered the room carrying a broom and hit the man over the head with the broom handle. He staggered for a moment and then regained his composure, turning around to try and knock the broom out of Beatrice's hand. As he did so Jane pushed hard against his naked body moving him towards the door which had remained open after Beatrice's entry. She stood aside and helped Jane push him further into the corridor. Once they had pushed him all the way to the living room, Jane went back into the bedroom to gather up his clothes and throw them at him. "Get dressed and go," she said. Beatrice then hovered over him still holding the broom while Jane regained her composure, went back into the bedroom and got dressed. The man started to get dressed. He put his trousers and shirt on but then a feeling of rage seemed to overcome him. He looked at Beatrice and saw a slight tender woman – not someone who would be able to resist an attack – and lunged at her knocking her over and sending the broom flying out of her hand. He then picked up the broom and started moving towards Beatrice threateningly – a look of smug satisfaction coming over his face as he contemplated bringing the broom down upon her. It only lasted a few seconds, though, as Jane emerged from the bedroom with the bedside lamp in her hands and gave him a whack across his right-hand side. It had the effect of sending the broom flying again. Beatrice regained her composure while Jane struck him again with the lamp. She opened the front door of the flat and between the two of them they bundled him outside. They then slammed it shut and Jane put the lock on. Both sat down exhausted. Within seconds, there was a furious rapping on the door followed by a shout of "I'll get you, you bastards".

"I suppose we'd better give him his shoes and socks back," said Jane as she got up and walked towards the bedroom. Coming back with the aforementioned items she opened the door and quickly threw them outside. "We've called the police," she said firmly before closing and relocking the door. "Gosh," she said as she sat back against it. "What was all that about?"

"I haven't a clue," said Beatrice.

"I think," said Jane, "he just wanted to take out his frustrations – whatever they were – on a woman." They listened in silence for a moment and then Jane thought she could hear footsteps making their way downstairs. "I think he's going," she said. "His wife's probably walked out on him – or they've had a row. He just wanted to get his own back." she sighed. "Luckily, he's the last client I'll ever have." Then she added with a smile on her face: "Or never had, thank goodness."

Beatrice got to her feet and disappeared into her bedroom – re-emerging about a minute later.

"Let's have a cup of tea," she said. She appeared relaxed now.

"Or something stronger," said Jane. She got her own way.

• • ● • •

"We're getting nowhere," said Green as he sank back in his chair. "Two hours of questioning them and we're no nearer pinning anything on them."

Francesca nodded in agreement. "At least we can still hold them," she added, "on the assault and incitement charges."

"That's not going to cut any ice with him upstairs," said Green.

"No," replied his detective sergeant. "Where do we go from here?"

"I don't know," he said very deliberately. With that, he threw his pen across the table. Francesca picked it up for him. "At least they don't have any alibis to put themselves in the clear for the nights of the murders," he said.

"Except each other."

"That's worth sweet Fanny Adams," said Green.

"I must say I find Philip Rivers' argument that they don't have a car quite compelling," said Francesca. "You said that they could have taken Hedger and Peacock hostage and forced them to drive them to the wasteland. I don't see it, though."

"If Mr Rivers is so keen to put down our arguments, what remedies does he suggest himself?"

"I don't think he does, sir," said Francesca, "but he's still going to carry on investigating the case himself."

"You like him, don't you?" said Green.

"Sir?"

"I meant nothing by that," said Green, "but if you could ring him and ask him if he's got any leads it might help."

"We're that desperate, are we, sir? We have to beg a private detective to solve the case for us."

Green ignored her last remark. "Remember," he said, "those who were investigating the original Ripper killings were led a merry dance for much longer than we were. They'll probably be laughing at us from their graves. Why the Pratt should think it's easy to bring a Ripper killer to justice is beyond me. It's the indiscriminate nature of the thing. Makes it very difficult."

"I'm ringing Rivers, sir." said Francesca. It did not take the private detective long to answer the call. "Oh, Philip, I just wanted to share things with you," she told him. Green began to impersonate her as she made the phone call. "We've had a very frustrating afternoon interviewing Jenny Creighton and Gary Cole," she said. "Neither of them has admitted anything and we don't believe we've got any evidence to charge them yet."

"I rather thought that might be the case," he said.

"Are you pursuing any line of enquiry?"

Rivers sighed. He did not want the police to get involved in his operation just yet. A ham-fisted approach might ruin what he had set up. "I think I'm onto something," he said. "I can't tell you what just yet – but the position might be clearer in about an hour."

"Can you ring me when it is?"

"Yes, certainly," he said. "I might even need your help by then."

He switched his mobile phone off and put it back in his pocket.

"Francesca?" asked Nikki.

"Yes," he said. "They've drawn a blank. It looks like we're the only show in town."

"Nothing to report as yet, sir," said Francesca to Green, "but he thinks he's on to something and he'll ring us when he's got anything."

"Great," said Green in a tone which was heavily laced with sarcasm.

● ● ● ● ●

"We have lift-off," said Rivers as he spotted the crumpled figure almost staggering from Jane's block of flats.

"Goodness, he must have had a good time," said Nikki.

"I don't think so," replied Rivers. "It looks as if he's been duffed up – or something like it."

The crumpled figure rested his back against the wall of Jane's flats. He took his shoes off and pulled his socks up. After he had done that, he put his shoes back on and did up their laces. He grimaced as he tucked his shirt further into his trousers and then ran his hands through his hair. Having managed to make himself a trifle smarter than he had looked on emerging from the flats, he strolled over to where his car was parked, got in and drove off.

Nikki made as if to follow him but Rivers laid a restraining arm on her shoulder. "No, wait," he said. "We follow whoever's following him."

Sure enough, another car soon emerged from the driveway which led down to the garages. It was getting dark by now so Rivers could not make out who was driving the car. The trio of cars turned out of the estate and made their way back to the nearest main road. The lead car headed north towards Finchley – presumably to the home that Jane's client lived in. The driver of the first car seemed oblivious of the convoy behind him and just kept going along the main road. At one stage the second car appeared to swerve a little but the driver soon regained control of it.

"What was that?" said Nikki.

"He was distracted by something," said Rivers. "Could have been a mobile going off or something like that."

After about four miles, Jane's client took them on a journey through a few back streets – eventually coming to rest in a quiet no-through road. He parked on the street – the house he had parked outside already had a car in the driveway. He got out of his car and locked it but before he could make his way up the driveway to the house the driver of the second car got out, swiftly came up behind him and hit him over the head with some object and then quickly delivered a second blow. The man fell to the floor with a gasp – which, Rivers reckoned, would have been inaudible to anyone inside any of the houses in the street.

"Time to act," said the private detective. "Ring Larry Green or Francesca and tell them where we are. I've got to stop this." With that, he jumped out of the car and shouted at the man with the blunt object in his hand who, by now, was dragging the body of the other man towards the boot of his car. "Stop that," yelled Rivers. "Philip Rivers, private detective, who are you?"

The man dropped the body he was dragging and turned round to face Rivers. "Tom Harris," said Rivers recognising his face. The other man did not respond but moved towards Rivers with the blunt object in his hand. Rivers moved his hand up to protect his face. "I wouldn't try that," he said. "The police are coming. You don't want to get yourself into any more trouble." The words sounded hollow to Rivers even as he spoke them. After all, the man in front of him was probably responsible for two murders. "It's all over now, Tom," he said. "You might as well put that thing down." By this time, Nikki had also got out of the car and came over to see what she could do to help. Rivers

269

waived her back. "It's all right," he said. "I think we've got things under control."

"I don't have any quarrel with you, Mr Rivers," said Tom. "Jane reckoned you were one of the good guys." He tossed the blunt object – which looked like a door stop – on to the ground."

By this time, the commotion had resonated with the families living in the street. A couple stood in their front garden across the road and one woman went over to Laurie Fishlock's body to see how badly he was hurt. "I'm just a neighbour," she said to Rivers. "We know Laurie and Mary quite well."

"Best look after him," he said. She nodded and lent down beside the fallen body.

"I phoned for an ambulance as well as the police," said Nikki as if to reassure the woman.

Rivers was just beginning to wonder what more he could do to keep Tom Harris from running off when he heard the sound of police sirens becoming ever louder as they neared the scene.

To Rivers' surprise, Tom Harris was making no effort to extricate himself from the proceedings. It was as if he had heeded Rivers' assertion that the game was up.

Soon Larry Green was by his side. "Thank you, Philip," he said. "We'll take over from here." He walked over to where Tom Harris was standing. "If you would accompany me down to the station," he said. A police constable came forward with a pair of handcuffs in his hand and escorted Tom to the waiting police car. Before he left the scene, he turned to the woman whom he wrongly assumed was Fishlock's wife. "If you knew what he'd done, you'd understand," he said.

Larry Green turned to face him. "That's enough, sir," he said. "If you wouldn't mind just getting into the police car." He then turned to the woman. "And you are?" he said.

"A neighbour," she said. "He's still alive. I can feel a pulse." As she spoke, he appeared to regain semi consciousness. He started groaning in a low voice. By this time, the ambulance had arrived on the scene. Green turned round to another of the police constables. "Go to the hospital with him," he said. "Let us know when he can be interviewed." He turned to the woman. "Do you know where his wife is?" he asked. "We should inform her."

"She's staying at her mother's," said the neighbour. "They had a row about a week ago."

Green nodded.

"I dare say he won't want to be interviewed," interjected Rivers, "and the fact that his wife's gone probably explains why he was consorting with a prostitute – and maybe why he was violent."

"Why won't he want to be interviewed?" Green sounded irritated.

"Come off it. Consorting with a prostitute without his wife's knowledge? Tricky situation. Not likely to bring the wife running back."

"I don't suppose it'll matter. We've got a witness to the assault," said Green. "You. All in all, a good night's work. I can report to the chief super in the morning that we've cracked it. The murders of Hedger and Peacock, too."

"It's not over yet," said Rivers.

"What do you mean?"

"Ask yourself; how did Tom Harris know to attack this guy but leave me and Toby Renton alone after we'd left Jane Harris' flat."

"Well, you didn't have sex with her, did you?" said Green.

"Toby did. No, the answer is he must have had an accomplice."

CHAPTER TWELVE

"I've had his text messages checked," said Francesca as she joined Green and Rivers outside the interview room.

"And?" queried Green.

"He received one just about fifteen minutes before the attack which just said 'violent'."

"Who from?"

"I don't know yet."

At this stage Rivers intervened. "I think the best way to find out would be to go round to his flat and ring the number that texted him," he said. "It's got to be Beatrice – the lodger – or Jane. Assuming it's a comment on the nature of his victim, they would be the only ones who knew what went on between Jane and this client."

"We've scrolled back on his text messages and there are a couple from just over two weeks ago which say 'peaceful'," Francesca added.

Rivers thought for a moment. "That would coincide with when I went to visit her," he said, "And I know she had a visit from Toby Renton round about the same time. Both of us had the feeling we were being followed when we left Jane's flat."

"Right," said Green. "We should go round and interview them now. Before they realise there's anything wrong. Tom Harris can wait. We've got him bang to rights."

"One thing," said Rivers. "Do you think I could come with you to interview Beatrice and Jane?"

Green shot a glance at Francesca. "What do you think?" he asked.

"It's just that I know Jane," Rivers began.

"Do you mean in the biblical sense?" said Francesca tartly, interrupting him.

He ignored her remark. "I think I developed a rapport with her when I interviewed her," he said.

"Well," said Green after a moment's hesitation. "I hate to say it – but you've been a great help to our investigation so far. The police force isn't supposed to like private detectives but I think you could be helpful in questioning Beatrice and Jane."

"Thank you."

"You can come with us," said Green and with that the three of them repaired to Larry Green's car and drove round to Jane's flat as quickly as they could. Green knocked forcefully on the door. It was opened by Beatrice who seemed surprised to see them. "Can we come in?" said the detective chief inspector. Beatrice ushered them into the living room. "Are you on your own tonight?" asked Green

"I am at present," she said.

"Where's Jane Harris?"

"She's just popped out." Beatrice noticed they were not questioning her about Tom's whereabouts. That either meant they knew where he was or their enquiries had nothing to do with him. The latter, she felt, was unlikely.

"Do you know how long she's likely to be?" asked Green.

"I could ring her."

"No," said Green quickly. "We'll wait."

"Can I get you anything?" she asked ushering them into the living room to sit down.

"No, that's all right," said Green. "Can you tell me where you've been this evening?"

"That's easy," said Beatrice. "I've been here all evening."

"Can anyone confirm that?"

"Well, Jane could," she added. "She's been with me until about half an hour ago." Green nodded. Rivers noticed Francesca was taking her mobile phone out of her pocket. He wondered if she was going to try the number that had texted Tom Harris and shook his head firmly in her direction. It would be better to have both of them there before they tried to confirm the text. They did not have to wait long before Jane applied her key to the lock and entered the flat.

"Beatrice, I think ..." she began before she noticed the other three occupants of the flat. "Oh," she said, "what are you three doing here?"

"What were you just going to say?" said Rivers.

Jane hesitated for a moment. "I was going to say I thought there was something wrong with the car," she said. "It's why I've been such an age." With that, she plonked a bottle of wine down on the table. "I've just been out late night shopping."

You were going to say you thought there was something wrong, thought Rivers, but I bet it wasn't with the car.

Green took charge of proceedings. "Your brother has been arrested, Miss Harris," he said. "He has confessed to the murders of John Hedger and Danny Peacock – and to the attempted murder of Laurie Fishlock."

"Murder? Tom? No," She seemed genuinely surprised by what Green had said.

"He was actually caught in the act of trying to murder Laurie Fishlock – by Mr Rivers here. Mr Fishlock had just come from your flat."

"Yes," confessed Jane. "I know that. He was an awful man. We had to get rid of him." She paused and then – realising her words could have been misconstrued – added: "From the flat, I mean."

"He was violent," said Beatrice.

"Violent?" said Rivers. "Not peaceful, then?"

"That's a strange word to use," said Jane.

"We believe your brother had an accomplice with these murders," said Green. "Someone who directed him to do what he did."

"Well, we've both been here all evening," began Jane.

"That's not a defence," said Green. "You could have done it from here."

Francesca got her mobile out of her pocket and this time Rivers did not stop her from dialling the number. The tone of a mobile phone ringing sounded from Beatrice's pocket. Rather than try and answer it, she froze to the spot.

"You see," said Green. "We've had possession of Tom Harris' mobile phone. Someone texted him from that number – (he pointed to Beatrice's pocket) – to say the word 'violent' and he was nearly killed. Would you give it to me, please, Madam?" He held out his hand and Beatrice reluctantly pulled the mobile phone from her pocket and handed it over to him. "What's your full name?" he asked.

"Beatrice Rosen," she replied.

"Beatrice Rosen," he said, "I'm arresting you on suspicion of conspiracy to murder Laurie Fishlock." He then read her rights and turned to Francesca. "Would you order a police car?" he added. "I think it would be too cosy if we all trooped back to the police station in my four-seater."

"All?" said Jane.

"Yes, we have some questions to ask you as well – like where were you when we arrived here this evening."

"I was out getting a bottle of wine."

"Bit late for that, isn't it?"

"We've had a trying day. I was attacked by Mr Fishlock, remember? I also thought Tom would be back soon."

"And he would have had a trying day, too – clobbering Mr Fishlock over the head, and then, if he had not been interrupted, killing him and cutting his penis off."

"That was not what I meant, Inspector."

"You have a few questions to answer – which can best be done back at the station," he said. By this time, a couple of police constables had presented themselves at the door. They took charge of Beatrice and Jane and whisked them back to the station in their police car.

"So far so good?" said Green looking at Rivers as if he wanted confirmation of what he had just said. Rivers was deep in thought and did not respond.

• • ● • •

A police constable entered Tom Harris' cell soon after he had been brought to the station. "They're ready for you now," he said. He got to his feet and resisted an attempt by the constable to shepherd him into the room. Once inside, he sat down at the table waiting for his interviewers to arrive.

"He seems very calm," said the police constable to Green as they met outside the interview room. Green nodded and walked into the room. He was carrying a folder which he opened out and looked at as he sat opposite Tom Harris.

"We'll wait until Detective Sergeant Manners arrives for the formal interview," he said. "You've turned down the offer of a solicitor, I understand?"

"Yes, I don't need one."

Green eyed him curiously. "You do realise the situation you're in?" he asked.

"Yes, and I intend to make a clean breast of it."

Green shrugged his shoulders. At this juncture, Francesca appeared in the doorway. She motioned to Green to come outside for a moment. "Would you excuse me?" he said to Tom Harris. Tom nodded. It was polite of Green to ask permission to leave the room – almost quaint. Tom realised he had to accede to the request.

"Odd one here," said Green to Francesca when they were out of earshot of Tom. "It's got the atmosphere of a vicarage tea party in there – rather than a murder investigation. I think I almost prefer the ballsy insolence of Jenny Creighton."

"No, you don't, sir," said Francesca. "Look I just wanted to tell you I've ordered a search of the Harris' flat and their two cars – the one at the block of flats and the other at the scene of the arrest. The searches are going on now."

"Good," said Green. He turned round to go back into the interview room again. "Let's make a start." He sat down and switched on a tape recorder. "We want to talk to you about the murders of John Hedger and Danny Peacock and the attempted murder of Laurie Fishlock."

"Yes, I'm responsible for all three crimes," he said. "I killed John Hedger on June 11th and took his body to derelict wasteland where I disposed of it. I did the same with Danny Peacock. I would have killed Laurie Fishlock tonight if Mr Rivers hadn't stopped me."

"Why?"

"I deplore violence towards women. All three had attacked my sister Jane. I was not going to let them get away with it. I've seen too much of the effects that violence can have on a relationship."

"Your sister was a prostitute."

"And that makes it okay to beat her?"

"I'm not saying that," said Green, "but to talk of the effect that violence has on a relationship is a little off beam in the circumstances."

"The relationship I was talking about was my mother's and my father's. He was constantly beating her."

"So why didn't you go to the police then instead of starting on a killing spree of totally innocent men?"

"I reject any suggestion these men were innocent. All three of them attacked my sister. They probably attacked other women in the course of their lives, too. They deserved to be punished."

"To die? Even though they hadn't killed anyone?"

"I don't regret what I did."

"You say you abhor violence to women but you seem to tolerate it against men. These were particularly brutal crimes.

Both Hedger and Peacock had their penises hacked off. A particularly cruel form of torture?"

"If they had been alive, yes, but they were both dead by the time that happened."

"Why did you do that?"

"The hacking of the penises was a statement. You will not use this to bully women again."

"But they wouldn't have done. They were both dead."

"It helped underline the fact these men were sex pests."

"And the hacking of the penises was your idea?"

"As I said, it was a statement saying they would not use them to bully women again."

Green shuffled the folder on his desk. He brought out the leaflet by the North London Women's Revolutionary Action Group. "Have you read this?" he asked.

"No."

"Look at it a little more closely," said Green, "and then answer me."

Tom Harris picked it up and scrutinised it. "No, I can honestly say I've never read it."

"You see, it's calling for indiscriminate attacks against men in revenge for violence towards women. That's just what you did."

"Not because of anything the writer of this article said. I've never read it."

"But your sister would have done. She was a member of this group. Perhaps she read this and thought it was a good idea – particularly because of what your father had done to your mother. Perhaps she suggested that you should go on this killing spree. She would have liked to have gone on a killing spree herself – but realised she didn't have the physical strength to carry it out. So she asked you to?"

"My sister had nothing to do with this. I acted on my own."

Green relaxed at this point. "But that's just not true, Tom, is it?"

"Yes."

"We know that just fifteen minutes before you carried out your attack on Laurie Fishlock you got a text saying just the word 'violent'. There were earlier texts – coinciding with visits by Philip Rivers and a Toby Renton to your sister – saying 'peaceful'. In fact, even now, we are trying to retrieve earlier texts sent to you and I would lay odds that we will find two coinciding with the days that John Hedger and Danny Peacock were clients of your sister saying 'violent'." Green stared at Tom Harris but there was no response. "What's the matter?" he said, "Cat got your tongue? I thought you said at the beginning of this interview that you intended to be straight with us. I don't call this straight."

"You don't know those texts were connected with the murders," said Tom.

"Oh, so we will find the other two texts, then," said Green. "Thanks for that."

"They could just be referring to the experience my sister had had with her clients. It was my decision to kill them after receiving those texts not...." He suddenly stopped in mid-sentence.

"Not Beatrice's? Is that what you didn't want to say? Don't worry. We know she sent the texts."

"And not my sister," he said emphatically.

Green looked at Francesca. Tom seemed at pains to distance his sister from any involvement in the murders. After an initial attempt at concealing Beatrice's involvement, he seemed less reticent about shopping her. "True," said Green, "but you are asking us to believe that she read this article about killing men indiscriminately, did nothing about it – and simultaneously her brother, who had never read anything about it – suddenly took it upon himself to start bumping off men randomly. Bit too much of a coincidence, that? Jane must have discussed the article with her friends. Perhaps they agreed with its sentiments and got you to put it into practice?" I would dearly love to get Jenny Creighton tied to this conspiracy, thought Green.

"That's not the way it happened. It was because of my father."

"So you say." Green paused for thought. "How long had your father been hurting your mother? She's been dead for some time now. It couldn't have happened recently. Why only start your killing spree now?"

"My father was admitted to an old folk's home," he said. "He was senile. We'd had nothing to do with him for years but then Jane felt morally obliged to go and visit him while he was dying. That's what triggered me off." He began to show signs of emotion. His voice started to falter. "You see, she even showed kindness towards him despite what he'd done," he said. "She wouldn't have had the stomach to do what I've done."

A thought struck Green. "Have you killed before killing John Hedger?" he asked. "It would be one way to prove that this article had nothing to do with the killing spree if you had. Maybe it wasn't on my patch." Tom Harris remained silent. Better to leave the seed in Green's mind that he had killed before, he decided, than to come out with an outright denial. "Let's get on to Beatrice, then," said Green. "Why did she become involved in these killings?"

"She loves me." The words came out before he could think. He bit his tongue. He had incriminated her.

"So, she did become involved in the killings?"

"She didn't harm a hair on anyone's head," said Tom.

"No, but she didn't have any qualms about passing the information on to you to carry out the killings. Even if she didn't realise you were going to kill the first one – John Hedger – she must have realised by the time you had Danny Peacock in your sights."

"I repeat – she never harmed a hair on anyone's head."

"You stick with that thought if you want to," said Green. "I think you have just given us enough information to charge her with conspiracy to murder – on all three counts." He could see Tom Harris squirming in his seat. "What's the matter?"

said Green "Telling the truth not as easy as you thought it would be?"

"I acted on my own," he said defiantly.

"Let us be the judge of that," said Green, snapping his folder shut. "I have to tell you that you will be formally charged with two murders and one attempted murder in the morning. In the meantime you will be returned to your cell." Francesca then followed Green out of the door while a police constable entered the room to take Tom back to his cell. "What do you make of that?" Green asked Francesca when they were on their own back in his office again.

"Beatrice must have known what her texts meant."

"And Jane?"

"Difficult to believe that she was living in a house where her clients were being bumped off by the two people she shared with – and she knew nothing about it."

At this juncture, one of the detective constables attached to the station came up to Green. "We have some results from the search of the Harris' flat and their cars," he said.

"And?"

"Nothing incriminating found in the flat," he said, "but weapons in both of the cars – a sort of machete in Tom Harris' car – and a sharp knife in Jane Harris' car."

"So what was Jane Harris doing with a sharp knife in her car?" mused Green.

· · ● · ·

Tom Harris sat back in his cell thinking about his encounter with Green and Francesca. He had been told his fate had been settled – he would be appearing at the magistrates' court in the morning and that he would in all probability be remanded in custody to a prison. He sighed. It was all over now – and he realised he had to take what was coming. In his mind's eye, though, he had not let go of the thought that the world was a better place without the likes of John Hedger and Danny Peacock (and Laurie Fishlock if he failed to pull through) and that his actions had probably saved several women from violent beatings. His father was dead now, Jane was giving up prostitution. Hopefully that would mean she would never be involved in a violent relationship with a man again. His campaign against violent men was over. It was just a pity that he had fallen at the last hurdle – caught in the act of meting out justice to Laurie Fishlock. A pity, too, that the police had established a link between Beatrice and the killings. He realised he had been on flimsy ground arguing that she did not realise sending the texts to him would mean murder if she identified Jane's client in question as "violent". It was easy, he thought, to let slip information unintentionally when you were being questioned by experienced detectives like Green and Francesca Manners. He would no doubt be questioned by them again. He began thinking. There was only one way to ensure he didn't let anything more slip or say something innocent which was misconstrued by detectives who seemed hell-bent on proving a link between Jane and the killings and that was by killing himself. He looked round his cell. It would not be easy. There was a light fitting in the centre of the room and he had a shirt which he could tear into ribbons to hang himself from the light fitting. He was just taking his shirt off and contemplating going ahead with the plan when he thought again. What would be the impact on Jane – and Beatrice? They had enough to cope with without him saddling them with remorse over his death. What had seemed like the best way out a moment ago faded from his mind and he started to button his shirt up again. He had just finished when he realised there was someone looking in at him from outside the cell. The police sergeant was doing his rounds. "Are you all right, sir?" came the question.

"I'd hesitate to say that, Sergeant," said Tom.

The sergeant smiled. "All right," he said and continued on his rounds.

Tom lay back on the bunk – in the knowledge now that even if he had gone ahead with his plan it would have been futile. The sergeant would have found him and saved him before he could have gone through with it. Best just to stiffen his resolve and try to take all responsibility for the murders himself.

• • • • •

Beatrice looked nervous as she was led by a police constable to the interview room. Her eyes furtively glanced from side to side as she made the short walk from her cell to the room. Once inside, she was offered a seat at the far end of the table – which she took, nervously drumming on the table with her fingers. Next to her was a duty solicitor with whom she had had a brief chat earlier. She did not know him and gained no confidence from his presence. She stopped her drumming as Larry Green entered the room followed by Francesca. Green looked at her. She would be easy to intimidate, he thought. She would not hide behind a wall of silence.

"Your full name," he said.

"Beatrice Claire Rosen."

"How old are you?"

"Twenty-one."

"Occupation?"

"Student."

"Thank you, Miss Rosen," he mopped his brow which was beginning to sweat with all the work he was putting in that evening. "Miss Rosen, I want to convey the seriousness of your situation before I start this interview. We believe you formed part of a conspiracy – a conspiracy with Tom Harris to murder two men, John Hedger and Danny Peacock. You also took part in a conspiracy to murder Laurie Fishlock although he was rescued by a member of the public. We shall start by questioning you about the attempted murder of Laurie Fishlock this evening. Where were you all evening?"

"At home in the flat I share with Tom and Jane Harris."

"Can anyone vouch for this?"

"Jane."

"Except she was not there when we called to speak to you earlier this evening."

"She had just popped out."

"Why?"

"She told you. It was to buy a bottle of wine. We had had a stressful evening and we needed to unwind."

"What was so stressful?"

"Jane was attacked. I had to help get him off her and throw him out of the flat,"

"Why was it that it was a good three hours later that Jane went out to buy this bottle of wine?"

"I don't know," Beatrice stammered. "We did have some in the flat which we finished off first."

"So Jane would have been driving under the influence of drink."

"We didn't have that much." She glanced at her solicitor who sat there stony-faced.

"No," said Green. "Of course not. She wouldn't have wanted to risk being stopped by the police on her journey."

"She was only going to the off licence."

"So you say but we can attest that – considering evidence already given by you and the time we spent at the flat – it took her at least 45 minutes to complete that journey. Seems a bit implausible, that."

"There may have been traffic."

Beatrice's solicitor put a restraining hand on her arm. "You don't have to answer Detective Chief Inspector Green's asides if you don't want to," he said.

"Oh, no, of course not. I'm sorry." She smiled at Green. He looked down at the folder in front of him on the table.

"Let's get back to slightly earlier in the evening - 8 o'clock to be precise. You sent a text to Tom Harris saying 'violent'. Why?"

"He was very protective of his sister. He always wanted to know how her encounters went."

"Encounters?"

"With clients."

"She was a prostitute?"

"Yes."

"And what did you expect him to do as a result of receiving this message."

"I don't know. I suppose he knew he would have to be sympathetic and comfort her when he got home."

"How touching," sneered Green. He looked down at his folder and picked up a scrap of paper. "We have checked through both your and his mobiles for text messages and it seems you sent a similar text to him on the night that John Hedger died and another on the night that Danny Peacock died." Beatrice remained silent. "I note you don't deny that," he said.

"There would be no point," she said resignedly. "You've got the text messages."

"As you say, we've got the text messages." He remained silent for a moment and – when he spoke again – it was in a more commanding, authoritarian voice. "Are you extremely dim, Miss Rosen?" he said.

"I beg your pardon."

"Are you a bit short of the full picnic?" She looked bemused. "It's a phrase we older people use to describe people who are not all there. Bit backward, maybe."

"I don't understand."

"Well, I can just about accept that you send the text the first time and a man gets killed, you didn't know that would be the outcome of what you had told Tom Harris. But a second time and a third time. You must have known what would happen."

Beatrice moved forward as if to say something. Again, the duty solicitor put a restraining hand on her arm. "If you don't know what you want to say, don't say anything," he said.

"Who suggested you send these texts to Tom Harris?" continued Green.

"He did."

"And the ones sent on the days that Philip Rivers and Toby Renton visited Jane Harris which said 'peaceful'. Presumably that meant he shouldn't attack them?"

"Yes," said Beatrice.

Green's eyes gleamed. "So, you're admitting that sending a text marked 'peaceful' was a way of conveying to Tom Harris that he shouldn't attack the person concerned."

Beatrice looked alarmed. She shot a sidelong glance at her solicitor.

"I think what my client meant was 'yes' to the first part of your question – that she sent the 'peaceful' texts after the visits by Rivers and Renton."

"Did you?" asked Green, fixing his stare on Beatrice.

"I meant..." She turned to look at her solicitor. "I meant what he said I meant," she finally concluded.

"But you can't quite remember what that was," said Green. "We'll go on, then," he said. "What was your relationship with Tom Harris?"

"He was my boyfriend."

"He's substantially older than you – fifteen years, twenty years."

"He's still my boyfriend."

"But probably has great influence over what you do." Beatrice had the sense to remain silent this time. "Why did you stay at home with Jane Harris every time she was entertaining a client?"

"It wasn't every time. I had my studies."

"Most times, then."

"So I could protect her."

"But she had been a prostitute for far longer than you had been a lodger at the flat. Before your arrival on the scene, she would have had to take care of things herself. Isn't the truth that Tom Harris asked you to stay in the flat when she was entertaining clients."

"He might have had the same reason – to protect her," said Beatrice defiantly.

"Isn't the truth that Tom Harris' father had recently come back into his life - the father who ruined his mother's life, the father he felt he should have stopped from beating his mother when he was a young kid? He was so affected by this – and the fact that Jane was putting her life in danger every day of the week – that something snapped. He felt he had to rid the world of men who behaved towards women in the way his father had behaved towards his mother. As a result, he asked you to tell him whenever anyone acted violently towards Jane. Jane couldn't suffer in the same way that his mother did. He would kill anyone who made her suffer."

Beatrice started crying at this juncture. The duty solicitor then addressed Green: "I think my client has taken enough, Chief Inspector. Could I ask you to bring your questioning to a close?"

"I haven't finished yet," said Green tersely. He opened the folder on his desk and took out the leaflet from the North London Women's Revolutionary Action Group, He pushed it across the table to Beatrice. "Have you ever seen this article before?" he asked.

Beatrice blew her nose and started drying her eyes. She squinted at the leaflet. "No," she said.

"Thank you," said Green withdrawing the leaflet from the table. "And another thing – can you tell me why Jane Harris would take a sharp knife to the off licence to buy some wine?"

"I don't know," said Beatrice. "Perhaps to protect herself with? It was late at night and she had been attacked earlier in the day."

Green nodded. "So she was guilty of driving whilst over the

limit with alcohol and possessing an offensive weapon," he said. "Anything else? Do you remember if she went out on either the night John Hedger or Danny Peacock was killed?"

"I'm sorry – I can't remember."

"I think you can but you're just not telling me. You can't convince me that those nights don't loom large in your mind – nights when you played your part in a conspiracy to murder the two of them which was successfully carried out by your boyfriend – as you call him – Tom Harris."

"I don't know."

"All right, we'll leave it there for the moment," said Green. "On the basis of what you've said I now feel we have enough evidence to charge you with conspiracy to murder John Hedger, Danny Peacock and Laurie Fishlock." Beatrice started sobbing again. She was then led out of the interview room by a police constable. Green turned to Francesca. "Two down, one to go," he said. "And that's going to be the most difficult one."

"If she did it," said Francesca. "And if she didn't may I remind you of the old Meat Loaf number – two out of three ain't bad."

Green chortled. "Let's take a break for some coffee before we start questioning Jane Harris," he said.

• • ● • •

Laurie Fishlock was on his own when he came round in his hospital bed later that night. He rubbed his eyes and looked around him. There was, though, a woman police constable sitting by the side of the bed. "Where am I?" he suddenly asked.

"You're in hospital," she said. "You've been attacked. You were lucky. They got the man who did it. A brave man who happened to be nearby managed to stop him from killing you."

"What are you doing here?" he asked.

"I'm a police officer," she said stating the obvious. "My detectives will want to question you about what's happened."

"No," he said. "I don't want to talk to them. Tell them not to bother."

"It was a pretty serious attack," the police constable said.

"Well, tell them I can't help them. I didn't see anything. I was attacked from behind."

"I can tell my boss that," she said, "but he will want to interview you sooner or later. Besides, they have caught the man who did it. We do have the assailant in custody. So there's no need to fear you may be attacked again. And we have the eye witness who made a citizen's arrest. Now, if you'll excuse me, I have to tell the detectives that you've come round."

"You're not listening," said Fishlock adopting a more assertive tone. "I don't wish to press charges."

The constable took out her phone and telephoned the police station. She was put through immediately to Larry Green. "I don't think he wants to co-operate with any police enquiry," she said.

"I'm not surprised," said Green. "This all stems from the fact that he was with a prostitute earlier last night. His wife probably doesn't know about his nocturnal habits. It doesn't matter. The assailant's confessed and we have an eye witness – but we will want to speak to him at some stage."

"I'll pass that on." The constable moved over to the side of Laurie Fishlock's bed. Laurie sat motionless in the bed and the police constable began to address him. "Just to say, sir that they will want to talk to you at some stage but it's not urgent. Best you get some rest."

At that stage, a nurse came round to the bed. "I just want to have a look at my patient." The constable left the scene and the nurse felt his bandaged head. "That's a whopping great bruise," she said. "You've been lucky. You could have been killed by that force of blow."

"How long will I have to stay in here?" he asked.

"I can't really say sir, but I would have thought you'd have had to rest up for a couple of days."

"Free from pressure?"

"You should avoid all stress."

"Can you keep the police away?"

"You can tell them yourself that you can't help them," she said. "I can't do that."

"Will I be successful, though?" he asked.

"I can't say," said the nurse.

If I'm not, the questioning by them will be as nothing to that of my wife when she realises what has happened, he thought to himself. She's bound to find out with the publicity that will be given to the assault. She'll never come back. He decided to stick firmly to a policy of non-cooperation with the police.

• • ● ● •

"Don't worry about it," said Green when Francesca raised the question of Laurie Fishlock's reluctance to co-operate with their investigations. "In the end, he won't have to testify. Tom Harris has admitted the offence. Philip Rivers witnessed it. If he thinks by non-co-operation he'll manage to keep it from his wife that he was consorting with prostitutes, he'll have another think coming when he reads the papers tomorrow. We've got more pressing things in hand. I've just arranged for Jane Harris to be taken down to the interview room."

She was sitting across the table – looking quite composed. "Inspector," she said, sitting upright in her chair as he and Francesca sat down opposite her. Francesca started the tape recorder.

"Miss Harris," Green replied. "I'm sorry to keep you but we have had pressing matters to attend to. Your brother has confessed to the murders of John Hedger and Danny Peacock and to the attempted murder of Laurie Fishlock. Your lodger, Beatrice Rosen, is being charged with conspiracy to murder in all three cases. That only leaves you. You're an intelligent woman.

You must have realised something was going on - two of your clients being murdered and a third being near death's door."

"I didn't lose too much sleep over their deaths," she said quietly but firmly."After all, they had attacked me."

"Where did you go when you drove away from your flat yesterday evening?"

"You saw the proceeds from that journey,"she said. "I bought a bottle of wine."

"You need a knife to buy a bottle of wine?"

"I beg your pardon, inspector?"

"You need a sharp knife to buy a bottle of wine, do you? One was found in your car - one which would have been sharp enough to cut someone's penis off."

"I'm sorry, Inspector. I don't know what that knife was doing in my car. Maybe it was still there from a picnic some time ago. I don't know. I certainly didn't cut anybody's penis off with it. I think I would have remembered that."

She's too confident, thought Green. Trying to give the impression of being open and helpful. She'll slip up."It took you 45 minutes to complete that journey– at least – by our reckoning. It should only take 10 minutes."

"You're right, of course, Inspector,"she said."I had had a hard evening. I sat alone in the car just collecting my thoughts before I started the journey. I wasn't able to do that in the flat. Beatrice was there."

"Shall I tell you what I think you did?"

"Please do, inspector. I'm all ears."

"I think you drove to the waste ground where John Hedger and Danny Peacock's bodies were found. I think you had a pre-arranged agreement with your brother, Tom, that – in the event of a client turning vicious – you would meet him there. Tom would supply the body. You would supply the finishing touches. The mutilation."

"You must think me cold and calculating, Inspector."

"It doesn't matter what I think of you. It was a sort of ritual – a statement if you like. You wanted people to know these men had been violent towards women and were being punished for their sex crimes. Cutting their penises off seemed the right way of drawing attention to that."

"Except that I didn't. Don't take my word for it. Have a look at Mr Fishlock. His penis is intact, I believe?"

"I haven't said anything about the state Mr Fishlock is in. It strikes me you would only say that if you had been planning to mutilate his body but failed to do so."

"He's alive, isn't he, Inspector? You said my brother had been charged with his attempted murder."

"His body could still have been mutilated even if he had survived the attack. You would only know it couldn't have been if you knew that – in these murders – the mutilation was the last act. The men had been murdered beforehand."

"I repeat. I did not mutilate Laurie Fishlock's body."

"But you did John Hedger's and Danny Peacock's?"

"You have evidence that I made a late-night journey and I had a sharp knife in my car on the nights those two were murdered?"

He had to admit he had not. He decided to change the subject. He looked down at the folder on his desk and took out the article from the North London Women's Revolutionary Action Group. He pushed it towards her. "Have you read that article?" he asked.

"Yes," she said.

"And what did you think of it?"

"Not much. I don't agree with its sentiments."

"You don't agree with the killing of John Hedger and Danny Peacock?"

"I told you before, Inspector. I wept no tears over the death of those two men."

"They were indiscriminate victims – a sort of tit-for-tat for Jack the Ripper's murders."

Here her voice started to crack. "You can use that language if you like, Inspector. They were two violent men murdered – murdered by my brother. He always found it difficult to come to terms with what my father had done to my mother."

"And you?"

"I'm sorry?"

"You found it easy to come to terms with what he had done?"

"You're twisting my words, Inspector. Or rather reading too much into them." She reflected for a moment. "No, I wouldn't let my father die alone," she said, "but that doesn't mean I in any way exonerated him for what he had done."

"What did you think had happened to Hedger and Peacock? You must have thought their deaths were connected to you. Did you not realise both the other occupants of your flat were involved in their killings? Did it not make you want to give up prostitution that so many people could come to your flat and find themselves murdered at the end of the day?"

"I have given up. Laurie Fishlock was my last client."

"Going out in style, then?"

"This is not a joking matter, Inspector. Two men have been murdered. I didn't go out in style. He was just punished for what he did."

"So you approve of what happened to him?"

"It is neither here nor there whether I approve or not. The point is you have no evidence to suggest I had any role in his attempted murder – or the killing of the other two men. We are just going round in circles, Inspector. Unless you can produce more evidence to link me to the murders, I suggest this interview is coming to an end."

Masterful performance, thought Francesca. I can see why she waived her right to a solicitor. She didn't need one.

Green looked at his watch. "Yes," he agreed. "I think it is time to pause. You can go back to your cell now but we will want to question you again tomorrow." He opened the door and summoned a constable to take her down. "What do you make of that?" he asked Francesca.

"She was right. We were going round in circles."

"I'm not finished yet," he said as the two of them walked out of the interview room. "I want you to look at surveillance cameras along the route to the off licence and around the waste ground. Look at them at the waste ground for the night of John Hedger and Danny Peacock's murders."

"We've already done that," said Francesca.

"Well, just do what you can," he shouted as he made his way back to his office.

Francesca turned to go to hers but noticed as she passed the front counter that Rivers was still there. "I take it from that noise that it didn't go well," he said.

"I don't know whether it went well or not," said Francesca. "It went well for her but I haven't the faintest idea whether she knew about what was going on or not. It almost beggars belief that she didn't but she was so forceful and persuasive in the interview."

"Let me have a listen to the tape," said Rivers. "I might be able to pick something up."

Francesca nodded. It was worth a try, she thought.

• • ● • •

Tom Harris and Beatrice stood side by side in the dock that morning. The hearing only lasted three minutes as the charges were put to them and they were both remanded in custody. There were no applications for bail.

"They don't look like a couple of people who plotted murder," Rivers said to Francesca as the hearing came to an end.

"No," she had to agree.

Beatrice reached out to hold Tom's hand as they were being

led from the dock. One of the warders yanked Tom ferociously away. "No touching," he said.

"Hey, there's no need for that," said Rivers angrily. The warder gave him a cold stare and then took Tom downstairs from the court room.

"They are murderers," said Francesca.

"I bet Beatrice didn't realise what she was doing until it was too late," said Rivers.

"Oh, you don't think they discussed it beforehand- what they were going to do – with Jane?"

"You haven't proved that," said Rivers tersely. He had to admit to a gut feeling. That Jane was fundamentally a good person. He thought Tom probably was, too. The words "while the balance of his mind was disturbed" suddenly came into his head. "Do you think Tom will plead insanity?"

"Too planned. Too calculated," said Larry Green.

"Tell them not to be too harsh on Beatrice," Tom told his solicitor once downstairs. "She really didn't know what she was letting herself in for." The solicitor nodded soothingly and made his way upstairs to pass this message on to Green.

"I don't believe him," said Green. "She's not an imbecile. She must have known what the results of her actions would be."

Francesca added: "I have some new evidence. His sister, Jane, said she went to the off licence to get some wine yesterday evening – yet there is no CCTV footage of her car anywhere near the off licence nearest to her home." She turned to face Tom's solicitor. "Can your client explain that?" she asked. She went on: "We do, however, have footage of her car in Colliers Way – which is near the deserted wasteland where the first two bodies were discovered. There is no CCTV available near the actual site but can you explain why she might have gone near there last night? It would be a long way to go from Hampstead."

"She's not my client – and my client doesn't have to explain that," said the solicitor turning on his heels.

"I'm trying to prove a conspiracy between the three of them," Green shouted after him. When the solicitor was out of earshot, he turned to face Francesca . "Colliers Way isn't that near the wasteland, though, is it?" he asked.

"It was worth a try."

• • ● • •

"The detectives will see you now," said the police constable to Jane Harris as she opened the door to her cell.

See me now, thought Jane. Sounds as if I've arranged an appointment with them rather than the fact they have kept me waiting for hours locked up in a sparsely furnished cell. She walked with composure to the interview room and greeted Green and Francesca with a cheery "good morning" as they entered the room after her.

Green set the tape recorder up again. "We have just one or two more questions for you," he said. "I have to ask you again: do you wish a solicitor to be present for this interview?"

"And I have to tell you no, inspector. I do not need one."

Francesca gulped down some coffee from the cup in front of her rather too quickly. Jane was right about that if last night's performance was anything to go by, she thought.

"Your brother has been remanded in custody on two counts of murder and one count of attempted murder. Beatrice Rosen has been remanded – also in custody - on three charges of conspiracy to murder."

"Poor Beatrice," she said.

"And no sympathy for your brother?" asked Green.

"A lot of sympathy," she said, "but Beatrice is an innocent abroad. Even the most hard-hearted of police officers - and I mean you no disrespect by saying that - must have realised that."

"Two people plotting, talking about murder in your own flat. Killing people you knew."

"I wouldn't say I knew them." Jane sat back in her chair. "Inspector, we're going over old ground again. I would have thought you had more pressing things to do with your time."

"Then let's cover some new ground. Do you know Colliers Way?"

"Yes."

"Would you agree that it's nearer to the wasteland where the two bodies of your brother's victims were discovered than the off licence nearest your home?"

"As I have never visited that wasteland, I don't in fact know. I'm prepared to take your word for it."

"Why was your car spotted on CCTV there yesterday evening?"

"Because I'd driven there presumably."

"Why? I've had police officers scouring the neighbourhood round there this morning and I would have to say there are no superior off licences around there to the one nearest your home."

"You're probably right, inspector. Anyhow, I did buy the wine from the off licence near my home. If you let me go home, I could probably produce the receipt to show you."

"Your car doesn't show up on CCTV cameras near there."

"That's because there are no parking spaces nearby. I parked a couple of streets away and walked the rest of the distance - obviously out of the gaze of any CCTV cameras."

Green did not challenge this. The CCTV cameras had not given a clear definition of anyone entering the off licence. "So why Colliers Wood?"

"The wasteland is not the only place it's near to," she said. "It's near to the retirement home where my father died. I'd had a stressful day. I'd been attacked by a client. I decided to give up prostitution. I felt quite emotional. He was partly the reason why I went into prostitution. I drove around to think about what had happened and ended up outside the retirement home. That's why it took me longer to get home than you think it should have done."

"Why didn't you tell us this before?"

"I didn't think I needed to. It was personal and I thought I'd dealt with all the points you'd raised adequately."

Oh, you'd certainly done that, thought Francesca. She looked at her boss to see if he was giving any indication as to where they going from here. As far as she was concerned, it looked like game, set and match to Jane.

"Yes," said Green non-commitally. He shuffled the papers on his desk - not for any reason except that he, too, had reached the same conclusion. "Well, then," he said. "I have to say you're free to go. I will arrange for you to be escorted from the station."

"Thank you, inspector." She got up from her chair.

"We could offer you a lift home, Miss Harris," Green added.

"I don't think so, inspector. The police are not my biggest friends at the moment, I'm sure you'll understand. I don't think I'd be relaxed going home in a police car." With that, she left the room - anxious to leave the station as soon as possible.

Green turned to Francesca. "I had to let her go," he said. "We had no evidence against her. What little we had related to the attempted murder and you never know - there may be difficulties with that charge if Laurie Fishlock continues to refuse to co-operate. We're rock solid on the two murders with Tom and Beatrice, though." He grinned. "As you said last night - two out of three ain't bad," he added.

· · ● · ·

Jane walked up to the custody sergeant. "Jane Harris," she said. "I've come to collect my belongings."

The sergeant looked at some papers in front of him. "Yes, you've been freed to go. I'll just go and collect them."

Jane turned around as she was waiting for his return and

heaved a huge sigh of relief. She collected her belongings. As she walked out via the front desk, she noticed Rivers. "You still here?" she asked.

"Can't drag myself away."

"I'm free to go." she said.

"Yes - congratulations."

"Congratulations?"

"I've been listening to the transcript of your interview last night. It was quite a performance."

"It wasn't a performance, Philip. Every word I spoke was the truth."

"Well, you convinced them of that. Or at least to the point where they believed they had no evidence against you. And this afternoon?"

"Not so much of an ordeal. They were obsessed by the fact that my car was spotted in a street near the wasteland where the murder victims were found. I managed to convince them it was also near the retirement home where my father was living and that was it."

"Presumably they thought you were driving to the wasteland to take part in the ritual mutilation of your brother's last victim?"

"Presumably."

"And were you?"

"Philip, I thought we were friends."

"Oh, make no mistake, Jane, I like you but I'd still like to know."

"If you won't accept it from me, accept it from the police: I had nothing to do with the murders."

"A very diplomatic answer." He thought for a moment. "I wish I could give you a lift home," he said. "Drunk driving charge, though. Can I at least take you for a coffee? It'll be easier to talk there than here in the police station."

"That would be nice, Philip."

Once they were sitting in the cafe with cups of coffee and

a couple of pastries, Rivers took the lead in the conversation again. "You know, I can't believe you'd be involved in a murder plot," he said. "All that stuff about offering intimate relationships - it made it sound as if you relished warmth in relationships. Painted you as a warm person. Not someone who would be involved with violence and killing."

"In defence of my brother, the people he killed were involved in violence. Who's to say they would not have killed at some stage in the future if they were left to their own devices? Warmth and intimacy in a relationship breeds warmth and intimacy. Violence breeds violence."

"And that's OK then – to kill them?"

"It's inevitable, Philip."

Rivers nodded. Her answer appeared to him to have been very carefully worded. He was satisfied, though, there was no point in probing any further as to whether she had been involved.

POSTSCRIPT

The headline glared at Rivers from the local paper: Councillor gets life for murder. He felt a certain sense of satisfaction for the part he had played in John Morgan's downfall. Morgan had failed to convince the judge and jury that the killing of Brian Jones had been an accident. The judge had been particularly harsh on him in his sentencing remarks. He had spoken of him ruling his family with a rod of iron. Perhaps this was the reason why both his wife, Emily, and son, Jed, had both been given suspended sentences for their parts in disposing of Brian Jones' body. Some justice there, thought Rivers, particularly in the case of Emily Morgan. He had seen enough evidence during the course of his investigations to show how reluctant she had been to go along with her husband's cover-up.

· · ● · ·

Similarly, the words of the judge had rung in Tom Harris' ears as he was taken down to the cells at the court and had to wait for transport to prison. "Yours was a heinous, cold, calculated crime in which you not only bludgeoned your victims to death but also mutilated their bodies," he had said. Life would mean life, he had added. In this case, too, there was some sympathy for the co-conspirator, Beatrice whom, the judge said, was under the spell of the older man she had fallen in love with and – as a result – was hardly aware of the implications of what she was doing. She had been given a three-year sentence. Tom could hear a commotion outside and thought he detected Beatrice's voice as she was presumably being shunted off to prison. He wanted to shout out an encouragement to her. She had already served six months in prison and would no doubt be a model prisoner if she could escape the taunts of her fellow inmates. She need only serve less than a year more of her sentence, he reckoned. He would write to her. Jane would be able to get her address even if he couldn't. She shouldn't wait for him, he decided. She was a young woman and could start life afresh when she got out of prison. He sighed. He wished he had not involved her in his crimes. He had no remorse for what he had done (a fact that the judge had picked up upon in his summing up) but he did have remorse about involving Beatrice.

His thoughts turned to Jane. She had been at the trial every day. She had not been called as a witness. She was merely there to support him. She was a beautiful, fine, sensitive woman, he thought. Thank goodness she was not tainted in any way by what had happened.

While he was waiting for his escort back to the prison, Larry Green was leaving the court with a smile upon his face. "It's all over now," he said beaming to Francesca. "I'm done now. Retirement. Glad we sorted all that out before I went. I hope you get on with the next DCI that you get."

"Thanks, sir," she said.

"Thanks, Larry, now," he replied. His thoughts were interrupted by Jane Harris bustling by on her way out of the court. She did not stop to speak to either of them. Larry Green stared after her. "You know, I've still not made my mind up on that woman," he said, "But it's not my problem anymore."

"Or anybody else's," said Francesca. "There was no evidence against her."

• • ● • •

"What are you doing here?" Hilary asked curtly as Jenny entered the hall.

302

"I saw a poster about the meeting."

"We thought we ought to meet again to decide what to do with the group," said Hilary. "If it's just the three of us I suggest we disband the group." Angela was also present in the room. "I doubt whether Angela or I have any stomach for working with you in the future."

"All the charges were dropped," said Jenny. "I did nothing." In truth, Larry Green had told her she was free to go as there was no evidence of any conspiracy between her and the actual murderer. It would just have been a separate case about the freedom of the publishers of the pamphlet to print what they liked and the Crown Prosecution Service appeared to have little appetite for that.

"That's right," said Hilary, "and – as a result – Angela got her head kicked in. Just go, Jenny. We don't want you here."

Jenny looked up at Angela who was trying not to show any emotion. "All right," she said. "I'll go." She turned round and trudged wearily out of the hall. As Hilary watched her go, she thought to herself that something was missing. There was no swagger to Jenny's step. She was no longer the bolshie feminist fighting her corner. The events of the last few months had taken their toll of Jenny Creighton.

"And then there were two," said Hilary.

"One," corrected Angela. "I'm going more mainstream. I've had a chat with James and he's quite okay about me getting involved in things now."

"That's big of him," said Hilary. "So, what are you going to do now?"

"I'm thinking of getting involved in local politics."

"A thankless task round where you live, isn't it? They're all Conservatives."

"No. Not all."

"So who will you be standing for?"

"It's not as easy as that: I'll have to get involved locally first before I put my name forward to stand – for the Labour party naturally."

"Naturally," said Hilary with a hint of sarcasm in her voice. Inwardly, she said to herself: Oh, God, you'll be disappointed.

"We can remain friends, though?" enquired Angela - a note of apprehension appearing in her voice."

"Yes, of course," said Hilary. "I'd lead a pretty barren existence if I only associated with people I agreed with."

Rivers had some time on his hands the morning after Tom Harris had been sent down. On impulse, he decided to go and visit Jane Harris. He had read of Tom's sentence and thought he would go around and see how she was. She looked surprised at seeing him when she answered the door to his knock.

"Do I have to be on my guard?" she asked only half-jokingly.

"No, I thought I'd come and see how you were."

"Come in," she said. As he made his way into her living, he was surprised to see Toby Renton sitting on the sofa. Jane walked over to him and took his hand. "We're an item," she said. "You seem surprised?"

Rivers tried to pretend that he wasn't. "No," he said – without conviction.

"I know there's quite an age gap between us," she said, "but (at this juncture she held Toby's hand more firmly) Toby's a sensitive soul and a sensitive soul is just what I need right now."

Toby grinned. "And I need help to grow in confidence. Jane can help me there."

"I hope it works out for the two of you," said Rivers. Jane then volunteered to go and make some tea – leaving Rivers and Toby alone in the living room. "Christ," said Rivers. "You don't half like to live dangerously. I reckon I should ask your parents to keep me on a permanent retainer."

"What?"

"You heard. You don't have a violent streak in you, do you?"

"No, of course not." replied Toby indignantly. "Well, only towards that Rudolph fellow – Gabi's boyfriend – but he hit me first."

"I should keep it buttoned."

"It's very good of you to be concerned about my welfare - but there really is no problem."

"No," said Rivers, "probably not. I doubt if your parents would see it that way, though. Still, what do I care? They've only been paying my bills." He stayed to drink tea with them and then decided to leave. "Look," he said, "I really hope you two work it out. I really mean that."

"Thank you," said Jane as she showed him to the door. She stepped outside with him as he made his way to the staircase leading to the hallway. "Look, it really is all right," she said. "I'm starting a new life. No more prostitution. No more violent men. Just one loving relationship."

He took a few strides down the staircase and then turned to face her again. "I suppose I'll never really know everything that happened here," he said. "I've got my gut feelings, though."

"Yes."

"And – despite everything – I think you will make a go of it."

"You know," she said before he departed for the last time. "You might find out what happened. I'm writing a book about it – which can only be read after my death. I'll be leaving it alongside my will."

"An honest book?"

"Yes, totally honest."

"What's the title?"

"Guess."

He thought for a moment. Then the tabloid treatment of the case came back to him. "Jill the Ripper?" he said.

She smiled an enigmatic smile and – with that – disappeared back into her flat.

Also by Richard Garner

RICHARD GARNER

BEST SERVED
COLD

A thriller of revenge and corruption

Journalist Roy Faulkner is the prime suspect in a murder inquiry
when Kate Williams, the fellow journalist he accompanied to
a night club appeared to disappear from the face of the earth.
Worse still, he finds the detective who is investigating the case
harbours a long-standing grudge against him dating back to
their teenage years in a rock band. As evidence piles up against
Roy, he is charged with the murder of Kate. Private investigator
Philip Rivers faces a battle against time to find out what really
happened before Roy is found guilty.

£8.99   ISBN: 978 1 910074 13 8